All Thy Sons

by

K. M. Breakey

ALSO BY K.M. BREAKEY

The World Clicks

Creator Class

Johnny and Jamaal

Never, Never and Never Again

"I began to sense faintly that secrecy is the keystone of all tyranny. Not force, but secrecy...censorship. When any government, or any church for that matter, undertakes to say to its subjects, "This you may not read, this you must not see, this you are forbidden to know," the end result is tyranny and oppression, no matter how holy the motives. Mighty little force is needed to control a man whose mind has been hoodwinked."

~Robert A. Heinlein

Contents

Prologue
Vancouver, B.C.
July 10, 2031

Not so long ago, people thought Canada was safe. That was when sovereign nation-states were a thing and people of the Western World assumed civilization was the natural order. They believed it would go on forever.

The further they were from the advancing chaos, the more they believed the fairy tale, and the more aggressively they defended it. They demanded it be nurtured and fed.

This pattern played out across the globe as bit by bit, day by day, the madness inched forward, claiming new ground, gaining strength, until one day it reached critical mass and took hold.

Canada was one of the final dominoes to fall. A blessing or a curse? Probably neither – everyone ended up in the same place, though some were luckier than others.

I don't pretend to understand the dark forces that conspired to drive Western Man into his peculiar dysphoria. Some blamed migration, some Islam, some felt inept leadership was to blame. I suggest all of the above, and more.

I'll tell you about it. Perhaps together we can figure out what happened, and how it was *allowed* to happen. Was it deliberate? An elaborate conspiracy? Or divine destiny? The hell if I know.

Either way, the grand charade collapsed in a heap. The pillars of modern civilization – democracy, science, Christianity – were systematically hollowed out until they became façades. They had no substance, no integrity, and thus no defense against the advancing disease. In the end, they simply disintegrated.

Some warned of the approaching calamity. Some tried to stop it. I was one of them and for that, I paid a dear price. To some degree, I still do.

The name's Anthony Fierro – *I mostly go by Tony* – and it's a miracle I'm here to tell the tale. But here I am, sixty-six and living among the chosen. The majority are not so lucky. For them, life's an adventure, survival, a gamble. Many meet a violent end in the flush of youth. The weak and infirm are exploited and culled, as in primitive times.

Some thrive, however, like my Number One Son, Vincent. He chooses to be there, wouldn't have it any other way. I gave up fretting over him decades ago. In the Unprotected Zone, he wields power merrily, with a firm but fair hand.

Without Vinny, I wouldn't be here. Through trials and tribulations, he was often the difference between survival and a cruel, violent end. Truth.

Vinny's life in 2031 was not all that different from a dozen years ago. He was into gang warfare before it became *de rigeur*. He was up-and-coming HA. A full patch by twenty-five, and damn proud of it. I was proud, too, in a twisted and morbid way.

He did the dirty work (which I try not to think about) and he still does, albeit from a higher perch. Vinny was never shy with foot and fist, and whatever else he got his hands on. Vinny was never shy about anything. People loved him, too. He's a funny guy. Downright comical.

My phone buzzed. Speak of the devil, Vincent was on his way. My mood brightened, as it does when Vinny's around. I cherish my boys, those that are still alive. I cherish family in general.

That's the Italian way, and I'm a purebred. My boys are only half, mind you. Lisa, may God rest her soul, was anything but. She was run-of-the-mill *mangiacake*, white as the driven snow. Not a scrap of Dago blood running through her veins.

Her English genes scarcely penetrated the DNA of Vinny and Julio. Vinny was stocky and thick, beefy as they come. Five-ten with shoes on, olive-skinned like me. My youngest, Julio, *may God rest his soul,* was my clone, though that's not why I loved him most. I swear.

Leonardo was odd man out. The dreaded middle child. He was blonde and fair. Lisa had to watch him in the sun, load him up on sunscreen or he'd burn to a crisp. He was also emotional, prone to theatrics and hysteria. I hate to say it, but he was a bit *girly* for my taste. Sometimes I wondered if he was actually mine, but I never dwelled, and never will. I wouldn't taint Lisa's memory with such selfishness.

Vinny appeared in the flesh, reckless and grinning, barrel-chested and crazy-eyed. "Ciao Papa, how you doin'?"

"Ciao, il mio ragazzo." *My boy.*

We embraced and ran through ritual greetings and jokes.

"You get that situation on *The Drive* sorted?"

"You kiddin', Papa? It ain't never gonna end. *Porco dio!*" He balled up a beefy fist. "Those sons a bitches by SkyTrain, they think they can leach our turf past First Avenue."

"Neutral territory there, no?"

"It's the freakin' Drive, Papa. *That's ours.*"

"Can't the Peacekeepers take care of it?"

He scoffed. "Hey, I take care a my own neighbourhood, and I don't take shit. We gotta make 'em pay, huh Papa? An eye for an eye."

"Be careful, would ya?"

He grinned mischievously. "I got it covered. Don't worry about it."

I slapped palm to forehead in mock exasperation, and Vinny let fly the laughter. One day, he'd retire to safety. That's what I told myself. Hopefully before I was dead and gone. *Or he was.*

After the seismic shifts of 2030, loose equilibriums had formed in the Unprotected Zones, but stability was an illusion. Vinny's world was primal. Ruthless gangs roamed the streets. Stick to your tribe, or you were toast.

Peacekeepers wielded the ultimate power – *even Vinny knew that* – and they reinforced the notion with occasional demonstrations of force. They tended the peasants as one would a caged animal. They kept the lights on, the supply chain flowing. People didn't go hungry. They had clean water and sanitation. But their lives were nasty, brutish, and often short.

Maria entered the living room and began fussing over Vinny. She doted on children – *even adult ones.* She reminded me of my own Mamma in that respect. I smiled at the memory, and got to thinking about the good old days.

The recollections were strong, and they took me back to high school. I'll tell you about it. Probably best you know the full history, get the full perspective.

It all started back in...

Chapter 1 – Adolescence
East Vancouver, B.C.
September, 1979

Some kids dreaded high school. The thought of it instilled panic. Fear of teachers, bullies, fear of the unknown. Not me. Templeton Secondary was a tough school with plenty of tough characters, but I had two things going for me. First, I was tough – already tall as a grown man, and just as strong I figured. Second, I was Italian. Back in the day, we looked after our own.

What a time to be alive. The information age hadn't kicked in. No computers, no video games. Forget the Internet, we had one goddamn phone in the house. A rotary beast stuck to the wall in the kitchen. Papa took it off the hook at suppertime.

We didn't wear seat belts, we rode bikes without helmets. When we came home with scrapes and bruises, our parents didn't panic. You've heard the stories. Everyone smoked, including me, though I was smart enough to quit eventually.

We had a tough neighbourhood, but not much crime. The community was tight-knit. Neighbours treated each other like family. Us kids, we played *kick the can* and *British Bulldog*. When our parents weren't looking, which was often, we played *truth or dare* and *spin the bottle*.

Wandering the halls of Templeton those first few days was a treat, 'cause Italians like me dominated the place. Ah, but don't think we had the place all to ourselves. There was no shortage of English, Irish, and German. Polish, Ukrainian, you name it.

They were all *mangiacake* to me. Cake eaters we called 'em, but with no real animosity. Perhaps a little mockery, but no prejudice. It was just, well, we kinda figured we were a cut above those candy asses. Sorry, just being honest.

There were other ethnic groups, too. The Greeks, the Portuguese. They were like us, only lacking the prestige. *The coolness.* Then there was the ever-growing Asian crowd – Chinese, Korean, Filipino. East Indians, too, and they were new. Those bastards took abuse in the early going.

That was my first experience with racism and I confess I was witness and perpetrator. I blame youth and peer pressure, but I wasn't near as bad as some. Rico Berutti was the worst. That kid was a menace to anyone in his path.

Did I miss anyone? Ah yes, couple First Nations kids in my class – Indians we called 'em back then. Nice fellows, but kinda messed up. One had terrible teeth, the other was spaced out half the time. We also had the obligatory Black kid. Not many Blacks in Vancouver then. There still aren't.

Darnell was popular, outgoing, funny. Amazing athlete, too. Ha, while we're on the topic of stereotypes, I should mention the Chinese kids were rockstars at math. All the clichés came to pass in my world. God's honest truth.

To be clear, the racial mashup was new. Back in primary, my class was lily-white (not counting olive skin like mine). It reflected 1970s Canada – also lily-white, but changing fast.

Immigration was finding its groove. Visible minorities were turning up in droves, though Vancouver had not yet transformed into a city of extreme ethnic diversity. It was coming. Anyone with half a brain could see that.

I was cool with it. Heck, Italians were still viewed as foreigners in some circles. Mistrusted and feared, even despised. Especially the dark ones, which I wasn't. And these Asian newcomers, they were *really* different. They looked different, they spoke different languages, they observed different traditions.

Guess what. Canadians got used to it. I certainly did. Having Dhanesh Singh as a best pal certainly helped. We called him Danny back then, and he was a slick dude. I didn't give a fuck if he was East Indian. Neither did my family. Mamma doted on Dhanesh, she loved to feed him. Okay, she loved to feed anyone, and she made the best pasta. Lasagna to die for. *Danny Boy* would agree.

Despite the onset of multiculturalism, I still figured Italians ruled the world. Definitely they ruled the East End, especially on the Drive. *Commercial Drive*, that is. Little Italy. Papa hung out there in the coffee bars and pool halls, smoking and shooting shit with his countrymen and longshoreman pals.

At World Cup time, you couldn't buy a table at Luigi's, but we always got one. Papa had connections. Italy did okay in 1976. *The Azzurri* gave us paisanos something to cheer about, but host Argentina was not to be denied.

I brought Dhanesh now and again. He almost passed for a dark Italian – *almost*. As I introduced him to my culture, he did likewise for me with the Indian way of life. His family spoke Punjabi and they fed me curry, butter chicken and aloo gobi.

When Dhanesh's cousin got married, I discovered Indians had bigger weddings than Italians, which was saying something. Theirs lasted several days and participants wore elaborate costumes. I was impressed.

My other best buddy *was not*. Ivan was of Hungarian descent. Before he was born, his parents risked everything to escape the Communist regime. They slipped through the Iron Curtain, and embarked on a long and arduous journey, including time in an Austrian refugee camp.

When they arrived in Canada in the early '60s, they were forever grateful. But also fearful, and they imparted their suspicion of government to Ivan. As for his arrogance, I'm not sure where he got that from.

He enjoyed verbal swordplay but was vulnerable to taunts. I knew just the buttons to push, and did so rarely. Dhanesh wasn't always so kind.

Where I raved about the wedding, Ivan mocked. He called Indian traditions primitive and archaic. Beneath his culturally superior station. Didn't faze Dhanesh, and he dished back as appropriate. He could match wits with anyone.

"What if your parents pick an ugly girl for you?" Ivan asked. "You guys do arranged marriages, right?"

"Nope, but we'd consider it for you. Could be the only way *you* ever get married."

Ivan ignored him. "You'll probably get one from the old country. Some peasant who grew up in a mud hut."

"That's rich coming from a guy who never actually grew up." Dhanesh waved his hand at the *four-foot-nothing* level. Height jokes were a staple.

"If she's ugly, don't worry. Maybe you'll get some goats in the dowry. Maybe some cute ones, eh?"

"I'll keep you posted, Ivan. No doubt you'll still be a virgin."

I refereed the sparring, but it rarely escalated. Ivan meant no harm with the ethnic comments. He was just getting used to multiculturalism. We all were. I compensated in the other direction. I bent over backwards *not* to mention race. I barely noticed I was doing it, which was typical. Soon enough, East Indians would become a dime a dozen in Vancouver. But in '79, they stood out.

We became the three musketeers – *Tony, Ivan and Danny.* An unlikely trio, but inseparable. The friendship lasted well beyond high school. Those adolescent bonds are always the strongest.

We were good kids. We avoided the burnouts, the bullies, the wannabe and *already-were* criminals. I figure it's 'cause we had good parents. *Parents who cared.* Full stop.

With apologies to Bryan Adams, for us it was *the summer of '79* that seemed like it'd last forever. The memories were fresh and vivid. We rode bikes to New Brighton Pool, or if we felt adventurous, maybe Kits Beach. We noticed girls in bikinis as if for the first time. *How's that even legal,* Ivan used to say. I had no answer.

We played pick-up soccer at the field by Templeton Pool. I remember the disappointment when darkness put a stop to it. I had enough energy to go forever. Canada was this great hockey mecca, but I never played. Not even street hockey. Papa put us in soccer and that was that. That's what Italian families did.

Turned out, I was pretty good. I played for Grandview Legion and we kicked ass. Not to brag, but I was head and shoulders the best on my team. It did wonders for my popularity.

And my ego.

I remember that first high school game like it was yesterday – the freshly-cut grass, the late summer sunshine. It was a September to remember. We were playing some pampered West Side pussies. Had to be a cake walk, right? No chance these spoiled *white* kids, from swanky parts of town like Shaughnessy and Point Grey could compete with our gang.

I was a natural midfielder, but Coach started me striker that day and I scored two beauties. I felt like Paolo Rossi, and I pretended there were throngs of cheering fans sporting the Azzurri blue.

Alas, those rich kids could play. They took us down 3-2, and it solidified them as my mortal enemy on the pitch, a rivalry that lasted many years. Every last one of them was a white Anglo-Saxon. Somehow, that intensified my hatred.

Their star was a rangy, waspy kid named Charles Kennedy. He had the blonde hair, the money, the pedigree. And *goddamnit*, he had the game. He ran their midfield with poise and vision, and sported a lethal left foot.

He was a racist ass, too. He called Rico Berutti an ape and Dhanesh a Paki. Taunts like that were common in '79. Truthfully, there wasn't much genetic disparity between the groups, Dhanesh notwithstanding. Maybe that's why things never got too out of control. They cussed, we cussed. When the ref threatened us with red cards, we got on with the game.

Still, we were tribal in adolescence, and these boys weren't my tribe. My tribe was working-class East Van. All the better if you were Italian. Was I racist toward non-Italians, toward guys like Charles? Possibly, but my contempt was more rooted in class than race. They were filthy rich. We weren't. Was there a better source of resentment?

You may have noticed, I talk a lot about race. Get used to it, this is a story about race. Also, culture, diversity, and privilege – a host of taboo topics. Before Transformation, few discussed such matters with any degree of honesty, though they pretended to.

I wish race wasn't such a divisive characteristic, but I can't change nature. No matter what rubbish the PC crowd once espoused, human interaction will probably always be shaped by race.

Don't blame me.

Chapter 2 – Young Adulthood
Vancouver, B.C.
Spring, 1985

Straight out of high school, I went to work on the docks. Papa got me in the Union, and it was a damn good gig. Course there nutjobs aplenty, and an HA presence that everyone gave a wide berth. Papa filled me in. He was well-liked, a company man through and through. A lifer.

The boss seemed to like me, told me one day I'd be shop steward. Almost like he started grooming me from day one. I think Papa dropped a hint or two. I was interested, but I had some living to do first. I was twenty years old, for Christ's sake.

They were paying me $25 an hour, and I was booking plenty of overtime. I bought a brand-new Camaro Z28, I started wearing designer clothing – Polo, Tommy, Oscar de la Renta. The ladies flocked. The world was my oyster.

Compared to Ivan and Dhanesh, I was rich. At least for now. Those bozos took the university route – Dhanesh CompSci, Ivan Finance. The culture gap damaged the friendship not one iota.

We palled around constantly. We played soccer, we chased women, we discovered nightclubs and boozing. Man, we were living. Nothing finer than a night out, drinking beer, shooting pool, scoping chicks.

For me, the scoping part didn't last. I found the right girl practically straight away, before my twenty-first birthday. I had no regrets, at least while it lasted.

The night I met Lisa was a night to remember. Our gang started at Swangard Stadium watching our beloved 86ers take down the Edmonton Brickmen 4–2 in front of 8,000 fans. My favourite player, Domenic Mobilio, netted a pair. What can I say, I cheered for the Italians. It was a good omen.

From there, off to the Keg for juicy steak and cocktails. Then, the main event. *Diego's*. The Burnaby nightclub was our go-to hotspot. We coulda hung at *The Sport*, or *The Lougheed* but we were a cut above that riffraff, when we wanted to be.

Diego's was a young crowd, a mix of cityfolk and suburbanite. A few greaseballs. Always, a ton of hot chicks. Your typical meat market. We'd been doing our share of gallivanting – getting wasted and trying to get laid. God, that sounds terrible.

There were barfights, too. Not my thing, but I could handle myself. Rico Berutti stirred it up constantly. He hadn't changed since high school, except now he was huge. A *roid monkey*, rumour had it. I never thought of him as a friend – *he was too crazy* – but he took our side in any beef. Like I said, us Italians stuck together.

By the mid '80s, Vancouver's march to multicultural Valhalla had picked up steam. In East Van circles, the number of Chinese was astonishing. The expression *visible minority* was starting to sound ridiculous. Meantime, Surrey was morphing into Little India, as opposed to the misfits and lowlifes it traditionally attracted.

I had no concerns. Commercial Drive was still Little Italy. We had ours, let them have theirs. Why not? And honestly, everyone got along. Sure, flickers of racism flared. The age of PC hadn't yet choked the cheek out of people. Ivan still openly mocked and teased.

"You Hindus keep stinking up neighbourhoods with your goddamn curry," he'd say to Dhanesh. Sounds bad, but it was meant in jest and taken as such.

"Someone's gotta bring a little colour to the neighbourhood."

"Hey, hey," I protested.

Dhanesh grinned. "Love the Italians, but imagine a neighbourhood full of people that looked like that." He pointed jeeringly at Ivan.

"Without people like me, you'd be a Himalayan goat herder."

Dhanesh sneered. "You really got a thing for goats, eh Ivan?"

"Oh, did I upset you, Danny Boy? You're not gonna bomb my house are you?"

"I'm not an Arab you moron."

"Close enough."

An on they went. I sometimes wondered why they were friends. But they were, and the friendship was enduring. I got a good laugh out of their antics. The comedy of the day was raunchy and provocative, never pandering.

Ivan attacked everyone with equal fervour, and occasionally went too far. He wasn't the toughest guy around, and I looked out for him. Dhanesh did, too. But mostly Ivan knew where to draw the line, though the line was always shifting.

Take the C-word – *not the one for female anatomy* – the hateful slur on Chinese folks. It was common in the '70s, but ten years on, off-limits. *Toxic.* Not quite N-word territory, but close. Even now, I recoil at the word, perhaps because I grew up among Asians.

No one predicted how poisonous the N-word would one day become. Heck, no one predicted the absurd language rules that would soon descend. In 1985, no one would have believed it.

Vancouver took a good run at multiculturalism. Through the'80s, the '90s, the 2000s – the lore of peaceful diversity was formed. I swear to God, everyone got along. Wasn't my little gang proof? The Hindu, the evil Hungarian, and me – the greasy Wop.

We also had Asians coming and going, some great pals. *The best.* And – *shocker of shockers* – we even had white kids. I never thought of myself as white, but through the '90s, I realized the world sure did. Us Italians, *ha*, we never quite qualified for the *People of Colour* designation. Probably on account of our European heritage.

Back in the day, Canada had a thriving middle class. Well-paying jobs for anyone willing to work, college degree or otherwise. People were making *mucho dinero* and the cost of living was manageable. For the slackers, there was welfare. A few of my old Templeton pals tapped it, I know that for a fact.

As for my family, Papa worked and Mamma took care of us kids. She cleaned house, she cooked dinner. Her pasta was legendary. We were a typical Italian family. I figured everyone was Catholic and that me and my pals were hooligans. *Ha*, we weren't. The anchors of family and religion kept us on the straight and narrow.

Society was stable. The Western World was excelling. Nobody gave it a second thought. Nobody worried the government might transform us into a socialist hellhole. No one feared creeping anarchy, or mob rule. We were civilized and enlightened. What could go wrong?

They were the *good old days*, and I knew they'd last forever. Man, was I naïve? I wonder if I sensed they were slipping away. If their *fleetingness* made them all the more special.

Of course, I saw the good old days through rose-coloured glasses. Indigenous people might have a different take. Same goes for gays and lesbians. There were other factors, too, chipping away at the era's innocence. Crime was up. The Downtown Eastside was slipping into squalor. And the Hell's Angels had arrived, with their Harleys, and their colours, and their drugs and violence.

Still, no Vancouverite fretted law and order was at risk. Our town was peaceful and tolerant. Heck, the biggest bullies around were still the Italians. Not gonna lie about that.

One thing I knew for sure – when it came to race relations, we were streets ahead of our southern neighbour. America just couldn't figure out the *Black White* thing, not for lack of trying. Just when you thought the racial strife was getting better, some Black guy would come on TV to confirm it was worse than ever.

But this was 1985 and things *were* better. Unfortunately, the race hustlers didn't want you to know it. They were finding their stride. It was the dawn of identity politics, of the victimhood industry.

For the record, I didn't care two shits about politics in '85, but Ivan did. He kept me up to date, whether I liked it or not. He was a staunch conservative, shockingly knowledgeable, opinionated as the day is long.

Evidently, the Cold War still raged. The fall of the Berlin Wall was still a few years off. I didn't know much about the Soviet Union, except they had great hockey players who rarely smiled. The 1972 Summit Series was epic, even for a soccer guy like me.

Other notable markers: the conservative fat cat Brian Mulroney was starting a nine-year run as PM. Ivan loved him. Papa hated him. I was indifferent. In America, Ronald Reagan had started his second term and his wife was telling everyone to *Just Say No*.

My favourite TV show was *Family Ties*, starring lovable conservative Alex P. Keaton. Had Alex existed in the age of Trump, he would have proudly donned a MAGA hat. He also would have been called every name in the book and kicked off TV in Season 1.

Ah, *Mamma mia!* I got sidetracked. Where were we? Ah yes, Diego's...about to meet my future wife. A far more entertaining tale, I promise.

Chapter 3 – Gallivanting
Burnaby, B.C.
Spring, 1985

We arrived at ten and the place was hopping. We skirted the line-up thanks to a bouncer we knew, a friend of a friend. An Italian thing, what can I say?

It was me, Ivan, and Danny. A few other *goombahs*. We claimed real estate near the pool table which afforded a view of the lower bar and dance floor, where the fine ladies perched. We bided time, drinking, shooting stick, posing. Some of the boys lit up – smoking was permitted back then. No one gave it a second thought.

I surveyed the scene with as much nonchalance as I could muster. *Then I saw her.* Jesus, how could I not? She was tall and blonde and curvaceous. The dress was frivolous and brightly coloured, sexy to the point of being obscene. She was attracting attention, and I could tell she was used to it. She had a haughty air of confidence, as if she was a little too good for everyone. It was a beautiful thing to see.

The male brain is shockingly efficient – I picked all this up from across the room in a nanosecond. I also took in the less attractive friend – why do they travel in mismatched pairs? On second glance, the friend wasn't so bad, it was the contrast that did her in. Again, why?

When it came to wooing the fairer sex, I didn't lack confidence. Not to brag, but I was blessed with great hair, great skin, a great build. I was no pretty boy, mind you. I sported a manly look – big jaw, big brow, my nose had a prominent Roman bridge.

Whatever I had seemed to work for the ladies, and I exploited my looks shamelessly. Nothing to it really. I turned up, made eye contact, smiled. God did the rest. Worked most every time. I had a boyish grin, and I always found the right things to say. What an arrogant ass, some of you may be thinking. I don't blame you.

I found Ivan in deep discussion with a non-descript regular. "Hey chooch, what'd I miss?"

"Can't ya see I'm talking here?" Ivan feigned irritation.

"Oh well *hey*, sorry to bother the big man. *He's talking...*" I scoffed heartily. "How you expect to get laid hangin' out this side of the freakin' bar?"

"We always hang on this side."

"I rest my case." I nodded toward the dancefloor. "Follow me, *ciccio*. Some ladies we need to meet." I needed a wingman to occupy the homely friend. Hey, all's fair in love and war.

Ivan glanced at his buddy. "Why not? I talk to youz later, Pauly." Ivan always tried to act Italian. It was pathetic.

Off I went on a mission, Ivan hot on my heels. He wasn't the most attractive fellow, short and pudgy, with droopy hound-dog eyes and a perpetual five o'clock shadow. Already his hairline was receding.

He made up for his deficiencies with enthusiasm. He brought energy, and he was a stylish dresser to boot. He wouldn't embarrass me, but he also wouldn't compete for the prize, if ya know what I'm saying. I picked Ivan over Dan the Man for a reason. I'm not stupid. Dhanesh was a handsome specimen and had more luck with the ladies than me, though I never set out to be a Casanova.

The dancefloor was packed, and the object of my desire had shaken her fabulous booty more than once, each time with the friend. She'd turned aside a handful of suitors. I missed nothing.

I pushed through bodies, male and female. Strobe lights flashed, couples gyrated, music blared – *Let's Dance* by David Bowie. Ironically, I had no desire. I only wanted to meet, to flirt, to bond.

My confidence was surging and as if to bolster it further, a pathway opened direct to the blonde. I seized the opportunity. Our eyes met, her beauty assailed me with a physical force. She shone. She glowed. She looked away.

What the fuck?

My ego was hit. I was wounded, but barely broke stride. With Ivan in tow, I trudged on like nothing happened. I didn't stop until we reached Lino's mob in their usual alcove. I made a great show of hugs and handshakes and high-fives, but from the corner of my eye, I kept tabs.

Then it happened. *She glanced over. She was checking me out.* Oh, she tried to disguise it, but I caught her red-handed. It told me everything I needed to know.

My response was to up the ante on theatrics. I held an animated discussion with Luigi on Italy's chances in Mexico, and whether Paolo Rossi was past his prime. I was play-acting.

Finally, Ivan intervened. "*Tony,* you mentioned some ladies?"

"Patience grasshopper."

He gave me an eyeroll, which I deserved. The ladies in question were on the floor shaking what God gave them. I discretely pointed them out.

"Which one's mine?"

"Take a wild guess."

"What if *I* like the blonde?"

"What if she sees your *facia brutta?* Then what?" I pinched his cheek and he stood down with a grin. "The other one's cute," I added. "Also, not six inches taller than you."

"Okay, okay." He was zeroing in, and I was too, unabashedly studying the blonde's sultry moves. They were causing chemical reactions in my body.

When I made my move (for the second time), she met my eye contact with a clear and steady gaze. The mutual appraisal was successful.

"You doing laps?" She asked.

"Just trying to get some exercise." I jogged on the spot for effect, and shot her a zany grin. "Soccer season's coming up."

"Ever heard of the gym?"

I tapped my watch. "It's closed." I extended my hand. "I'm Anthony."

"Lisa." She held out hers and I kissed it dramatically. By now, Ivan was entrenched in conversation with the friend. Gotta love a wingman.

"You're not a regular?" I ventured.

"First time."

"Ah, lucky I'm here to take care of you."

She smiled with faux skepticism. "Helen warned me about this place."

"Ah, Diego's is harmless."

"Uh-huh, lots of players I hear." She raised eyebrows. "Are you a player, Anthony?"

"I'm a *soccer* player."

She groaned. This is what I pass off as charm.

By now, I'd taken full stock and she was a sight to behold. A blue-eyed blonde, with perfect white teeth and a silky complexion. Fair, but not pasty. Light freckles around her nose, under her eyes...*exquisite*.

I was back to cocksure and cool as a cucumber. I got that trait from my Papa. The kind of confidence that told people I deserved the best.

Lisa brought her own brand of swagger, but was content to let my masculine energy drive the bus. I rambled on about this and that. I played the big dopey Italian. It came natural to me.

I caught her checking me out – my gold necklace, the swirl of chest hair (not a shag carpet like some Italians), my height, my broad shoulders. What's not to like? But she was coy. I'd have to work for this one.

When Ivan dragged Helen to the dancefloor, I made no similar overture. I'd show my moves later. I wanted to find out who this chick was.

"You're not a Burnaby girl."

She shook her head.

"West side?"

"Lucky guess."

"You got the look."

"What look?"

"Money." I rubbed my thumb across the tips of my fingers. "Where'd you go to school? Magee? Point Grey?"

"Little Flower."

"Of course, had to be private school."

She scoffed. "Where you from, the ghetto?"

I burst out laughing. "Pretty much. East Vancouver. I went to Temp."

"Oh God, an East Van boy. Italian, too, if my eyes don't deceive."

"Full on." I laughed some more. "Don't let that scare you."

"I'm not scared. You seem nice. And trustworthy, I must say."

"I am. Scout's honour."

The song changed, and Ivan and Helen stuck it out.

"High-school friend?" I motioned toward Helen.

"God no, she's from Burnaby. Our moms know each other. We grew up together."

"Coolio," I said, and switched focus back to Lisa.

I learned a bunch. Her family was well-off (very wealthy, I'd soon learn). She had a younger brother named David. The Dad was a lawyer, the Mom a socialite. It dawned on me, she was the same waspy ilk as those West Side boys I despised in high school. For Lisa, I was willing to set prejudice aside.

When *Tainted Love* came on, I gestured toward the floor. "Shall we?" The song was all the rage in the '80s.

We rendezvoused with the others, and had a grand time showing off dance moves. Time passed quickly. Maybe it was wishful thinking, but I already felt like Lisa was my girlfriend.

"What say we get the heck outta here?" I casually offered. "Go get some food, huh?"

Blessedly, the girls agreed.

Chapter 4 – Bino's

At my behest, Lisa rode with me, Ivan with Helen.

"You okay to drive?" Lisa asked.

"F-f-f-fine," I slurred, and added a wobble to my gait. "I've had like—" *hiccup* "—two pints. Is oannnnn-ey....a few brocks."

She giggled. "Seriously, *are* you?"

"Course I am." And by the standards of the day, I *might* have been. The '80s were a drinking and driving heyday. *Everyone* did it. The laws were toughening, but change takes time. I rarely gave it a second thought, but I wasn't a big drinker, not like some of the goombahs. Not like Rico Berutti, I'll tell ya.

My Z28 was pure East Van, right down to the soccer boots hanging from the rear-view. Not remotely Lisa's style. "Whadaya think of the ride?"

"It suits you," she said politely. "How fast does it go?"

"Wouldn't you like to know?"

Her eyes sparkled with anticipation, so I dropped a gear and punched it. The 5.0L V8 roared savagely and we were forced back in our seats – the feeling never gets old.

Alcohol on board or otherwise, Kingsway at 2:00 a.m. was neither the time nor place for such shenanigans, and I settled back to the speed limit.

Lisa was laughing hysterically. "Do it again," she said. "Do it again."

"I'll show you more some other time."

"You will, will you?"

"Lots of stuff I can show you." It came across thick with innuendo, and I cleared my throat. "Maye on our second date."

"This is a date?" She smirked.

"Uhhhh..."

"Where we going, anyway?"

"I got just the spot. An East Van institution."

"Oh God."

Bino's was our goto for late-night grub, open 24 hours. It was diner-style, kind of a lesser version of Denny's. I realize how shitty that sounds.

"The food's better than the décor, I promise."

"Uh-huh."

"It's cheap, too."

"You trying to impress me?"

I slapped my forehead. "Come on, I'll get us a table by the window."

Ivan and Helen turned up and small talk ensued, repeated introductions. Conversation was light and friendly as we perused the menu.

"See something you like?" I shamelessly posed. "On the menu, I mean." I'm insufferable at times.

"Not yet."

"Ouch."

She smiled. "Any recommendations?"

"I always get the $4.99 all-day breakfast. *Bada bing, bada boom.*"

Ivan shook his head. "Don't worry, you get used to him."

The girls ordered tea and a side of fries. I got my bacon and eggs, Ivan went with his trusty BLT.

"You enjoy fine dining, Anthony?"

I laughed boisterously. "One day I take you to Nick's Spaghetti House on the Drive. The owner's a friend of the family. We go soon, yes?"

"Hold your horses. How about we make it through Bino's first?"

"*Buono!*" I drew a breath. "So ladies...*tell me.*"

"Tell you what?"

"*Everything,*" I made an expansive gesture. "I wanna know it all."

Ivan jumped in. "You guys go to school? Ya work? What?"

Lisa raised her hand. "UBC."

Helen: "SFU."

"What're ya studying?"

"English Lit," said Lisa. "Do you like to read, Anthony?"

"Sure I do."

Ivan roared with laughter.

"What? *I read.*"

"Comic books don't count."

"You hear this? Comin' from frickin' Shakespeare over there."

"He likes to read but his lips get tired."

"Hey, hey."

"Who's your favourite author?" Lisa ventured.

"That's tough." I grinned sheepishly. "So many to choose from. How 'bout you?"

"I'm studying modern classics. Hemingway, Orwell, Fitzgerald."

"Love those guys." The names were vaguely familiar.

"But I'm a romantic at heart – Bronte, Jane Austen. Tolstoy."

"Me too," I said dreamily.

"Tolstoy?" Ivan was animated. "He's from my part of the world."

"Russia?"

"Hungary. Close enough."

"I know very little about Hungary," said Lisa.

"I'm hungry." Everyone groaned.

"He's *never* used that one," said Ivan. "Hungary's amazing. Budapest's the most beautiful city in Europe."

I scoffed. "Try Rome, Florence, Venice." I put on an accent to bolster my argument.

"You've never been to Budapest."

"I'm Italian. When I go to Europe, I go to Italy."

"*You're* Italian?" Lisa feigned shock. "I never woulda guessed."

"I went to Italy once," said Ivan. "Beautiful place. Only problem...so many goddamn Italians."

I scoffed. "Yeah, and he's never used that one." I looked at Lisa. "And you are?"

"Canadian."

"No really, what are ya, Scottish? Irish?"

"My family's from England, originally – both sides. But we've been here a hundred years. My great grandad was one of the founding members of the Jericho Tennis Club."

"Hey, I'm a member."

"I doubt it."

"As you should." I grinned. "My family's from Naples, originally."

"How long they been in Vancouver?"

"*Heya, we ah jus' arriva lasta weeka. Buongiorno.*"

"Come on."

I giggled. "Nah, we been here awhile. Not a hundred years, though."

"You speak Italian?"

"O ma certo. *Of course.* Why am I gonna stop?"

"Good for you."

"And you, any other languages?"

"Je parle Français." She smiled "We vacation in France sometimes."

"I took French in high school."

"We all did, thanks to Trudeau."

"I'm not into politics, but I hate that guy."

"How come?"

"'Cause my Dad hates him."

She giggled. "So does my Dad."

"Hey, something in common."

We spoke not of Justin, but of *Pierre Elliott*, who declared in 1971 that Canada would adopt multicultural policy. Little did I know his mutant offspring would soon come along and attempt to destroy Canada. In that moment, I cared not two hoots.

I was wallowing in Lisa's beauty, mesmerized by it. The harsh fluorescent lighting couldn't dampen it. She glistened and glowed. An English rose, with a personality to match. She was quick to laugh, as if always on the verge, and not shy to toss a friendly jab. She'd fit in at my family's dinner table. But would I at hers?

"Tell me about your family," I said. "What's your Dad like?"

She smiled modestly. "He's amazing. Both my parents are. I'm super lucky."

"And your brother? He's what, seventeen?"

"Eighteen."

"Does he play soccer?"

"David's not into sports."

"*Everybody's* into sports."

"Nope."

"What's he into?"

"We're not quite sure."

I didn't press further. I started to ask if she knew Charles Kennedy, but caught myself. The thought of Lisa with that pasty-white rich bastard made the chip on my shoulder grow three sizes.

We cleared out of Bino's by 3:00 a.m. The alcohol had worn off, but I had the energy of coffee and euphoria. Like a good gentleman, Ivan walked Helen to her car while I loitered near my Camaro. Blessedly, Lisa stayed. When I saw her shiver, I had my opening.

"Chilly all of a sudden." I draped an arm over her shoulder. She shot me a scolding grin, but didn't pull away.

"Maybe, uh-uhmmmmm, maybe we go on a real date sometime, huh?"

She shrugged. I wasn't used to girls playing hard to get.

"Is that a yes?"

"We'll see."

"You're not seeing someone, are ya?"

"Not really."

"What does that mean?"

She ducked out from under my arm. "Are you the jealous type? That's an Italian thing isn't it?"

"God no." I took offense, but backed off. Truth is, I never had cause to be jealous. "I just kinda like you."

"I like you too," she said, and my heart soared.

"Can I get your number?"

"Gotta pen?" No smartphones in '85. Stone age times.

With Ivan wandering back, I reached for Lisa's hand and laced my fingers through hers. "Until we meet again, Madam."

"Are you always so dramatic?"

"Only when I'm in a state of shock. I never thought I'd meet someone so gorgeous."

She scoffed. "You sound like a Harlequin character."

"That's good, right?"

"You look like it, too. And *that's* good."

I raised my arms in victory. "Hurray."

"Ever consider a career in theatre?"

"My life is theatre."

"Okay well, this movie's over. Time to go." She gave me a wink, and began to sashay across the parking lot

"I'll call you," I yelled, and she acknowledged with a wave.

Meanwhile: "Dude, open the goddamn door." Ivan was back. "I'm freezing my balls off."

A few blocks into the journey home, we commenced the post-mortem.

"How'd that go?" I asked.

"Meh."

"You get her number?"

"No."

"Well, I'm gonna say it didn't go well."

"Maybe I'm not interested."

"You're interested in anything that moves."

"You're thinking of Danny Boy."

I chuckled. "What happened to the D-Man?"

"He found one that moves." Ivan eyed me. "How 'bout you, big man? You get the digits?"

"Course I did, *stoopido*." I cuffed him playfully.

"She's a hottie. Maybe a keeper?"

"She might be, pal. She might be."

That night my mind raced. I envisioned bringing Lisa home to meet Mamma and Papa. Lisa was far from Italian. *Christ sakes*, I didn't even know if she was Catholic. I just assumed everyone was.

Papa might corner me and say something like: "What, you can't find no Italian girls?" Mamma might gently enquire about Lisa's religion. My parents were old school, what can I say? Heck, so was I.

I laughed out loud. *Hold the phone, paisano...you ain't getting married yet.* Solid point, but I was feeling rather besotted. Infatuated. Love-struck. You name it.

But what was that talk of another guy? *What if it was Charles Kennedy?* I shuddered. God wouldn't do that to me. Would he?

I had a lot to learn about faith. I still do.

Chapter 5 – Courtship

The following day, I was up by seven. I rarely slept in – Papa didn't tolerate it, not under his roof. My mood was part ecstasy, part panic. I had to have her, and I was bitterly jealous of a potentially non-existent guy.

But she blew me a kiss. No girl with a boyfriend would do that. Right?

By eleven, I was crawling the walls. Calling now would break every rule in the book. I had to wait a few days – that's what the cool kids do. Show 'em you don't care, you got better things to do.

Fuck that.

"Miller residence." A high-pitched male voice answered first ring. The brother? I asked for Lisa.

"Whom may I tell her is calling?"

"Anthony." Already, I didn't like this guy.

He called her in a sing-songy voice. *Good Lord.*

"Guess who?"

"Is that you, Peter?"

"No."

"Matthew?"

"No."

"George?"

"It's fucking Ringo." I snorted. "*Che palle*. Come on, Lisa, you know who it is."

She giggled. "Hello Anthony. How are you?"

"I *was* good."

"I knew it was you."

Bless her.

We swapped stilted small talk, but eventually got the electricity back. *The passion.* Most importantly, we got a date booked. Lunch tomorrow. UBC.

Perfect. I had Mondays off all summer. I was on top of the world, with energy to burn. Thank God, I had soccer that afternoon. A distraction, mental and physical.

I played for Columbus, a storied Vancouver side dominated by – *you guessed it* – Italians. I wasn't Mobilio's level, but I could play. That afternoon, we were hosting a friendly with a Select Team from Surrey.

I still recall the moment I took the field. Jesus, their whole team was East Indian. They were jabbering away in whatever language it was – *Punjabi?* All I could think was, *am I in Canada?*

I'm no racist – never was, never will be – but that was my reaction. Woulda been anyone's. Don't forget, this was 19-*fucking*-85. And don't forget, this is a story about race and culture. We're gonna talk about this stuff, even when it's uncomfortable. Anyway, was a good run in the sun and we took down the Surrey lads. A sound thrashing which I took it as a good omen.

Monday rolled around on schedule. The sun shone, the birds sang. For the first time in a while, I said my morning prayers. Life was too good not to honour God. After brekkie, I killed a couple hours at the gym. Biceps, quads, traps, lats, abs. I was a vain bastard. I still am.

Finally – *finally, you hear me* – time for our date.

I was to pick her up at two at the corner of University Boulevard and West Mall. I was early, so I parked illegally and threw on the hazards. My car stood out among a myriad of Japanese compacts and beaters. I got a few suspicious stares. I felt like a tough guy.

There was no shortage of scenery. Glorious specimens of every colour, shape and size. I rubbernecked shamelessly, but my mind settled on the race issue again. *What's wrong with me?*

The West Side was lily-white ten years prior, and still not far from it. But here today, wow, Asians aplenty. Definitely more Chinese than Italian, but I felt no racial threat. I was seen as white, and white was dominant. These things were unspoken in 1985, but the seeds of *white guilt* were being planted.

There were also more guys than gals strolling about, I'd say 60-40 minimum. Ah, the white male – Western society's apex predator. Fast forward thirty years, and how time would change. Circa 2019, I recall an article in The Sun: *Only 1 in 8 UBC students Is a White Male*. It was presented as a happy story. Clear progress toward...*what*? Toward getting rid of us evil bastards?

No such hostility in 1985, and certainly no fear of it.

I digress.

I spotted her. Man, I could spot that sashay a mile away. She was decked out in a bright floral number, and strutting like a catwalk model. Her hair was pulled back severely, and she wore large-framed glasses. But her beauty could not be hidden.

I hopped out and ran around the car. "Hello, Darling." I offered a big smile and a hug, nothing over the top. I had to show her I could button it down, fit in with the highfalutin intellectuals.

"Where we going?" I asked.

"I thought *you'd* have something planned."

"Hey, it's your neck of the woods."

"Touché. I know just the spot. We'll get away from the riffraff."

"Does that include me?"

"I'll make an exception for you."

"Thanks." I opened the car door. "Where to M'Lady?"

"Arbutus Club."

"Well, la-di-da."

It was a short drive through the Endowment Lands, Point Grey, to the edge of Shaughnessy. The Club was exclusive, and they liked it that way. A sizable entrance fee and lengthy wait lists kept the unwashed rabble at bay.

I pulled into the parking lot and felt a twinge of self-consciousness. Row upon row of Mercedes and BMW, and those were the crappy cars.

The digs were swanky. Money had been spent. Lisa knew almost everyone, and she made a few awkward introductions. Nothing but Caucasians. Upper crust. Arrogant. No doubt connected and wealthy. I was hyper-aware of my East Vancouver heritage. And my *Italianness*.

We got a primo table at the members-only bistro, overlooking the tennis courts. A foursome of middle-aged females, immaculately dressed in white, played doubles.

"You play?"

I shook my head. "I'm guessing you do."

"A little. How's Ivan, by the way?"

"Was Helen asking?"

Lisa smiled sheepishly. "Actually, no."

"She wasn't diggin' him, huh?"

"She said he was trying too hard."

"Or was it 'cause he's ugly?"

"He's *not* ugly."

"He's no Robert Redford."

She giggled. "You're mean."

"Don't worry, he knows it." I bellowed laughter

"Beauty's in the eye of the beholder."

"Says the most beautiful girl I've ever met."

She blushed. "Flattery will get you nowhere."

"It's not flattery if it's true."

"*Puh*-lease. What's up this week for you?"

"I work for a living. I took today off on account of this being a special occasion."

"I'm deeply honoured." *Sarcasm.* "Where do you work?"

"On the docks. Port of Vancouver."

"Cool. What do you there?"

"Longshoreman."

She grinned. "I repeat, what do you do there?"

"Nothing to it really – load and unload cargo. The containers come in, we use cranes, forklifts, *our muscles...*" I struck a pose, "...we get shit on and off the boats. Or the trains, or the trucks. Basically, we move stuff. We're like movers." I laughed. "Honestly, I do whatever they tell me."

"You like it?"

"You kiddin'? It's a great gig. I'm lucky. I make top dollar. I got my medical, dental, you name it. I'm in the freakin' Union. I'm on easy street if I play my cards right."

Lisa chuckled – she was finding this amusing. "What are your co-workers like?"

"Ha, you sure you wanna hear?"

"Go on, I'm a big girl."

So many ways to answer. They were crass and vulgar – the stuff they said wasn't fit for a lady's ears. But they were also good and capable men, most anyway. There was a dicey element lurking. Heck, even a criminal element. Papa told me straight up, don't mess with those guys.

"Regular guys like me. A little rough around the edges."

She smirked at the non-answer. "Like you?"

"Worse than me."

"Where is this?"

"Waterfront, down off Commissioner. That's my stomping ground."

"Nice."

I nodded. "Yeah I'm on mornings this week, 6:00 a.m. to 2:00 p.m. Last week it was nights. Us newbies, they keep us on our toes."

She raised her eyebrows. "Hard to plan weekends?"

"No way, I call my own fucking shots." I said this louder than necessary, and several patrons glanced over. I covered my mouth. "Sorry, I'll try to keep it down."

"Maybe tone down the F-bombs," she said with a light-hearted smile.

"Right, where was I?"

"Calling your own shots."

I nodded. "I got some say. They like me, they treat me well. Ha, they wanna make me shop steward one day."

"You'd be good at that."

"Really?"

"Yeah, you've got a strength to you. An honesty."

"Thanks Lisa." I couldn't suppress a grin. "I been there a year. Papa got me the job. He worked there since 1960."

"Wow," she exclaimed. "What's your dad like?"

"You got a couple hours?"

She grinned at me.

"Where do I start? Italian as they come, what can I say?" I gestured emphatically.

"You guys get along?"

"I love my Papa. He might look at me and say. *Ma boy, you a crazy. You gotta rocks ina you head.*" I laughed. "But he loves me. He's proud of me."

"And you're proud of him, I can tell."

"Of course. Papa don't care what people think. He loves life. He loves people."

"The apple didn't fall far from the tree."

"*Grazie.* I think a you eeza right."

She smiled. "Maybe one day I'll meet your family."

"Ya, maybe." I pictured bringing Lisa for dinner. Papa was embarrassing at times. He had the habit of shoving a forkful of pasta in his mouth right before launching into a story. On hot days, he walked around in his underwear, usually not when we had company. He was a character, too. He'd flirt with Lisa shamelessly.

"And maybe I meet your parents, huh?"

"They'll ask about you tonight."

"Huh?"

"See these people, all so civilized, so well-behaved." She flitted her eyes about the room. "They gossip like high schoolers. My mom'll know about our little *date* before dinner." That was saying something. Remember, no cell phones, no social media.

"Sounds like Papa and his buddies on the Drive."

The time flew, and we got along like a house on fire – not even counting the sexual tension, which was off the charts for me. We cleared out at quarter past four.

When I dropped her at UBC, I got another hint of her wealth. She drove a 325i convertible, a metallic blue beauty that brought to mind the famed Azzurri jersey.

"Nice ride."

She ignored the comment. "Thanks Anthony, I had a wonderful time."

She stood not six inches away. It was my moment to steal a first kiss, but I decided a peck on the cheek was enough. A gentleman I was.

"See ya next time, Beautiful."

"Can't wait," she replied, and my heart soared.

Chapter 6 – Dhanesh

That evening, Dhanesh talked me into a burger and beer at the North Burnaby Inn. It would be the extent of my evening, but mere warmup for the D-Man. Earlier that day, he wrote his last final exam and was looking to run riot. *To feed the beast.*

In the 1980s, strip clubs were a dime a dozen, and red-blooded Canadian boys like us were fans. How could you not be? The peeler bars had no cover and draught was *cheap like borscht.* The '80s were glorious.

Dhanesh and I had catching up to do. Me with the Lisa thing, him with his latest floozie. He was also taking a job at IBM. A summer co-op, a glimpse of the successful career he'd soon enjoy.

When I picked him up, he cut to the chase. "How was she?"

"Don't you mean, *how are you?*"

He grinned. "Tell me how *she* was, and I'll know how *you* are."

"I just met her. No sex yet, bud."

"Nothing?"

"Nothing. And might I add, *minda yo fuckin' business, paisano.*"

"Hey, hey, hey." He slapped hands together, right knuckles on left palm.

"We talkin' 'bouta ma future wife." I looked away and added. "You believe this guy? *Va fongool.*" The playful mafia-speak was a favoured activity.

We waltzed into the NBI like we owned the place. It was dimly lit and not exactly rocking. But the entertainment never let up and the stage was alive with feminine flesh. Dancers here were second-string, which offended us not in the least. A naked woman – *any naked woman* – was worth watching.

We found a table twenty feet from the stage and ordered a pitcher. Dhanesh picked up where we left off. "Your future wife?" He scoffed. "Gimme a break."

"Already decided, I'm gonna marry this one."

"That's crazy talk. She's fine, granted. But ya know what my cousin says about hot chicks."

"What?"

"Someone's sick of fucking her."

"*You* say that."

"It's true, pal. *Variety.* That's the spice of life. That's why chicks dig me. They like the brown skin, not that pale ass white shit." He preened. "They don't get this everyday."

"I'm almost as dark as you." I placed my forearm alongside his.

"Yeah, not even close."

I chuckled. "Who you bangin' these days, big man?"

An essay question for Dhanesh (and incidentally, I apologize for the crude talk – *striving for authenticity is all*). Danny usually had a main squeeze with side dishes lurking in the shadows. I tried not to judge, but my morality leaned toward the prudish, side effect of my Catholic upbringing.

Don't get me wrong, I was no virgin when I met Lisa. I surrendered that distinction at seventeen. I had no choice – those high school chicks were aggressive, they literally threw themselves at me. That type of behaviour was unthinkable a few decades prior, when women would have been shamed and ostracized for such antics.

Ha, even sex before marriage was unthinkable not so long ago. But the progressives called this ludicrous, a holdover from the puritan age. In fact, so was marriage itself, they said. The anti-Christian narratives grew more outrageous as the years passed. Soon, nothing would be off-limits.

I used to wonder if the sexual revolution was a good thing, all this godless depravity. It felt a lot like Satan's calling. I didn't wonder anymore.

Where were we? Ah yes, Dhanesh.

The boy was *not* encumbered by religious restraint. He rejected Hinduism outright, along with most of his Indian heritage. He was first-generation Punjabi-Canadian. His parents came in 1964 and were fairly Canadianized. But their old country ways were close at hand. I gave that no second thought. My parents were the same. So were Ivan's.

But Dhanesh rejected his culture with a peculiar zeal, and I chalked it up to the racist taunts of his early days. He was often the only brown kid in class, and he got teased, sometimes worse. I even took a run from time to time. Not proud of that.

Ask him about his Indian heritage and he'd say: "Fuck you, I'm Canadian." He might add: "Sikhs, Hindus, it's all bullshit. Don't get me started on the goddamn Muslims."

For the record, in 1985 there were practically no Muslims in North America. Europe, too, was mostly untouched. Back then, few Western thought leaders were conscious of Islam's destructive potential. That would soon change.

Everything would soon change, and it was interesting to watch Dhanesh evolve. Before long, he would come to embrace his heritage. He'd listen to Bhangra music, he'd seek out Indian cuisine, even date Indian girls. I suppose he had to wait until his culture was cool. We all have our battles.

That aside, in '85 Dhanesh was having more fun than all of us put together. He was a big good-looking kid, a lady's man, a straight-A student with the world by the tail. Being a *person of colour* (a phrase yet to be coined) held him back not one iota.

No one knew it at the time, but POC status would one day be practically essential for success in Canadian culture. Hard to believe eh?

Chapter 7 – Culture Clash

I never set out to meet the girl of my dreams at twenty. Sometimes I wish I'd had more time to sow oats, but I got my decadence vicariously through Dhanesh. And Lisa was good for me. She helped me grow up, gave me a much-needed dose of humility. Before her, not many called me out on my bullshit.

Well, Mamma and Papa did. *And my priest.* But I barely listened. My ego was out to here. I knew what I was doing. I was King of The World.

Well, guess what. Relationships have a way of exposing flaws. "You're selfish and immature," Lisa told me.

"Says the spoiled rich girl." It was a cheap shot.

Her parents had done something right. Lisa knew how to behave, she knew how to treat others. I came around, too, eventually. Perhaps the groundwork was already there, a solid base. Say what you will about religion and strict parenting, they produce upstanding and productive citizens.

Still, we had to work through a culture clash. Lisa was raised in wealth and figured money grew on trees. The Millers were loaded. *Loaded you hear me?*

Me, I made a good living. I enjoyed life's finer things. But I had a healthy dollop of frugality in my character. Got it fair and square from Papa. He was cheap as the day is long, though to his friends he pretended money meant nothing to him, and that he had plenty.

Lisa and I got through it. Not everyone's built to be an adult in their twenties. Turned out I was. *Shocking*. We were gonna make this work. The world was ours for the taking. Though we did get off to a rocky start.

I was too *ghetto* for her parents, she was too *not Italian* for mine. Mr. and Mrs. Miller were high-brow, some might say snobby. They had reason to hold their noses in the air. They were old money. They lived in a century-old Tudor in Shaughnessy, one of the finer mansions in that oh-so-posh Vancouver borough.

They were skeptical of me. Perhaps they thought I was a gold-digger? Or they didn't like my Italian heritage? Maybe they just wanted the best for their daughter? Whatever the case, Lisa was a darling through it all. She tuned out negatives and embraced positives. A helluva skill, not one I was blessed with.

But no matter what, Lisa's parents were always tolerant. I can't stress the word enough – *tolerant* – because its meaning would soon be stretched and distorted and perverted beyond recognition, like so much of the English lexicon.

My parents were tolerant, too, in their own peculiar way. I'll leave it at that. Didn't take long for Lisa to win them over. So she wasn't Italian? And *good God*, not Catholic either. She was a Christian, and a damn sight better Christian than me. Mamma spotted that. Meanwhile, Papa shamelessly fawned, like he did over all beautiful women.

Lisa handled it like a pro. She loved how friendly and unpretentious my parents were. Hers were great, too, but uptight in comparison. My opinion.

The most friction I had was with her younger brother. *What a piece of work.* Try as I might, I found no common ground with David. He tested my tolerance and showed little of his own. Simply put, he was a spoiled brat in dire need of a thrashing.

First couple years, the little bugger tagged along everywhere. Even by nineteen and twenty years old, he was our third wheel. What, he had nothing better to do? *Mannaggia!*

Lisa indulged him without restraint. She knew it was a sore point, but family came first. I understood that. Heck, I supported it.

And David was ahead of his time. He was a shrill social justice warrior before the term was ever invented. In '88, he took a PoliSci course and found his calling, insofar as he'd *ever* find a calling. Ten years on, he was still in search of a degree. He pawned himself off as an intellectual, but he was just another perpetual student living off his folks, nothing more.

When Ivan and David met, it was hate at first sight. Ivan was just two years older but miles – *light years* – ahead in maturity. Ivan was already in his third year with Deloitte. A worker bee with a nose for money. Other than the colour of my collar, I was the same.

By that time, Ivan's political savvy was legendary. He leaned right, and he knew his shit. He despised liberals, and had talent for calling out phonies. The pretenders, he called them. Hypocrites all.

Unfortunately, that was David to a T, and Ivan thrashed him regularly. David was poster child for the emerging loony Left. An idealist, peace and love for all. He had no solutions to messy problems. He was prone to vague statements like *we all just need to love each other.* They were as irrefutable as they were useless.

Ivan took a pragmatic approach. He understood the difference between *persecuted minority* and *professional victim*, even in the late '80s. He was prescient in that regard.

But even he had no idea how epidemic the clashes would become. That they would eventually tear the Western World apart.

No one did.

Chapter 8 – The March of Time

I bought my first house in 1990. I'd been waiting for the Vancouver market to tank, but it never did and never would (at least not until *Transformation*). So, in I plunged. Best move I ever made, financially that is.

I was a humble longshoreman, keen to invest my pay and build my future. Papa taught me well. I had zero interest in politics, nor motive to cultivate interest. The world was a sane place, even Ivan thought so.

The house was mine and mine alone (okay, Papa lent me twenty grand, and we both knew I'd never pay it back), but the place had nothing to do with Lisa, not on paper. Off paper, we'd live there once we were married. That was my unspoken plan.

So of course, Lisa took an interest in *helping* with the search. "Ever consider West side?"

I looked at her like she was a space alien. "I'm not West side material."

"What does that even mean?"

"I don't fit in."

"Nonsense, you're there all the time. No one bats an eye. Except at your silly car." She grinned. "No offense."

I stroked my chin. "I can't afford West side. *Whadayathink*, I'm made of money?"

She produced a list of properties. "Lots of homes here in your range. So your mortgage is slightly higher. You're young." She winked at me. "Young and strong and handsome."

She knew I was susceptible to flattery. "Let me have a look." I scrutinized the list and was pleasantly surprised. Expensive as hell, but what the heck, maybe possible. I was making seventy-five, and the places were going for low to mid threes. East Van was a hundred K cheaper.

"Always figured my kid would go to Temp."

She chuckled. "*I* always figured *my* kid would go to private school."

"East Van looks good on you, Baby."

She scoffed. It was abundantly clear – Lisa had no intention of living in East Van. *Ever.* She felt about East Van how I felt about Surrey. For some reason, I didn't resent her for it. I actually understood.

In the end, she talked me into West side. I picked up a modest Fairview bungalow for $329,000. I was scared shitless, but when Papa gave the deal his blessing, I knew I'd be okay.

Was I ever.

Best money I ever spent. I made a hundred K in three years. *On paper.* In thirty years, the property value increased tenfold. Not that I owned it that long. We moved further west, where I made far more profit. In 2026, my house was assessed at twelve mil. That was the peak.

Even when shit began hitting the fan in the late 2020s, the West Side held value much longer, almost right up until Transformation. After that, traditional economics went out the window. We'll get there.

Back to 1990, Ivan and Dhanesh helped with the move. That's what friends did in my day. I supplied pizza and beer. That was a given.

Presto, I had a new lifestyle. A *homeowner* lifestyle, just like a real adult. My commute got worse and I started looking at my monthly gas bill. I started watching the market, even compared notes with Mr. Miller, on occasion. He had ten times Papa's net worth. Heck, maybe a hundred.

Inklings of the Miller family wealth leached out. They had the Whistler chateau, the Mexico beachfront. Lisa was raised with riding and tennis lessons, private schools, fancy holidays. I could get used to it. I'd have to if Lisa was my wife. Such sacrifices I would make.

She did become my wife, you probably figured that out. I'll gloss over the proposal – yes, it was romantic, yes she got a helluva ring, *yes she said yes*. I had no fear of commitment. Oddly, I think I feared not committing.

The proposal gave Lisa license to help furnish and decorate my new place. My priorities were a top-notch hi-fi system and a big-screen TV. Essentially, a giant mancave. A month in, my compound was mostly barren of furniture. I had people sitting on foldout chairs. Minimalism was a 90s thing, but this was ridiculous.

Lisa brought sanity to the process. She knew her way around an Ikea. "For a rich chick, you're a damn fine bargain hunter."

"My Daddy didn't raise a fool."

"Yes, he did." It took her a second to realize who I meant. "That's my brother."

"He's widely considered a moron."

"By you guys," she scoffed. "Give David time, he'll be fine." She said it without much commitment.

Incidentally, Lisa was also familiar with Vancouver's ritzier shops and not shy with a credit card. For house-warming, she got me a fancy living room set. I didn't ask how much. It was a lot, I promise you.

"We're gonna need a good, solid bed, too," I winked.

"I see where your priorities are," she admonished playfully.

Lisa wasn't Catholic, and ultimately no prude, but she was proper. We waited to consummate the relationship. I pushed at every turn, but her restraint sat well with my pious sensibilities.

We fooled around like tomcats, but when it came to the age-old act, we held off. Out of respect for each other, for God, whatever it was, we resisted.

The dam burst after I proposed, and once she came unleashed, good God, Lisa was a tiger. For a few weeks, we had a free-for-all as we sated pent-up demand.

She spent many a night, but didn't move in 'til after we married. We kept up appearances. Everything was on the down-low, and a poorly kept secret. Her car parked on my street was a dead giveaway.

Chapter 9 – The Wedding

We got married the summer of '91, and planning the wedding was an ordeal – no shortage of angst and culture clash. We Italians love our weddings big and loud.

Obscenely so.

If we had it our way, we would have rented a massive banquet hall, decorated it to the hilt, and brought in a band to cover classic rock, with a nice mix of Italian folk songs. We'd have partied like maniacs, had way too much food and booze. There might have even been a fight or two. The English, shall I say, were a tad more reserved.

The day was an exercise in compromise, with only a smidgeon of resentment here and there. We capped the list at 250, half what my parents wanted, but we didn't compromise on the ceremony. It was a Catholic affair at Our Lady of Sorrows, smack in the heart of East Vancouver. The church was an Italian-Canadian institution, with roots back to the 1940s.

Ivan was my best man, even though Lisa was developing a dislike for him. She bit her lip. Dhanesh was my number two, and I agreed to David's objectionable presence at the head table. The lengths I went.

There was debate over who'd pay for the wedding. Papa had money, but as Father of The Bride, Mr. Miller insisted. *It's tradition*, he argued, and Papa relented. I shudder to think of the final tally. No expense was spared.

There was an air of British pomp at the reception, but also a generous helping of Italian flare, including a multi-course feast featuring various pastas, veal, prosciutto, salami. Also, a steady flow of red wine from renowned Italian regions like Veneto and Tuscany. We even snuck in some traditional songs from the old country and each time the dance floor went mad.

I thought Papa might say something embarrassing, but he buttoned it down. In fact, the two Dads bonded beautifully on the day. The culture gap wasn't big, and both sides were willing. What more do you need? The biggest source of friction was Ivan. He was a prickly sonofabitch, God love him, and never one to keep opinions to himself.

Surprise, surprise, it started with something or other political. Some tediously boring provincial issue. *Provincial, you hear me?* Good fucking Lord. And this was 1991. The gulf between Left and Right was not yet a gaping chasm. Not a looming civil war. Sure seemed like it the way Ivan and David ranted and raved.

Foreshadowing future Facebook battles, they descended into insult swapping. Ivan suggested there was a village that could use David's services. "In fact," he added, "you got enough idiocy to supply a few villages."

That spawned a temper tantrum, a preview of the obnoxious SJW David would become. Or was he one already? Ahead of his time? Interesting thought.

Meanwhile, Ivan smugly spouted more insults, *and more facts*. He knew his shit.

When Lisa intervened – *I think that's enough political talk, boys* – things went further south. "Doesn't she know the men are talking?" Ivan asked.

Full marks for comic timing, but *OMFG*. Ivan had come into his own. He had a steady girlfriend now and was smoothing over his ungainliness. If the measure of a man was *know thyself*, Ivan was ten feet tall. He didn't lack confidence, though tact was in short supply. He could be a real asshole, and he'd be the first to tell you.

I tried to make amends. "Whoa Ivan, that's my wife you're talking to. Show a little respect would ya? *Dio mio!*"

I looked to Dhanesh for support, but he was off gallivanting. He was the only brown guy in attendance, and he was playing it to the hilt. Surprised there weren't more given Vancouver's shifting demographics. For what it's worth, there *were* a few Asians. But yeah, whites and Italians were dominant.

Not necessarily true in Vancouver anymore, or much of the Western World. Immigration was picking up steam. By now, Britain had a sizable Muslim population, France was loading up on North Africans, and the rest of Europe was keen to get in on the act. Few anticipated what was coming. The thought of millions descending on Europe's shores was beyond inconceivable.

In America, Blacks were hitting the mainstream, and not only for athletics and music – they'd been doing *that* since the '50s. Now they were professors, mayors, and judges. The civil rights movement had worked wonders, and affirmative action did its part, too.

Perhaps it was time to shut that down? Hell no. Black America was just getting started. They'd learned that victimhood was currency, and that White America would submit at every turn. It was only fair, because, you know, *slavery*. No one could have predicted how bad the nonsense would get.

Then there was Canada. Beautiful. Peaceful. Multicultural. We were showing the world how it was done. For a spell, even Ivan was lulled into that belief. He kept me appraised of everything. He always had the inside track, and this was pre-Internet. We got our news from TV and newspapers and conversation.

Hey, what happened there? Wasn't I supposed to be talking about a wedding?

Chapter 10 – The Nineties

Ten years flew by. That's how life is, ask anyone. Birthdays, anniversaries, christenings, always something. I barely clung to the reins.

Married life suited Lisa and me. No more shuttling back and forth, no more false pretenses. We worked, we partied, we planned and dreamed and schemed. We had youthful exuberance in those pre-kid days, and we thought it would last forever.

On my 29th birthday, we threw caution to the wind – no more birth control. Turned out we sucked at Vatican roulette. Vincent showed up nine months later and *Christ on a bike*, what a handful he was. I contemplated a vasectomy.

We went back to protective mode until 1997. Again, pay dirt in the form of Leonardo. We were a growing family and Lisa suggested I trade the Z-28 for something sensible, like a wagon or an SUV.

I felt my youth slipping away. My freedom. I played up that line of BS to all who would listen. Gone were the days when I'd drop Lisa at UBC and burn rubber on the way out, just to show those snobby intellectuals what real life looked like.

I was due for a new ride. My twelve-year-old beauty was past its prime. Honestly, even I found it tacky and dated. A Beemer, I decided, was more in keeping with my new station. More suited to my new identity.

At work, they made me shop steward and were grooming me for higher union positions. One day, I'd go full white collar, toiling not on loading docks but in boardrooms. I was okay with that. I got a kick out of the theatrics.

Meantime, Lisa worked her way up the academic ladder. She was a sessional instructor, guiding newbies toward useless degrees while she herself pursued a PhD in English Lit. The pay was borderline, but Daddy-O (*hers*) was sliding over a nice little stipend every month on the down-low. I didn't complain.

My girl was a serious bookworm, she always had a book on the go. I was no illiterate, but the books I'd read would fit in the glove box of my Trans Am. Somehow or other, she got me hooked.

She started me slow and easy, like a drug dealer. Cussler and Crichton, with a side of Grisham. I plowed through *The Firm* in a weekend. Next, I tackled a couple of Michener beasts. I felt cultured.

The hobby improved my vocabulary, as did being around Lisa, and that was a valuable addition to my professional toolbox. Collective bargaining was a contact sport, but in between haymakers, appearing erudite never hurt a position.

Through it all, I kept playing soccer. Eventually, I swallowed pride and downshifted to Div 2. The body was looking good, but the fire in the belly was cooling. I got some back when young Vinny turned five, and I started coaching.

Lisa kept in shape at the Club, working out, swimming lengths. In summers, she took to the ocean and when we moved to Point Grey, that pursuit increased given proximity to Jericho. She even got me in the water sometimes. Damn it was cold.

You heard right. *Point fucking Grey.* Swanksville. Once we had child number three, *Young Julio*, Lisa talked me into the upgrade. We got ourselves a ritzy house in a ritzy neighbourhood. Not bad for a kid from East Van, a dock worker no less. Not that I was ever destitute. Papa did right by us. He put food on the table, a roof over our heads. We never wanted for anything.

Still, I felt a tad out of my league. My neighbours were doctors, lawyers, and CEOs. They drove fancy cars, they wore fancy clothes. Their kids wore fancy clothes. I got used to it soon enough.

In the *it's-a-small-world* department, who do I bump into? My old soccer nemesis, Charles Kennedy. He was a lawyer now, a partner at some highfalutin downtown outfit. He lived a few doors down, in the nicest house on the block. It was worth a couple million, I was told. Its value would ultimately peak at 117 mil in 2026. Not a bad ROI if you time it right.

Charles and I had some good chats. We talked Whitecaps, we reminisced on the glory days, we lamented lingering injuries.

"We didn't like you West Side boys much."

When he smirked, I saw a flash of the waspy arrogance. He covered it with good manners, but he didn't fool me. *Bastard.*

He was a good neighbour. A good citizen, too. He was planning a run for office. "Make sure you vote for me," he said.

"I'll think about it." Laughter. For some reason, friendship never blossomed. Some things were never meant to be.

Like friendship between Lisa and Ivan. She tolerated him, and for that I was appreciative. He was married now, and it helped that Petra was an agreeable sort. She had to be to marry Ivan. They had a kid, too. A boy named Sasha. I remember wondering if the youngster might turn into an opinionated ass like Ivan.

I also wondered, at times, why Ivan was my friend. Ha, I knew why. The friends you make when you're young are always your best friends. They know all your secrets.

Between Ivan from the Right, and Lisa from the Left, I was getting a well-rounded political education. The chasm grew by the day and I tried hard to see both sides. The approach worked well, until the disease of Liberalism deemed logic to be racist. I'm not kidding.

Ivan kept me abreast of political drama all over the globe – Bosnia, the Middle East, South Africa – but my naivety was epic. "Nothing bad ever happens here," I once declared.

"Complacency is the enemy of freedom."

I smiled condescendingly. "Give it a rest, dude."

"Never."

If there'd been more skeptics like Ivan, we might not be in the state we were in. He proclaimed socialism was the road to ruin, and communism was worse. He despised liberals, and seemed to sense the dangerous forces that were lurking.

Lisa figured he was nuts. I settled on cynical, perhaps slightly neurotic. I don't feel that way now. I feel only admiration for his prescience.

But not even Ivan anticipated the extent of the depravity, the lies, the deceit. By the time he did, it was too late. The Western World was on a suicide mission. People tried to stop it. I was one of them.

Race was always the driver, because it was just so untouchable. *I don't see colour* was the acceptable position for whites. The only one. Whites clung to the idea even when racial division and tribal conflict couldn't be ignored. Even Ivan treaded lightly in this minefield.

On its face, diversity appeared wonderful. A mosaic of people and cultures living in blissful harmony. What's not to like? That's what we were taught, that was my experience, that's what I believed. Who cares if the experiment failed every time it'd been tried. This time would be different, right?

During high school, we *did* get along. That was my recollection. But in high school, minorities weren't told they were victims. In high school, the government didn't actively recruit immigrants that would be burdens on the state. *Ah hell,* maybe they did, but back then they weren't numerous enough to do much damage, or alter the host culture.

By the time problems emerged, everyone was indoctrinated. Mass immigration was good – anyone who said otherwise was bad. Racist. Xenophobic. A Nazi.

Those who went a step further and suggested maybe, *just maybe,* all cultures were not equal, or heaven forbid, maybe all people were not equal – good God, *that was hate speech.* Punishable by law. Ostracism. Imprisonment.

Whoops, getting ahead of myself again. I keep doing that. Let's get back to the 1990s, shall we? Back to my pal Dhanesh – the brown Casanova, my token Indian friend. He was still living at home and why not? He lived like a king and paid no rent. Why move out?

He was thriving at IBM, and breaking hearts. He was God's gift to women of all colours, just ask him. Truth be told, he'd slowed. He had to, we were in our 30s for Christ's sake. But there was more going on with the D-Man. *Oh yeah.*

By the late '90s, there were a great many Indians in the Lower Mainland, and suddenly Dhanesh was embracing the culture. The same culture he'd vigorously rejected as a teen, and a twenty-something.

Nowadays, brown was hip. Brown was cool. Dhanesh spotted the trend and went all in. Minorities were numerous and had become aware of their political clout. Dare I say, some took note of the struggle of American

Blacks, and hints of victim status started appearing in non-Black persons of colour. The dawn of identity politics.

I recall Dhanesh announcing, out of the blue: "Maybe one day I'll run for office." Ivan fell out of his chair laughing, but in retrospect he saw the potential. People vote along tribal lines, Ivan said. Always have, always will.

Soon, everyone would join the victimhood movement – *except whites of course*. First Nations peoples were still top of the totem pole, and perhaps the only group with a legitimate beef, a right to complain.

There were hints of the victimhood epidemic in the 1990s, especially in America. The O.J. Simpson murder trial exposed the racial divide. *The chasm*. When O.J. was acquitted by a mostly-Black jury, everyone knew he was guilty. *Everyone*. Yet Blacks celebrated. They couldn't hide their delight, and didn't bother trying. *About time a Black man caught a break*. It was an obscene spectacle, and a learning experience.

Black America learned that if enough fuss was made, they could get literally away with murder. The victim card was just that powerful. That was the start of the madness, the day America realized – whoa, maybe this thing ain't gonna work after all.

The preposterous verdict coincided with an explosion of Black culture. Rap and hip hop were all the rage, and White America was fascinated. They even got in on the act. Vanilla Ice hit big with *Ice Ice Baby*, and went on to become a punchline. A few years later, Eminem released *Slim Shady* and was deemed the real thing.

In other news, South Africa became a democracy – a feelgood moment for everyone, including many white South Africans who bought into the dream. Unfortunately, it was a sham and the unravelling began immediately. People pretended not to notice, until that was no longer possible.

Meanwhile, the European Union debuted with a mission to promote social, political and economic harmony. They produced lofty doctrine, but they were just another sham. A bloated, corrupt mess intent on destroying Europe. My opinion.

What else? Y2K ran rampant and Microsoft released Windows 95, their answer to Apple. They didn't get it right, but they got closer. The Internet arrived and dramatically altered human behaviour.

Instant access to infinite information seemed like a good idea, and it was. Unfortunately, it opened a Pandora's Box of hyper-Orwellian surveillance that was impossible to turn off.

Whoops.

Chapter 11 – September 11, 2001

I was working the early shift, and up well before sunrise. *Living the dream.* For my 6:00 a.m. start, I showed up early to sip coffee and bullshit with the boys. Lest you think I'm a hero, I often left six hours into my eight-hour shift. I had a good gig.

Can you believe it, Vinny was already in grade two and making a name for himself, not always a good one. Young Leo was a year away from Kindergarten, and Christ was that kid a *Mamma's Boy.*

Lisa was expecting our third child and I was curious what might come out. Vinny and Leo were as different as chalk and cheese. I wasn't anxious about the pending birth, but it was on my mind as I strolled into the work yard, swapping jabs with co-workers. I had no idea the enormity of the day ahead. That in a few short minutes, America would be subjected to horrific attacks no screenwriter could ever imagine.

As I contemplated a day of tracking and moving containerized cargo, American Airlines Flight 11 crashed into One World Trade Center, the North Tower. The second plane had yet to hit.

"Hey Big Shot, ya hear?" My buddy Aldo loved the gossip. "Freakin' *aero*plane crashed into the goddamn World Trade Center."

"*Ah cazzo!* Get the fuck outta here."

"No kidding. My wife called, it's all over the news. The whole fucking building's on fire. Like a goddamn towering inferno." We swore a lot in my line of work.

I pondered what I'd heard.

"It ain't no little fire, Tony. The whole thing's smoking like a fucking chimney."

An unease descended. A premonition something monstrous had occurred. "How about we get another coffee, Aldo? Maybe take a peek at the TV?"

"You're the boss."

I consulted my watch. A new batch of containers was due at eight. We had time. "Let's go take a looksee."

We waltzed into the coffee room where a handful of guys were crowded round the TV. "What, you guys got nothing better to do?"

Heads turned in my direction, but no trash talk came back.

"You gotta see this, Tony," someone hollered, and several men repeated what Aldo had told me. The group was boisterous. Questions and opinions flowed.

"Know what I think? I think it's one of those motherfucking terrorist kamikazes."

"How many people in that building?"

"Oh fuck, *thousands*. They're three hours ahead in *New Yawk*, and those fuckers get up early."

He was right about financial professionals. Ivan was at his desk by seven every day. He lived and breathed the market. If it was up, he was happy. Otherwise, not so much.

"How you put out a fucking fire like that?" Someone said. "Whadaya, drag a fucking hose up there? Get a massive fucking ladder?"

Good question. Helicopters maybe? *Jesus, look at that thing smoke.* The contrast between blue sky and black smoke was startling. Mesmerizing. I couldn't take my eyes off it.

I thought of Lisa and stepped away to call. She picked up first ring. "I'm watching," she said. "Mom called ten minutes ago."

"Where are the kids?"

"Leo's playing downstairs. Vincent's at school."

"I gotta bad feeling, Baby. This ain't good."

"Me too."

I asked how she was feeling. Her due date was near, and I was on light standby. I hung up and went back to the TV, where the gathering had strengthened in numbers.

At 9:03 a.m. eastern, there was a massive and horrific flash of orange flame as United Airlines Flight 175 disappeared into the South Tower. The guys went ballistic.

"Holy. Fucking. Shit."

"This can't be happening."

"We're under attack. *This is crazy*, it's goddamn war."

"It's fucking terrorism. It's gotta be. No doubt."

I didn't say anything. I was in shock. We all were. Ivan called a few minutes later.

"What'd I tell ya?" He ranted for a while about various conspiracies, but I barely listened. I felt like I was watching a movie. Except it was real. A harsh new reality was settling in.

Maybe one was an accident. But two? *No way.* And Jesus, was it even over? What was next? Both fucking buildings hit. What landmark would they go after next?

The talking heads on CNN speculated. Back then, CNN was a respected news authority. Some of you younger folks may find that hard to believe.

I called Lisa again. My emotions were at the surface. *I'm coming home, Baby. I'll get Vincent. You talk to your parents again? Can you call Nonna...make sure they're okay?*

I had to make sure all my loved ones were accounted for. Jesus Christ, was this real? The crowd had thinned. Had they gone to work? Or gone home? I thought of the containers waiting to be processed, but I had neither the intention nor the capacity to work. Hell, they might even close the Port.

"Those crazy motherfuckers," one man barked. "They finally did it."

"Who you talking about, Frankie?"

"You know *goddamn* well who I'm talking about. *We all know*. Those crazy fucking Arabs."

"Shut up, Frankie. You're talking outta your ass. Coulda been anyone."

"Goddamn right I know. We gotta teach them ragheads a lesson. We gotta bomb the shit outta 'em, and we gotta do it now."

Reactions like this played out all across the Western World. I felt them myself. I was scared, but my blood was boiling. I wanted revenge. Payback. I wanted to see them suffer. Outwardly, I remained calm.

"That's enough, Frankie," I admonished. "Capisce?"

"Christ," someone said. "What about the people in those buildings? Imagine being above that? *Look at that smoke.*"

I shuddered. Watching the towers burn was surreal. I can't describe it. Hollow emptiness mingled with morbid fascination.

George W. Bush came on the screen, and I heard snippets: "...a national tragedy...apparent terrorist attack...conduct full-scale investigation...full resources of the federal government...we're gonna hunt down and find the folks who committed this act."

Did he say folks?

When they cut back to CNN, more anger erupted from Frankie. "We gotta take these fucking terrorists out. We gotta bomb 'em, and we gotta bomb all the fucking countries that support 'em."

Several men agreed and Frankie took license to continue. "And we can't let any more of 'em in our fucking countries."

I didn't bother interrupting. Why was I still here? I looked at my watch. 6:35 a.m. I arrived an hour ago, but it felt like a lifetime.

Then more horror. *Huge fire at the Pentagon. What?*

Everyone shut up. Even Frankie. "Massive plume of smoke...impossible to say what happened...getting reports the Whitehouse is being evacuated."

The Pentagon? The Whitehouse?

"Associated press is reporting a plane has crashed into the Pentagon."

"Oh my *fucking* gawd."

"These guys mean business. This is World War Three, guys. It's on, baby."

My bright red anger intensified. So did my fear. What was happening? No one knew. Would it come here? I was overcome with emotion. My eyes watered. When I tried to speak my voice caught.

I had to go home. I had to be with family. See my wife, hug my kids. I wasn't the only one. Within fifteen minutes, the room was deserted.

I picked up Vinny on the way and he was unusually well-behaved. Kids sense a parents' mood and he knew I was worried. All the parents were. Grave expressions all around.

On the drive home, NewsTalk 980 reported the South Tower had collapsed in a cloud of steel and concrete. People nearby ran for their lives. One-hundred and ten stories, *gone*. The thought was incomprehensible.

When I pulled into the driveway, Lisa rushed out to meet me. I hugged her fiercely, then scooped up young Leonardo.

"They were jumping out of the buildings," Lisa whispered.

"I heard."

She was near tears, and there was a tremor in her voice. "The South Tower's gone."

I nodded.

"I wonder how many people died."

"A lot."

"There might be more planes. That's what they're saying."

I nodded again. *God help us.*

The rest of the day was a blur. The North Tower collapsed. A fourth plane crashed in western Pennsylvania, eighty miles outside Pittsburgh.

We hunkered down. The whole country did. Canada and America both. The whole world. We tried to put on a brave face for our kids, and failed.

When I talked to Ivan, he had lots on his mind. He had it all figured out. Conspiracy theories. Islamic extremism. Osama Bin Laden.

I listened with little emotion as he raged. I had no awareness Islam was at war with the West. Islam barely registered on my consciousness, save an athlete or two. Muhammad Ali, Kareem Abdul Jabbar. Those guys didn't seem like our enemy.

"How you gonna fight someone who's not afraid to die?" Ivan continued. "You can't negotiate with 'em. You just gotta wipe 'em out."

"How would we do that?" I asked.

"Nuke 'em, that's how. It's the only way. You let this cancer grow, it'll kill us all." Brief pause. "We ignored the signs, we shoulda seen this coming. What did we have? The U.S. Embassy in Kenya, the attack on the USS Cole. They already bombed the Towers, when was that? The '90s?"

I'd heard enough. "I gotta get back to Lisa, bud."

"I hear ya. Petra's waiting on me."

"How is she? And Sasha? Everyone okay?"

"We're good, thanks for asking. We're blessed, my friend. You hear me? *Blessed.*"

I couldn't agree more. We lived idyllic lives in a peaceful paradise. We never gave it a second thought.

Until now.

Would it always be like this? Or would the evil find us? According to Ivan, it could and would. *They hate us*, he said. *They hate our way of life. You can't imagine how much they hate us.*

I spent the week trying to process what happened. I was reeling from the images, from the depth of the attack. The World Trade Center was gone. The symbol of capitalism and freedom. *And the Pentagon.* It was too much to comprehend.

On Friday, there was a Day of Prayer and Remembrance. Memorial services were held throughout the world – London, Paris, Ottawa. It took a couple weeks for any sense of normalcy to return. The world became a different place on September 11, 2001.

2,996 people perished. Countless others were injured, some horribly maimed and burned. 9/11 was the deadliest attack on U.S. soil since the War of 1812. Lower Manhattan was a wasteland of rubble and debris, and human remains. It was *Ground Zero*.

Heroes emerged, and America was keen to celebrate them. Firefighters were at the head of this group. Those brave men who voluntarily went up the Towers as the public went down.

There were stories of miraculous escape and tragic tales of death, of loved ones lost. There were makeshift memorials, and posters of the missing. Mayor Giuliani emerged a hero as he spoke calmly, and with authority and compassion.

The resilience of New Yorkers was on full display. The grit to carry on amid unspeakable grief and sadness. The people of New York and all of America bonded in the days following. I still recall David Letterman's somber monologue, not for what he said, but how he said it.

There was a feeling of unity – *of all for one, and one for all.* It transcended race and colour. The divisions were there, but for a precious few weeks, they were invisible. The Union lived in harmony.

American flags were everywhere – on cars, houses, and buildings. People sang *God Bless America* spontaneously. They united in patriotism, but also grief, determination, and a common enemy. The line between good and evil was never clearer.

We felt it in Canada. For a while, *we felt American*. Bound by powerful uniting forces, the same forces that forge great nations. What happens when those forces go away? Do great nations wither and die? Do they fall prey to predatory forces?

The solidarity was fleeting as old grievances came to the fore. I believe that brief window following 9/11 was America's last great show of unity. 9/11 was also the ultimate wake-up call, yet no one woke up.

I thanked God for the Western World and the gifts it bestowed, for the protection from madmen. We were good. They were evil. But as time passed, doubts formed. Who were *they?* Who were *we?* What have we – *the Western World* – become? We were not without sin. We were certainly not without enemies.

Anti-American forces were gathering, and not only in dusty desert compounds of the Middle East. Criticism, verbal attacks, threats – they came from Iraq, Iran, North Korea. They came from Russia and China, and pockets of Europe.

But they also came from within. *America was never great,* the voices said. *America stole this land. She enslaved Africans, she brutalized Natives, she bombed the innocent. America must pay for her sins.*

To make matters worse, the Bush Administration wanted vengeance – they wanted the scalp of Saddam Hussein or Osama bin Laden – preferably both. They invaded Iraq to seize weapons of mass destruction, 'cause obviously Iraq had them. And *so what* if they didn't – they were a rogue state and they had it coming.

Five years later, the conflict raged on and no one was happy. America needed a sea-change. Politicians on both sides of the aisle felt it.

Chapter 12 – The Times They Are A Changin'

9/11 changed us. Despite assurances from politicians, naïve illusions of safety vanished. We were vulnerable. Soft targets were everywhere. Security ramped up all over the place. Air travel got complicated.

But America moved on and so did we. Like all good humans, we ignored the danger. Before you knew it, 9/11 was in the rear view. The Iraq war, a minor distraction.

We had enough to worry about. Lisa was a West Side snob at heart, and she desperately wanted our boys to attend private school, preferably St. Georges. I knew two things about the institution: 1) it was nothing like Templeton and 2) it cost a fortune.

We settled on Vancouver College, which was a fraction cheaper, and Catholic. A small victory, not that we were in competition.

We weren't.

Sounds like a cliché, but Lisa and I were best friends. Hard to believe, seventeen years since we got hitched. I say it again, time flies. My boys were growing up. Vincent was fourteen, Leonardo eleven, and Young Julio about to turn eight. *Unbelievable.*

Equally unbelievable, Vinny was already like a man. He was always thick and sturdy, but puberty unleashed a torrent of testosterone. At five eight, he'd practically reached full height, and he was intimidatingly broad-shouldered. He was shaving at twelve and his facial hair now rivalled my own.

School was not Vinny's strong suit. His grades were terrible and his behaviour worse. "Look Ma," Vinny would say and knock on his skull. "It's too thick. Nothing gets in, *hahahahahaha.*"

Lisa labelled him high-spirited, occasionally naughty, but in truth she was horrified by her firstborn. *So was I.* But I'd seen many like him from my own high school days.

Vinny got kicked out of VC – *correction*, the headmaster suggested he might not be a good fit. After a spell at a West Side public school, I packed him off to Templeton. Vinny held the place in high esteem after hearing me rave about it for years.

Four months in, he was sort of fitting in. At least he was trying. Spoiler alert, he never graduated high school, much less any institution of higher learning. Vinny drank beer and cavorted with boys two and three years his senior. They were generally up to no good.

He was a life-of-the-party type, with a short fuse. At a young age, he developed a reputation as someone not to mess with. He earned it with fists and feet, and a damn fine wit I must say.

At home, I kept a close watch. Back in the day, Papa kept me in line with threats of *the dreaded belt*. He even used it on occasion. Didn't work with Vinny. He barely flinched, and truth be told, I feared an eventual reprisal. Not kidding.

Vinny had a tendency to bully his younger brothers, especially poor Leo. Vinny ridiculed him relentlessly. He roared with laughter at Leo's effeminate ways.

I used to wonder, what will become of Vinny? Will he end up on the docks? That was the best I could hope for. I worried about a criminal destiny. He just didn't give a damn. I never figured that kid out, and I'm still trying. I still love him to this day.

I loved all my kids, but I ain't gonna lie – Julio was my favourite. I'd never say it out loud, but he was my golden boy. I burst with pride at his exploits on the pitch and in the classroom. He excelled at everything, especially life.

Believe it or not, one of Julio's classmates (and teammates) was Charles Kennedy's boy. *They were friends.* Weird how this guy kept coming in and out of my life. We chatted on the sidelines, around the neighbourhood, and still friendship never blossomed. I just couldn't let go of the childhood animosity. By now, Charles was into politics, a rising star in the Conservative Party. He made life look easy.

Julio was the same. He was blessed with the good-natured demeanour of someone you knew would do well in life. A *can't miss.* He attracted attention wherever he went. Lisa and I fawned over him, so did his teachers and coaches. Through all his winning ways, few were jealous. Leo had his moments, mind you.

Julio, bless him, looked upon me with such love and adoration. I was his hero and I did my best not to disappoint. If ever I had a bad day, Julio's smile took it away in a heartbeat. I get choked up talking about him.

Better move on.

Ah Leonardo. The dreaded middle child. Where to begin? At eleven, he was still fair, with a shiny mop of blonde hair. He was a quirky little fellow, slight and unathletic. He enjoyed video games, writing in his beloved journal, various other flights of fancy.

He was a *Mamma's Boy.* Soft, you might say. Delicate and fragile. Definitely not rough and tumble like Vincent and Julio. I didn't know what to make of him, but I loved him anyway. Lisa did, too. She probably gave him extra love, 'cause he seemed to need it. Lisa was an amazing mother.

She was an amazing *everything*. Man, I lucked out. I mentioned we were best friends, but we were also passionate lovers. If I'd lost a step in the libido department – *I'm not saying I had* – Lisa was still a tomcat. Sexier now than the day I met her. No lie.

Home life was good – lots of drama raising three boys. Work kept me busy and out of trouble. I didn't work the yard anymore, I'd been a desk jockey since 2005. I spent my days scrutinizing grievances and attending disciplinary hearings.

I found my calling in the collective bargaining process. Turned out, I was a good negotiator. Tough and fair, manipulative as hell. You had to be going toe-to-toe with management, 'cause they were conniving snakes. When I shared war stories with Ivan, he delighted in calling me a socialist.

Speaking of Ivan, he'd come into his own. He was making *mucho dinero* managing stock portfolios, including mine. He and Petra had just the one child, Sasha, and no desire for a second. Dhanesh figured Ivan was too selfish.

Travel became Ivan's hobby, his mode of relaxation. He took oodles of time off every year, and since his wife didn't work, they enjoyed frequent excursions. 9/11 deterred them from flying not one iota. They'd been to Europe more times that I could count. France, Italy, Spain, Greece. Hungary of course. The list was ever-growing.

Vacation-wise, Lisa and I stuck to the beaten path – Hawaii, Mexico, the Miller family cabin in Osoyoos. Ivan regularly invited us to join them farther afield, and I always said *one day*. Well, one day we did, and I still lay awake at night wishing we didn't. We'll get to that.

Besides travel, Ivan was non-ostentatious. He lived in the same *Vancouver Special* he bought in '97. He rented a suite downstairs, not that he needed the money. He was just naturally industrious. He inherited his father's Eastern European aloofness, a temperament many mistake for rudeness. But underneath the crunchy exterior, a large and loving heart thumped. He was surprisingly caring with family. Lisa actually warmed to him over the years. Ivan was an acquired taste.

He remained a relentless political beast, ranting and raving about all manner of the Canadian body politic. American and European, too. He was remarkably knowledgeable and remarkably pessimistic. The world was going to hell in a handbasket, he figured.

I listened. Occasionally, I probed. Occasionally I believed. In 2008, I was liberal as the day is long. Most Vancouverites were. Most would be until it was too late.

Ivan had a bigger audience now. Facebook had exploded, and he preached and prattled about all manner of fact, rumour and opinion. You wouldn't find me there for a few years yet. Pretty Boy Dan was there, and he had more friends and followers than Ivan, many of them Indian. His content was lifestyle, as apolitical as you could get.

For now.

Dhanesh also had a steady girlfriend. An Indian lass, far younger, ultra-traditional. A girl his parents approved of. *Selected*, if I believed Ivan. Prisha was a sweetheart – too good for that rogue. When Dan the Man told me he no longer kept secret lovers, this only meant he kept them on the super-duper down low.

He still talked of a run at politics. *It's our turn to run this place*, he was fond of saying.

In other news. Saddam Hussein was executed, Hurricane Katrina almost wiped New Orleans off the map, and the iPhone showed us how crappy Blackberries were. Facebook, Twitter, and Google were taking over the Internet. No one could imagine the power these behemoths would soon have.

One more thing, fairly significant. That sea change America needed? That balm for her wounds?

She got it in 2008, in the form of Barack Hussein Obama.

Chapter 13 – Barack Hussein Obama

We were changing fast, and it felt like for the better. We were entering a new phase, a more enlightened phase. More open, more honest. Everyone – *I mean everyone* – would get a fair shake at opportunity. Utopia was within reach.

Wasn't the election of the 44th President proof?

He was Black.

That meant everything in America, and America was the Western World's barometer. America would finally purge her original sin. Racial grievances would vanish. They'd become a relic, a distant footnote of a distant and best-forgotten past. Post-racial harmony would emerge, just like we enjoyed in Vancouver.

LOL.

That's how I felt January 20, 2009, and I wasn't the only one. America desperately wanted Obama to be good, *and he was*. He was handsome and presidential. Intelligent and smooth. The guy had no flaws. So smitten was the press and the fawning public, no one questioned the bizarre rush to bestow upon him a Nobel Peace Prize. What great deed made him a deserving recipient?

He was Black.

What other justification was there? Part of it was anticipation of what he might do. Had to be.

But my God, Obama was slick. He even charmed Ivan. He oozed charisma. He was inspirational, intelligent, articulate. *And regal.* He would surely return America from the brink and unite the world.

If that sounds hyperbolic, I swear it's not. In fact, it hardly captures the euphoric spirit of optimism gripping the U.S., Canada, and the world. Obama would right the economic ship, heal domestic wounds, build bridges of peace to Islam. He'd probably eliminate world hunger, while he was at it.

CNN drooled over his every utterance. They went wall-to-wall-Obama, and so did the other stations. Obamamania was in the air. So much so, we were having an inauguration party at Lisa's parents' place. There were fireworks, of course, and they started with Ivan.

"Hey, I like the guy," Ivan explained to David. "All I'm saying is, if he's not a natural-born citizen, he shouldn't be President."

David scowled. "If he was white, you wouldn't question his birthplace."

"I wouldn't question his birthplace if he produced a birth certificate."

"He has, jackass."

"What took so long? And where's the long form? Even you could make that one in Photoshop. Okay, maybe not *you.*"

"You're a real asshole, Ivan."

"Got a job yet, David?" Ivan snickered. "Or still studying."

David stormed off to his bedroom, the same one he occupied as a teenager. I may have been a liberal, but I had a hard time with David. A self-righteous, part-time student living off the good graces of his parents. At forty fucking years old.

"Lighten up on him, hey pal." I said.

"I said I like the guy," Ivan replied. "I just wanna know he's a real American."

"I meant David, dumbass." I gestured like a crazed Italian. "*Va fongool.*"

Ivan pressed on grinning. "I got other concerns, too. Not just the birth certificate. Or lack thereof."

"Like what."

"He's green, man. Ya see his resume?"

"He's a lawyer, isn't he?"

Ivan scoffed. "He practiced a couple years. He was a street organizer, too, then some sort of junior senator. Out of the blue, he's running for president. Forty-five years old. No executive experience, no foreign policy. Does that sound thin to you?"

"He'll be fine. Listen to him speak, he's brilliant."

"I hope he's got the chops," Ivan said smugly. "'Cause he certainly ain't got the experience."

"Sshhh," said Lisa. "They're doing the oath of office."

CNN cut to a live shot with Diane Feinstein introducing the Honorable John G. Roberts. An immense crowd had gathered outside the Capitol Building. Reporters and dignitaries stood at attention. Everyone wanted to witness history.

Obama appeared on screen, sanguine, polished, *presidential.* No fault to be found. The two men got straight to business, and immediately fumbled. Obama began speaking before Roberts was finished. No problem, they were pros. They moved on.

But the gaffe flustered Roberts, and he misplaced the word *faithfully* in the next sentence. Obama hesitated, as if aware, and Roberts attempted to correct himself. Obama then repeated the sentence in its incorrect form. It was bizarre and slightly comical. You certainly couldn't fault Obama.

They completed the task without further incident and the crowd cheered. Cannons fired, the band played, flags waived. This was America. Land of the free, home of the brave. These folks knew how to do it right.

But troublemakers speculated: was Obama *really* president if the oath wasn't properly taken? It was a silly thing, but Ivan pounced.

"A bad omen," he declared. "Already Senator Obama's showing he's out of his depth."

"That's *President* Obama," David bellowed. He was back.

"Not yet," said Ivan. "He needs to take the oath."

"You're such a racist ass, Ivan." Smoke was pouring out of David's ears.

"Easy guys," I said. "How about another beer?"

Ivan enjoyed pushing David's buttons for entertainment. He was a jerk that way.

On the screen, James Taylor sang *America the Beautiful,* and I vaguely wondered why him. Blessedly, Obama came back, lean and strong and handsome, as if he'd stepped from the pages of GQ. His voice soothed, it instilled confidence. You wanted to believe the guy. I *did* believe the guy.

How far America had come since the days of MLK. *A Black man in the oval office.* Unthinkable not so long ago, yet there he was. This was the pinnacle. Proof of post-racial harmony. More than that, I got the sense – it's finally over. *Finally,* we can put the bad feelings behind us. *Finally,* we can all just get along.

Not so fast.

What had David just called Ivan? *Racist.* It was a harbinger. The squabbles would not only continue, they'd worsen. David's reaction was the start of a pattern in which any critique of Obama, or any Black person, was not only in poor taste, it was vile racism.

Nonetheless, Obama didn't disappoint with his Inauguration speech. He spoke of unity and action, of prosperity and freedom. And he didn't shy from tough topics:

"Our economy is badly weakened, a consequence of greed and irresponsibility on the part of some, but also our collective failure to make hard choices and prepare the nation for a new age. Homes have been lost, jobs shed, businesses shuttered."

Obama called for hard work, bold and swift action. He talked of duty and responsibility, of hope and courage, of American values. Around the living room, we heaped praise. David was moved to tears. *What a drama queen.*

When the celebrations were over, and the fawning waned, Ivan injected some unwelcome reality. The markets were tanking, fortunes were eroding.

"He's in tough," Ivan stated. "Canadian banks should be fine – *thank you Stephen Harper* – but south of the border? They're on the brink."

"That's not Obama's fault," David shrieked.

"Don't worry, son, your allowance should be fine." Heavy on condescension.

"*Asshole,*" was all David could come back with.

"Why should we believe you, Ivan?" I asked. "My portfolio's getting killed. That's on you, dude."

"Have you seen the Dow? It's under 8,000. It was double that a year ago."

"*I know.* You're taking me to the poorhouse."

"Me too," said Dhanesh.

"Both you bastards are beating the market. I've shown you. *That's* on me. But if the financial system collapses," he hung his head, "it'll be hard to keep working my magic."

"There's gotta be someone we can blame," I said. "Jesus, there's gotta be someone we can *shoot.*"

Ivan nodded. "I suppose we can blame *Double-ya.* He's a convenient scapegoat. But it's left-leaning policy that's the culprit."

"Oh, gimme a break," David howled.

Ivan ignored him. "They created the subprime market. They pressured banks to make risky loans because of uhhhh...*equality.*" He made air quotes. "Well guess what? When you get rid of oversight, bankers run hog-wild. They sold millions of bullshit loans, then covered it up. Eventually, the schemes fell apart. They ran out of other people's money. Now, the big banks are wounded. That's what happened, folks."

"Okay expert, what happens now?" Lisa chimed in.

"Yeah, *tell us* expert," David added. He was such a pipsqueak.

"Let me look into my crystal ball." Ivan put his hands beside his eyes and began speaking as if in a trance: "I see Obama sprinkling fairy dust on the markets. I see him asking us to believe things will get better. We must *believe, believe, believe.* I see Obama as our white knight."

"You mean Black knight?" Everyone but David laughed.

"Seriously Ivan," Lisa persisted. "What's next?"

"I'm halfway serious. Markets are emotional, they respond to confidence, and Obama's got plenty. Then again, what the hell does he know about finance?"

"You're only saying that 'cause he's Black," David snarled.

Ivan made the *shush* gesture. "There's gonna be some sort of bailout. Something artificial. Has to happen. And uh..." he drew a deep breath, "...I hope like hell it works."

Ivan was a smart cookie. He called it. The markets kept tanking into February of 2009. Each passing day the Dow found new bottoms. The TSX, too. Markets flirted with dotcom lows. It was grim, and Obama's pep talks – *inspirational as they were* – had little impact.

Jobs evaporated, banks collapsed. Detroit's big three were on death watch. My investments got pummeled.

On February 17, 2009, Obama signed into law the Recovery and Reinvestment Act, a massive stimulus package to rescue the economy. It was a Hail Mary.

Emergency surgery to save a dying patient. No one knew if it would work.

Lo and behold, two weeks hence the Dow hit bottom and bounced. *Grazie Dio!* Within a year, it crested 10,000. By the end of Obama's first term, it closed on 14,000. The bull market would charge on many years.

Unfortunately, other vital signs took longer to come around and key indicators stubbornly exposed economic woes. Labour force participation plummeted. Food stamp use skyrocketed. Healthcare costs, well.... that was a whole new ballgame.

But to Obama's credit, a full-blown financial collapse was averted. America dodged a monumental crisis. Ivan called it Obama's only victory.

I tended to agree, especially with the luxury of hindsight. The weight of expectation was heavy on Obama's shoulders. For Christ sakes, they awarded the guy a Peace Prize because they expected miracles. At the end of the day, he delivered division and hostility, and little else.

If it's any consolation, his foreign policy was equally bad. The Iraq withdrawal, the Red Line debacle, the Benghazi attack – the list of blunders was long. He certainly brought America's credibility down a few pegs. Almost felt like that was the goal.

Sorry folks, Obama sucked.

Again, I'm getting ahead of myself.

Chapter 14 – Something Is Amiss

Time advanced like an invading army. By the end of Obama's first term, I was within sight of the dreaded fifty. Damn near a senior citizen. *Jesus.*

Life was good, but not without worry. Vinny had me on edge, though his happy-go-lucky nature tempered my anxiety. He worked only sporadically at the docks, and always had a ton of dough. Go figure.

When he had run-ins with the law, I asked myself *where'd I go wrong?* I asked myself that for many years. Our kids are not blank slates. They come hardwired, some more than others.

Leonardo was the polar opposite. A rule-follower, a studious bookworm. He was set to start university, and would take to Leftism like a fish to water. At the time, it worried me not in the least. Julio was on the crest of puberty, still my golden boy.

Meanwhile, Vancouver continued to diversify. No one batted an eye. Multiculturalism was in our blood, preached to us since childhood. Every red-blooded Canadian knew our country was built by immigrants, and that diversity was our strength. Commenting on emerging ethnic enclaves was not only in poor taste, it was racist. So much easier not to notice.

But I noticed. Surrey had become predominantly Indian. Richmond was a Chinese city, where English signs were a rarity. These changes happened in a blink. Ivan called it colonization.

At least Commercial was still Italian, right? *Right!* Not so fast. There were hints of a once-dominant Italian culture – *we still had Italian Day in June* – but The Drive was a racial mashup. Even white people roamed about from time to time. *Che sorpresa!*

The changes seemed to happen slowly, but they were anything but. It was, in fact, the fastest demographic shift in the history of time. *Anywhere.*

No wonder I noticed.

But like I said, we were expected *not* to notice. People pretended not to, including me. I thought about it, though. Couldn't help myself. The changes were so *in-your-face.* I recall Christmas shopping at Metrotown in 2012. The place was a gong show as usual, but something struck deep.

Every. Single. Person. Was. Asian.

All of them.

Fine, I reasoned. *Perfectly fine.* I presented myself with familiar arguments and catchphrases. *We live in a colour-blind society. We're all members of the human race.*

Who cares if most of the people are Chinese? They're gentle and compatible and industrious. I wasn't at risk of violence or persecution. I felt no physical threat.

But the experience unsettled me. It intimidated me. Was that not a natural reaction? Would not any white person feel the same? And if they said no, would they be lying? Or brainwashed?

I couldn't shake the primal sense of...*a threat.* Or was it shock, fear, sadness? Hard to say. But it was there.

I scolded myself. I searched and scoured my soul for an explanation. I had nothing against Asian people. I loved people of all races. Were my feelings rooted in nature? A tribal instinct encoded in my DNA, the product of tens of thousands of years of behavioural evolution?

Or was I a racist?

The Metrotown moment stuck. A vivid memory encoded in my brain's hippocampus. Vancouverites were lucky. Asians were extremely compatible with Western ways. Was that part of a grand plan or blind luck? Rhetorical question.

A few decades prior, we were ninety percent white. Before that, *ninety-eight.* Canada's English and French heritage shaped our traditions and values – they made Canada a highly desirable destination for immigrants. *Right?*

I knew the counter arguments – that our founding fathers stole the land, that they violently displaced the Indigenous. Be that as it may, they also settled an undeveloped continent and built a thriving and productive civilization. A beacon for freedom, no less great than our neighbour to the south. Greater, in fact. We were never fouled by slavery.

White people, and white people alone, did this.

Eeesh.

I was programmed to recoil from such statements. I could hear the attacks, the accusations. *White supremacist. Nazi.* You can't talk about Canadian heritage without including Indigenous peoples, and you certainly can't talk about white skin.

It was forbidden.

But the truth was there, and I glanced at it occasionally. I pondered it out of curiosity.

But what did it matter? Would we not all be mixed race in a few generations? Eurasians? *Wasians?* Mulattos? They were growing in numbers.

Canada and America were melting pots. The Italians, the Brits, the Germans? Did they not have their own countries? Same for the Irish and the Swedish. *Ha,* so I thought at the time.

These were my first naïve stirrings of racial consciousness. I was beginning to realize *Western culture* was a gift passed down by our ancestors. An heirloom to be treasured and protected.

My awakening was evolutionary, a process I resisted at every turn. But jarring red pill moments were inescapable. With Ivan around, I was swimming in them, which may have actually desensitized me. Ha, I considered Ivan *the boy who cried wolf.* An alarmist. A bit of a crackpot.

He scoured the globe for wanton threats. Presently, his soapbox was the evils of Islam. He steered me to such luminaries as Mark Steyn, Pamela Geller, and Douglas Murray. An eclectic mix if ever there was one. There was still no mainstream awareness of Islam as threat. Not in Canada. Not in my world.

Ivan had also grown suspicious of Obama, and the *dangerous false narratives* of the Black community, as he put it.

"If I had a son, he'd look like Trayvon." The words of Obama on the shooting death of a 17-year-old Black youth.

I saw nothing untoward. Nothing to fear. But in hindsight, I saw the moment as a trigger for change. The case itself was complicated. Trayvon was no angel. Neither was Zimmerman.

But with a simple statement, Obama stoked racial grievance. He stoked hostility. He divided Americans. The Black community embraced the message and white liberals blindly followed, even it meant self-flagellation. A campaign of white demonization crystallized.

Even Ivan didn't know all that in 2012. No one did. But by the time the Michael Brown drama unfolded, Ivan figured it out.

"He's a bully." Ivan declared. "A thug. Guy commits robbery *on video*, and they want us to feel sorry for him? Fuck that."

The video was bad. Mr. Brown roughed up the tiny shopkeeper and robbed him. He looked like a thug. Period. *Black Lives Matter* told us otherwise. Michael Brown was a victim. *Hands-up-don't-shoot* found purchase and never went away. No one cared if it was false.

I tried to accept the lie, that was the groupthink at work. The brainwashing, the indoctrination. But I was conflicted. Especially when I watched the riots, the looting, the arson. And their cause célèbre? The martyr for which these *activists* destroyed their community?

A criminal.

Not only were we to excuse the criminality, we were to hold the criminal in high esteem. In the same regard as Emmett Till and Rosa Parks. That was too much.

And what of BLM? What did they stand for? Black empowerment, I suppose. What did they stand against? Blacks being targeted and killed by police. Rampant white on Black violence.

But but but...the statistics told a different tale. Ivan laid it out for me. Black on white violent crime was astronomically higher than the opposite. By some estimates, twenty times higher. By others, 200. Not 200%. *200 times.*

Ivan showed me Colin Flaherty's videos, and I swallowed another red pill. A big one. This guy had been documenting the problem for years. Relentless Black violence and hostility. Endless and shocking brutality.

"Why's this shit not on the news?"

Ivan laughed. "The news has nothing to do with reality."

"How long's it been going on?"

Ivan raised his eyebrows. "Years? Decades?"

I thought about Ferguson, about what I'd heard on TV. I thought about Obama's lofty idealism. Was it all a sham? A big fucking charade?

Ivan watched me think it through: "Unspoken rule when you travel to the States – if you're white, know where *not* to go. The danger zones are everywhere, pal."

"We don't have them in Canada."

"Toronto does."

"Well, we don't have 'em in Vancouver."

"Not yet. *Not that we know of.* Think the media would tell us? You think you're getting the truth? Ha, you're getting fairy tales."

"What are they hiding?"

He scoffed. "You got a few hours?"

"Vancouver's peaceful. Always has been."

"The city you know is fading fast. Wait 'til we get some Muslims." He grinned evilly. "Wait 'til we get a few more Blacks."

"What do you got against Black people? *Racist.*"

He laughed out loud. He was pushing my buttons, and it was working. No question, Blacks had been through hell. Slavery, Jim Crow, the list goes on. But this BLM crap was disturbing. Were cops really that bad?

Maybe some. Trust me, I knew about the bad apples. Some of my pals growing up, they told me stories. They got beat up. *Some got beat up bad.* And they weren't Black. They were Italian, like me. Or white.

Well guess what, I never had a run-in with a cop 'cause I wasn't involved in a bullshit lifestyle. I had *respect* for the law. Heck, even the worst hoodlums of my day did, too. Or fear, maybe. Today's Black urban youth had neither. They were nasty and mean and entitled. The carnage I saw on Flaherty's channel, those videos shook me to the core.

Ah, but life is never simple and God showed His twisted sense of humour by blessing me with Vinny. Violence was part of my eldest son's lifestyle. He was an adult now, twenty years old. Cops pestered him relentlessly. It bothered me, but I knew he deserved it. He was a troublemaker. He'd had a few scrapes, but so far nothing stuck.

I loved my kids fiercely, and I tried to do right by them at every turn. I tried to instill values and I wasn't afraid to dole out punishment. But like I said, Vinny laughed in my face.

I wondered where I went wrong. Vinny was my firstborn. I was proud of him. I dragged him into work on occasion, and he was captivated by the hooligan element. The crazies, the goons, the gangsters. I thought it was cute.

I didn't realize it'd be a pattern. Many a day, I've beat myself up for exposing him to bad influences. But my kid had a screw loose. I've come to believe that no matter what I did, Vinny was gonna gravitate to the underworld. He was hardwired. Was it the money, the women, the power, the drugs? All of the above? Who knows?

Vinny's descent into to gangsterism seemed his destiny. Like I said, he was no blank slate. He had a don't-mess-with me demeanour. He dealt with enemies swiftly and ruthlessly.

But he had plenty of Italian warmth, too. He made friends wherever he went. I loved him no matter what. Still do to this very day.

Chapter 15 – Red-Pilled

By 2014, I was taking a keener interest in world affairs. Ferguson opened my eyes to the media's denial, deceit and delusion. I began asking questions. I began listening to Ivan's diatribes.

The more I explored, the more disturbed I became. Take Islam, a faith boasting child marriage, female genital mutilation, and wife-beating. *I know, I know, not all Muslims.* But when enough congregate, those negatives – *and others* – seem to come to the fore. Look at Europe – cars burning in France, rape gangs terrorizing Britain.

There had to be a silver lining. An upside. "Surely there's a moderate form of Islam." Ivan and I were out for a beer after a 'Caps game.

Ivan shrugged. "From what I can tell, moderates are almost always extremists-in-waiting."

"David says it's our fault. That Christian nations attacked and crippled Muslim nations."

"David's a drooling idiot."

"But is he right?"

"About as often as a broken clock." Ivan smirked. "It's complicated, but even if that's *partly* true, are we supposed to roll over and take it up the ass?" He made a rude gesture. "People like David don't *want* Islam to be evil, so they pretend it's not. And they attack anyone who says it is." Ivan scoffed with disgust. "They'd throw him off a building, and he'd defend their right to do it. Dude, *Sharia ain't compatible*. Muslims don't answer to our laws, they answer to Allah. That's it."

"Last I checked, no shortage of crazy Christians roaming the planet." *Devil's advocate.*

"False equivalence, Tony. You're comparing molehills and mountains. Look, the Old Testament had issues, but Christianity matured, it softened. The New Testament was transformative. The Quran does the opposite. Islam's going backwards."

"How bad is Europe? You're always saying England's lost. Why doesn't the government do something?"

He bellowed laughter. "You don't get it, man. The government, the British elite, the police. They *are* the danger. Not Islam."

"Why isn't this on the news?" *Sarcasm.*

"You're catching on, son. The Europe of old, the one that drafted the Magna Carta and spawned the Enlightenment – the one that gave us Mozart, Shakespeare, Dickens. It's dying."

"It won't happen here." I shook my head adamantly. "We have no issue with Islam, not in Vancouver. I've never even *met* a Muslim."

"Trust me, they're around – check out North Van – and they're fine, 'cause there's not many of 'em. But they're coming, mark my words. Count the mosques. It's simple arithmetic."

I waved him off. Justin Trudeau wasn't yet on the scene, and Islam was a muted presence. That'd change in a hurry.

"Speaking of Britain, you're still coming next year, right?"

"That's the plan."

"You have to see London before it goes dark."

I scoffed.

"Think I'm kidding?"

"I think you're *exaggerating*." I checked the time. "*And* I think it's time to go. Early start tomorrow."

"That's cool." Ivan checked his phone. "I got notifications to catch up on."

"How do you get anything done? You're on Facebook 24-7."

"Doing my part to save the world."

"Good luck with that."

In 2015, I finally relented and joined Facebook. I was sick of my family making fun of me. They were all there, except Vinny who lived incognito. Electronically, he was invisible. He had an encrypted cell, that was it.

I began posting family shots, I commented, I liked shit. I even sent the odd happy birthday wish. Mostly I lurked, and I was struck by the political tirades, not just by Ivan. Some people had time to burn. I got into it a couple times, and always regretted it. As a union man, I had to keep controversial opinions to myself.

Meantime, Ivan and David were content machines. David virtue-signalled like a champion. It was nauseating, and he was becoming progressively more unhinged. Even Lisa noticed, but she was protective, as always.

I took perverse delight in watching Ivan trounce him in debate. Ivan would dismantle David's position, whatever it happened to be, then destroy him with vulgarity as the dialogue degenerated into ad hominem attack. David always took it on the chin, which is exactly where Ivan suggested he rest his balls. From there came accusations of bestiality and pedophilia, and worse. Ivan had no fear of the taboo.

Somewhere along the way, I turned conservative. Don't get me wrong, my values were Classical Liberal – tolerance, civility, compassion. Problem was, the Liberals moved hard left. It was bad in 2015, but boy was I in for a shock. They'd barely scratched the surface of irrationality.

I wondered how any sane person could *not* turn conservative. I suppose they ignored the nonsense. Take my lovely bride. Lisa had no interest in conflict, so politics was out-of-bounds. For her, trust in government was an article of faith.

She focused on the good parts of life, which was the privilege of an insulated liberal. But as Leftist absurdity crept into our lives, it was getting harder. She was adept at parroting the clichés: *I don't see race. I don't see colour.* She might as well say I don't see gravity.

Then there was Dhanesh. My lifelong bud was still a strapping lad with flowing locks and a desperate need to preen. We were tight as ever, but old Danny Boy was changing. *Oh yeah*, in all sorts of ways. For one, he married the Indian girl which necessitated he tame his wandering eye – though truth be told, he never fully stopped the shenanigans.

But he was changing in other ways, too, and I wasn't sure I liked how. He dragged me to a Canucks game one night, and I actually enjoyed it. A helluva barnburner, though our boys came out on the wrong end of the scoresheet. Later, while drowning sorrows at the Shark Club, we got into it.

Did we ever.

We got to discussing the *hands-up-don't-shoot* lie, and – *fuck sakes* – Dhanesh actually believed it. He didn't want to hear contradictory facts. He was impervious to them.

"People of Colour are oppressed," he said. "We always have been. What's so hard to understand?"

Was it just me, or was the term *People of Colour* vaguely offensive?

We had it out and got nowhere. Dhanesh had no ground to stand on, but he was smug and condescending, like he was winning the debate. Like he was perched on higher moral ground.

"We've had discrimination forever," he proclaimed. "We finally point it out, and you guys can't take it."

"*You guys?*"

"White people."

"I'm *Italian.*"

"You're white, Tony. Get used to it."

"Since when are *you* discriminated against?"

"Are you serious? You forget what I went through growing up."

"You got called a few names a hundred years ago. Big deal, so did I."

He laughed arrogantly. "You wanna talk a hundred years ago? Let's talk about the *Komagata Maru.*"

I shrugged.

"In 1914, she sails into Vancouver with 376 Sikhs on board, subjects all of the British Commonwealth. What happens?"

"Pray tell."

"Majority-white Canada says *no*. Not you fucking guys. They got forced out by the Canadian Navy."

"That sucks, dude. But times have changed."

"That sorta shit went on a long time. 'Til the '70s, it was impossible for people like me to get in this country."

"Now you're taking over. You colonized Surrey."

"Beautiful thing, ain't it?"

"Not many whites left out there."

He smirked. "You guys'll be in a museum someday."

"I don't know about that."

"Your numbers are shrinking. You better hope we're nice to you."

He was joking obviously, but it was a chilling remark. "Aren't we all just Canadians?"

"I'm *Indo*-Canadian."

"Well whoop-de-*fucking*-do. I'm *Italian*-Canadian. My people had challenges. I don't worry about that now."

"You're white, Tony. It's not the same."

Porca vacca! This was my boy Dhanesh. *Lecturing me.* It shouldn't have come as a surprise. Why would he *not* embrace victimhood? There was power there, and white males had no claim to it – none. Oh, how the tide had turned.

This was the new and improved Dhanesh, replete with fancy talking points. He was right about the *Komagata Maru.* The story got headlines when our obnoxiously incompetent PM decided a formal apology was necessary. The Grinning Idiot was apologizing to practically everyone – LGBTQ, First Nations, the list goes on.

There was something insincere and dirty about Trudeau's antics. He took every chance to divide by race, religion, and gender. He preached Canada's history was shameful, that it should be condemned and dismantled. He actually claimed our country had *no core identity, no mainstream.*

This guy, what a piece of work.

By now, the absurdities were infecting everything. They had been for a while, I just hadn't noticed. Ivan had. Ivan was a voice of reason before Jordan Peterson arrived on the scene. Ivan knew the Left was hollow and amoral, that their positions couldn't stand the slightest scrutiny. That their only defense was to name-call – racist, sexist, homophobic, transphobic, Islamophobic.

Things really went sideways when my Number Two Son Leo started his Liberal Arts program at UBC. He was deeply indoctrinated by the time he got there, and about to get worse. They were poisoning minds, no two ways about it.

I loved Leo, of course. *Always.* But it wasn't easy. He knew where I stood politically. He also knew Ivan was my friend, *perhaps my best friend,* and he hated that. I was starting to catch Leo's virtuous ire, and it was pissing me off. Not so much his ridiculous opinions, as his bogus *morally superior* attitude.

I was his Papa for Christ's sake, show some goddamn respect. We were family. Blood. Where I came from, that trumped all.

Chapter 16 — Bizarro World

One lovely late Spring Friday, we hosted Ivan and Petra for a barbeque. Julio was at a friend's place. Leo was at some sort of political rally. Vinny was *always* out. A hint of summer was in the air, and we were in a festive mood. Especially once we got into the vino.

Leo had just completed first year studies, and figured he was an expert on everything. He was talking nonsense, but I tried to cut slack. At eighteen, I also knew it all, and I knew my old man was clueless. But this was different.

Sure, Vinny was off the rails, but at least he wasn't an imbecile. Vinny had common sense. Leo, on the other hand, was borderline cuckoo.

Not so long ago, I made a joke about safe spaces and microaggressions. When Leo defended them, I got my ire up: "This is what they teach you? This what I'm paying for?" It didn't go over well. Questioning his lunacy never did, so I usually bit my tongue. I curbed my urge to slap him upside the head.

With Ivan in the house, all things politically incorrect were fair game. Before we sat for dinner, we'd hashed out carbon footprints, pot legalization, and the mysterious rise of LGBTQ.

"You're not saying it right, bigot."

"What?" I asked. "*LGBTQ.*"

"They added a few letters." He laughed out loud. "They're not done yet, either."

"Ah, Jesus."

"Try to be more inclusive, would ya?"

"He calls it LGBTQ-LMFAO," Petra said, with a giggle.

"They don't like that."

"*David* didn't like it," said Lisa. "He tore a strip off you on Facebook."

"David doesn't like much."

"He said you were marginalizing the non-binary people of the world. I have a feeling Leo would feel the same."

"I have a feeling Leo *is* the same. No offense."

"Easy," I said. "Enough outta you."

Ivan had touched a nerve. *On purpose.* Leo's sexual orientation was a matter of debate and curiosity. If he was out, he wasn't out to us. Definitely not me. The little bastard had me blocked on Facebook and Instagram.

A gay son – *not that there's anything wrong with that* – would take some getting used to. I was old school. Couldn't help it. Thank God for Julio, my normal son.

"Problem is," Ivan was saying, "the education system's been scrubbed of religion. These kids got nothing solid to hold onto. No moral bedrock."

"You're not exactly a hardline Catholic."

"I try," said Ivan. "Look who's talking."

"So they take out religion and they start peddling gay sex?"

"They peddle it *everywhere*. I mean, must we have a gay character in every sitcom?"

"When I was a kid," Lisa said, "we recited the Lord's Prayer every morning."

"So did we," I said, looking to Ivan. "Remember grade three, Mrs. Channing? She had the Ten bloody Commandments at the front of the class."

"She wouldn't get away with that now," said Petra.

"A copy of the Quran might fly."

Laughter all around. Not the joyous kind.

"Mrs. Channing was old school. She was teaching in the 1960s."

"Different world back then."

"They weren't handing out condoms."

"Imagine bringing her in now. She'd have a heart attack."

"I think she *did* have a heart attack."

"It's not just the gay thing," Ivan continued. "They push *all* the asinine left-wing ideology."

"Teachers have no choice. That's the curriculum."

"You talking K-12?" Lisa asked. "Or uni?"

"They plant the seeds in grade school. In university, the seeds flower. They preach the hate with fancier language. It's pure groupthink."

"How's Sasha doing at Temp?" Ivan's kid was at our old school.

"Temp ain't what it used to be. It's all diversity and inclusion now."

"What's wrong with that?" Lisa asked. A little friendly button-pushing.

Ivan scoffed in disgust. "My kid lives in fear of perpetrating a microaggression. He asks questions like *how do we fix white privilege?* What am I supposed to say? Don't try so hard? Hey, he's smart like me. Course he's gonna do well."

"Wait 'til he gets to college."

"I've seen the courses. *Critical Race Theory. Open Gender Studies. Advanced Grievance Analytics.* What do you do with degrees like that?"

"Dismantle the patriarchy?"

Ivan laughed. "They make it sound like thoughtful, reasoned analysis, but it's nothing but layer upon layer of horseshit. Logical fallacy. Circular reasoning. Indecipherable gibberish. Makes me angry."

"How you think I feel? I'm *paying* for it."

"They're fraudsters, man. They're bilking ya."

"The deeper Leo gets, the angrier he gets."

"That's the game plan. They can't win the debate, so they yell and scream and slander."

The front door creaked, and I looked at Lisa questioningly.

"Speak of the devil," she said.

"Leo? What's he doing home?"

"He said the event might wrap early."

"What was it, an Antifa mixer?"

"Don't start, Ivan." Petra scolded.

"Yeah, leave my kid alone, ya bully."

Ivan grinned and reached for the wine. "Refill anyone?"

Leo strolled in wearing jeans and a t-shirt. A bright red cardigan draped across his shoulders reminded me of the preppy stage Dhanesh sported thirty years back. I used to make fun of him. *Pussy.*

When Leo spotted Ivan, his expression turned sour.

"How'd it go tonight, sweetheart?" Lisa asked.

"Was okay."

"Still solving the world's problems?" Ivan volunteered.

"It's not easy with so many assholes around."

"Language, dear."

"Sorry, Mom."

"What do you think of this Jordan Peterson fellow? Is he an asshole?"

"Total asshole. Like you."

Ivan chuckled. "I think he's great."

"Thank goodness you're an old white man. You'll be dead soon and so will he."

I laughed out loud. Because it was funny or to ease tension? Not sure.

"That seems vaguely inappropriate," said Ivan. "Especially since I'm not that old. A few clicks on the odometer, but the engine's running smooth."

"I think your engine's growing." I pointed at Ivan's expanding girth, but he ignored me.

"Got an argument against Mr. Peterson, Leo? Or just skin colour and age?"

"I don't listen to old white men. With any luck, he'll be in jail soon."

"C-16 ain't law yet, thank God."

"It will be, you watch."

The Bill was set to force the use of non-gendered pronouns like *ze* and *zir*, if that's what a person desired. Don't comply, go to jail. A twisted application of human rights, and Jordan Peterson eloquently announced his refusal to comply. It was the start of his meteoric rise.

"What's your pronoun, Leo?"

"Why do you bring him here, Dad?"

"He shows up looking for food."

"*You're just like him.*" Leo's voice had turned whiny. "You just don't have the balls to speak your opinion."

"Don't speak to your father like that, Leo."

"Well it's true." He took a moment to stare daggers at Ivan and me. "I'm outta here." Off he marched in a huff, and we watched him go in silence.

"Couldn't leave it alone, eh pal?"

"He's far gone, Tony. You gotta sit that boy down."

"Ya think I haven't tried?"

Later that night – guests departed, dishes done – I nursed a whiskey and pondered. What happened to my middle son? How'd I lose him? He'd been drifting for years, but now he was out of reach.

Or had I changed? I *definitely* had. I no longer clung to the lies. *I refused.* I tried to stay quiet, but my opinions kept leaking out. The chasm between Leo and me caused friction with Lisa, too. She either gave me shit or the cold shoulder, even though I think she understood. Probably even agreed.

Ivan was my only sounding board. How's that for torture? He was always there to listen, to add value. Sometimes too much value. When he went on about Stalinists and Bolsheviks, or cultural Marxism, I tuned him out. I liked to keep things simple.

I envied the simple life Papa had. I wished, sometimes, I hadn't been red-pilled. That I could pretend all was well.

Something had to change, didn't it? We were descending into chaos and picking up speed. How could we turn this thing around? How could we get off this rollercoaster to insanity?

I didn't have the answer. Neither did Ivan. No one did.

Or so we thought.

Chapter 17 – Donald J. Trump

The answer came in the form of Donald J. Trump. On June 16, 2015, he descended Trump Tower's golden escalator to announce his candidacy. The crowd cheered, the media fawned, Trump stepped to the mic. It was more detonation than announcement:

"When Mexico sends its people, they're not sending their best...they're sending people that have lots of problems, and they're bringing those problems...they're bringing drugs, they're bringing crime. They're rapists. And some, I assume, are good people."

Whoa.

Reporters were aghast. Twitter went berserk. Certainly no one predicted he'd shake the GOP (and the Western World) to its core. Trump was a sideshow. A carnival barker. A *billionaire-real-estate-mogul-slash-reality-TV-star.* Evidently, a racist one.

This sampling of rhetoric set the tone for Trump's campaign. He would not mince words. *Hell no.* He'd tell it like it is. At first, the media didn't know what to make of him, as his popularity surged. *He's like a car accident,* they said. *You can't look away.*

Pundits warned the Trump Circus would damage the GOP, as if their reputation was above reproach. For the good of the party, best to eliminate him ASAP. He had no chance of winning the nomination, much less beating the great Hillary Clinton.

LOL.

Experts favoured Jeb Bush, with nods to Huckabee, Rubio and Carson. But experts were trapped in conventional thinking. They didn't know the force of nature they were dealing with.

They wised up quick. At debates, Trump humiliated opponents with wit, mockery and childish nicknames. *Low Energy Jeb* was dispatched, unceremoniously ending the Bush dynasty. *Little Marco* was next, then *Pathological Ben*.

At the Republican National Convention, Trump ousted *Lyin' Ted* and *1-for-38 Kasich* on the first ballot. The poor bastards had no chance. As official Republican nominee, Trump set his sights on *Crooked Hillary*. The nicknames were outrageous, hilarious, devastatingly effective. And so much fun.

No one had seen anyone like Trump before, and no one expected his incessant drive. *His relentlessness.* He attacked the political class with boundless bombast. He had no off switch, he was always ON.

His gaffes were legendary, and part of the fun. *I like people who weren't captured. She had blood coming out of her wherever. Look at my African American.*

Did I find Trump's comments offensive? Certainly some, but I also found him refreshing. I couldn't help but think – *finally, someone's speaking from the heart. Finally, someone's telling the truth.* Meanwhile, Hillary regurgitated content-free platitudes. Scripted and scrubbed and tested.

Trump shot from the hip. He was playful and fun. He adlibbed, he joked, he insulted. His rallies were rock concerts and oh, the gems he came up with: *lock her up, fake news, build the wall, Mexico's gonna pay.*

It was red meat for his base, which had magically
materialized. They weren't alone anymore. They weren't
strangers in their own country. They'd found a voice of
sanity. If that voice was occasionally vulgar, they didn't give
a rat's ass.

Pundits doubted he could win. Mainstream media said
no chance, and they had the polls to prove it. Even Fox and
Breitbart weren't bullish.

"If Hillary wins," Ivan said, "and let's face it, she probably
will – there'll never again be a free and fair election in the
United States."

Ivan's ideas were radical, but this one was downright
ludicrous.

"I'm serious," he continued. "Trump's thrown a scare into
them. They'll rewrite the rules."

I chuckled. "America's not a banana republic yet."

"They've shown their cards, dude. They despise the white
working class, the freedom-lovers, the gun-toters. Hell, a
few more years, they won't even have to rig the elections.
They'll have the numbers, they probably already do."

On Ivan rambled. He spoke of the elites, he harped on
the stench of Never-Trumpers. Weasels, he called them.
Faux conservatives.

"They stand on their high horses, they spout their mealy-
mouthed rhetoric, their pathetic bullshit. It's like they're
intent on *not* winning."

"So whadayasay...does Trump have a chance?"

"We'll find out Tuesday."

"You're coming over, right?"

"With bells on."

The Tuesday in question was November 8, 2016. We
gathered at my place for the big night. We ordered pizza
and I opened the wine cellar. We cycled between Fox, CNN
and MSNBC. We even glanced at CBC on occasion.

Leo had made himself scarce, but the lefty contingent
was still represented by my flaky brother-in-law.

Presumably, David had come to gloat. Because seriously, everyone knew Trump would lose. In fact, he would get his ass royally spanked.

But something strange happened. Something truly amazing. The heartland showed up and let their voices be heard. Flyover country stepped up to the plate. They'd been played for suckers once too often.

At 7:39 p.m., Trump took Ohio, a swing state, albeit one he was expected to win. *Big deal*, said David. At 7:53, he took Florida. You hear that, *Florida* – a must-win he wasn't supposed to win. CNN could barely bring themselves to say it. Next came North Carolina, Utah, Pennsylvania.

Holy shit.

Trump was gonna win.

And he did.

What a glorious moment. The polls were an illusion, the blue wall, a fallacy.

David's scowl set in immediately. "This is crazy," he shrieked. "It doesn't make sense, he's not even a politician."

"Thank God for that," Ivan replied.

This was Armageddon for the Dems, and most of the mainstream media. The ultimate cognitive dissonance, where reality stopped matching the illusion. It made for compelling television.

Not many Trumpsters in the house, not open ones. Heck, I kept my celebrating to a minimum, but not Ivan. He was over the moon. I'd never seen him so animated. *Ever.* By contrast, David was inconsolable, much like the wingnuts on TV having temper tantrums.

No matter whose side you took, emotions ran high. You'd almost think this was *our* election, which said a lot about the relationship. America was loud and boastful, like Trump himself, but America was our protector, our big brother. Also, our neighbour and best friend. When we dashed off to Seattle for a weekend, we weren't visiting a foreign country, we were visiting family.

Ivan stayed late that night. We sucked back beer and shot the shit – he had a lot on his mind. I finally had to punt him out. "I start at six, dude. I gotta go to bed."

"I'm too excited," he said. "A brand-new world starts tomorrow."

Was he right?

In the weeks following Trump's historic win, experts scrambled to explain themselves. They blamed pollsters, they blamed the Democratic Party, they blamed Hillary. *Perhaps Hillary wasn't so great*, they said. *Perhaps, she was...dreadful.*

Haha, conservatives had been saying that all along. So had Ivan. *So had I.* For my money, Hillary was the worst candidate in history. Watching her hobble to podiums to flash fake smiles and bestow scripted fiction – was there any worse torture?

But the media focused their ire on Trump. They called him a wildcard who played fast and loose with the truth. They were right. Trump was a salesman, and this time his product was America. He set out to sell America to itself and the world.

Hollywood came out swinging. They attacked with vulgar insults and threats of violence. They attacked Trump's base. It was like a competition, and they tried to outdo each other. DeNiro was an early frontrunner. He called Trump *stupid. A punk. A dog. A pig. A con. A bullshit artist. A mutt.* Just like in his movies. He wrapped up with *I'd like to punch him in the face.*

Meryl Streep used her Golden Globes pulpit to sanctimoniously condemn the President-Elect. Everyone piled on – Alec Baldwin, George Clooney, Madonna, Alyssa Milano, Cher. The hypocrisy was astonishing, and would get worse.

Meanwhile, north of the border, a bumbling moron was leading Canada into the abyss. Through malice or incompetence, I couldn't tell but what an embarrassment.

Canadian politics was normally dull, not to mention irrelevant on the world stage. Deck chairs on the Titanic, if that. Even Canadians didn't follow it closely. For all the wrong reasons, Trudeau changed that.

When Fidel Castro died, world leaders condemned him as a ruthless dictator who presided over executions and human rights abuses. Trudeau lavished praise. He called Castro *a remarkable leader, a legendary revolutionary and orator*. Justin was soundly ridiculed.

When Trump and Trudeau went head to head on NAFTA, Trudeau led with ostentatious virtue-signaling. It seemed his default, almost a cover for shocking ineptitude. Trump was not amused. He dissolved the agreement with barely a nod to our Drama-Teacher-in-Chief. Next.

Where Trump was a cheerleader for America, Trudeau thought Canada sucked. He showed contempt for the country, its founders, its people.

Where I come from, we loved Canada, and I mean the Canada I grew up in, not the shapeless, rootless Canada Trudeau envisioned. How'd this guy get elected? How had he *not* been tossed out on his ass?

Friendly press, that's how. CBC was worse than CNN and MSNBC combined. The others fell in line obediently, aiding and abetting the clownshow.

Except Rebel Media, that is. They were truthtellers, *the Canadian Breitbart*. Or as MSM might put it, a far-right political website – definitely not members of the *respectable press*. Sure, they had cowboys, they had political incorrectness. But their leader Ezra Levant was a tireless voice of reason. From Rebel's sober perch, I promise you there was plenty of room to the right.

No matter the outlet, Trump was a news-making machine. A money-making machine, too. The markets were shooting like a rocket – so much for the jokers that predicted an unrecoverable crash.

But what could America expect come January? No one knew for sure.

Perhaps Trump didn't either.

Chapter 18 – A Family Divided

People soon stopped wondering. Trump made shit happen fast. Conservative judge appointed to Supreme Court – done. Illegal border crossings – down. Unemployment – down. Stock market – way, way up. Jobs coming out the ying-yang. Good ones, too. Manufacturing, construction, high tech.

Promises made, promises kept. Tax cuts, deregulation, surging growth. Intangibles, too. Trump asked questions like *why's the deficit with China so huge? How come no one else pays into NATO? And what's with this ridiculous Paris Climate Accord?*

Trump's performance was breathtaking, and the Left hated him all the more. They despised the sound of his voice. If he cured cancer, they'd call it racist. They'd demand a right to die from the disease. They'd bemoan the lack of attention given other diseases.

The successes kept coming, and it was difficult to spin them all into negatives. But the media managed by using every trick in the book. They omitted facts, they used circular sources, they amplified stories that boosted acceptable narratives. People built careers around attacking Trump.

They wrote hit pieces packed with undisguised vitriol. Condemnation came from all corners, including the Canadian media. God, they sickened me. Sometimes the prejudice was blatant, sometime sneaky and underhanded – buried in gesture and facial expression, nuance and tone. A wink here, a nudge there. A raised eyebrow, a knowing smirk.

The weatherman, the sports guy, they were all in on it. The message was loud and clear: *Trump's a moron. That's what we think, and you should too. Trump's base? Ignorant bumpkins. Clueless hillbillies that were blessedly diminishing in numbers.*

A new disease emerged – *Trump Derangement Syndrome* – and it was rampant in the Democratic Party. Five years prior, the Dems spoke of the need for border security. Now they sought to abolish ICE.

Overt and unapologetic socialists came out of the closet. Free tuition and healthcare for all, illegals included. *And stop calling them illegals. They have every right to be here.*

To challenge their policies was to invite accusations of racist, xenophobe, white supremacist. In the emerging *Newspeak*, Ivan informed me, racist meant *uppity white person*. Yes, he said uppity.

Disagreements between Left and Right were no longer minor. They were profound ideological clashes. A battle to the death was brewing. A war between capitalists and socialists. You could feel it.

The fight wasn't confined to America, but there was a sense if America lost, all would be lost. Trump was the one man standing between us and lawless chaos. That's how I saw it. That's why I loved him.

But I loved him in stealth mode, 'cause supporting Trump had become taboo, *verboten*, even in Canada. Friendships fell apart, families were divided. Mine included, sad to say.

Our dinner table was sacred – no phones, no TV, only the breaking of bread, talking, laughing, rejoicing. Maybe a glass of vino, why not?

Ah, but kids grow up. Times change. A Leo appearance was rare, Vinny even rarer. Thank God for Julio. He was my constant. He was still in high school, still a baby. A big beautiful precious baby, and he never let me down.

One evening in July of 2018, Leo graced us with his presence – *by request* – and Lisa made her specialty. Meat pie, mashed potatoes, all the fixings. Not an Italian dish, but still a family favourite. Better than the usual British fare – overcooked roast beef with potatoes and Brussel sprouts. The British and their food, I tell ya. Worcestershire sauce? What was that crap?

On the agenda that evening, planning for the big trip – yes, we were going to England. Fourteen days of fun and sun (*hopefully sun*) and sightseeing. Also, much-needed family bonding. Too many squabbles of late, too many spats. There'd be no talk of politics. Nary a mention of Trump.

We were set to leave mid-August and I was on top of the world. Lisa and Julio, too. Primed and full of chatter and sass, except Leo. He was his usual pissy self.

"Come on, Leo." Lisa gave him a motherly stroke. "Where's your enthusiasm, love?"

He managed a smile for his Mum.

"We need you, son. All for one, one for all." I figured an extra push couldn't hurt. I was wrong. Leo couldn't wait to unleash his vitriol.

"Does Trump feel that way?"

"Who's talking about Trump?"

He scoffed. "As long as the *Orange Moron's* in office, we have to talk about him. Does he feel that way when he's breaking up families? When he's putting kids in cages?"

"Hey, you and me, Leo. We gotta put that behind us, eh?"

"Why Dad? You don't like families being torn apart?"

"Come on, Leo. Lay off." Julio rarely got between us, and anger flared in Leo's eyes.

"What, you're a Trump supporter too? Jesus Christ, what a fucking family."

"I'm just saying lay off, that's all."

"Why? Don't you think those families should have the same rights and freedoms we have?"

"Sure." Julio's tone was sarcastic. "They should get hotels, too. Like Trudeau's doing for our illegals."

Wow, one of my talking points. Julio had been listening. My heart swelled with gratitude and pride.

Leo scoffed. "Listen to *Mr. White Privilege.* You got a house, healthcare, schooling. Plenty to eat. You never worked a day in your life."

Julio had worked summer jobs, but he ignored the lie. "Papa paid for the house. He worked hard for it. I admit, I'm blessed. Blessed to have the best Papa in the world. So are you, and you don't even know it."

"Gimme a break."

"That's enough, boys," said Lisa. "*Please.*"

But Julio continued: "How's your car running, Leo? You know, the one *Papa* bought you."

"You're not answering the question."

"No, they shouldn't get the same rights and freedoms."

"That's rather heartless."

"Someone comes to Canada illegally, and you wanna give 'em a free house? How many we gonna do that for? When does the money run out?" Julio waited a few beats. "I'm not heartless. Neither's Papa. How 'bout we solve real problems? How about we *talk* about real problems?"

"*Everyone* deserves housing and healthcare. That's a given."

"Everyone deserves to work, too. And obey the law."

"Easy for you to say. You never had a hardship in your life."

"I'm lucky, already said so. But Papa had hardships. So did Nonna and Nonno. Our family worked hard to get where we are."

Leo glanced at his mom, as if to say *she had no hardships.* But he didn't go there. He never spoke against Lisa. "Everyone deserves a chance. We're a nation of immigrants, we always have been."

"Fine, come in legally."

"Why? Not like we settled this country legally."

"You can't compare 2018 with three hundred years ago."

"I just did."

"There *was* no country when the Europeans got here. They weren't immigrants, they were explorers. They tamed the land, they brought civilization."

"They were invaders. They stole the country. Face it."

"Yeah," – *sarcasm* – "did they take advantage of the welfare and free tuition?"

"Don't be an asshole, Julio."

"I'm asking a question."

"*Obviously,* it was a different era."

"You made the comparison. Why can't I?" Julio thought further. "And it's not like the Natives were pacifists. Some of 'em were brutal."

"Check your history, dude."

"Not all, *but some.* I've looked into it."

Leo scoffed with disgust.

"Come to think of it, why *didn't* they accept us? Show tolerance?" Julio was pushing buttons now, and I was letting him. I was enjoying this. "Imagine if we shot immigrants with bow and arrow. Or scalped them. Ever think of that, Leo?"

"They were defending themselves, *you idiot.* They were being slaughtered."

Julio sighed. "It wasn't pretty on either side. I'll tell you what. They were lucky enlightened Europeans showed up, and not Muslims. Or Zulus. *Or Genghis Khan.* Could you imagine?"

"I don't believe it. My younger brother's a Nazi."

"That's enough, Leo," I said. It was one thing for Leo to take shots at me.

He scoffed. "Course you take his side. You're a frickin' Nazi, too."

"I'm not taking anyone's side." I drew a breath. "And you better watch your tone. *And your mouth.*"

"You always take his side." Leo's voice was shaking. "He's always been your favourite."

"Leo," Lisa pleaded. "We don't have favourites. We love you all."

She attempted to stroke his head, but he ducked away. "I'm outta here. I don't need this."

"Don't go, Leo. We need you here."

He rushed out and Lisa gave chase. Momentarily, we heard tires squealing on the driveway.

Lisa was always the peacekeeper, calming storms and simmering tempers. Many's the day she'd shielded Leo from Vinny's abuse, but subtly, so as not to strip his dignity. But Leo was a different person now. He was irrational. Unstable. This incident felt like a watershed.

"We're losing Leo," I muttered.

"No Papa, he'll be fine," said Julio. "He just cares so much about people. I do, too. But..." he hesitated, "...I worry about our country. I hear you and Ivan talk."

I took him in a friendly headlock. "You listen too much, my little paisono." He grinned up at me.

"Let's have a sip of the vino, huh?" I poured myself a generous glass, a much smaller one for Julio.

"Leo'll be okay, Papa."

"I hope so." I sipped wine. "But I'm not so sure he'll be joining us on our trip."

"We're still going, right?"

"Damn right we are."

"He's too old for a family trip anyway," said Julio. "He's twenty-one. He's an adult."

Julio always made me feel better. To be honest, I was relieved Leo wasn't coming. Julio was, too. Maybe even Lisa, though she'd never admit it.

The problem was, I'd been red-pilled, and you can't turn that off. Not a good thing for my relationship with Leo. Politics in 2018 was hazardous. People picked sides, and there wasn't much common ground. I was sick to death of it. I didn't wanna lose Leo. *So he was a brainwashed moron.* He was still my son.

For the good of family, I resolved to take a step back. I'd focus on the big trip, catch a Whitecaps game or two, maybe even get out on the golf course. There were many healthy distractions.

Could I heal the division with Leo? He wasn't coming on the trip, that much I knew. *Not in a million years* was the phrase he used. Obviously, Vinny was never in.

I felt bad for Lisa. She'd long since abandoned the *perfect family* dream, but she desperately wanted this *perfect family* vacation. We'd make it happen, just the three of us. A helluva trip it would be.

Like I always said, thank God for Julio.

Chapter 19 – Leftism Everywhere

For the rest of the summer, I tuned out. I stopped watching news, I got off social media. Ivan began calling me *the ostrich*, and it caught on with Dhanesh. *Bastards.*

But I was still getting the gist, because the absurdity was unavoidable. Just when I thought Trudeau couldn't sink lower than changing our *national fucking anthem*, he upped his game. Evidently, whites needed another reminder of how much we suck. How about a new stat holiday to mark the legacy of residential schools?

Would this help anyone? Would this help the country? No. It had one purpose – to shame European-Canadians. Trudeau's shitty government was about blame and division. About keeping wounds fresh and alive.

And the echo chamber press was a willing accomplice. One night, Julio and I were chilling, having a beer – *me not him* – and the local news was on. CTV? CBC? Global? Makes no difference. The anchorman was dutifully dispensing state-approved propaganda – *oops, I mean news.*

This one was a white male. Clearly gay. His lispy voice and effeminate manner were a dead giveaway. I found him shrill and unpleasing, but this was the only breed of white male they hired these days, so said Ivan. Visible minorities and women were all the rage. I know this sounds petty and prejudicial. Just tellin' it like it is.

This particular talking head was bemoaning a spate of racist attacks, and my *spidey sense* tingled. They cut to a clip of a drunk white guy cursing a group of Indo-Canadians.

No context was given, but the reporter wondered, *was the behaviour Trump-inspired? Was it part of a larger trend?* He set everyone's mind at ease by confirming the poor dummy would be prosecuted under hate speech laws.

Talk about a manufactured crisis. Where were the stats? Where was the meat in this fairy tale? I re-watched the clip. No one was scared, except the pitiful white guy. He was lucky he didn't get his head kicked in. And if he did, *no one* would rush to his defense, his attackers wouldn't be punished. They'd he hailed heroes.

And I'd bet money this was *the best* example of white racism they could find. What did Ivan say recently? The demand for white racism always exceeded the supply. Meanwhile, amid media silence, whites were decimated by violent crime in America and Europe. Definitely in South Africa. Point that out, you're a white supremacist. What an upside-down world we lived in.

I flipped to a Blue Jays game. Good Lord, I needed a vacation.

Chapter 20 – The English Countryside
August 22, 2018

On departure day, I was calm and relaxed. Earlier that week, a cordial visit with Leo put me in a good headspace. He actually made an effort and it warmed my heart beyond belief.

He promised to keep an eye on the place, which was unnecessary. In a different part of the world, I might worry about vandals or burglars. Not Point Grey. We had virtually no crime. I might also have been concerned my kid would have a house party. Not with Leo. He wasn't the type.

Our flight was 3:20 p.m. local time, and – *miracle of miracles* – Vinny volunteered to drive us to the airport. Spending time with my Number One Son was always a treat. He did his own thing and I didn't ask questions. I worried about Vinny, but he put my mind at ease whenever I saw him. He was a big friendly joker, though he could kill you with a bear hug.

I heard his Harley in the driveway – *actually heard it a mile away* – and we wandered out to greet him. "Ah, my long-lost son."

"Papa." He came at me with fury, and we embraced. Next, he picked up Lisa and spun her around playfully. My God, he was a brute.

"And who's this kid?" Vinny stepped toward Julio. "Look Papa, he's taller than me. What, are you some sorta tough guy?" Vinny assumed a boxer's stance and stalked Julio. "Ya think you're tough, eh?"

Julio responded gamely. "You wanna have a go?" He puffed up his chest and flexed.

"Whoa, you been working out, too."

"Comes natural to me," said Julio.

"C'mere paisano." Big hug. "Look at you. Shaving, too."

"And he's got a girlfriend," Lisa chimed in.

"What?"

"Oh yeah. *Monica.* You have to see the way they make goo-goo eyes at each other."

Julio was embarrassed only for a moment. He wasn't the self-conscious type. "Wait 'til you meet her, Vinny." Julio kissed his fingertips and exploded them in the classic Italian gesture. *"Bravissimo."*

"She's a knockout," I added.

"Smart, too," said Lisa.

"Bravo, Julio. You finally getting some?" Vinny made a rude gesture with fingers and thumb.

"Vincent," Lisa admonished.

"Sorry Ma," he hung his head for all of half a second, then calmly lit a cigarette.

"Those'll stunt your growth," Julio said.

"Watch it punk."

"What'd you top out at, five-six?"

"Tall enough to hurt you." Vinny held up a beefy fist "And I'm five-eight, so fuck you." He blew a stream of smoke at his younger brother. "When we leaving, Papa?"

"Soon." I glanced at my watch, grinning at the spirited banter. "Our flight's at three."

"Sure ya trust me with the Beemer?"

"I have no choice." My heart was bursting with pride. My boys were rough-and-tumble, and they had love in their hearts. Lisa and I did something right.

Upstairs in the master bedroom, sealing up suitcases, Lisa got sentimental. "When we get back," she said, "Julio starts university." She pretended to sniffle. "He's not a kid anymore."

"Nope."

Julio was set to start Engineering at UBC in the Fall. It'd be a brutal workload and tough competition, but Julio would take it in stride. In addition to his many gifts, he was smart as a whip. A straight-A student. No flies on this kid. Eighteen years old, his whole life ahead of him. Oh, to be young.

"We've had our ups and downs," Lisa continued, "but we did alright. Our boys turned out fine. *Even Vinny.*"

"And *even Leo*," I added, and she admonished playfully. Her protective instincts were always close by.

"We did okay, too." She leaned over and kissed my cheek. "You and me."

"We did amazing, Darling." I pulled her close and gave her a passionate kiss. "Thanks for putting up with me for thirty-three years."

"Was my pleasure."

"Speaking of your pleasure," I gestured toward the bed. "How 'bout a quickie?"

"Excuse me, I'm not that kind of girl." She feigned offense, and I forced her roughly onto the bed. She fought like a damsel-in-distress. It was a familiar game, one of many in our arsenal to keep life fun and interesting.

Our bond was always growing, always being reborn in different forms. Never did I take her for granted. Sadly, the amorous interlude didn't go the distance. We aborted after a bit of naughty mischief and made our way downstairs, eyes twinkling.

With Vinny behind the wheel of my X5, we made it to the airport without incident. I commented on his conservative driving.

"Hey," he said, "when you've had as many run-ins with the law as me, you don't wave the red flag."

I nodded sagely and said a silent prayer for him. I didn't care to know the depraved details.

The flight, too, was uneventful but grueling. I actually managed some slumber time, a rarity for me. Arriving at Heathrow, I felt light and fresh and ready for adventure.

Before you knew it, we were blasting up the M11 toward Cambridge, right on track with Lisa's detailed itinerary. Through her work, she had an impressive network of contacts there and we got the royal treatment. We took in the architecture, the famous buildings, the storied lecture halls.

We lingered at The Sidgwick Site, home of the Faculty of English, also once home to Thackeray, Forster, and Nabokov. The names meant little to me, but were Gods for Lisa.

Thirty-six hours hence, we were back on the road, venturing deep into the English countryside. We traversed winding roads in places like Essex and Cheshire. The names stirred something in my soul, and I was Italian for Christ's sake.

We saw farmhouses and ancient woodlands. We saw stately homes and castles on hills. England was a magical, peaceful land. *Enchanting.*

I felt reverence for iconic towns like Liverpool and Chelsea. I knew them through football, and I wasn't even an EPL guy. I favoured La Liga and Serie A.

The English won me over. I had thought Brits arrogant and unfriendly. Rude, even. Nothing was further from the truth. Delightful people, kind and gentle and peaceful. Always eager to help. I even warmed to their dry sense of humour. It was subtle, which was odd to an Italian like me who's anything but.

In Manchester, Lisa had distant family relations and she'd arranged a visit. Amazingly, they couldn't wait to spoil us rotten. They treated us like gold. I never drank so much tea in my life.

They brought out the British in Lisa, as if drawing out a deep ancestral memory. I watched her sparkle and shine. I was so blessed to have her in my life, and I thanked God for about the millionth time.

Our mood was carefree and lighthearted. We reminisced. We told tall tales from across the decades. We laughed about Vinny and Leo, about each other. *The Vin Man* always got the biggest laughs.

Not for the first time, I told Julio about my high school escapades. The three musketeers – Tony, Ivan and Danny. Lisa said nice things about Ivan, if you can believe it. She also recounted the night we met, and I corrected details along the way.

Julio had heard the story, but never tired of it. We coaxed him for details on Monica. *Where did they meet? How did they meet?* Ha, he picked her up Kits Beach. A chip off the old block, he was.

Everywhere we went, we dined at fancy restaurants. Civilization was always close at hand. Makes sense when you're in its birthplace. The Brits had come a long way from fish and chips, and kidney pie. You name it, they had it. One night, we found an Italian joint that served up amazing Veal Scallopini. I claimed it was the best I ever had, though I was exaggerating. As for the curry, no exaggeration necessary. Best on the planet. Better than India, so they said.

By Labour Day weekend, we were back in London. We'd gone full circle and our spirits had dimmed not one iota. I wasn't yet dreading a return to work – we still had a few precious days to savour iconic sights. Big Ben, The Tower of London, Buckingham Palace. They were all on the list.

A visit with Ivan was also on the list, but for all our planning we only managed a one-day overlap, which suited Lisa. Especially when she learned it was *only* Ivan.

"Change of plans, Petra's not coming."

"What?"

I shook my head. "Yeah, they're still in France, they were booked up with something or other. Ivan's making a special trip, *just for us.* What a guy, eh?"

"Oh, brother."

I grinned. "He's coming in on the Chunnel."

"He's a Prince."

I laughed. "It's one afternoon, Darling. We're going to an English pub to watch football. Can't get more British than that."

She slapped her palm to forehead. Just like an Italian.

"Here's the plan. You and Julio chill at the hotel. *I'll* battle the traffic, pick up Ivan at London Bridge Station. Then we all meet back at The Brighton Pub. It's just off Oxford, five minutes from the hotel."

"We're gonna sit in a pub all afternoon?"

I laughed. "Did you hear me? Oxford Street. You can duck out any time and go shopping. If that's what you want."

"I think that's what *you* want."

I shot her a look of shock and hurt. She didn't buy it for a second.

Chapter 21 – London

I was getting handy at driving on the wrong side of the road, and I made good time. I beat Ivan's train by ten minutes, which gave me time to change into suitable gear for the match.

When I exited the men's room, like magic, there he was. We greeted each other like long-lost pals, but we didn't linger. Within minutes, we were back in the car.

"So...*tell me*. The trip. How's it been?"

"What can I say, amazing. Every place we went, *amazing.*"

He nodded knowingly.

"You keep telling me this country's falling apart." I shook my head. "England's still England, pal. It ain't never gonna change."

He shot me a cheeky look. "*London's* a shithole."

"Doesn't look like a shithole." I gestured about. "Looks like the same jolly old England it's always been."

"For sure, look at all the Englishmen." We happened to be passing a mosque, and the sidewalk was awash with Muslims.

I grinned. "Bad timing. Doesn't prove anything."

"*Riiiiight,*" he said sarcastically. "Hey, not many Frenchmen in Paris, either."

"Give it a rest, Ivan."

"*I'm serious.* Europe's getting Africanized. Hell, you saw the French national team."

"Huh?"

"World Cup, dude. It's a contest for who has the best Africans." He chuckled. "Another plus for immigration. Increase your odds of winning on the big stage."

"That and the ethnic food." I got in the fun.

"*Totally* makes up for the car fires and the riots."

"Good God, you been saving this shit up?"

"Hey, you missed a lot with your head in the sand. Trump was here a few weeks ago."

"I heard they were flying a Trump Baby balloon."

Ivan chuckled. "They thought that was brilliant. But the Sadiq Khan *revenge balloon* was a disgrace."

"How was Trump's visit?"

"Ah you know, lots of whining and complaining, lots of protests. England's lost. They're a laughingstock. A country of cucks."

"Say what you really think, Ivan."

"You heard what Trump said, right?"

"Tell me."

"He called Sadiq's London a shithole. Said the little man's doing a terrible job on crime, yadda yadda."

"Did Khan respond?"

"Called him a racist."

I laughed out loud.

"Brilliant coming from a guy who says terror attacks are *part and parcel of living in a big city.*"

"Khan's right, though." I said.

"Unfortunately, he is. Did you hear? Couple weeks ago, a migrant smashed his car into some cyclists outside Parliament."

"*Jesus.*"

"Exactly. Meanwhile, the fake news merchants spread their bullshit and white Brits get tossed in jail for saying mean things. What a country."

I shook my head.

"If ya can't silence 'em through harassment and intimidation, why not jail 'em?" Ivan's ire was up.

"Like Tommy Robinson."

"I took your advice, by the way. Steered clear of Luton."

"Ah yes, Tommy's hometown. You hear he's out on bail, eh?"

"Nice to see. Maybe logic and reason will prevail yet."

"Don't hold your breath."

"There are some bright spots. I see *my* home country's fighting back."

"Salvini's a hero. We need more like him."

"Hey man, you didn't come here to talk shit."

"Fuck no. Get this beast parked and let's start drinking."

I got that job done and we made it to The Brighton ahead of Lisa and Julio. Ivan claimed it was the best place in London to watch football.

The sun shone and people were out in droves. Despite the bustling crowds, I felt peace and joy, almost too much to bear. I smiled at a young family passing by, their rambunctious toddler making a fuss. How quickly the years pass. Two of my sons were men, and the third was within shooting distance.

"Where are they?" Ivan asked. "The game's about to start."

"Relax, pal. They're on their way." I, too, was getting a thirst for the beer we were about to drink. Ivan was downright antsy.

Finally, they arrived and we endured the hugs and handshakes, the usual small talk.

"Are you joining us for the match, dear?" I asked.

Lisa shook her head with a smirk. "We're going shopping. Gonna give my credit card a workout."

"The British economy could use the help," said Ivan. "Where you off to?"

"We're going to wander up toward Regent, see what we find."

"Only about 300 shops between here and there."

Lisa rubbed her hands together in greedy anticipation. Oxford Street was the heart of London shopping. It had the landmark brands, the designer outlets, even bargain fashion. Something for everyone.

"You're not taking the boy are you?" Ivan gave Julio a friendly punch in the arm.

"Who you calling a boy?"

"Good point, you're old enough to drink in these parts."

"You guys are on your own," Lisa said, and linked arms with her youngest. I felt a surge of happiness, but also a trace of melancholy, as if I knew the moment was fleeting.

"I can't change your mind?"

She shook her head decisively. "Watch out for soccer hooligans. They get a little rough sometimes."

"We grew up in East Van." I flexed a bicep. "They better watch out for us."

She frowned, but it was an act. She never worried much about me. She didn't have to. I rarely worried about her, either.

Perhaps I should have.

I stepped forward and kissed her cheek. I patted Julio on the shoulder. "Take care of your mother, would ya?"

"You got it, Papa."

"Meet you back at the hotel?"

"Can't wait dear." Lisa blew me a kiss, and I pretended to catch it.

I watched them go. Lisa never looked more elegant. *And so very British*, in her floral print dress and extravagant beige sunhat. She'd bought it the day before, at great expense, and I kidded her *will you ever wear it?*

She looked a work of art, I remember thinking. My heart had swelled with pride. Julio was right. We'd get Leo sorted. We'd get it all figured out.

Ivan snapped his fingers in my face. "Hey, *wakey wakey*. You ready for a beer?"

"Try four or five."

"Lightweight," he scoffed. "Follow me."

The pub had all the essentials – TVs galore, hot waitresses, raucous clientele. Somehow, we scored VIP seating on the deck – football on one side, Oxford Street on the other. Within minutes, two pints of draught arrived.

As the Brits say, *brilliant*.

The game in question? Crystal Palace vs Liverpool. The crowd was boisterous. Lots of trash talk, banter and bravado. I heard one guy yell *fuck off ye daft cunt* and another *up yer arse, ya bloody wanker*. All in good fun, no punches thrown.

Just a bunch of blokes watching football with their mates. A gathering. A meeting place. Part of England's social fabric. A great atmosphere, not to be missed by any tourist.

As if to prove Ivan's point, the best player on each team was an African. An Ivorian for The Eagles, an Egyptian for The Reds. When Wilfried Zaha scored a few minutes in, Ivan bellowed: "What I tell ya about those Africans?"

I motioned toward our empty glasses. "Round two?"

"Bring it on."

I glanced down at Oxford, scanning the sidewalk for Lisa and Julio. Ha, I'd have more luck finding Waldo in the bustling crowds. I was feeling no pain. The football, the beer, the *bonhomie*. Life was good.

Then I saw it.

Something was amiss. Vehicles emit a body language, just like people, and the large white van was loudly proclaiming: *I'm up to no good.*

It stopped at a weird angle, blocking two lanes. Immediately, the cars behind expressed displeasure. Ivan turned to have a look. Soon, everyone was looking with expressions of shock and fear.

"What's that fucking idiot doing?" Someone bellowed.

I was afraid to answer.

Chapter 22 – Horror
September 2, 2018

Time slowed to a crawl as the van awkwardly circumnavigated a system of traffic bollards, and climbed the curb. A cop ran toward it, gesticulating, but he was ignored. The van was a predator stalking prey, and its path veered ominously. The wide and busy sidewalk was there for the taking.

"What's he doing?" A women screeched. "*Oh my God.*"

What happened next was a blur. The van accelerated into a crush of pedestrians. Those who saw it scrambled, but many were oblivious, or slow to respond. I remember trying to yell out, but my voice wouldn't work.

I saw a series of grotesque impacts, like a bowling ball knocking down pins, leaving a trail of broken bodies in its wake.

"*This can't be happening,*" someone yelled.

But it was. Witnesses later described the sickening thuds and crunching noises as the van mowed down everyone and everything in its path. Even from a distance, we could hear the screaming. It was contagious, and spread immediately to our patio. A chilling chorus of shock and horror.

Something clicked in my brain, more instinct than conscious thought. I leapt up and raced toward the stairs. Ivan shouted after me, but I ignored him. At street level, panic was in the air. People ran about chaotically, unsure where to go, how to help.

I sprinted toward the mayhem. I assumed Ivan was following, but couldn't be sure. Bodies were strewn about, the injuries catastrophic. Twisted and tangled limbs, dismemberment, blood flowing freely.

It was ghoulish work, but I scanned each victim. I had no choice. I studied each broken body as the dreadful thought ravaged my consciousness. A thought so appalling, I couldn't voice it.

Couldn't be. No. No. No. No way. Not a chance.

I continued through the horror. The crime scene covered many meters. One man had been trapped under the van and dragged. He was ground to a pulp by asphalt. It was beyond grotesque.

I kept moving, scanning amidst the cries and groans, the anguish of the witnesses. Sirens wailed, I saw the white van not twenty yards in the distance. Stationary. Commotion surrounding it. I sensed police attempting to restore order.

My nervous system jolted, as if a surge of electricity shot through me.

Lisa's sunhat.

Unmistakable. There on the pavement, quietly delivering the news I feared more than anything. It was a bad sign and I braced myself, but hope still flickered.

It's only a hat.

Then a sickening despair engulfed me. I saw Julio, a young couple grimly hovering over him. He lay peacefully, his body seemingly intact. For a moment, hope cruelly flared.

But the man's face grew grimmer, as I approached. Did he sense I was the father? I ignored his pleas, his attempts to stall, to warn.

I knelt beside my youngest and saw the carnage. The horror of the injury overwhelmed me. Julio's skull was destroyed. Bits of brain matter mingled with skin and bone and blood.

I kissed him gently and sobbed. I whispered messages of encouragement, in case he was still alive, but I'm afraid I failed him. My words were incoherent and laced in panic.

Ivan was with me now. He had marshalled paramedics, and a fresh-faced young man pushed his way through. I reluctantly surrendered my vigil. The boy, barely older than Julio, dutifully observed protocols.

Moments later, he shook his head. Julio was dead. No vitals, the man solemnly stated.

A new thought entered with fury. *Lisa! Oh my God, where is Lisa?*

Ivan placed a hand on my shoulder, as if he knew. "She was hit too, Tony. I'm so sorry." He wiped his own tears and tried to draw me into an embrace.

"Where is she?" I demanded. *"Where?"*

He led me to the fateful spot. Lisa's left leg was twisted grotesquely. It looked as if it might tear away at any moment. There was no movement. No sign of life. Her hair was bloodstained, her expression frozen in terror. It would torment me for the rest of my days.

The EMS crew tended, but I knew in my heart there was nothing they could do. I prayed for a miracle anyway, but when they told me the news, I collapsed again in anguish and despair. I buried my face on her broken body and sobbed.

I cried until I was exhausted with agony. Ivan had a hand on my shoulder, but I asked him to go be with Julio while I stayed with Lisa. I couldn't be with both at once, and I didn't want either to be alone.

When they began covering the dead, I didn't want Julio and Lisa covered. Ivan had to coax me away, with the help of a gracious constable.

I later learned Lisa was also dragged. The skin on her back and buttocks was mostly gone, ground by friction. The pain would have been unbearable. When she was finally set free, a rear wheel came across her midsection, crushing internal organs, causing hemorrhaging. She died of blood loss on the scene.

I won't go into more detail. What I saw was too much for any man. Ivan wasn't known for his warmth, yet he consoled: "They're with God now," he said. "God was with them when it happened."

The words provided momentary comfort, and I felt my faith flicker. But I rejected it. I wasn't ready to speak with God. I wanted only pain. I needed to suffer.

The wail of sirens was constant. They came to cart away the wounded, to restore and mend them.

Not my Lisa and Julio. They were gone. Departed. They would never again grace this earth. I wished I was gone, too. My suffering was unimaginable. And I knew it would get worse.

Chapter 23 – Grief

Leaving the scene, we saw grieving relatives, but also tearful reunions. People relieved to find loved ones safe. I would never find relief. I would never have peace. My life had been destroyed.

I barely recall what happened after that. How we got to the hotel, what interactions I had with police. Ivan helped me into bed. He tended me as one would a small child. A doctor gave me something to sleep, and I didn't resist. I craved the oblivion. I needed a break from...*the horror.*

Dawn came, and the pain found me. I heard car horns and London's incessant bluster. The tragedy was not mine alone, yet the streets were noisy and bustling. The crime scene remained active, but makeshift memorials appeared. People placed flowers and wreaths, messages of sympathy. They held vigils and lit candles.

September 2, 2018.

Would I mark the date each year? Would I relive it? When would the pain cease? I felt old and weak and beaten. I prayed God would take me.

Government officials and the press pleaded with the public not to jump to conclusions. *The motive is unknown,* they said. *An investigation is underway.* They stressed the need for patience. Some outlets conjectured it may have been an accident. Twitter was alive with speculation.

Positive messages flooded the airwaves. *This is an attack on all of us. Diversity is our strength. London Strong.* Very little news leached out. The van, described as a 7.5 tonne lorry, was seized as evidence. It had been hired the same day.

Witnesses saw the perpetrator emerge from the van, his face shiny with sweat, his eyes transfixed with a madman's determination. He waved a gun and bellowed in a foreign language – *I'll let you guess which one and what was said.* He was shot dead on the scene.

He was an immigrant. A Muslim. Two days after the attack – *I was already back in Vancouver* – the media identified him as *Faizan Zayyir Farooq.* He'd trained in Syria with the Islamic State, and had served time in British prison. His rap sheet was long. The press emphasized his struggles with mental illness.

Condolences poured in, but I couldn't look at them. The pain was too raw. People came to express sympathy. They brought cards and flowers and food. None of it mattered. I saw only the image of Lisa and Julio wandering away happily, not knowing a gruesome death was minutes away.

Julio. He was the one for me, I've said it many times. My Golden Child seemed blissfully unaware of his beauty. What would he have become? A doctor? A lawyer? An engineer? Or would he have joined me on the waterfront?

I'll never know. His potential will forever go unrealized. His bright light will no longer shine. My boy will never age, he'll be forever young and beautiful.

And Lisa, my lovely Lisa, lost. I could accept losing one, maybe. *But both?* My grief was unimaginable. Lisa was gorgeous, that was undeniable. It's possible I married her for her looks – we are shallow in these matters. But I was lucky. I discovered so much more than beauty.

Lisa was an unlikely mixture of sweetness and charm, of grace and poise. She was still youthful and vibrant. She was my lover, my best friend, my life partner. The mother of my children. My rock.

Well-meaning people said I must be strong for my remaining family. They implored me. They told me to lean on my faith, that they'd be there for me. *Was there anything they could do?*

It was a sad joke. I was left with two sons, one I didn't care for, one I didn't understand.

I was broken. Physically, emotionally, spiritually. The lure of despair was strong, and I succumbed the fourth night. I downed the whiskey with destructive abandon. I was so desperate to numb the pain.

Later I vomited violently, and sobbed. Again, I had failed them. Soiled their memory. I resolved to accept the agony without sedatives, a small sacrifice in their honour.

Family members stepped up. Ivan and Dhanesh, too. Those two stalwarts took turns spending nights with me. They helped me through that first week. I knew I would soon spend nights alone, that the loneliness would spread its darkness into every corner. These thoughts frightened me.

For the funeral, I wore my black suit, the one I reserved for such events. I shaved, I attempted basic grooming. It didn't help. I looked haggard and unkempt. My eyes were swollen and bloodshot, devoid of spirit.

At the church, a large picture of Lisa and Julio was set up in the foyer, their likenesses serenely gazing out at the mourners. It was a recent photo from a summer gathering. They were happy and smiling, no sign they knew the end was near. They smiled with careless abandon, certain of their immortality.

I stumbled about in a daze, and my loved ones kept watch. Ivan and Dhanesh repeatedly assured me: "Anything you need, pal. *Anything.* We're here." There was nothing they could do.

In the front row, my boys flanked me. Leo bawled throughout the day, not haltingly, not reluctantly. He blubbered like a schoolgirl. Leo loved his mother, as much as I did and possibly more. When I tried to console him, he brushed me off.

It angered me, and I almost asked if him he also grieved for Julio. That would have been petty and mean, and I held off. Nonetheless, the chasm between us grew. I was starting to doubt our bond could be restored.

Vinny came with his biker friends and, aside from manner of dress – lots of leather and gangland insignia – you'd never find a more respectful bunch. They were used to funerals.

When I hugged Vinny, I felt his overwhelming grief. We shed a tear together, and it took me by surprise. Big tough Vinny was hurt bad. Devastated. His pain was a new wound for me to bear.

"Sometimes life is sad and tragic," the Priest sermonized. "It is never our place to question God."

The statement upset me. Who then do we question? Who do we hold to account for the evil among us? My rage flickered, and I swore a solemn oath on the souls of Julio and Lisa – as God is my witness, I would get justice. This led to soul-searching guilt as I realized I had no means. I would let them down again.

In the receiving line, I saw faces old and new. Workmates, classmates, teammates. My neighbour and one-time nemesis Charles Kennedy was there, polished and composed. "I'm so very sorry, Anthony." I could tell he meant it, and my opinion of him went up a notch.

But grief and despair overwhelmed all. They would forever haunt me.

Evil had won.

Chapter 24 – Dark Days

I lurched through the first few weeks like a zombie. I have no idea what I did. Nothing of consequence. By October, I was trying to participate in life – *I'd go crazy if I didn't* – but it took enormous energy. People tiptoed around me, as if I might fall to pieces. *Just act normal*, I wanted to scream. At night, despair and loneliness came calling.

I was off work, with time to fill. Ivan kept me abreast of the political world, north and south of the border. It was a welcome distraction. I noticed he steered clear of all things British.

In the leadup to the American midterms, the gloves came off. The Democrats were hateful and vicious and would stop at nothing to win, so said Ivan. Lie, cheat, steal – for them, the ends justified the means.

Skipping ahead, Trump held his Senate majority, but the Dems *recounted* their way to sizable gains in the House. America got one step closer to a permanent democratic majority.

Up north, Trudeau continued embarrassing himself on the world stage. His hallmark was signaling virtue and stammering. He was consistently cringeworthy.

I looked on indifferently. What did I care? Since my regrettable alcoholic binge many weeks prior, I'd abstained admirably. However, one rainy Thursday, Dhanesh dragged me to a pub and we slugged back a few. The Canucks were taking on the Blackhawks and we made efforts to shoot the shit, like old times.

Was nice to be out, nice to see my old friend, but a distance had grown. Dhanesh had changed. He was *woke.* He was *down with the struggle.* He despised Trump, and advertised that opinion to the world. Most people did. The Left demanded it.

These thoughts, pressing as they were, didn't consume me. I was stuck in a well of misery. Contrary to popular belief, time does not heal all wounds. Or did I just need more of it?

Memories of Lisa were everywhere. In the bathroom, her mysterious potions stared up at me as I shaved. In the bedroom, her jewelry perched on the dresser, seemed to wonder if it might one day see limelight. And her lingerie – I knew the drawer she kept it – would be forever retired. I didn't dare look.

Her walk-in closet, I hadn't touched. I couldn't bring myself to disturb her many frocks and garments. I was fearful of finding some sharp memory that would cut deep. One lonely night, I rummaged through the bedside table and found her journal. I stared at it for five minutes before summoning the courage to open it. I was brought to tears after one sentence. I couldn't read on.

Perhaps one day I'd clear these things away. At that moment, I would never have survived such an ordeal.

Nonetheless, I felt myself getting stronger. By late November, I returned to work. Three days a week to start, but I bumped it to five almost immediately. Idle hands were the devil's tools.

Leo stopped by rarely. We dutifully exchanged pleasantries, and avoided topics of conflict, which didn't leave much to say. I suspected his visits were for economic reasons. He'd never held a job and was dependent on me financially.

Conversely, Vinny took care of his own finances, and visited frequently. Two, three, four times a week. Not sympathy visits, either. He brought energy and cheer. He often brought friends. A motley and diverse cast of characters. No Rotary Club members. I was happy for the company. Vinny always put a smile on my face, even if I worried about him, which I did.

Grief and despair still attacked in the night, sometimes with crushing force. I was getting used to the demons. They were now, I assumed, part of who I was.

I felt something had to change or I'd grow old quickly. I prayed it was not already too late.

I needed a purpose, a reason to carry on.

Chapter 25 – What Now?

I was coming to terms with God. The loss caused me pause, but my faith never broke. As Father Fazzio stated, *it's never our place to question God.*

God is good, though not always responsive. Sometimes, however, He answers quickly and with precision. I sought purpose? A raison d'être? He supplied a tall order. If I had understood how tall, I may never have accepted. You'll see what I mean.

Indifference and apathy had been my twin demons. When Ivan preached, I listened blankly. He railed about Democrats. He railed about Trudeau. What did it matter? I couldn't summon conviction or fortitude, much less anger. I was withered and beaten.

Ivan missed nothing, and gave me a nudge. "You do recall our chat about England?"

I glared. He knew the topic was off-limits.

He gestured apologetically, but pressed on. "We covered a lot of ground that day."

I sighed. "I remember."

"You said *England's still England. It's not gonna change.*"

"I changed my mind. I *get* it now."

"I know you do. But," index finger aloft, "how about Canada? Have we changed? Are we changing?"

"Dude, we talked about this. Demographic change. Look at Surrey, look at Richmond. Look anywhere. I still never met a Muslim. At least our minorities – okay, they're *not* minorities – at least they're peaceful."

He patted me on the back. "The most words you've strung together in months. Nice to see your brain still works."

I held up a threatening fist, but smiled in spite of myself. "What can I say? No Muslims in Vancouver."

"Not yet, but Ontario's at five percent, and Québec ain't far behind. Those are dangerous thresholds if I believe Mark Steyn, and I do."

"Last I checked, we live in B.C."

"Two percent, and growing fast."

"Maybe we're different. Who says we'll have problems?"

"I just told you, dummy. *Mark Steyn.* He's not the only one."

"I'm getting a beer, you want one?"

"Been waiting for the offer."

When I returned, Ivan didn't miss a beat. "You're aware our Minister of Immigration's a Muslim refugee?"

I took a swill. "Of course."

"A fox in charge of the henhouse, ain't it?"

"*Racist.*"

He shrugged ostentatiously. "Oh, good point. *Conversation over.* You win the debate. Let me hang my head in shame."

"As you should." I felt feisty for the first time in a while.

"All I'm saying is, we're going in a bad direction. England's lost. Great chunks of Europe are lost. Parts of Paris are like a different country, and no one says shit."

"They don't wanna be called racist."

He nodded. "Or get thrown in jail. Not every country has the First Amendment. We don't. We got hate speech laws, just like the goddamn UK. We got M-103 calling out Islamaphobia."

"That's not a law."

"Baby steps, bud. Hate speech laws are sharia in disguise. Never forget that."

"You think I don't know?" I gestured emphatically. It was the Italian in me. "I know it well, Ivan. I know Islam ain't compatible with *our* way of life. To them, we're infidels. Unbelievers. Not even human. *The Quran says so.*"

Ivan blinked theatrically. "You been taking smart pills?"

I chuckled. "What's that saying? To learn who rules you, find out who you can't criticize."

"You're catching on." He nodded. "We're going down a dark path, my friend."

"You really think the nonsense is coming to Vancouver?"

"Question is, is it already here? Things change fast, dude. One day, we'll wake up in a different country."

I shuddered. "I feel like I'm trapped in one of your Facebook debates. Ranting and raving and name-calling. And for what? Nothing ever gets resolved."

"Just drawing you out, pal. Been watching you mope for too long. And..." He paused dramatically.

"*What?*"

"Listen, your name was in the news a lot after...*what happened*. That was big news. People know who Anthony Fierro is, and they're on your side."

"So?"

"So you got currency. Our country's getting ruined. It should be all hands on deck to save it. Someone's gotta speak up."

"Why not you?" I challenged.

"Have you seen my timeline?"

I chuckled. "Sure, when you're not in Facebook jail."

"Look at Danny. Don't get me wrong, love the guy, but suddenly he's all over the *people of colour* victim message."

Ivan scoffed. "He's no victim. He's one of the luckiest people on the planet."

"Is he what you call a useful idiot?"

"I usually reserve that for white morons, like your brother-in-law. Or your...uh—"

"My kid?"

"Sorry about that."

"I know he's an idiot." We sat in silence and sipped beer. "You say I should speak up. What am I gonna say? Who am I gonna say it to?"

"I don't know, man. But it'd do your soul some good to unload."

I drained my beer. "Round two?"

Ivan nodded and made tracks for the bathroom. I pondered further in the kitchen. I thought about Lisa and Julio. I missed them every day, and would for eternity. I ached for them. I thought about the hollowness and the pain of knowing justice would never be served.

Then, I remembered the solemn oath I swore to avenge their deaths. But how? I felt confused. And weary. But I also felt a stirring of...was it anger? Yes, but something more. Something I couldn't put my finger on.

I was jolted from my reverie, someone at the front door. Vinny? He usually texted first. Hopefully not Leo, not with Ivan in the house. Sure enough, Leo and Ivan entered the living room simultaneously. Worst case scenario.

"Hey Leo, how's life on the frontlines?"

Leo ignored him. "Dad, I just came by to get that cheque. I was gonna visit but," he glared at Ivan, "I think I'll be on my way."

"You sure? I could barbeque some steaks? Ivan was just leaving." I glared at him, too.

"Yeah," Ivan said cheekily. "As soon as I finish this brand-new beer you gave me. How's school, Leo?"

"Go fuck yourself. I don't have to be nice to you anymore."

"Hey," I snapped. "You gotta be civil in this house. I don't care who you're talking to."

"Pretty fucking hard when you hang out with racist assholes, Dad."

"*Leonardo.*" I pointed at him accusingly. "What would your Mamma say? May God rest her soul."

He shot me a dirty look. "Don't you dare bring my mother into this."

I looked at him in bewilderment. *Who was this person?*

"I'm no racist, Leo," Ivan said. "But your mother and brother were killed by a racist. How do you wrap your SJW head around that?"

"*Ivan.*" I barked. "*Enough.*"

Leo scoffed in disgust. "You have no idea what Faizan Farooq went through. You don't know what pushed him to get behind the wheel of that van."

Leo used the murderer's name in my house. Va fongool! It was worse than blasphemy.

"I know he didn't belong in England," Ivan replied.

"Who says? Maybe you don't belong in *this* country."

"People like Farooq like to throw people like you off tall buildings. Ever run that through the old noodle?"

I knew Leo was gay, but it went unspoken between us. Now Ivan decides to out him in my presence? This was a nightmare.

"I'd throw *you* off a building if I got the chance. *I'd shoot you like a dog.*"

"Yeah, and you'd go to jail. You got a lot of growing up to do, Leo."

Leo was hysterical now. "I loved my mother more than anyone. *Definitely* more than him," he pointed at me, and I was too stunned to counter. "But maybe what happened was necessary. Maybe these incidents can show us the way. Maybe they're the growing pains we need to get to the promised land – equality for all."

Who was this person? What book was he reading from?

I snapped. I walked over and cuffed Leo. He's lucky I didn't knock him out. "*A fanabla.* Get the fuck outta my house." My hate was sharp and pure in the moment. I could accept he was a moron, but I could never accept betrayal.

He gave me one last pathetic look, a mixture of shock and hurt, then turned tail.

"Don't come back," I yelled. I felt no remorse for a very long time.

Chapter 26 – Waking Up

They say a conservative is a liberal who's been mugged. It's the final straw, the crucial red pill. But what does it take to push someone to action? To risk stepping up and demanding change? The betrayal of a loved one might do it.

Who was our enemy? I wondered. *Islam? Or Leftism?*

I didn't know much about Islam and I sure as hell didn't understand it. But Leo was flesh and blood, and he'd been taken by enemy forces. He'd become the enemy.

The episode pushed me into new territory, a new way of thinking. Leftism was the disease, and people like Leo were the cancerous tumour. He had to go. It ripped my heart in two, but I had no choice. I could not abide by treachery.

My ire was fresh, but I also had clarity. A heightened state of awareness and lucidity. I noticed everything. The spin, the bias, the full-frontal attack on cultural traditions I held dear. Obliteration of norms was the new normal. It had been for a while.

I zeroed in on Canada's elected representatives. The image of Trudeau berating an elderly Québécois woman for daring to ask a question. For her troubles, she was humiliated, manhandled, and smeared.

Trudeau had an army of minions. One of his rising stars was Esther Hermilus, a Woman of Colour, but not a Muslim. Haitian by birth, her success paralleled that of our Minister of Immigration. Both seemed to believe racism was Canada's biggest problem.

Islamaphobia was her signature issue and she professed deep love for Muslims. Why? POC solidarity, I had to assume. Unless it was the FGM, the child marriage, or the wife beatings.

To lefties, Esther was a precedent-setter, a role model for People of Colour. She was so *woke* she dropped ghetto lingo in parliament – what better way to bond with the masses than to sound like a gangbanger? *Ha,* just another way to defile and cheapen our sacred traditions. I found Ms. Hermilus disgusting. *Disgustoso!*

She perceived everything through a racial lens. *Everything.* Under this lens, whites were at the bottom, and only their replacement would remedy the problem.

As she planted seeds of division in every act and utterance, no one called her out. On the contrary, they pretended she was smart and noble. What fruit would her work bear? Incivility? Tribalism? Race wars? Was that her goal?

Trudeau's merry band of misfits seemed intent on dismantling Canada's pillars. They were openly disdainful of old stock Canadians, and they lobbied diligently for open borders. An oxymoron, incidentally. They preached the desperate need for immigrants, illegal or otherwise.

Their scariest weapon was their army of white liberal enablers. *The Leos of the world.* These good folks couldn't wait to smear and demonize any who called attention to the threat, or so much as asked a simple question, like the Québécois woman.

The disease had infected our government, our schools, our young people. And of course, our media, who happily disseminated propaganda disguised as concern and feel-good non-partisan politics.

Deny, deceive, delude. Spin, confound, obfuscate. These were their tools. It was journalistic malpractice, funded by the taxpayer. Meantime, "small c" conservatives cowered. They dodged topics like white privilege. They tiptoed around immigration.

This was Canada in late 2018. This was my starting point.

What could I do? I didn't wanna be like Ivan, venting on social media, fending off haters, fending off suspensions. For what? The ROI was nil. It dawned on me – I, too, would attract haters. I'd be attacked and smeared. I was a sympathetic figure for the moment, but that would quickly be forgotten.

I was expected to slink away quietly. If I spoke, I should condemn hate, I should caution against prejudice, I should show forgiveness. That was the accepted model.

My mind spun with doubt and fear. If I was a crusader for truth, what about my real job? Would they fire me? *Could they?* And if they did, could I find another job? And if not, did I have enough tucked away to survive the rest of my life?

At least they couldn't destroy my family, I realized grimly. But what about friends and colleagues? What about my soccer and high school pals? They'd see the smears. Would they believe them?

Jesus, what about Dhanesh?

Would he support me? He was like a brother, he'd have my back. Wouldn't he? I wasn't gonna do anything wrong. I was gonna speak the truth. But in this day and age, the truth was a matter of opinion.

Dhanesh was in the outrage business now, and it was booming. I might lose him, I realized. He might disavow me. A lot of my friends might.

I became uncertain, not only of my plans, but of my fortitude. My courage and stamina. I wallowed in indecision, but then an image hit me with a physical force. Lisa's broken body. And Julio's.

Resolve returned with a vengeance. I wouldn't let fear and doubt deter me. I wouldn't let down the people I loved.

I couldn't.

Chapter 27 – Taking Action

Our lives are brief, our societies fleeting. Cultures not cherished and protected risk extinction. They risk lapsing into oblivion. The nonsense arrived with shocking suddenness and people hardly noticed. They were busy making ends meet, raising families, living lives. Once the common man noticed, it felt inappropriate to say anything. Perhaps even illegal.

Only yesterday, I was in grade eight and my world was stable and safe. There were two sexes and children recited the Lord's Prayer. Neighbours watched over each other and random street violence was vanishingly rare. People walked at night without concern for personal safety. We were all on the same team, a team rooted in sanity and reason.

What happened? How did it unravel? And could we stop it?

I didn't have the answers. No one did. But was that reason to stay quiet? Not in my books.

What was my message? Was I anti-Islam? Anti-immigration? Anti-diversity? *No.* Call me old-fashioned, I still believed in MLK. *Content of character, not colour of skin.* I was pro common sense. Pro free speech. Pro *common decency.* I wanted to be fair, to see all sides.

A radical Muslim murdered my loved ones, but Islam wasn't the root problem. No, it was the dark forces of Leftism that were driving us on a march to chaos and anarchy.

Trump couldn't stop it. The resistance expanded in direct proportion to his efforts. And when Trump was gone, what then? Would another take his place?

I didn't see one. Trump was a bluebird. *A unicorn.* He showed us how to fight, how to confront the evil. He inspired. Without Trump, there would be no Salvini in Italy, no Bolsonaro in Brazil. But I feared he was a speedbump on our descent, because the Left is a virus that never goes away. Its disease runs deep.

So why bother? Why not live out my days comfortably? Because I'd made a vow. And maybe, *just maybe*, my voice would be heard. I had a feeling in my heart it would.

I didn't want Canada to follow Britain. I didn't want to descend to the violence of South Africa, or the chaos of Venezuela. But that was our path. I saw it with crystal clarity.

I would come up from the grassroots, wage my war bottom up. What that looked like, I had no idea. I'd be feeling my way in the dark. Ivan would be my support team and I would actively leverage his knowledge. When I told him my plans, he was rather shocked at their scope.

First things first, I negotiated a leave of absence from my job, twisting management's arm on a few clauses and restrictions. They trusted me unreservedly. I told them I needed personal time, and that came with full pay and benefits. I wasn't lying.

The gravy train would eventually run dry, but that was a battle for another day. I had a sinking feeling my choices would cost me money in the long run, perhaps a lot of it. I was navigating unchartered waters and I ignored the ripple of fear running through my nervous system.

I sprang into action. I signed up for Twitter and tweeted a series of short sharp thoughts, a stream of consciousness:

> *Our country is broken. How do we fix it?*
> *#CanadaFirst*

> *Who is our enemy? What can we do about them?*
> *#CanadaFirst*

> *Diversity is strength? Tell that to my wife and son.*
> *#CanadaFirst*

> *Society is unravelling. Does anyone care?*
> *#CanadaFirst*

> *I cannot sit idly by and watch my country collapse.*
> *#CanadaFirst*

It was a style I would come to embrace. Simple, plain speech. I didn't hide behind an alias. I showed name and face to the world. I would speak the truth, and stand behind my words. Doxing, a term Ivan enlightened me on, would never be a threat.

Besides, my name had *street cred*. After the attack, Canada's liberal media churned out sympathy stories. Lisa and Julio were the only Canadian victims, and the Fierro name got *muchisimo* airplay, not just in Canada. It was a global story through several news cycles. I was known far and wide. I was a victim, to be treated with respect and kid gloves.

I was painted as a strong father figure, a union man, a descendant of Italian immigrants. A lot of love came my way in the weeks following September 2, 2018, not just from family, friends, and co-workers. I got a letter from the Prime Minister, himself.

For a spell, the media was relentless. When those vultures smelled a story, they pursued aggressively. They desperately wanted a quote, a sound bite, anything. Not just Canadian media, but the big leagues – CNN, Fox, the BBC.

At the time, I declined all interviews – *I was a zombie* – and the attention waned. New victims emerged. New stories.

Well, guess what. I was ready to speak, and my tweets reignited interest, especially among Canadian media. They also raised eyebrows, but no one dared attack. Not yet. I booked two interviews – one with CTV, one with Rebel Media. A lefty and a righty, both close to home.

Game on.

Chapter 28 – Meet The Press

2019 was upon us and I was on a mission from God. The interviews were back to back. CTV was first, and they sent a young Asian named Amy Chin. She looked like a fresh-faced teenager but was probably mid-twenties. The older I got, the more young adults looked like children.

Amy was sharp as a tack, but green in the business of human nature. In the *interview before the interview*, she tiptoed around me like I'd collapse in a stiff breeze. She didn't sense my new vibe, my new sense of purpose. I felt great stores of boldness and energy, and I was getting my sense of humour back. Damn, it felt good.

I let Amy lead, this was my warmup. She nodded to the cameraman and we were off to the races.

"Amy Chin, reporting live from Vancouver, B.C. I'm here with Anthony Fierro, husband of Lisa, father to Julio, both of whom perished in the tragic events in London four months ago. Thank you, sir, for inviting me into you home. I know it's been a difficult time. May I ask, how are you doing?"

"Getting stronger every day."

She nodded with an expression of sympathy. "I'm so happy to hear that. You have the support of the entire country."

"Thank you."

"Where do you find the strength?"

"I'm a man of faith. I reach out to God every day. May sound silly in this day and age, but that's what I do."

"Doesn't sound silly at all," she said with a straight face. "What would you like the world to know about Lisa and Julio?"

I was so ready to be *badass*, I didn't prepare for a tearjerker question. I thought for a moment. "Lisa was beautiful inside and out." My voice caught, and I swallowed hard. "She loved life. She loved her family. She gave so much to so many. Ask anyone. She had no enemies."

"Says here you were high school sweethearts. What's your favourite memory of Lisa?"

There was an infinite supply, and I rambled on for several minutes. I touched on how we met, how we came from different backgrounds, how our parents initially disapproved. I talked about our wedding, summers at the cottage.

"I could talk about Lisa all day. She filled my days with joy and happiness. She was the light of my life."

"That's so beautiful." Amy wiped a tear. "And Julio? He was a sportsman I see, and a scholar to boot. Quite a kid."

I saw an image of Julio's grinning face and chuckled before answering. "He was a star, that's all I can say. He was too good for this earth. I think God wanted him back."

"Wow." Amy sniffled. "So beautiful. What's that you've got in your hand?"

It was a smaller version of the photo displayed at the funeral – Lisa and Julio happy and smiling in our backyard. It was my enduring image. They would never change. I said something to this effect, and it resonated with Amy.

"You're gonna make me cry."

"Don't get me started," I said. "I'll never hide from their memory. I'm grateful for the time we had together. I only wish it was longer."

"There must be so many memories, so many reminders around the house."

That got me. "If you only knew."

"Your family has such a beautiful story. You're the son of immigrants, correct?"

"That's right. My parents came from Italy. I grew up in East Vancouver."

"Ahhhh." She smiled wistfully. "The classic Canadian story. We're a land of immigrants, are we not?"

I shrugged noncommittally.

"Have you thought about the man who did this? I won't mention him by name. Obviously, I read your recent tweets."

Wow, what an opening. I could have charged in like a bull, but I refrained. I decided, *for this interview*, to stay clear of controversy. It was a game time play call. Why not stoke the fire of compassion and sympathy first? I was gonna need it.

I sighed and covered my face, as if the question upset me greatly, *which it did.*

"Oh, I'm so sorry, Mr. Fierro."

I looked up. "It's hard sometimes."

"I understand," Amy said. "And I think we've taken enough of your time, sir. I know this was not easy, and we thank you. On behalf of everyone at CTV, we wish you all the best."

I nodded solemnly and the tape stopped rolling.

"I'll check in with you in a few months." She shot me her friendliest smile. "Just for good measure."

"Thank you."

Mission accomplished. The interview aired on the Six O'clock News and I was hailed a model of grace. The Globe wrote a glowing piece for their Weekend Edition. I trended on Twitter as social media saluted my humility and dignity.

Would be a shame to spoil the impression, but I had a message to share. I got none of it out in the CTV interview.

The next day, Monty McEvoy showed up. Once a reporter for the Toronto Sun, McEvoy was known for irreverence and boldness, common among Rebel Media staff.

McEvoy was Amy's polar opposite – relaxed, informal, longer in the tooth. Closer to my vintage. And oh yeah, *a white male.* Sorry if that offends.

He shook my hand firmly and we swapped small talk. He expressed condolences, but didn't dwell. He was keen to cut to the chase, as was I: "Nice work with CTV," he said sincerely.

"Thanks, I was speaking from the heart." Big shrug. "Guess I gave 'em what they want."

He nodded perceptively. "What do you think my audience wants?"

"Something a little different?"

He beckoned me to continue.

"Less grace, more anger?"

"Now you're talking. None of that came across with Amy."

"She didn't ask the right questions."

"Are you angry?"

I looked at him like the question was preposterous. *"I'm incensed."* I snarled when I said it. "And I need to say so publicly. Canadians need to hear it."

McEvoy chuckled. "Maybe we should turn the camera on."

"Any time."

He motioned to the cameraman. "All set Pete. Lights, camera, action."

McEvoy blasted through his intro like a pro. He reminded viewers who I was, what had happened. "Last night, we saw Mr. Fierro's humble side. We heard about the loved ones lost, we saw the love and grace in his heart."

Then he hit me with a fastball. "Let me ask you, sir. Do you also have frustration? Enmity? Malice? *Anger?*"

My blank stare lasted only a moment. "Feel free to go straight to the hard questions."

He gestured apologetically. "I can go easy."

"No, no. Like I told you, some things I need to get off my chest." I cleared my throat decisively. "Of course, I'm angry. *Who wouldn't be?* I lost my wife and son to a madman who should not have been in that country. He mowed people down because he hates us."

"Who is us?"

I smiled gamely. The question was laser-focused, and I ignored it for the moment. "My family meant everything to me. *Everything.* I didn't think I could go on. I contemplated ending it all." I rubbed my face with both hands in exasperation. "But that would have dishonoured Lisa and Julio's memory. It would have dishonoured my surviving family members. It would have dishonoured God."

"So instead you got angry?"

"I did, but anger alone is toxic. It eats you up. I need to channel the anger. I need to find a way to use it for good."

"I see where you're going. You wanna use it for good..." he gesticulated wildly, "...in England? Or here in Canada?"

I laughed involuntarily, and it dissolved any remaining tension. I was light and calm. "I'll let ya know. I'm feeling my way through. I don't have a playbook. Not yet."

"Could an attack like this happen in Vancouver?"

"Of course it could, and it probably will. Look what's happening in Toronto."

"The Danforth shooting?"

"Yeah that, but the violence in general. Toronto's descending. Everyone knows it. Are we next? Of course, we are. We're bringing dangerous people in. Look at this animal who murdered Marrisa Shen. That happened twenty minutes *thaddaway.*" I pointed east. "In Burnaby, you hear me? *Burnaby.*"

"You blame Trudeau?"

I snorted in disgust. "What are his priorities? A gender-balanced cabinet? A seat at the UN? Tearing down statues? He's a clown. He has no business being PM."

"So you *do* blame him?"

I shrugged. "All I know is, under his watch we bring in unvetted migrants and plunk them in beautiful, safe, placid neighbourhoods. Does that sound like a guy who cares about Canadians? Or a guy with contempt for them? *Contempt for Canada?*"

"Tough words."

"Someone's gotta say 'em. Go ahead, pack me off to racial sensitivity training."

"Trust me, it's overrated." A small chuckle.

"Look, it's not all on Trudeau. Sure, he's an incompetent imbecile who got elected 'cause of his last name. *That's obvious.* But I blame a lot of people. I blame everyone who looks the other way 'cause they're scared they'll be called racist."

"Here, here."

"All I want is a safe and peaceful country. A *viable* country."

"You don't think we have that?"

I scoffed. "Ask the Shens."

"I'm asking you."

"Look, there's nothing magical about this land." I pointed at the ground. "This soil we live on. The reason Canada's safe and prosperous is our history of government. The people who founded the country, who built it. And yes, they were all white men. *All of them.*"

"That's rather inconvenient."

I nodded.

"And our Liberal government might disagree," McEvoy continued. "They mint new citizens every day by the boatload."

"And that makes us stronger?"

"That's what they tell us."

"If we transplant thirty million people from Pakistan, just like that." I snapped my fingers. "Or Somalia, Haiti, Sierra Leone? Do they magically become Canadian? Do they inherit our values? Do they declare their love of hockey and maple syrup?"

"Of course not."

I frowned at McEvoy. "The question was rhetorical."

"My bad."

"On the other hand, sure we can bring in a few families from a war-torn country. That's fine. That won't change Canada. Where's the happy medium?"

"You tell me."

"All I know is, it's ridiculous to force incompatible groups together in close proximity. It's evil, as if powerful people are doing it for entertainment. Like a cruel joke."

"You might be onto something."

"If you bring in the Third World, you *become* the Third World. Bring in people who hate our culture – *who hate us* – don't be surprised if they drive vans into crowds."

"*Who's us?*"

"Us is *our way of life*. Our respect for each other, for human rights. How we treat women and children – the elderly, the disabled, the disadvantaged. It's respect for rule of law. *Not Sharia.* It's safe streets, politeness – we're known for politeness, right? It's helping neighbours, it's high trust. Does that make sense?"

McEvoy nodded. "Good answer."

"Thanks." I sipped coffee. I felt fearless.

"Okay, I have a question."

"Shoot."

"What do we do about it? What are *you* gonna do about it?"

"The million-dollar question."

"Can we do anything?"

"We have to try. *I'm* gonna try. I told you, Toronto's going south. Everyone's looking at each other asking, *where'd all these problems come from?* They came from neglect and indifference. They came from the seeds we've been planting *and nurturing.*"

"You think Islam's the problem?"

"Islam's an *issue,* but the real problem is silence and denial. When no one calls out absurdity, it grows into a beast. And we're supposed to pretend it's not there. If we don't, we're racist." I shuddered. "I'm not singling out Islam, I'm singling out *absurdity.* You wanna see where it leads, look at the UK, look at Sweden. Hell, look at South Africa."

"And the solution is?"

"We need to speak up."

"People lose their jobs when they do that. In the UK, they go to jail."

I acknowledged his point with a weary sigh. "We gotta find a way."

"Tommy Robinson went to jail for pointing out a child rape epidemic."

Another sigh.

"And the media piles on." McEvoy shook his head slowly. "They call him a ruffian, a hooligan, a lawbreaker. Obviously, a racist. I know Tommy personally. He's no racist. He's a truth-teller. A damn courageous one. A hero."

"He is."

"Maybe you can be the Canadian Tommy Robinson. You're a man of the people, Tony. A working-class hero."

"Hey, easy. I don't dwell on Islam. I'm pro West. I'm anti-Left. I'm anti-stupidity. I also don't wanna go to jail." I laughed nervously. "I'm not the Canadian Tommy. I'm Tony Fierro. *Capisce?*"

"Well said, Tony." He nodded appreciatively. "And on that note, I think we can call it a wrap. Thank you for your time, sir."

I was pleased with how it went. I felt virtuous and invincible. I was thinking clearly, I was polished and eloquent. Cool and dry.

McEvoy raved. "This is gonna be huge. *Huge*, I tell you."

When the interview hit the airwaves – *i.e. all manner of social media* – the blowback was instant. The Twitter Hate Machine came at me thick and fast. Nothing prepares you for a pitchfork mob. They were hurtful and nasty. They called me a far-right provocateur, a troll, and worse. They were out for blood.

Delete your account....crawl back in the sewer where you belong...kill yourself you worthless POS.

These were not the worst. In the Leftist handbook, I was no longer a good guy. I was the enemy, and thus fair game.

My life was forever changed.

Chapter 29 – Rise

I couldn't fight off all the attackers, but I went after a few. I would *not* bow to the mob. Ivan helped. He was a veteran of social media blood sport, though even he was surprised by the vitriol. A few days passed, and the attacks dropped off. I breathed a sigh of relief.

Then the mainstream media got hold of the story. *Boom.* Attack mode back on.

But something else started to happen. Something remarkable. In addition to the venom, I was getting messages of support. They came from everywhere. Okay, mostly Canada – but also America, Europe, Australia. There were even POC in my corner.

I couldn't possibly read all the messages, much less respond. I had an instant and ardent fanbase, not to mention allies in the burgeoning alternative media. I was humbled and grateful. A week after the McEvoy interview, I tweeted a message of gratitude:

> *Thanks everyone for the love and support. It means everything to me.*

Interview requests poured in, and I accepted several. I kept pushing on social media, too. I had a message to deliver and I felt a sense of urgency. We had to stop the nonsense before it got a foothold. Slay the beast before it got big.

I started popping up everywhere. The media compared me to Tommy Robinson, along with less favourable comparisons. For a spell, they sprinkled in the odd supportive editorial, they reminded the public of my loss. Those sentiments had a short shelf-life. Soon, nothing but attacks and hit pieces.

Fuck them. That's what they do. Smear, shame, repeat. But as the backlash grew, so did the adulation. It was exhilarating. I found myself wallowing in affection, soaking it up. I had the faith and self-awareness to not let it go to my head, though.

I was God's humble servant, spreading His word. He kept me grounded, He insulated me from swirling doubt, and foreboding. This wasn't about me, or my ego. This was about protecting Canada. The Canada I loved. This was about alerting an apathetic Western World to a sickness that would surely destroy us all.

After a couple months, the grind became second nature. I was in the trenches. It was one street fight after another. My stamina was limitless, and my skin grew thick. I was immune to the slings and arrows.

But I grew restless. The clock was ticking and things weren't changing. I was a conservative voice among many, preaching to the converted. I went in with a message but not a plan. Or a goal. Okay, my goal was to change hearts and minds. To change policy. But that was vague.

I needed a focal point. Something tangible. Not surprisingly, the answer came from Ivan. He'd been watching my ascent with fascination and wonder. Perhaps a hint of jealousy, though he'd never admit it.

Dhanesh was watching, too, but that was a whole new ballgame. *Big news on the Dhanesh front.* We'll get to that.

First, Ivan. He'd been supportive throughout my rise. A sounding board. Occasionally an insufferable ass: "Everything you know, you learned from me."

This was a common refrain, and he was right to a degree. "You could have done it yourself, but you were busy on Facebook."

He scoffed. "What, throw myself into the fiery pits of hell? No thanks."

"Is that what I've done."

He chuckled. "Let's hope not, for your sake. But you have become rather infamous."

"Try notorious." My turn to chuckle. "I was under no illusions. I knew what I was getting into. This is my mission, my life's work. You know why I'm doing it."

He nodded.

"Remember when I started? Everyone's telling me, *stay out of it, it's not your fight.* It's like they were saying. *Don't worry, we're safe. It can't touch us.* Guess what, it touched me." I scoffed with disgust. "What, did they forgot about Julio and Lisa?"

"The media sure has."

"No shit. Like, overnight."

"I warned you about all this, but I never told you not to go for it."

"Dhanesh did."

Ivan scoffed. "He's a little bitch. He's gone full socialist. ND fucking P."

We dragged Dhanesh through the mud for a while, then proclaimed our love for him. Yep, we were conflicted. I assumed Dhanesh was, too.

"I gotta say, I'm feeling a bit stuck. Stalled out, man."

"What do you mean?"

"I wanna take it to the next level. But how?"

"You're *at* the next level, my friend. You're huge. You got the Twitter following, your YouTube's blowing up. Fuck, that interview with Ezra? Most viewed Rebel video ever."

Ivan was right. I spoke the truth in my one-hour sit-down with the great Ezra Levant. *Yeah, I was once Liberal. Yeah, I was once lukewarm to Trump. Was the murder of Lisa and Julio my red-pill moment? No, it was the catalyst for me to do something.*

"But who watches Rebel Media?" When he didn't answer, I answered for him: "*People like us.*"

"Good point. I have noticed your mentions going down." He was warming to the topic. "I suppose they're trying to marginalize you. And if they absolutely *must* mention your name, they do it with scorn."

"Or mockery."

"That, too."

I felt anger rising. "I point out obvious truths, and they call me racist. The irony is, it's racist *not* to talk about these problems. It's racist *not* to notice the shit going down. I'm trying to do the right thing, the noble thing. I wanna make sure Lisa and Julio didn't die in vain. I want their deaths to inspire change."

"I know, bud."

"I'm way out on a limb here. Would be nice to have something to show for it. I been at this six months straight. We're halfway through 2019. When's it gonna make a difference?"

"Patience, my son. Are you not following God's will?"

Ivan enjoyed ridiculing my faith. "I am. You're sure as hell not."

"Sometimes." He grinned wickedly, then cocked his head and his expression changed. A smug smile soon appeared. I hated that smile, but it was often accompanied by impressive insight. "By George, I think I've got it."

"Got what?"

"An idea, grasshopper."

"Uh-oh."

"A big idea, all for you."

"Give it to me."

"You're aware our Federal Election is approaching."

"Well, duh. When is it? October—"

"Twenty-first, dude. Three months away. And obviously, we have to oust the sock puppet moron."

"Obviously." I said, and frowned. "Not sure I love our chances with our current front man."

Andrew Scheer was the Conservative Party leader. A standup guy, decent and honest. And geez, I hate to slag a good man, but he was a tad light on the old charisma scale. A "small c" conservative, to boot. Wobbly and weak on *sensitive* matters. Definitely unwilling to question the *Diversity Is Strength* maxim.

Sometimes I felt it didn't matter a rat's ass who was in charge. They all quaked in their boots at the slightest whiff of the R-word. It rendered them powerless, and the enemy knew it. Would Scheer not take us to the gutter, just like the Grinning Idiot, albeit at a slower rate?

We needed street-fighters. Guys unafraid to get down and dirty in the trenches. The high road wouldn't work with lefties. Only a Trump clone could stem the disease, much less reverse the damage. And Trump was one in a million.

I became aware Ivan was speaking. "Earth to Tony, anybody home?"

"Sorry pal, daydreaming."

"You ain't gonna fall apart on me are ya?"

I scoffed. "Go on, man. Tell me your big plan."

"My goal is to kick Trudeau to the curb."

"No shit."

"That's where you come in. You're gonna bring out the vote."

"Go on."

"So, the media trashes you, yet Joe Six-Pack loves you. We gotta leverage the dichotomy."

"How?"

"A one-day event." He rubbed his hands together. "A *huge* event. *Yuge.*"

I shot him a dubious look. "I've done the freakin' townhalls, the meet-and-greets. Done 'em all over the country. A lotta work, not much return."

"Aw, is *widdle* baby tired? Does he need a *nappy wappy?*" Ivan sniffled.

"Do I look tired?" I said it with hearty gusto, and flexed a bicep.

"Just checking. You seem to be holding up well. *Shockingly.*"

"Man, I got energy to burn. I don't know where it's coming from. Straight from the Almighty, I presume."

"Says the guy with no day job."

"I have a job. My job is to save the world." I scowled at Ivan. "You gonna tell me your cockamamie idea or what?"

He nodded and drew a breath. "I'm talking about a *coming out* party – not for gays – *for conservatives.*"

"Hmmmm." I was skeptical. "Like the Walkaway movement?"

"Bigger. *Much bigger.* Walkaway on steroids. Our movement will involve *everyone.* We'll go after the majority. The grassroots. The taxpayers, the people that raise families and work hard. The bedrock. The people that love Canada." He was warming to the topic. "Hell, our target may be Canada – and the *Babbling Idiot* – but fuck it, we'll go global."

On he went, ranting and raving. I asked questions, I probed. The idea was sinking in, slowly taking shape. I had to admit, I liked it.

"Not bad," I said. "Not bad at all. And we're doing it all in one day?"

"That's our starting point. We're gonna shake the snowflakes to their core."

"You gotta name for this thing?"

"Not yet."

"A date?"

"July 1, 2019."

"Canada Day?"

"Yeah, baby. We'll steal Mr. Dressup's thunder."

"Shit dude, that's a month away."

"We better get busy."

"We?"

"Well, *you*. But don't worry, I'm gonna help."

Chapter 30 – Unsolicited Advice

That evening, I tweeted the following:

July 1, 2019. Save the date. We're taking it all back, folks. Please Retweet. #HowTheWestWasWonBack #DayOfTruth

I always got action on my tweets, thanks to a few hundred thousand of my closest friends – followers, fans, my troops. They worshipped me, they loved my ideas, even the crappy ones.

This was different. This tweet shot like a rocket, 10k retweets the first hour. Trump territory. The next day, 50k, and my follower count through the roof.

What the holy hell?

Already, it felt like a movement. *A crusade.* Who knew the announcement itself – *forget the event* – would set the world on fire. The support came thick and fast, and with a new trend: *video testimonials.* People were laying it all out. Taking the gamble.

It confirmed what I knew. People were desperate for truth, desperate for common sense, desperate to attack and ridicule *Prime Minister Peoplekind.* Who knew so many "Big

C" conservatives were closeted? Our like-minded brethren, once too timid to speak, swarmed from the woodwork.

"Just like the Trump Train," Ivan said. "They were always there. Jesus, maybe you oughtta run for PM?"

"I'm no politician."

"Neither's Trump."

"I'm no Trump."

"True."

I had to hand it to Ivan, he nailed it with this idea. The throngs were coming out ahead of schedule. The critical mass of rank and file were roaring: *We are conservative. We are angry. We will no longer be silent.*

When the press finally deigned to comment, they smeared and slandered. They called it naked white supremacy. They ignored the support I got from Asians and other Persons of Colour. *God, I despised that term.*

The media was livid and they were just getting started. The Left came hard, too. They attacked me, they attacked my supporters. One of my more fervent followers, a fireman, spoke with a little more candour than they deemed acceptable. For his troubles, the mob destroyed his life. He was fired after twenty years service. Freedom of speech was dead and gone.

Perhaps my nastiest detractor was – *get this* – my middle son. Leo lost it entirely, and I felt no remorse casting him aside. After what he said, I didn't want him back. He was no longer family. He was the enemy.

But others spread my message with religious fervour, not only in Canada. They spread it like it was God's word. I was excited. Also, nervous. The big day was drawing near, and I was in demand.

As much as the media skewered me, they courted me with equal zeal. The attention came from all over the planet. Even politicians, perhaps thinking they could ride the wave? Or talk me out of my silliness? I ignored them.

Except for one.

Dhanesh Singh. Haha, lots to cover with the D-Man. He was still married to Prisha and she was still a sweetheart. Still traditional. They had a two-year-old and another kid on the way. Imagine starting a family in your 50s, I thought.

But Prisha was just thirty-three, and God bless Dhanesh, he didn't look much older. He was still the big, good-looking Indian kid I grew up with. Flowing hair, silky skin, winning smile. He was almost *too* good-looking. The kind of good looks that make you suspicious, make you wonder if you can trust the guy. His *Rob Lowe sizzle* seemed to improve with age.

Good looks can hamper a white politician, but not a Person of Colour. On the contrary, Dhanesh traded on them. That's right, he was a politician.

That's the big news.

Back in 2012, he moved to Surrey to be near his wife's family. Two years later, he ran for City Council and won in a landslide. He worked the municipal game like a master. He always got his name out there. Charity events, print media, even front and centre on the Six O'clock News. Dhanesh was always *on*, always blathering about the dreary details of city politics.

The camera loved him, and the feeling was mutual. Alas, that pond was too small for his ambitions and in 2019, he tossed his hat in the Federal ring, running for MP in the Surrey-Centre electoral district. His sense of entitlement was matched only by his thirst for power.

And OMFG, he was running under the ND freakin' P. The Socialists. The Marxists. The sworn enemy of logic and reason. I swear, Dhanesh was once a Capitalist, a guy who eschewed liberal fairy tales. That's how I remember it.

The incumbent was another Indo-Canadian, a turban-clad Liberal, ten years Dhanesh's junior, the son of Sikh immigrants. They were all Indian in Surrey. Running a white guy was unthinkable in an age where democracy was racial headcount. Ivan claimed Dhanesh was a shoo-in. He had unstoppable mojo.

Dhanesh was a busy boy, what with photo ops, ribbon cuttings, plenty of events cloaked in poisonous identity politics. The South Asian community mostly, but he mixed in events for Chinese-Canadians, for First Nations. He touched all the POC groups. That's the kind of selfless guy Dhanesh was.

I watched in fascination. Dhanesh was still my boy. A fellow musketeer. I still considered him a best friend. *Family*. But we hadn't talked in months, and distance grows with time. Bonds weaken, sometimes they break.

Especially when subjected to trauma. My recent activity made it tough on *Dhanesh the politician*. The press had gotten wind of our history, and demanded he disavow me. Dhanesh obliged like a pro. He acknowledged the relationship, hit me first with praise, the obligatory condolences. He was a persuasive speaker, and if he was lying, I couldn't tell.

Then, under the bus I went. He condemned *my movement*. Called it openly racist, offensive, counter to the spirit of our country. The media loved it and they pushed him further up the ladder.

When pressed in subsequent scrums, Dhanesh refrained from comment. The media painted this as dignified and heroic. One pundit enthusiastically proclaimed: "We rarely see this level of honesty in our political leaders. We should humbly thank Dhanesh Singh. He's a shining light. A beacon of hope for us all."

Also, a talented political animal.

Which is why I wasn't super-surprised I heard from him. A phone call out of the blue, an invitation for coffee. I accepted, and of course consulted Ivan.

"When did you last see him?" I asked.

"Maybe a week ago. We keep in touch, you know that."

I nodded. "You figure he misses me? Or he wants something?"

Ivan smirked.

"I know, I know. But what's his game?"

"No idea. Danny's a good man, but he's slippery. I'd love to be a fly on the wall."

"Don't worry, you'll get the details."

We met a quiet JJ Bean, not far from our high school stomping grounds. There were no disguises, no subterfuge, but we were low-key. Semi-incognito. We embraced like long-lost friends, which we were.

"How ya holding up, pal?" He asked. A reference to Lisa and Julio.

"Good days and bad."

"Gotta keep on keepin' on. Make 'em proud."

I nodded. "Tryin' to. I sorta started this new...uh...project. You may have noticed."

He wagged a scolding finger. "I wanna talk about that."

"Is that why we're here?"

"No, dude. *No.*" He feigned deep offense and we fell into the embrace of familiar banter. We bashed Ivan, we bashed each other, we reminisced.

"How's the family?" I asked.

"Amazing. I shoulda had kids twenty years ago. *Like you.*"

"Does your kid call you grandpa?"

"Hey."

"Think he'll visit you at the old age home? Think you'll live to see him graduate?"

He scoffed. "I'm younger than you, Tony. I'll always have that."

"Two freakin' months."

"Doesn't matter."

"Least we don't look like Ivan." This a belly laugh, and spawned a healthy round of *Ivan abuse.* We insulted his looks, his character, his body parts. Just like old times.

But it wasn't old times. Things had changed. Soon enough, Dhanesh steered us to business. *Of course, that's why we were here.*

"Quite a stir you're making."

"Thanks for sticking up for me, by the way."

He shot me a winning grin. "I coulda said worse."

"*Whatever.*"

His expression grew serious. "I had no choice."

I scoffed.

"You're going out on a limb, Tony. *Way out.* I mean, I sort of understand, but come on. It's political suicide for me *not* to condemn ya."

"How about loyalty? *Fuck*, how about honesty?" I paused. "Or maybe you *were* being honest."

"Still love ya, buddy. You know that. I got a game to play and you put me in a tough spot."

"That's what happens when you join the NDP."

He bristled. "You shouldn't knock it. Have you read our policy papers? Do you know what we stand for in 2019?"

"I'm a union guy. I voted NDP my whole life, even though I knew they were bad for the country. *But now?*" I shook my head. "You guys make Trudeau look conservative. You pretend to be a normal party, you got this outward appearance of legitimacy. But all you wanna do is tear everything down. Burn it to the ground."

A look of sadness spread across Dhanesh's face. If it was phony, he was a hell of an actor. "You need to take a closer look, pal."

"The closer I look, the more repulsed I become."

"You been listening to Ivan too long."

"*Ha*, I agree with that."

I was trying to cut tension, but Dhanesh didn't take the bait. He drew a breath, as if readying himself to *really* sell me on the vision. This oughtta be interesting.

"It's not the NDP you have an issue with, Tony. It's the changes happening all around you. Society's changing, bud, and you don't like it."

I laughed bitterly. "Changing? How's that for a euphemism."

"I think it's changing for the better, and you...well...geez you better get used to it."

I let his words hang in the air. What was I supposed to say?

"Change ain't always comfortable, dude. Sometimes it's *uncomfortable*. All part of the process."

"*The process.*" I scoffed. "Another brilliant euphemism. When exactly does this process end?"

He smiled warmly. "We'll see."

"What does Canada look like when it's over? What's the fucking world look like, for that matter?"

He chuckled. "Can you be more specific?"

"What's it look like when all the statues are gone? When Christianity's been yanked out by the roots? When our—"

"Whoa, whoa, that's not—"

"When you've destroyed all the institutions, and all the traditions? When you've killed off every last white male, and God himself is dead and buried. What'll Canada look like then?"

He laughed out loud.

"You think I'm joking?"

"I hope so. 'Cause that's a pile of nonsense. Sounds like pure Ivan." He stroked his chin, then abruptly raised an index finger. "Let's ignore that silliness for a moment. Try this instead."

"You don't like my question, so you'll answer a different one?"

"Hear me out."

"Go ahead."

"We grew up together, right? East Van, went to Temp, the toughest school in the city. Lots of tough kids. *Fucking Rico Berutti.*"

"He wasn't the toughest. He was the loudest."

"A tough school, but everyone got along. Am I right?"

"That's how I remember it."

"Exactly. That's how *you* remember it. Guess what. That's not how *I* remember it."

"Here we go."

"I'm serious. You guys treated me good, *obviously.* I was one of the gang, one of the musketeers."

"Obviously."

"Well, it wasn't like that everywhere. *Fuck no.* In elementary school, I got racially bullied every fucking day. Even you bullied me."

"Bullshit."

"Call it what you want, I remember. *I was there.*"

"You're worried about an issue from primary school?"

"You *do* remember?"

"I picked on you a couple times. *Vice fucking versa.*"

"Not like that." And off he went, retelling of a trivial grade three dispute in which I evidently called him a Paki. I remembered. Those words were tossed around like candy back then, including the N-word, though no one admitted that now.

"Get over it, Danny. *Jesus Christ.*"

He shot me a smile. "I'm just sayin' acknowledge it. People like me were marginalized. We still are."

"Didn't you call me a honkey? And white trash?"

"So what if I did?"

"It pissed me off. You shoulda called me a Wop. *I'm Italian.*"

Again, I was trying to lighten the mood, but his sense of humour was AWOL. He was off again, dredging up old slights, the minutiae of our formative years. He had the tropes mastered, and he used the appropriate amount of righteous arrogance. Had I interrupted, he might have hit me with: "Shut up and check your privilege."

The effects of the abuse, he claimed, were still with him. They affected his self-esteem. *Give me a break.* Dhanesh had one issue with self-esteem – way too much.

"You don't believe all that."

"Course I do."

"Seriously, *you don't.*" I pointed at him accusingly, as you do a close friend who's feeding you bullshit.

There was the smile again. "I believe it will get me elected."

Aha, now we're getting somewhere. Dhanesh had it figured out. He didn't need to debate issues or defend positions. All he needed was a narrative that couldn't be challenged. It sure made life simple.

He was right, too, society *had* changed. Here he was, sincerely trying to explain injustice to me, a guy whose family was slaughtered in the street. I didn't go there. No point.

Dhanesh had embraced the insanity, nothing I said would talk him out of it. There was too much at stake. The narrative paid handsomely. Money and power were his for the taking. Jesus, maybe one day he'd run for prime minister.

We chatted almost two hours and when it was time to wrap, Dhanesh tried to make peace. "I understand why you're doing what you're doing." He put a hand on my shoulder. "And don't worry about the crap I say in the press, I've always got your back."

"Try not to throw me right under the bus."

"You got it, pal." We had a good laugh. "We shoulda went for beer not coffee. That was an intense discussion."

"I'm gonna need a couple beers to sleep after all this caffeine." I drained the last of my third cup.

"Can I count on your vote in October?"

"I don't live in Surrey."

"But if you did."

"If I did, I'd vote for the brown guy."

He burst into laughter. "Which one?"

"The good-looking one."

"Now you're talking." He grinned ferociously. "Ya know, Tony, we may disagree on politics. I say big deal. We put it behind us. We move on, right?"

I nodded faintly. He made it sound like a minor disagreement, and not a profound difference in belief systems.

"Love ya, brother." He came in for a hug.

"Love you, too, my man."

But the lovefest felt hollow. Our little pow-wow was a long time coming, but I came away wondering if there'd ever be another.

Chapter 31 – More Unsolicited Advice

A few days after the Dhanesh sit-down, another politician called out of the blue – my old nemesis, and my neighbour to boot. Strange how Charles Kennedy kept coming in and out of my life.

He was a conservative MP now, a backbencher, a likely cabinet minister should the Conservatives ever stumble back into power. His party was sensitive to my activism. Initially, some spoke of me publicly, bestowing support and praise, cautiously and with caveats. I soon dropped off their talking points.

On the one hand, my movement was a rallying cry for a great chunk of their base – a call to arms. *A call to battle.* On the other, my movement was toxic. If they showed support, they were crucified by the Liberals, the NDP, the press. Even members of their own party.

My positions were taboo in the Canadian political sphere, miles outside the Overton window. To a white male like Charles Kennedy, they were Kryptonite.

So why reach out? Ivan and I tried to figure out his angle. For starters, he knew me. We had history going back to the '70s, and we'd been neighbours the past twenty years. But why? A fishing expedition? See if there was a way to leverage my following? Maybe cleanse my message?

I was willing to listen, though I still harboured ancient resentment. He was still the arrogant, waspy, white kid. The *mangiacake*. The bastard who beat us in soccer.

These were childish things, and it dawned on me – this character flaw could shed light on the resentments minorities carry. *Whoa, that was deep.* But *my* grudge didn't rule me. It wasn't the central organizing feature of my life. It was practically insignificant. Except at this moment, haha.

Charles' life was unfolding on schedule, as you'd expect of a privileged rich kid. He was a politician to watch, a partner in a prestigious law firm. Fabulously wealthy. He had a wife and two kids, which only sharpened my resentment. No family member of his had been massacred by a lunatic.

I was still weak and vulnerable at times. I still had moments of appalling darkness. But I kept close contact with my loving God. I served Him, I served others. This helped immensely.

I entered the posh driveway and the wrought iron gate closed behind me. It was not yet 8:00 p.m., and shadows played against a lush landscape of shrubbery and stone. I followed a circular driveway into the loving arms of wealth and privilege.

It was a safe and private haven, consistent with Charles' message. He had requested confidentiality. If anyone asked, the meeting never happened.

I understood.

Charles greeted me with a friendly smile and a respectful handshake. His dress was casual. We swapped small talk as I took the place in. I'd been here before, years ago, for a team function. A haunting memory of Julio assaulted me, but I chased it off.

The foyer was stately and grand, yet restrained. Not remotely ostentatious. I was struck by the size. Literally acres of space. Space to burn. You could play a game of three-on-three and have room for bleachers.

We passed the pool, the squash court. So *this* was how the other half lived. Correction, the other one percent. His third storey office featured a stunning water and mountain vista. I thought *my* view was impressive.

"You're probably wondering why I invited you." He poured ice water from a carafe.

"I have my suspicions."

"You've attracted the attention of some powerful folks."

"Such as yourself."

He chuckled. "Above my level, I'm afraid." Charles wandered to the plate glass window and gazed out for several seconds. Finally, he turned and spoke with force: "Respectfully Anthony, we're asking you to slow things down a notch. Tone down the rhetoric. Tone down the radical talk."

"And if I don't?"

He smiled thinly. "Hear me out. This is coming from the top, by the way."

"Go on."

"I'm not sure what you're cooking up for your event. We simply recommend you go easy."

I shrugged, as if to say *what the fuck?*

"The thing is – *and this is off the record* – we actually *like* what you're doing. We like that you've rallied the troops. We even like your message, *for the most part.*"

"Why not say so publicly?"

His smile was condescending. "If I said that publicly, I'd be gone tomorrow. I'd never work in politics again."

I knew he was right. What a sick society we lived in. "You say go easy. What do you mean exactly?"

He sat near me, as if ready to really hash out brass tacks. "I'll start with an easy one. Lay off Andrew Scheer.

Stop knocking him. He's the best we have, and he's under the same shackles I am. You must know that."

"Hmmm."

"Why not endorse him? Give him a boost. Every time you knock him, Trudeau gets one step closer to a second term."

"I see your point."

"Give it some thought. Like I said, that's an easy one. A no-brainer."

"You want me to lighten up on Trudeau, too?"

He laughed. "That's an area we don't mind," he raised an index finger, "within reason."

"What does that mean?"

"Go easy on the diversity thing. Maybe stop saying it's destroying Canada. We're a diverse country, in case you hadn't noticed. You have to accept it, Anthony. When you knock diversity, you're knocking Canada."

My turn to laugh. "That's a good political line."

"It's the truth."

"All I'm saying is, take a pause."

"I'm not asking for deportations. Charles, I grew up in diversity. Not these lily-white parts, like you."

"Please, keep it in mind, if you would. That's all we ask."

I shrugged. "Anything else?"

"Oh yeah." He drew a deep breath and exhaled loudly.

"Something serious?"

He nodded. "Islam."

"What about it?"

"You need to slow down on the attacks. Look Anthony, we all know what happened in London, and oh my goodness, I am *so* sorry. I can only imagine what you went through, what you're going through."

I wanted to tell him *he had no idea*, but I bit my tongue.

"Brett and I speak of Julio frequently." Brett was Charles' eldest, born same year as Julio. "They were close."

"I remember." My emotions were firing, and I closed my eyes to ask God for guidance. "If we don't speak the truth,

Charles, the truth grows into a monster. And more people die. What's that saying? You can deny reality, but you can't deny its consequences."

"We just have to be sensitive. Islamaphobia is real, Anthony. Our government takes it seriously, no matter who's in power. We just ask that you go easy."

My anger flared. "And if I don't?"

"I think that might be a bad decision." He cleared his throat and leaned in close, his voice barely a whisper. "A *dangerous* decision."

"Is that a threat?"

"It's friendly advice, Anthony. As I said, we like what you're doing. But there are questions we should not ask, topics we must leave alone. Canadians know this. They *sense* it. You've been crossing the line, treading in dangerous territory."

We sat in silence. The conversation had taken a sinister turn.

"Look, by all means push the envelope but..."

"You're asking me to ignore reality."

"I suppose we are, I'm not going to debate you."

What the fuck, a moment of unguarded honesty?

"We show the public a version of reality." He chuckled. "You could call it a lie, propaganda. Hell, you could even call it *diversity porn*. It's what we do. And we'll continue to do it."

"Why not talk about the downside? The problems diversity brings?"

"Because...well, we just don't. It wouldn't be good. Again, these are questions that should not be asked."

"I notice you don't deny it."

He shrugged. "This conversation's off the record."

Wow.

Who was this guy? What was in his heart? I always considered Charles Kennedy a narcissist, a snobby elite, uptight and reserved. The kind of guy who'd never go by

Charlie. Not in a million years. I had him pigeonholed. Back in the day, I thought he was racist, too. *Toward me.* For my *Italianness.*

But this new perverted form was worse. He was murky and sinister, his playbook rife with contradiction and fallacy. Was this essential for a modern-day white male politician? They walked a fine line. Forced to trumpet diversity, yet their presence contradicted the message.

It took skill and cunning to navigate these waters. They had to be slippery and smart, sensitive to political wind, PC at all times. They must pretend to talk tough but never draw too hard a line against progressive hogwash.

I shuddered. It would leave a person's moral fiber in tatters. They would act out of fear and cowardice, and self-preservation. Were they all like that? If so, was it any wonder their behaviour was amoral and traitorous?

Charles had shown his cards. He was two-faced, not a denier of the nonsense, but ready to put personal ambition ahead of country. Just another "small c" conservative. A *cuckservative,* Ivan would say. I couldn't live like that.

We needed bold and fearless men to stop the madness, and they were in short supply. I'd be damned if some spineless bureaucrat would make me soften my message. I didn't answer to the party line.

From me, people would hear the truth, the whole truth, and nothing but the truth.

So help me God.

Chapter 32 – Backlash

Unfortunately, I was capturing the attention of more than just politicians. Like my bosses at work – they were none too pleased. In *union* culture, we're told when to show up, when to leave, what to do, and what to think. We're also told who to vote for. It's groupthink, always has been, and in these parts we vote NDP. They always gave us the most goodies.

So obviously, the suits weren't happy with my political activism – *ha*, understatement of the year – but I was still a member in good standing. Right?

Not so fast.

Everything came to a screeching halt a few days after I announced my *movement*. I got the phone call. *Come in, Tony. Some issues we need to discuss.*

My foreboding was justified. At the conference table, lawyers and bigwigs galore. A couple hardhat-wearing blue-collars, just to mix it up. Not a smiling face in the bunch. No gags, no horseplay. Grim expressions all around.

They didn't beat around the bush. "Unfortunately," they advised, "your time with the ILWU Local 500 is over."

They had mountains of paperwork, everything terrifyingly official. The shop steward across the table studiously avoided eye contact. I wanted to ring his scrawny neck.

Terminating a union employee was a nontrivial matter. The company had to have *just cause,* and the misconduct had to be serious. There was usually a grievance process, possibly arbitration. None of this was mentioned. In fact, besides the top dog lawyer, not much of a peep from anyone.

My alleged transgressions were many. A long list, and I knew they'd make 'em stick if they wanted to, *and they did.* No one mentioned the elephant in the room – *my activism.*

Their naked treachery was something to behold. These were men I knew, some of them friends. I suppose they had no choice.

I was toast. History. This was the path I chose and I knew it would come at cost.

For a fleeting moment, dark rage overwhelmed me. I wanted revenge, I wanted to hit someone. But I channeled God's will. I sought serenity and calm. I sought trust in His providence.

Their pathetic offer stared up at me. So much for a golden parachute. A paltry severance, and six months of benefits. *Brutal.* I'd like to say I left without fanfare, but alas, I said bad words. I hurled a threat or two, told 'em they'd hear from my lawyer. It was a lie.

This chapter of my life was over. I suppose I'd been expecting it, but it was still a shock to the system. I was a longshoreman. A union man. *A lifer.* That was my identity. Who I was.

Not anymore.

In the days following, I received a handful of support calls from longstanding workmates. They offered condolences and best wishes, but quietly. And privately. I understood.

Losing my job was the tip of the iceberg. Even before *the Main Event,* things were flying out of control. The trolls on social media were ever viler and more sinister. Death threats were common.

I occasionally fought back with logic and reason. When that failed, I went with insults. The exchanges were occasionally amusing, and people liked my fire. But I began to realize, they were futile and wasteful. And I had little time to waste.

I might have given up entirely if not for a promise made to my deceased wife and son.

My loyal supporters helped, too. They fed me strength every day.

Chapter 33 – The Big Day

July 1, 2019. Canada Day.

Our government had yet to declare the observance an abomination. *Shocker.* For me, what better way to celebrate than by saving the country itself.

Vancouver offered up a fine sunny day as it so often does this time of year. Highs of 28 Celsius, no sign of wind or rain.

The big speech, set for a 7:30 p.m. start, would be my first public appearance in a month. I'd toned down out of necessity – Antifa and other miscellaneous confused millennials had been turning up, doing their part to curtail free speech.

They didn't realize they were pawns in a much larger chess game. Pampered first-world softies, ill-prepared to do battle with the unsavoury elements they so desperately fought for.

Violent agitators were a common problem for conservatives, and I'd been comparing notes with contemporaries. I had a sizable number in my circle, an interesting and diverse cast, some obscure, some famous, some infamous.

Take the notorious Bucky Bradford, a good ol' Southern boy, country to the core. He was a hunter and a fisherman. A guy who believed in chivalry, manners, and the Second Amendment. He was also thirty years my junior. Leo's age for Christ's sake.

We were cultural opposites, but our values were virtually identical. Figure that one out. And don't be fooled by the drawl or the hayseed handle – Bucky was high IQ, smart as a whip, a philosopher. He was also a Trump supporter extraordinaire with a rabid following. He was furious with the course America was on, and not afraid to say so.

A guy like Bucky had no chance of escaping the R-word smear, though I promise you he was anything but. In our Orwellian world, venture too close to the right edge, you could easily fall off. You could risk being permanently smeared, permanently discounted. Tossed to the wolves, even by your own kind. Bucky travelled in that territory.

He taught me many things, including the importance of venue selection. How you must keep it secret, share only with trusted folk. How you must plan an escape route, and bring muscle. He'd been accosted many times, and unlike me, he carried.

I took Bucky's advice for the event, emailing particulars only to a carefully curated group. A trustworthy bunch, though you never know for sure. Ivan had evolved into my support team, and I ribbed him for it, but I counted on him. He was instrumental in pulling it together, including venue selection. Simon Fraser University was his Alma Mater, and he knew the place inside out.

On the drive up, Ivan merrily pointed out landmarks and reminisced. I nursed a coffee and listened to him ramble. I was sick and tired of reviewing my speech. In the back seat sat Igor the bodyguard. We hired him for contingency. Heaven forbid we'd need him.

He was a skookum fellow, though not huge. Not even my size, but well-schooled in the art of personal protection. He wasn't cheap, either. Thank God my Patreon was still operational and pulling in dough.

"How's the venue looking?" I asked. "Full up yet?"

Behind the wheel of his SUV, Ivan broke a few rules to consult his iPhone. "Three-quarters. People still milling about in the vestibule. No sign of the moron brigade."

"Thank God." I nodded toward Igor and he acknowledged stoically.

Ivan had booked a cavernous SFU lecture hall that serviced first year curricula. The university itself was perched at the top of Burnaby Mountain, a twenty-minute jaunt from Vancouver. Ivan maneuvered his Beemer into A-Lot and we began our trek toward the mall.

"Everything okay tech-wise?" I asked.

"Relax pal, we hired the experts." I would livestream on all the top platforms.

"Sweet."

My talk was the focal point for a day that had become known as Anthony Fierro's *Day of Truth*. There'd be a few hundred in attendance, but it was primarily an online event and millions would be watching.

I was feeling a hint of anxiety, and that was usually a good sign. Ivan gave me a pep talk. "You gotta knock 'em dead, dude. Take no prisoners. Dismantle and destroy the nonsense. Do it with logic."

"Maybe you should give the speech."

He chuckled. "I know it off by heart. Though knowing you, you'll go off script."

"I'll deliver my message, don't worry."

The *Day of Truth* had caught fire. I felt like we had the potential to make a difference, to spawn a paradigm shift. Leftist forces were doing everything to attack and suppress, but not even Twitter could hide our energy.

"We're trending huge," Ivan announced. "Number one in Canada. Number four in the States."

"Wow."

"How long you speaking?"

"Forty-five minutes, maybe an hour. You know the drill."

He laughed nervously. "You might wanna cut it short."

"Uh...*why?*"

"I have a feeling the nasty elements might turn up."

"That's why we brought him." I pointed at Igor, who maintained his stoic demeanour.

"Hopefully we don't need five Igors."

Any fear I felt vanished as I entered the Academic Quadrangle and saw supporters outside the lecture theatre. When they spotted me, a ripple of energy ran through them. By the time I was in in their midst, they were cheering, many were filming. I smiled like a politician, tossed out *thank-yous*, and made my way into C-9001.

As I strolled toward the dais, the crowd delivered more love and affection. Gotta say, it felt good. The President of the local chapter of the Young Conservatives stood to greet me. A rangy, nerdy kid named Chad. We swapped small talk, and made a few introductions.

Ivan huddled with the tech team, making sure the livestream was good to go, while Igor posted up at the main entrance. We were ten minutes from lights/camera/action, and I surveyed the crowd.

A good-looking bunch, young, smartly-dressed, *diverse*. Plenty of Asians in the house, and I mean Chinese-Canadians, not the UK's euphemism for Muslims. There was a burgeoning cohort of hard-right Asians in Vancouver, a demographic galvanized by the murder of thirteen-year-old Marrisa Shen. The accused was twenty-eight-year-old Ibrahim Ali, one of Trudeau's Syrian refugees.

Asians and conservative whites aligned on the incident, and they attempted to hold Trudeau to account. That went nowhere.

I had tremendous admiration for Chinese-Canadians. Their ancestors endured brutal discrimination in the early going, but rather than cry victim, these hardy and resourceful folks endured.

They worked hard, they saved, they took care of their families. By 2019, they were top income earners. Over-achievers with not a trace of self-pity. I was happy to see them represented. Indians too, and a smattering of other races. Having said that, I won't lie. The crowd was eighty percent white.

Ivan made his way to the dais and took his seat. "All systems go."

"Excellent." I glanced at Chad, and gave him the nod. He strolled to the podium with surprising poise.

"Welcome, patriots." The crowd erupted. "It's a special night indeed, and rest assured, we'll get to the main event soon."

Chad took a moment to build me up. He talked about my courage and passion. He called me a Canadian hero. A little over the top for my taste, and as he rambled on, I gathered my thoughts. I had my speech ready, but there'd be surprises. My off-script riffs were where I usually found my stride.

I said a quick prayer. I asked God for strength and wisdom.

Chad was wrapping up. "Without further ado, I give you the one and only Anthony Fierro."

"Go get 'em, Tiger," Ivan said. "Don't fuck it up."

Gee, thanks.

Chapter 34 – The Speech

As I stepped to the podium, the applause was loud and raucous, replete with whistles and shouts. A sense of calm descended. I was but God's humble servant. He would speak His message through me.

When I gestured for quiet, the audience complied. I surveyed the crowd for several seconds, then smiled directly into the camera.

> "Friends, Patriots, Countrymen – thank you for coming. We're not alone anymore. There are many like us. We could have filled Rogers Arena tonight, but instead we're here, because secrecy is needed to protect us from the bloodthirsty mobs."

> "Today, I speak forbidden truths. Our civilization is vanishing. *Civility* is vanishing. Once upon a time, I had liberal views. I still do. I support free markets, rule of law, and of course tolerance. I love people of all races and religions. But..."

I paused for drama.

> "...I also love my family. I love safe streets. *I love truth*. And I love my country. Canada was never

perfect, but I'm not looking to reinvent it. And I don't trust anyone who is."

"The dark forces of the Left have been chipping away at our bedrock, compromising our foundations. They care only about advancing their ever-changing agenda."

"Who the hell am I? On September 2, 2018, my wife and son were murdered by a madman. A man who hated the West. Part of me died that day. But part of me woke up and realized we were at war – and it was a battle to the death. For my country, and every Western country on the planet. Some conservatives think they can win by playing fair."

I made a face and a ripple of laughter ran through the audience.

"Our way of life is in grave danger, folks. We have to fight for it. I'm fighting for it. I'll sacrifice everything. I'll die for my country. Why not? The country I love is dying anyway."

"I barely recognize Canada today. It's not the place I grew up in. What happened to good manners, civility, *common decency?* We used to have faith in the people around us. Now, we have suspicion and mistrust."

"A massive cultural and demographic shift has happened, and we're not supposed to notice. We're *definitely* not supposed to care."

I paused to gather myself.

"The Left is everywhere, they've infected everything. Government. Corporations. Schools. Media. *Our minds.*"

"We live in the Twilight Zone. A dystopian nightmare. Up is down, left is right. They'll keep pushing their agenda, they'll keep pushing *us.* Further and further into the abyss. We're disintegrating in real time. Look at Britain. She ruled the world a hundred years ago. Today she's a laughingstock."

"A few decades ago, we were proud Canadians coast to coast – proud of our heritage, rooted in our French and English cultural origins. We were connected through blood and kinship and common values. We had traditions, a sense of unity, a national consciousness. We had God in our lives, and we built our societies around Him. Societies based on shared morals and principles. On high trust and high cooperation."

I shook my head dramatically and frowned.

"Times have changed. Today we're taught to be ashamed of our founders. We've cast God aside and given up on moral accountability. What's rushed in to fill the void?"

I scoffed loudly.

"Empty slogans like *diversity is strength*. Empty, you hear me. Meaningless. Actually, worse than meaningless. *False*. And everyone knows it. We're supposed to pretend race and ethnicity and culture don't matter, yet our eyes tell us a different story."

"These changes didn't happen overnight, but they've reached critical mass these past few years. They're impossible to ignore. Coincidentally, that's exactly when our wonderful Prime Minister arrived on the scene. He was certainly a man right for the time."

"My opinion on Trudeau?"

I laughed out loud, and the audience dutifully joined in.

"Put it this way. He's a treasonous imbecile hellbent on turning Canada into a shithole, either through malice, incompetence or stupidity. Probably all of the above. Hopefully that's not too ambiguous."

A few people snickered.

"It's nothing he hasn't heard before. You figure Trudeau notices the ridicule he attracts? You think he gives a damn? This guy, I'm tellin' you, is worse than Satan. Heck, sometimes I think he *is* Satan. Sorry, I know that sounds bad."

I made a show of trying to calm myself. I was strong and clear and confident in my message. Ivan's lessons had paid off. I could stand my ground in good faith.

"Modern Western government is not our friend, folks. *They hate you.* They want to destroy you. If you challenge their destructive policies, they call you un-Canadian. *Or un-American or un-British.* Whatever. Sometimes they call you much worse. Trust me, I know."

Laughter.

"Trudeau and his minions are working to undermine our unity and our sovereignty, the pillars of our nation. They're taking a sledgehammer to everything we hold dear. They're doing it every day, and with the full support of their Department of Propaganda – sorry, I mean the CBC."

More laughter.

"Every day, they gas-light us with a firehose of hogwash. Everything they produce – every statistic, every peer-reviewed study, every story – there's always a motive, always an asterisk, always a lie. And it's always in support of their destructive agenda."

"What's Trudeau's signature issue? *What is it, folks?*"

Someone way in the back shouted *diversity*.

"That's right, *diversity.* This is not a comfortable topic, nor is it one that we're allowed to freely debate in polite company. Or any company for that matter.

But today, I speak freely and without fear of censure. Today, I speak truth. Today, I say *diversity is not strength*. There's no precedent for it being strength. No evidence it could *ever be* strength."

"Diversity is division. It's tribalism. It's pitting groups against each other. It's disparate cultures vying for dominance. The only unity inherent in the Diversity Doctrine I see is *unity against whites*. Am I right?"

I scanned the audience.

"Diversity is code for less white people. Or even better, *no white people*."

I paused to let that idea resonate.

"No folks, diversity is not our strength. Our Christian principles, our shared values, our love of country and each other – *these are our strengths*. Until recently, Canada's been strong *despite* diversity. But the house of cards is teetering."

"I'm not surprised. Are you?"

I beckoned to the crowd.

"How do you maintain a nation of citizens with nothing in common? With no shared values? A nation where citizens treat the parent culture with disdain, scorn, and hatred. A nation that seeks immigrants who oppose our way of life. You know who I'm talking about."

"Despite everything I just said, diversity has become our God. Our Holy Grail."

I heard some jeering outside the lecture hall. Damnit, someone must have tipped off the lunatic fringe. Ivan warned me. So far, no trouble-makers in our midst. *Good Lord, I can't even give a simple talk in peace.* I made no reference to the disturbance. I walked calmly across the stage before launching back in.

"What causes diversity? That's easy, *immigration.* We're a nation of immigrants, they tell us. They say it repeatedly. They actually have the gall to say it about places like England and Germany. They'll say anything, I've come to realize. *Anything.*"

"When I was growing up, Canada preached multiculturalism over assimilation, and I used to think – *how charming.*"

I chuckled.

"It was a giant experiment. No one knew how it would play out and for a while, it was pretty cool. When problems began to emerge – here in Canada and other parts of the world – did governments put the brakes on? Did they say – *whoa, whoa, whoa* – let's take a pause. Let's get a grip on this before we continue. Let's allow some time for assimilation. Did they? *Did they?*"

"No."

"They doubled down. They increased the numbers and they upped the propaganda. They engaged in doublespeak. *Immigrants enrich us,* they said. *Immigrants add vibrancy to our communities. They do the jobs we won't do.* Of course, we were also told that the moment immigrants set foot on Canadian soil – no matter the war-torn hellhole they came from – these new Canadians inherit all our values. Even our love of maple syrup and Tim Hortons. I prefer Starbucks myself, just saying."

I smiled condescendingly.

"But that's what we're told. That's how Canada works, they say. Newsflash – if something sounds too good to be true, it probably is."

"Here's a crazy thought. What if the success or failure of diversity depends on the cultures and people involved? Hypothetically speaking, would we be better off with a million Somali Muslims or a million European Christians? What would be the long-term cost to the taxpayer? Yes, *I know* it's heresy to ask the question, but every single person knows the answer. We all know."

"What will become of Canada? *The True North Strong and Free.* Our white population is dwindling, that much we know. The Left constantly *and gleefully* reminds us of that fact. And we're expected to encourage and cheer and assist in the process."

I shook my head.

"What will become of Canada? If we don't make changes, I claim we'll become a Third World country. *Very quickly.*"

"What changes you ask? How about a time out-on immigration – *legal or otherwise?* How about stop bringing in migrants who fill shelters meant for our native-born homeless? How about stop bringing in people who have no intention, *nor ability*, to follow our laws and customs? How about stop bringing in low-IQ state-dependent predators?"

Whoa, did I just say that? I was deep in controversial territory.

"How about focus on existing Canadians? People already here? Sounds like a good idea to me. Surely our government would agree, right?"

"God no. Instead, they actively plan to bring in more and more, in ever larger numbers. They fight for it with great zeal. *Let's bring in new cultures, the more incompatible the better.* They nakedly weaponize migration against us. That's what this ludicrous Migration Compact is, folks. A weapon."

"By the way..."

I smiled brightly at the audience, as if ready to deliver spectacularly good news.

> "...if immigrants happen to be People of Colour – *they almost all are* – there are huge bonuses. *For them*, I mean. They inherit a rich legacy of grievances and reparations due from the evil oppressors. *Isn't that great?*"

Big smile.

> "Who are the evil oppressors, you ask? White people, of course. They're the source of all that is bad. *Everyone* knows that."

> "Of course the mere mention of *white people* makes everyone nervous. It also makes me a racist. Any critique of unchecked immigration, legal or otherwise? *Racist*. This is not a topic for debate."

> "Well, tough luck. I'm gonna debate it."

I grinned at the crowd.

> "What does all this mean for us? And by *us*, yeah, I mean white people."

My grin intensified.

> "Sorry if you're not white. Don't worry, you're welcome to listen. Hell, white people been listening to you guys complain forever."

That got a laugh.

> "So yeah, you heard me. I said it. *What's in it for whites?* Shoot me."

Ivan was frowning. I was way off-script, riffing on racism. I could see the headlines: *Fierro Advocates for White Ethnostate*. What the hell, I've come this far.

> "You've probably noticed, there's a rather prevalent anti-white narrative dominating the zeitgeist these days. We hear about the importance of political correctness. How we must go out of our way *not* to

offend people. And it's not easy. But here's the good news."

"There's still a safe place to vent. A convenient scapegoat. *Whites*. Have at her – belittle, slander, mock. If they push back, *Jesus Christ*, attack. Especially *old white men*. Those bastards have it coming. Thank God I'm not old yet."

A smattering of laughter.

"You laugh but I'm not kidding. Whites are demonized. According to the mainstream, whites are sinister, evil, and inhuman. And it's okay to say so. I ask you, what other race is used as a slur? Even *white people* use *white* as a slur against other whites. It's bizarre, folks."

"The only way white males get a pass in 2019 is through complete submission. Profess self-hatred, bow down and lick boots. Advocate for the black and brown, and bash any wicked white who doesn't. All the better if you do it loudly and obnoxiously."

"To be clear, following these rules doesn't guarantee you won't be arbitrarily demonized. That's only fair. I mean, look what your ancestors did."

"As for whites who don't toe the line? Whites who profess racial awareness? Or – *oh my gawd* – take pride in their race?"

I slapped my forehead.

"Obviously, they must be publicly humiliated. Professionally and financially ruined. By any means."

I drew a deep breath.

"It happens, folks. The Left wields this threat like a club and they use it without hesitation. The irony is how few white racists there actually are. Forget about supremacists, I've never even met one. *Never*. But the Left finds them."

I grinned.

"How, you ask? They make them up – the number of hoaxes is astonishing. They also expand the definitions. To be *anti*-anti-white is to be a White Supremacist. That's what it's come to."

"So essentially, whites have no power. *None*. We can't advocate for ourselves. We can't defend ourselves. The lunacy has spawned a strange abomination – the proliferation of *anti-white* whites."

Laughter.

"Everyone wants a claim to moral authority, I think it's part of human nature. For whites, disciplining other whites is the best they can hope for. These folks are the modern-day equivalent of a *house N-word*. Does that make sense?"

I raised my eyebrows and appealed to the audience.

"Whatever complex psychology's behind it, *I don't care*. It's creepy, it's dirty, it's self-serving. It's bizarre and amoral. Foul. Vile. I think you get my point."

"I ask, what's wrong with being proud of European ancestry? Everyone else celebrates ethnic pride, why can't we? Why is this basic instinct denied to whites, *and whites alone?* Is that not a denial of humanity?"

"Just spit-balling, folks."

Big smile.

"Here's what I think. Whites have to stop apologizing for our history. We have to start being proud of it. Why should we marginalize our achievements? *Which are unprecedented by the way.* Yeah, we invented a few things – cars, computers, the Internet, airplanes, space travel, radio, TV, film, newspapers. The light bulb. Modern medicine. And oh yeah, *democracy.* I could go on. *Bravo white people!*"

I laughed out loud for a few seconds, then turned serious.

"Look, I'm no white nationalist. I'm not pushing for a white ethnostate. I don't dream of a white Canada. Don't believe the smears. I dream of a safe and stable Canada. *Period.*"

My inner voice cautioned me. I was strolling around in dangerous territory. I pressed on, nonetheless.

"I think about race, though. I know I'm not allowed to. But yeah, race is the elephant in the room. It's not class."

I shook my head.

"Not culture, not religion. Well, I'll touch on Islam in a bit."

Laughter.

"No folks, race is the issue and everyone knows it. The ultimate untouchable. The issue that paralyzes conservatives in any rationale debate."

"We keep pretending that, aside from skin colour, we're all the same. *But we're not.* Everyone knows Germans are good at engineering. The Chinese are math wizards. Africans are outstanding athletes. What else?"

I chuckled.

"The English make a great cup of tea. The Irish love the drink. Swedish women are gorgeous. As for Italians like me, *Grazie Dio*, the list is long."

Laughter from the audience.

"Yeah, races and cultures are not only different, they're *radically* different. *But don't you dare notice negative traits. No no no.* That'd be racist. Well, here's a thought. I say it's racist *not* to notice. I'll repeat that. It's racist *not* to notice. Crime numbers for Blacks is the classic example."

"I say that and everyone takes two steps backwards. But they know exactly what I'm talking about."

I laughed mirthlessly.

"When people say they want an honest conversation about race, they don't mean crime stats. *Nope.* They don't mean IQ differentials. *Nope.* People get fired for hinting at such things."

I shook my head.

"That doesn't mean they're not there. What can I say, nature bestows gifts unequally. Don't blame me. Some groups are fast and strong, some are smart. Unfortunately, that means some are less smart. Not to get too technical, but on the intelligence scale some groups are a full standard deviation down the ladder, if you know what that means."

I shrugged ostentatiously.

"Basically, I don't. *Hey*, I'm not a math guy. I certainly don't go around bragging about my IQ."

I knocked on my head for emphasis, and the audience roared with laughter.

"But facts are facts. And with all that in mind, isn't it silly to expect equal outcomes?"

"And when we don't get equal outcomes, what happens? White people get blamed. White people get called racist. Here's what I think – white people are the *most tolerant* this planet has ever seen. We're the only ones who've ever even attempted to form multi-race societies."

I wandered across the stage. I was in the deep end now. What the hell, might as well keep swimming.

"I can hear the critics. You believe this guy? *White people.*"

I scoffed.

"Who are they to talk? Who are they to cry victim? White people stole this land from the Natives, right? *Right?*"

I gestured to the crowd.

"That's the conventional thinking. That's Canada's original sin – displacing this land's first inhabitants."

I stroked my chin as if pondering.

"But who did *they* steal it from? Or were they first? And if so, when did *they* get here? The truth is, they were here a blink ahead of the Europeans, on the big-picture scale. Around twelve to fourteen thousand years ago. Some would argue it's small-minded to think *they* have claim to the land."

I winked at Ivan. He was visibly uncomfortable with this latest change of direction.

"If that's the rule, *then Jesus*, it's been broken everywhere else. I mean Liberals don't seem to care about the rights of the Indigenous People of Europe. Not with any fervour. I wonder why?"

Deep breath.

"I haven't taken leave of my senses, folks. I wade in cautiously. I fully realize this is a sensitive issue, and an important one. But it's also an issue where accepted truths are selective. As I said already, today we're talking truth – forbidden or otherwise. No limits."

"So let's talk about European settlers, hmm? *Yes, I said settlers. They weren't immigrants.* Sorry. What do you think their first interactions with the Natives of North America were like? Remember, this was hundreds of years ago *and...*"

I raised an index finger.

"...the white men in question had not yet received their diversity training."

Laughter.

"And they'd *never* seen Native People. I know this sounds bad – but if they thought them inferior, you might understand, right? I mean, the people they encountered probably seemed, *to them*, like savages. Nomadic hunter-gatherers, a thousand years behind technologically."

"There are more charitable descriptions, and I realize it's blasphemy to say *anything* negative about North American Indigenous. But let's just say the people the white man encountered hadn't figured out electricity or indoor plumbing. Or democracy. Or the wheel. Or written language. Or...*you get my point.*"

"By the way, so far I've said nothing controversial. *So far.*"

"So how did the interactions unfold? The historical narrative has been carefully shaped – *evil colonizers* versus the *noble and brave indigenous* – I was gonna say savages, but I caught myself."

I smiled calmly.

"There are two sides to every story. Not all Natives were peace-loving saints. In fact, there was no shortage of brutal barbarism and cruelty on their part. It's there if you wanna look. I know it doesn't fit the narrative. Sorry."

"There are also countless tales of callous treatment of First Nations peoples. But again – *it was a different time.* You can't judge either side by today's standards. There was no Internet, and sadly, not many social justice concepts. Not in 1850."

"Here's the thing – there were shameful acts on both sides, the natives and the settlers. But one thing I've noticed – *this is gonna sound hollow and self-serving...*"

I could hear the counter arguments, and the anger.

> "...but...there *did* seem be an overriding benevolence on the part of white settlers, misguided and condescending as it may have been. It seems to me they were at least *trying* to do the right thing. They wanted the Indian people to embrace their way of life. Why not? They sincerely believed it was better. They knew it in their hearts."

> "Even in the case of Residential Schools, *fundamentally*, were their motives not altruistic? That *doesn't* mean I'm discounting the horrors and hardships, nor the actions of specific individuals."

> "Look, it's a long and complicated story. I don't pretend to be an expert. But one thing's for sure – no amount of bending over backwards...of catering to every whim...of indulging every frivolous complaint...will ever bring a people out of despondency. We'll never right every wrong, *real or imagined*."

> "Isn't it time we got the hell on with it? Isn't it time we let these good and noble people get the hell on with it? How about stop patronizing them? Stop with the freebies, stop treating them like dependent children."

> "No matter what we do or how much we give, it will *never ever ever* be enough."

> "How about we let our First Nations brothers and sisters prosper in dignity?"

Pause.

> "Okay, I better get the hell on with it. That was way more controversial than I planned."

At the back of the theatre, troublemakers had entered. At least ten by my count. *Che palle!* Igor was suddenly hyper-alert. Damn, I better cut to the chase. These bastards weren't known for their tolerance and kindness.

"Let's get back to the here and now. Back to the business of saving Canada. Of saving the Western World. How do we fight back?"

"It's not easy, folks. Like I said, if you don't follow the Left's maxims, you're in trouble. If you run *counter* to them, they will attack. They'll try to ruin you. They're ruthless and irrational and without mercy. And they'll never stop. They're like the Terminator."

"They're evil. They're anti-family, anti-freedom. *Godless.* They have no solutions. Nothing is valid or worthy for them. If I could distill Leftist policy to one slogan it would be: *Burn it down!*"

"And as they whine and bitch and complain, they enjoy life in the freest nations this earth has ever seen, with comfort and security unheard of through time. If they deign to debate, they do it with clichés and platitudes and slogans. *That's not who we are.*"

I said it mockingly.

"For Leftists, the goalposts are never fixed. They move them whenever and wherever expedient. They have no time for reason or rationale. *Or truth.* Truth is their enemy. To allow even a shred to leak out is too risky. So they squash you at the first sign of non-conformance. If they encounter a worthy opponent, they go straight to the R-word. And it works every time."

"We recoil and retreat. We can't risk our careers. Our safety. Even if it means risking the safety of our descendants."

I scoffed.

"How do you fight back when someone calls you a racist? *Haha*, it's not easy. A fundamental flaw in conventional conservatism – there's no provision to discuss race. Unless you're handing out goodies to people of colour, that is. Otherwise, conservatives simply pretend race doesn't exist, even as their enemies bash them over the head with it. It's a huge problem. It's probably why Western civilization will collapse. *Seriously*."

"If a white conservative complains about immigration, obviously they're racist. Obviously, they're scared the country's getting darker. Progressives make these accusations with gleeful tones. The conservative's only response is to deny any such feeling, and everyone knows he's lying. Because, despite all the high-minded thinking and education and moral handwringing, at a primitive level, he may very well be worried. How's that for a controversial statement?"

I seared the audience with eye contact.

"So what do we get? *Cuckservatives*. I hate that term but it's intensely descriptive. Cucks have no chance of saving Canada. They play along with the false narratives – *people of colour are oppressed, there's no such thing as anti-white racism*. They tremble at the thought of being called racist."

"And what happens? *They still get accused*. And what do they do? They bend and contort what's left of their spine to prove they're not. They play this unwinnable game over and over and over."

Scoff.

"Some stand up to the bullying – I guess that's what I'm doing today. But let's take a better example. *Donald Trump*. He's been calling out the nonsense for four years now. He's proof of just how hard the Left will attack. No politician has ever seen abuse like they've thrown at him. And he's still standing. Still fighting for his wall."

I chuckled.

"Well, not everyone's that strong. Definitely not everyone has Trump's wit, or his troll game. They definitely don't have his ego."

Laughter.

"His supporters will never desert him. They truly believe he's the one man standing between them and chaos. He showed us we're not alone. He showed us we have strength in numbers. That's the key, folks. Strength in numbers."

Just then one of the masked agitators began blowing a whistle – *insolent little prick* – and several more had entered. They sat ominously on the stairs. Igor had made his way down to stage level. I felt a premonition of danger. A sense I better wrap quickly. But there was so much I hadn't covered – nothing on Islam, nothing on Scheer. Ha, Charles'd be happy about that. I moved to closing comments, speaking now over an intermittent whistle.

"So I say to you tonight – not only my fellow Canadians – but all my First World brothers and sisters. *Which way Western Man?* We're in a battle for freedom. A battle between good and evil. A battle to the death."

"Some say collapse is inevitable, that we've passed the tipping point. Let's assume it's not okay. You with me?"

Applause.

"Let's assume we *can* come back from the brink. *I think we can.* But everyone..."

I pointed dramatically at random audience members.

"...everyone has to start contributing. Everyone has to start doing the right thing in all your encounters.

You'll sleep better at night. The only way to win is to fight as one. When we stand alone, we're picked off and punished. So we must stand together as one. And keep standing."

The audience members responded by standing. So did the Antifa contingent, and some of them started chanting *Go Home Nazis.*

"This is what we're protesting, folks. We won't let these clowns stop us, will we?"

This triggered a lusty roar.

"In times of crisis, courageous men and women step forward. Whatever your station, do what you can. Be humble, be kind, be respectful. But above all, be truthful. Don't sell yourself out, or your people."

"What's that saying? Evil reigns when good men do nothing. Stop cowering. Stop taking it. They can't fire all of us. We are the country. We are the tax base."

"The price of saying nothing is too high. Silence is complicity. Complacency is complicity."

"We must brave the accusations of racism. Show our intestinal fortitude. We can't live in fear of being called racist. Our *Day of Truth* doesn't end today. This is just the beginning."

I felt no fear, as if God was speaking through me.

"This freedom we have? You know, this thing we treat with casual indifference. It's precious and rare. A priceless heirloom."

I was bellowing to be heard over the racket.

"I empower you today. I give you permission. Speak now, or forever be silenced."

"Thank you, God bless you, and God bless Canada."

I was done. *Finito!* I got it all out and then some. A big fat middle finger to the establishment. Fuck Charles Kennedy.

Fuck Dhanesh. They didn't give two shits about the
country.

The crowd delivered lusty applause as I wandered to the
dais. Did I go too far? Too deep into forbidden territory? I
had no time to ponder such questions.

I had more pressing concerns. Like how to get the fuck
outta here in one piece.

Chapter 35 – Antifa

The standing ovation continued after I took my seat. I appreciated the applause, but couldn't savour it. The goons were circulating, and the chanting had grown louder. There was quite a number by now and, no doubt, more coming.

No sign of security. Not a cop to be seen. I wasn't feeling safe.

Chad took the podium like a pro. He spoke calmly: "We've got some Antifa, folks. Nothing to worry about, we've called the police."

Being the focal point of the venom was unsettling. I hadn't reached panic stage, but I could see it from where I was. I felt like chaos was about to erupt.

When Igor tapped my shoulder, I almost jumped out of my skin. "We go now, yes?" It wasn't a question.

I nodded and rose. Ivan did likewise. "Where are the cops?"

"Don't worry. You follow me, yes?" Igor marched with purpose to a stage-level fire exit. We followed silently, Ivan with a look of terror.

The parking lot was a ten-minute walk, and we managed a chunk of it through underground passageways. Igor knew the territory. Evidently, he was worth the hefty price tag.

Unfortunately, the secret corridors only went so far. When we climbed a concrete stairwell out to the open-air mall, Antifa spotted us and ran maniacally in our direction. Only a handful at first, but I sensed their numbers would increase rapidly.

"Should we run?" I asked.

Igor shook his head, but upped our pace. Meantime, the masked morons were already tormenting and harassing and threatening.

"Fuck off, Nazi piece of shit."

"Get the fuck off our campus."

"We're gonna fuck you up, you fascist fuck."

Persuasive folks, they were. And I thought *my* vocabulary was limited. I looked to Ivan, thinking to make a small joke, but held off when I saw his mask of terror. "Almost there, pal." I attempted a cheerful tone.

One fellow tried to start a synchronized chant: "*Nazis Go Home, Nazis Go Home...*" A few joined half-heartedly, but it never caught on. We were dealing with half-wits.

By the time we exited the mall, a good fifteen Antifa were hounding us. I avoided eye contact, but I noticed they were mostly millennial toothpicks. Sure, I was fifty-four, but I was six-three, two and a quarter. I could KO most of this rabble. Surely, Igor had made the same observation. I won't speak for Ivan.

But as their numbers grew, and threats intensified, my swagger eroded. Their faces were covered, but their eyes were grotesque with rage.

"Why do you cover your face?" I asked. I couldn't help myself. It was the East Van in me. "What are you hiding?"

"I don't have to show my fucking face to you, you fucking racist."

I should have known – never reason with a mob. Some of the little maggots began making forays into my personal space. Some brandished sticks and pipes. Igor gently discouraged them. One guy decided spitting was a good idea. He lifted his mask and let fly. I badly wanted to lay the bastard out.

"Ignore them," Igor said calmly, and I complied. My resistance was partly fueled by fear.

Igor's expression was grim determination. We could see the car now, about a minute away, tops. Any relief I felt was premature. The mob was twenty-strong, maybe thirty. They were loud and hostile.

Still no physical confrontation, but I sensed that could change. An ambush felt imminent. I wondered if Igor had a gun. I doubted it. That wasn't the Canadian way. Except for criminals, of course.

I felt the urge to run – to sprint for safety – but I sensed it would trigger a full mob attack. Ivan fumbled for his car keys but in his shaking, sorry state, dropped them on the pavement. One of the goons tried to kick them, but Igor neatly blocked him and scooped the keys.

"I drive," he said, and unlocked the BMW from ten paces. The vehicle lit up obediently and the mob surrounded it. One fellow gleefully keyed the drive-side door, raking deep into shiny black paint. Another kicked at the car pathetically. He was not a trained athlete.

We made it mostly unscathed, not counting the insults, the spit, the occasional shove. Now what? Would they let us get in? Or would it turn ugly? Igor didn't hesitate. He bore decisively through the hordes and opened the passenger door. "Get in," he said to me.

Ivan was quicker. He dove in ahead, taking the backseat of his coupe. I tried to follow, but one of their sturdier charge forced the door shut.

Matter-of-factly, Igor punched him in the throat, and the sonofabitch crumpled into a whimpering mess. Again, I contemplated Igor's high fee.

It was the first act of violence, and the more timid snowflakes scattered. But others were incited, including one punk who lunged in from the side and cracked Igor's head with a club. It triggered a lusty roar and stoked the savagery. These guys were out for blood.

Game on.

My adrenaline was so high, the first blows barely registered. I was also worried for poor Igor. But they didn't want Igor. They wanted me. I was about to be massacred by a bloodthirsty mob. There was no high road to take. Primitive emotions prevailed.

It had been eons since I'd thrown a punch, but I hadn't forgotten how. Blows were landing all over me. I prayed the guy with the club wouldn't take a crack. Ivan was screaming from the backseat: *"Get in the car, get in the car!"* His voice was shrill and panicked.

I swung hard at one of the masked figures, point blank, and the bastard went down like a sack of potatoes. My satisfaction was short-lived, as another began choking me from behind. Others pulled my hair and clawed at my neck. Christ, these weren't real men.

I shook the guy off my back, but another replaced him. Or was it two? Someone was hacking at my legs...I was in trouble...there were too many. Where was Igor? Where was fucking Ivan?

I squirmed and tried to run, but collapsed under the onslaught. The blows were thick and fast, and I curled into a protective ball, and that attracted more violence. I heard someone scream *kill him, kill him.* I had to get away, make one last valiant effort. Otherwise I was a goner. I summoned energy. I prepared for action. This was my last chance.

But something else...a new disturbance? A new presence? A new voice, loud and obnoxious. Threatening and authoritative.

Blessedly, the blows ceased. The bloodlust chanting fell silent. I could only hear this new commanding voice barking threats.

At Antifa.

The voice was familiar, though I couldn't place it. I was hyperventilating, my heart was racing. I rolled over to see what was happening.

Vinny.

Relief surged like a drug. I shoulda known. And he brought Vito, another scary-tough East Ender, crazier than Vinny. Put these bad boys together, you had a wrecking crew.

"Hey Papa." Vinny held out a thick, meaty hand.

I was shaking, but I nodded at my eldest and took his hand. I felt Vinny's raw power as he hauled me up. God, he was a beast.

"How'd you know?" I said.

"Little birdie told me."

I shrugged.

"Papa, I got friends on the force." He grinned. "They don't like me much, but they like you."

"*What'd* they tell you?"

His grin widened. "Ha, something about a stand-down order."

"What the fuck?"

"You been pissing off the wrong people, Papa. That's usually my job."

I tried to make sense of what I was hearing.

"Put it this way, Papa. They was giving these candy-asses a chance to take liberties."

"*Ah cazzo!*" I shook my head. "*Grazie.* I owe you bigtime."

"Don't mention it. How many times you bail me out, eh?" Vinny looked around. "I think you best get the fuck outta here. I'll give Vito a hand, then do likewise."

Some Antifa still milled about, but with Vito and Igor around, none were close to Ivan's car, or me. They hurled threats, but they'd lost their fortitude.

With shocking speed, Vinny rushed the closest agitator and the poor sap tripped over himself. Vinny could have destroyed the kid, but he went easy. A few cuffs upside the head, some manhandling. The young man whined liked a schoolgirl. "Time for you little fairies to go back to mommy's basement, eh? Past your bedtime, homos."

Vito and Igor laughed. I did, too. Yes, Vinny used homophobic slurs. In the heat of battle, PC didn't seem important.

By now, Ivan had left the safety of the car to get in on the action. "Time to go home and take off your Halloween costumes, *you pussyhat soyboys.*"

I laughed, not at the insults, but at Ivan's sudden feistiness. We jumped into the Beemer, with Igor behind the wheel. Vinny and Vito hopped on their hogs. Antifa was still barking, but I heard nothing but the thunderous rumble of the Harleys.

Igor deftly maneuvered out of the parking lot, and accelerated onto the main road. From the backseat, Ivan jabbered on about how we *showed those fascists a thing or two.* He was giddy, almost hysterical with relief.

I glanced at Igor, and noted the grotesque swelling at his hairline. The bump was an angry shade of pink. It resembled a tumor.

"You okay, brother?"

"Never better." He grinned and tapped his head. "I got Ukrainian skull. *Indestructible.*" With his Russian accent, I believed him.

I tasted blood in my mouth and remembered I had my own injuries to worry about. I took inventory. My lip was cut, still bleeding. I had bruising on my ribs and legs. The worst of it was the scratches on my neck and face. *Damn, those pricks.*

My adrenaline petered out quickly. When I was finally home, safe and sound, I tried to reflect on the speech, but it was useless. I couldn't concentrate. The trauma was too fresh. If not for Vinny, what would have happened? *Thank God for The Vin Man.*

I got in the shower and turned the water up as hot as I could stand. I wanted to wash away all the sweat and grime and blood. *And the spit.* I chuckled. Coulda been worse, I heard some protesters hurl feces.

I was ready for bed. I craved the oblivion of sleep, but I succumbed to curiosity and checked Twitter. My mentions were insane, but as I feared, the topic was not so much the speech, but the fiasco afterward.

Would that change tomorrow?

I doubted it. For some reason, I feared what tomorrow might bring.

Chapter 36 – More Backlash

When I awoke the following morning, memories flooded in. I wanted to relive the speech. Heck, maybe bask in glory. Our cumulative online audience was north of ten million. *Mamma Mia!* I was famous, but I had a sinking feeling the melee afterward would eclipse my message.

I hauled myself out of bed at 9:15 and sampled my notifications. Some expressed support, some told me to rot in hell, some asked if I was okay.

Nothing from Dhanesh or Charles Kennedy. Not surprising. I did, however, get an update from Igor. He sent a photo and boy did he have a goose egg for the ages. Nothing serious he assured me. No concussion. *Nothing gets through this Ukrainian skull.* He was quite proud of that, evidently.

Bucky Bradford was the first to call. He was like that. Not big on text or email, but quick to pick up the phone. He cared deeply. Had he showed up on an airplane, that wouldn't have surprised me. He was a committed Christian. All in.

"You're up to no good, I hear?" I loved his drawl.

"Who ya been talking to?"

"Doesn't matter." *Dudn' matter.* "Everyone's talking 'bout you. Y'all okay up there?"

I delivered a post-mortem. When I mentioned Ivan almost wet his pants, Bucky dissolved into tears of laughter. The conversation brightened my spirit.

Later that morning, I heard the distinctive *pop-pop-pop-pop* of Vinny's Harley in the driveway. I was expecting him, and had a couple Espressos ready. "Hey, look at fucking Rocky Balboa." He burst out laughing. Vinny was always jovial, always quick with a joke. "What's the other guy look like?"

"You mean the other fifty guys?"

"Whatever, they was pansies. Little fairy boys. They floated away once we showed up."

"That doesn't reflect well on me."

"Nope, *hahahahahaha...*"

"They weren't all pansies. They did a number on Igor."

Vinny nodded. "I saw that. We checked that guy out. He's a tough motherfucker."

I showed Vinny the goose egg, and he roared with laughter.

"How *you* doing, Papa? Looks like you were in a cat fight." More laughter.

"Tell me about it."

"You might wanna get a tetanus shot." He dissolved in convulsions of laughter, and I joined him.

After Vinny cleared out, I went online to see how things were unfolding. *Fuck*, condemnation of the Antifa scum was nonexistent. The goddamn Canadian media called them peaceful protesters. Painted them as little angels.

Meanwhile, they skewered me in their phony *we're-being-fair-to-everyone* style. They squeezed in all the labels. Far-right. Agitator. Provocateur.

Fuckers.

Here I am busting my ass to save our country, still grieving the loss of my wife and son. I barely escape the clutches of a mob, after hosting a historic event, and that's all they can say?

I wish I could say the rest is history. That my *Day of Truth* was a turning point, a wakeup call. I wish I could say all the sacrifices, the hard work, the scorn, the mockery, the ridicule, the loss of job and friends – I wish I could say it was all worth it.

I'd be lying.

The Big Day was a turning point alright – one hundred percent in the wrong direction. By end of week, the headlines were unambiguous.

From the op-ed of a prominent national newspaper: *This is What White Male Privilege Looks Like.* From a top American news journal: *Populist Activist Incites Hate in Canada.*

One particularly heinous blue checkmark called me a domestic terrorist. Even the spineless cuckservatives were condemning me.

Bastards.

The blatant dishonesty was surreal. Like they craft their headlines, *then* find a way to write the story. In Europe, the ink slingers were even more disingenuous, especially the Brits. You'd think they might take a pass given what happened a year ago.

Nope.

Overnight, I went from mildly controversial to the epitome of evil. A menace. Something had to be done about me. I felt a palpable sense of people pulling away, distancing themselves. My likes and retweets plummeted, as did messages of support and gratitude.

My base had become timid and meek, as if scared to speak out for fear of being similarly condemned. As if they might be *outed* as a bad person, and lose their job, or worse.

I was radioactive. It became fashionable to attack me, to mock and defame me. Everyone got in on the act, as if *not* commenting was to secretly support me. People were obliged and rewarded for their condemnations. I was thoroughly convicted in the Court of Public Opinion.

I was a racist, a xenophobe, a supremacist. Nothing new, but the tenor was different. Now they wanted to hurt me, to tear me limb from limb, to see me suffer. And they knew where I lived.

The death threats were almost preferable to some of the deranged messages. *Even your dead wife and son hate you!* I hid my account for a spell. The abuse was too much. When Leftists claimed victory, I stumbled back into the ring.

The press even dragged Vinny into the muck. That hurt so much I felt physically sick. Every aspect of Vinny's life was designed to avoid attention. Thankfully, they didn't persist with this dirty tactic. Why bother when they could pick on me?

Vinny didn't hold a grudge. The same could not be said for my neighbours when protesters showed up outside my house to scream obscenities. They threatened, they threw rocks, they spray-painted my driveway.

The cops removed them – such behaviour wasn't tolerated in Point Grey – but the resentment of my neighbours festered.

I'd given up fighting the personal attacks. And I noticed the smears were more cleverly articulated. Whereas once they were ham-fisted and easy to disprove, the new strain was more slyly crafted, harder to rebut without sounding defensive and petty. They were still laden with half-truths and lies, mind you.

My enemies were ideologically wrong and devoid of morals, but not stupid. They smeared through implication, innuendo and caricature.

I used to think *true* conservatives would always have my back. *Yeah right.* Top right-leaning thinkers everywhere were disavowing. Previously, there'd been talk of me guesting on Hannity and Tucker. I was stoked, Ivan more so. Bucky called me a God, said I'd knock it outta the park.

The phones went cold. I was left twisting in the wind. I'd crossed the threshold of acceptability. I was off the *acceptable list*.

Everything came crashing down. Rather than subside, the attacks escalated. The hit pieces were relentless. They called me every name in the book. They even called me a grifter. Said I was crooked. In it for money. It was a coordinated effort and it lasted right up until the Canadian Federal Election.

It took a toll. They had me on the ropes, feeling sorry for myself. I doubted my message. I doubted *myself*. My inner circle kept me sane. Ivan, Bucky, a few others. I began attending church again. I needed something solid to cling to.

How naïve I was. There was nothing solid left. I had no idea how bad things would get.

Chapter 37 – Downfall

My movement lost momentum. *I lost momentum.* I still had a following, but I rarely posted content and rarely engaged. My inner network kept me up to date. Bucky was as passionate as ever. The guy was fearless. *And tireless.* Then again, he was twenty-five and I was mid-fifties. My testosterone was on the decline.

I gave up on public appearances. Was it the Antifa thugs? The vicious online attacks? Or something else? A scary thought, but I was fearful of an increasingly hostile government. They appeared a sinister and ruthless enemy, no matter who was in power. The dark forces had been unleashed and nothing could stop them. Not me. Not Trump. Not anyone. The sickness was too thoroughly entrenched.

If Canada was going down, was I in grave danger? I was worried. For my safety, my finances, my freedom. Worried that one day jackbooted thugs would arrest me in the night.

Ivan disagreed, but didn't squash the idea with as much enthusiasm as I would have liked. Almost as if he'd rather not talk about it. Sometimes I felt even he was distancing himself. That scared me more than anything.

He wasn't the only one. I'd lost a long list of friends, on Facebook and in real life. Once-reliable contacts weren't returning calls. My supporters were backing away, they were deleting tweets with damning hashtags.

My star had fallen.

By early 2020, it got worse. The tech giants put their heads together and kicked me off their platforms. Coincidence? *Yeah right.* I was being erased from existence. Out you go, don't let the door hit ya.

Meantime, my idiotic Number Two Son merrily tweeted delusional messages of self-flagellation: *White people are disgusting. I hate white people. Ending white supremacy starts with killing white people.*

You get the idea.

YouTube kept me around, but demonetized my content. My *Day of Truth* speech had been driving $10k a month. Not anymore.

There was a brief crusade to save me. Respectable conservatives spoke on my behalf: *I may not agree with what Anthony Fierro says, but I defend his right to say it.*

Leftist thought leaders countered: *Private companies have no obligation to Mr. Fierro. It's a free market. He's free to choose a different service, or create one of his own.*

Some actually tried that, but the Internet had become rigid, resistant to upstarts. Especially ones power brokers didn't want.

At any rate, the uproar over my expulsion fizzled. It always does. Business as usual for the multi-nationals.

Of course, I did what all exiled conservatives do. I set up shop on the alternatives, like Gab. It felt futile. How long before they punt me right off the Internet? Ban me at the access level. Had to be coming, right? Just like China.

Like so many before me – *Milo, Alex, Gavin, Faith* – I was banished. De-platformed. Un-personed. As if I never existed. My content, lovingly crafted, was inaccessible to me or anyone else. The Left had claimed another scalp.

I shored up revenue with my Patreon, but alas, one day it too was abruptly terminated. Removed for violating – *you guessed it* – Community Guidelines. They informed me in the politest terms possible.

I was paying a steep price, and I worried a bigger one was coming. I was right. Several lawsuits came my way, including one from the parking lot incident. The Antifa asshole who Igor slugged was claiming I did it. He had witnesses and was suing for damages, demanding big money. *Can you believe it?*

Oh, and the CRA was auditing me. My assets were frozen, a lien placed on my house. I was forced to retain a lawyer and assemble a Statement of Financial Affairs, should my assets need liquidation.

They were choking me out, suffocating me, hounding me into poverty and isolation and despair. It wasn't enough that I go away, they wanted to thoroughly ruin my life. I must feel their wrath.

So far, they'd yet to charge me with a crime. Knock on wood.

Chapter 38 – Persecution

2021 inched by. My activism was limited to emails and phone calls, the occasional foray on Gab. My resolve had crumbled. I'd fought with all my heart, and they'd beaten the stuffing out of me. It took a toll on my health, mental and physical.

The online mob no longer terrorized me, only because they couldn't. I wasn't online. I actually began to relax, to feel a sense of calm. A spiritual tranquility I hadn't known for years. Ivan was right, fear of persecution was irrational. Perhaps, I could live out my days in peace.

Turned out *no*.

Gestapo-style, they burst into my home at 2:00 a.m. and hauled me from my bed at gunpoint. They cuffed me, they read me my rights.

"What's this all about?" I feigned indignance to hide fear. "This is outrageous."

The commander was unmoved. "Did you hear me? I said you have the right to remain silent."

"You're gonna march into my home in the middle of the night and talk about rights?"

The commander nodded at one of his charge. The young man methodically removed his baton and walloped the back of my legs several times. I yelped in shock and pain and my knees buckled. My feistiness vanished.

So, this was it. The government had been biding time, waiting patiently for their pound of flesh. They searched my house, they confiscated my phone. I wondered if I'd ever see it again. I wondered if I'd ever see Vinny again. Or Ivan. Or the light of day.

Was this North Korea? Was this an Orwellian nightmare?

When they marched me out, my driveway was lined with members of the media. The classic perp walk. To humiliate me, or a deterrent to my supporters? Probably both.

I was shoved into the back of a squad car, and we sped off into the night. I saw lights of neighbouring houses. My arrest would be all the gossip, and they'd be glad I was gone. Many still held a grudge, but now they could safely return to the comfort of their Utopian fantasy.

At the police station, I was struck by ancient déjà vu. I'd bailed young Vinny out of many a scrape. I had little time to reminisce. The sergeant glanced up from behind the desk and his eyes lit with glee. "Well, well, who do we have here?"

The commander shared a rundown and handed over paperwork. Soon after, they hauled me into an interrogation room, still cuffed. They grilled me for an hour. I didn't say much because there wasn't much to say. Everything I did was public record. I had no secrets.

That didn't stop the threats and intimidation. When we exited, the cops conferred again with the sergeant.

"I predict a long stay." He concluded merrily.

"Where we puttin' him Sarge?"

"Throw him in the tank with Hector. He could use the company."

The copshop doubled as storage facility for criminals awaiting trial. Conveniently, it was a stone's throw from the courthouse. Vinny told me it was worse than actual prison.

As I was frog-marched away, I asked about a phone call.

The cop turned to his partner. "He assumes he has rights." They laughed uproariously. "Those days are gone, asshole. Shut the fuck up and you might not get hurt." His partner didn't laugh as enthusiastically. Perhaps one of my supporters?

I'd already been scanned and strip-searched and humiliated. Upsetting, but it paled in comparison to my fear of the unknown. Who was Hector?

In we went. Row upon row of holding cells, stacked on top of one another, connected by utilitarian metal staircases. Everything cold and clinical, a chilling reminder of where we were.

I was struck by the lack of white faces. It was a primitive reaction deep in my nervous system. There were a few catcalls, not many. It was 4:00 a.m. Also, I was a big guy, pushing sixty, not some young fish ripe for bullying and intimidation and whatever else. That's what I told myself.

I figured out who Hector was. A large Native. Early 20s, but he looked forty and he looked mean. He had few teeth and a prominent scar down the side of his face. His menace was hard to miss.

He cursed and threatened from the get-go. He called me *sweetie* and rubbed his crotch. *Jesus Christ.* I prepared myself for battle.

"Hey Mike," said the guard who may have been a supporter. "Let's cut this guy a break. Throw him in number 7. It's empty."

"You heard Sarge."

"Fuck Sarge, we don't need the hassle."

Relief washed over me like a drug. In the empty cell, exhaustion took over. I slept fitfully for several hours on a rock-hard bunk.

They had trampled my rights – *ha,* except my right to a speedy trial. After two days in remand, I found myself in the prisoner's dock. Everything moved at lightspeed, fast and quiet.

I was charged with multiple counts of hate speech. This section of the Criminal Code had been thoroughly reimagined and rewritten, with provisions for astonishingly long sentences.

Ivan called the laws a thinly-veiled political weapon, a means to target dissent, but he assured me I was clear. *If they wanted you, they'd have got you by now.* For the first time, I realized Ivan didn't know everything.

Canada was well down the rabbit hole with insane asylums like the UK and Sweden. We had no First Amendment. I always felt we didn't need one. Times had changed. Canada was not only keen to follow totalitarian governments, they sought to be a leader. Perhaps they would set an example with me?

I was also accused of subversion, and they painstakingly listed my alleged subversive activities. Speaking the truth was a crime, evidently. Inciting others to do likewise, also a crime. The judge kindly stayed the second batch of charges, but they'd hang over me indefinitely.

For now, they didn't need them. I sensed an urgency to get this done. To get me out of the news, out of sight.

The gallery was sparsely populated – a show trial this was not. A few media types, a smattering of SJWs, some lookie-loos. Also, two of Vinny's boys in the back corner. I took intense comfort in their presence, for some reason.

It was a bench trial, so no jury to complicate matters. My lawyer was a public defender, appointed by the court on account of my financial woes. He inspired zero confidence. You get what you pay for.

There was no plea bargain offered. Through Vinny's travels, I knew they were the lifeblood of the criminal justice system. Without them, it would cease to function. In my case, the Crown wanted blood and they knew they could get it.

The prosecutor laid out his case thoroughly. He called witnesses and provided the court with copious evidence. My lawyer raised not one objection. It looked like a slam dunk.

When it was The Defense's turn, he called one person to the witness stand. *Me.* He asked basic questions about my background, my work. He explained to the court that, until recently, I was an exemplary citizen. A working-class man with no criminal record.

He questioned me on my motives, as if attempting to show I meant no ill will. He enquired about Lisa and Julio and established that I suffered daily from their loss, and that I did not forgive the perpetrator. This part of my testimony worked against me, I'm quite sure.

I tried to elaborate, to compensate for my counsellor's lack of fight and gumption. But neither judge nor prosecutor were about to let me grandstand, much less speak freely. I was threatened with contempt multiple times. This was a kangaroo court. Any hope of martyrdom was squashed.

When my lawyer ended questioning, the judge turned to the prosecutor. "Your witness."

"No questions, Your Honour." A bad sign.

The moment of truth arrived. Verdict time. "Will the defendant please rise." The words gave me a chill, but I obeyed. The judge reiterated the list of charges and their various counts.

"If there's no further evidence, I shall deliver my judgement." He made eye contact with my lawyer and the crown prosecutor. Both shook their head. "I find the accused, *Anthony Michael Fierro*, guilty on all counts." He paused to consult notes. "The court finds your actions abhorrent and indefensible. You are a purveyor of hate, a fear-monger, a threat to public safety. This court deems your foul acts worthy of a severe sentence, indeed the maximum penalty imposed by law. I hereby sentence you to twenty years, with no eligibility for parole until 2036."

I stopped listening. I was vaguely aware of more stern words. Something about deterrence. Finally, the judge slammed his gavel with authority and finality.

Oh my God.

This secretive charade of a court had convicted me within a week of my arrest. It went exactly as I expected, but was still a crushing blow. *Twenty years*, and still charges outstanding. I repeated the number in my head. *Twenty years.* I'd be seventy-six in twenty years.

Life was over.

There was no appeal. No time to dwell. The bailiffs escorted me from the courtroom to a waiting police van. I was whisked from the courthouse to... *God knows where.*

Prison? Fear of the unknown, perhaps the worst kind, took hold. Would I be beaten, raped, killed? Would a hundred *Hectors* be waiting for me?

I would be a caged animal at close quarters with other caged animals. The addicted, the mentally ill. Rapists, murderers, gangsters. Would I be targeted for my white skin? For my political activities? My mind spun.

I remembered Vinny's pals in the gallery. Vinny had connections in this dark world. Maybe – *just maybe* – he could get to the right people, make sure I was protected.

In the outside world, the media covered my fall from grace with headlines and few details. *Anthony Fierro Arrested and Jailed.* It was Breaking News. The perp walk made the front page, followed closely by the disheveled mugshot. My reputation was dead, this was the final nail in the coffin.

The only thing they hadn't done was #*MeToo* me. Not yet. I didn't put it past them. But at this moment, I had other concerns.

Like survival.

Chapter 39 – Prison
July 16, 2021

Vancouver wasn't known for sweltering temperatures, but we were in the third week of a July heatwave. The prison van was unbearable – probably high thirties, Celsius. I was told to settle in for a 90-minute drive.

I hadn't showered in three days and by the time we arrived, I was drenched in sweat and stinking. I knew a thing or two about prison through Vinny. Body odor, for example, was not appreciated.

The facility was Mountain Institution, a maximum-security penitentiary with a horrific reputation. *Ha*, was there a maximum-security prison with a good reputation?

I was confused and despondent, but mostly fearful. *Appallingly fearful.* On the drive, the fear attacked with corrosive strength. I became convinced my relation to Vinny would be very bad. That his enemies would use me to get at him. My imagination was fertile and ran rampant.

I pulled myself together. I was a big boy, and showing fear was not smart. Everyone knew that. During check-in, I was shuttled about like cattle, here, there, yonder. They told me what to, what not to do. They issued me freshly-laundered prison gear and a clear plastic bag. My kit: sheets, blanket, socks, underwear, soap, toothpaste, toothbrush, razor.

Two guards escorted me to my cell, which was in B-Pod. The place had six pods, each with separate bathroom and shower facilities. Common areas were shared. Each pod housed up to ninety prisoners, and they moved them around to minimize friction. There was plenty anyway.

I felt eyes on me. Scrutinizing. Sizing me up. New arrivals provoked gossip, speculation, suspicion. And aggression. A few remarks were made, not many. I kept my gaze straight ahead. I said nothing.

My cell was a decrepit six-by-eight enclosure, a bunk-bed, a toilet, a sink. My cellmate peered down cautiously from the top bunk. A white dude, maybe sixty. Scrawny and beaten and withered. His name was Steve, and I sensed his fear, which he was trying to hide. Relief washed over me. Temporary of course. Many unknowns lay ahead.

We were in the back half of 2021, and Vancouver was falling into dysfunction. We weren't yet overrun by lawlessness, mind you, not like some Western metropolises. We were still among the safest on the planet, not counting racially homogeneous cities in places like Japan and Poland.

But we were on the slippery slope. Toronto was already there. The migrants, the illegals, the entitled native-born – they roamed freely, persecuting the vulnerable, fighting tribal battles, complaining about racism. Whites remained silent.

Such dynamics were relevant to prison populations. In America, Black inmates mostly ran the show. They had the numbers and the demeanour. Sometimes it was Mexicans, depending on location. In the UK, Muslims held the upper hand. In South Africa, you can guess the power structure.

Lucky for me, penitentiaries in British Columbia weren't so bad, though demographics were shifting, not in my favour. The social experiment known as mass migration made that a certainty. The illegals, the *undocumenteds* – whatever you call them – they poured in. The media said all was well. We were a country of immigrants.

Like any prison, Mountain was profoundly racialized. Muslims didn't have the per capita numbers to dominate. Nor did Blacks, but that was changing. Africans were a new breed of inmate. They hailed from war-torn places like Sudan and Somalia. They spoke their own language. Many had no English, and no intent to learn.

They terrorized once-safe communities with violent home invasions, car-jackings, brutal assaults and random violence. They showed no remorse, or even understanding of the harm they inflicted. On the inside, they were ten times worse – fierce and violent, *barbaric* even by prison standards. Thus far, they had only loose gang affiliations with limited structure. But they were on the rise, and greatly feared. A wild-card.

Still, the groups that stood out in 2021 were the Indigenous and the Indo-Canadians. It was no coincidence they slotted me with Steve. Whites went with whites, like every other race. When it came to diversity and tolerance, in prison there was plenty of the former and none of the latter.

I was safe, right? *Ha*, not by a longshot. Prison was an ugly, dangerous place, no matter the racial breakdown. It was also disgusting. There was filth, repulsive smells, deviant sexual activity – I could go on.

I don't recommend it.

Chapter 40 – Guido

That night, there were catcalls, crazy talk, and other activities I won't bother describing. The Remand Centre was probably worse. Here, I sensed structure – not so much conscious insight as something I perceived. That may explain why I got sleep that first night. Deep and dark and dreamless.

Breakfast arrived at eight – eggs, toast, juice. We were still in lockdown. I devoured mine, and considered doing likewise with my celly's. Steve hadn't budged. I tested conversational waters. Nothing.

By 10:00 a.m., lockdown ended. We were free to mix and mingle in the common areas, and the commotion started immediately. Steve wasn't gonna show me around. He wasn't the type. In prison parlance, he was *a slug* – rarely venturing from his cell.

From my vantage, I could see and hear most of the activity. I had to go out, had to show my face, stare down whatever demons this place would throw at me. I also had to take a shower. I stank.

I took a piss, splashed water on my face, a little under my arms. There was no mirror and the water was icy cold. I swallowed hard and exited the cell. Having no particular destination, I sauntered casually. *I didn't swagger.*

I was immediately approached. An East Indian fellow, mid-twenties. A big dude, my size but juiced. Muscled arms. Ink everywhere. Fierce expression.

"You're new 'round here. I'm Mo." He gave me an appraising nod and a fist-bump. "Whatcha in for?"

Hate speech seemed like a bad answer. "I don't even know, to be honest. Don't think I'm supposed to be here."

He eyed me suspiciously. "That's what they all say. Seriously though?"

"I *am* serious." I looked him in the eye.

"Not a *chomo*, I hope."

"Pardon me?"

"Child molester." He pointed accusingly. "*Fucking* pedophile."

"No sir."

"Good." He stared me down a while longer. "Maybe we get a look at your paper, eh?"

I shrugged. "Maybe."

The conversation ran dry. "We'll chat again," he said, and nodded, half-friendly, half-ominous.

I discreetly watched Mo rejoin his group. Where to now? I spotted the facilities. They seemed my only option. Of concern, a clique of Natives milled about the entryway. I started slowly, but again I was stopped. This time, an old guy.

I put him mid-seventies. Stooped and gray, slow-moving. But his eyes were alive with curiosity and mischief, his expression friendly. "You got a minute?"

"Sure."

"*Tony*, I'm Guido from the neighbourhood. *Come Stai?*" He shook my hand warmly. No fist-bump from this guy. "Hey, sorry youz gotta be here, but welcome." His smile was genuine, his voice gravelly from a lifetime of smoking. I saw no lurking jailhouse motive.

Guido had the distinctive staccato delivery of an Italian-Canadian and despite myself, I felt a glow. A feeling of kinship. Around here, a feeling like that took on religious significance.

"Thanks." I decided to take the lead. "You been in a while, Guido?"

"Feels like forever."

"Yeah?"

The smile faded. "I'm doing *all day and a night*, as they say. Life without parole. I'll die here."

"Sorry to hear."

"Don't be. I get by. Been here since '79."

"Wow."

"I'm twenty-seven when I got here. Just a kid." He shrugged. "I don't know nothing different no more."

I nodded. "What'd they get ya for?"

He pointed at me, like I was talking out of turn. "Ha, they got me on a lot. We was gangbangin' hard in the '70s. I was a tough motherfucker. We battled the Riley Park boys, the Clark Park gang. We didn't take shit from nobody. Not even the fucking cops. We brawled, all fists and feet back then. No knives, no fucking guns."

Guido surveyed the pod and I did likewise. We were being watched. Mo and his boys, the natives, the other cliques.

Guido snapped his fingers. "Hey, hey. I'm right here."

"I'm listening."

"I hope so." He was only messing with me. "So I'm making a lotta money. More than my Papa – *by a lot*. I got more than I can spend. I'm wearing fancy clothes, going to fancy restaurants. Got the Rolex, the Caddie, always a stack of twenties. I was Vito Corleone, I tell ya. I probably saw that movie ten times."

"What happened?"

"Hey, patience. *I'm talking here.*" More mock anger.

I smiled appreciatively.

"Course I'm running the drugs – weed only then, and the stuff's terrible by today's standards. I figured it was honest work. When some fucking hoodlum tries to compete, get in my turf, I send a message, hey?"

I tried to picture Guido as a young tough, but couldn't. He was too caricatured, too set in his ways. Like he'd always been this way.

"I had big dreams, and a bigger ego."

I started to prod, then bit my tongue.

"I got busted a few times. Did time, learned the system. Then the gang stuff starts, mid-'80s. I'm thirty-five, I'm in on the ground floor. I'm set, hey? A made man. Nothing can touch me, right?"

"I guess..." I shrugged. "Or I guess not?"

"You guess right. Long story short, the narcs nailed me. I got set up. They got their people inside. They got me on everything, tied me to a list of murders – I never did 'em, I swear. But I took the fall. I couldn't rat out my boys, hey?"

I nodded in agreement.

"They appreciated the loyalty, lemme tell ya. To this day." He cleared his throat. "My lawyer tried to fight it, but hey – here I am. And here I'll be. That's okay."

I exhaled, a show of appreciation for the mini-life story. "Why you telling me this?"

"Hey, why not? I got time. So do you."

"True."

"Nah but, uhhhh..." he scratched his head. "I heard you was coming."

"You did?"

"I got connections on the outside," he bowed his head and waved dismissively, as if to say, don't ask how. "I use 'em here. *Inside.*"

He knows Vinny.

"Ya, I know your kid. Not personally, but I know 'im."

Guido had to be four decades older than Vinny. "May I ask how?"

"Dumb question." He frowned. "But you're in luck. Vinny said we should keep an eye on you." *Vinny had my back.* "Hey, I knew your Papa, too. From the Drive, back in the day. Both Sicilian descent, that stuff runs deep."

"Oh, I know."

We chatted awhile longer. Mostly I listened while he talked about the good old days on Commercial – Joe's Café, Nick's Spaghetti House. Finally, Guido made a move to end it.

"Look at me, taking up all your time."

"Like I got something better to do." We had a laugh. "Hey Guido, really appreciate the help."

"Don't mention it." He waved me off. "You have to excuse me, I gotta go feed the warden. Come by my house after. We'll do some real talk, hey?"

Chapter 41 – Learning the Ropes

Would I have survived without Guido? Luckily, I didn't have to find out. He took me under his wing, treated me like family. He let it be known, *don't mess with Tony*. That didn't stop everyone, but Guido wielded power and it helped.

He was gracious and wise, like Red in *Shawshank Redemption*. But whereas King's character knew *how to get things*, Guido steered clear of contraband. He trafficked in information. He was connected. With the gangs, the HA, the guards. Even the cops.

We took to meeting daily and had wide-ranging conversations. There were no gadgets or phones to interrupt the flow or dampen the connection. Guido schooled me on prison life. He laid out the rules, the framework for survival. Some I knew, some I didn't. Prison was a helluva way to live. Like I said, I don't recommend it.

"Don't show weakness," Guido stated. "That's number one. Don't strut like ya own the place, neither. Body language is everything. We're animals, never forget it."

I nodded.

"Don't let no one touch your stuff. Call 'em out if they do. Be ready to fight if they give ya lip. Be ready to fight, *period.*

It's not nice, but ya get used to it." He grinned. "Havin' fun yet?"

"Good times," I said, with as much joviality as I could muster.

"What's next. Ah yes, don't piss off the wrong people. Don't sit at the wrong table. That'll get ya a beating. A *severe* beating."

A lot of rules, started with the word *don't*, I noticed.

"Everything goes on racial lines, hey? We stick up for our own. We discipline our own." He raised an index finger. "Except snitches and chomos. Those fuckers are fair game. They never last."

"When we go to the chow hall, stick near me first few times. I'll show ya who sits where, who eats first. Ya gotta know the pecking order, gotta follow it."

I decided some levity might help. "How's the food? I like my steak rare."

Guido chuckled. "Get in line for that, *paisano*. You get meatloaf if you're lucky. Maybe a ham sandwich. You won't put weight on, I tell ya."

"That bad eh?"

"Ah, the chow ain't so bad, 'specially if ya know the right people. Ya get a little extra. Little bonus here and there. I don't go hungry." He patted his belly. "Don't knock the commissary, either. Sometimes a candy bar's the highlight of my day." He drew a breath. "Where were we?"

"The chow hall?"

"Right." He scratched his chin and pondered. "When we get supper tonight, I'll point out the shot callers. But don't go fucking staring, hey?"

I'd heard the term. "Shot callers?"

"They're the guys to watch for. Give 'em a wide fucking berth."

"What do they do?"

"They get final say on everything. They make the life and death decisions. *Like that.*" He snapped his fingers. "They ain't always the toughest, but they might be. They might be the smartest, or the best talker, or the meanest. *Or the craziest.*" He laughed. "There ain't no rules. If there are, they get broken."

"Are you..." I hesitated.

"Nah man, too much work. We got Curly. He does a good job. He's doing twenty-five to life, so he ain't goin' nowhere soon. He keeps me in the loop. This place is pretty stable. That could change tomorrow. I worry about the Indians mostly."

"The Natives?"

"No man, they're cool, but..." Another pause. "The fucking Hindus. You met Mo, hey?"

"I did."

"He's a loon, man. A hothead. Watch your ass around him."

"Yeah?"

"Oh yeah, he acts all Black, know what I'm sayin'." He bellowed laughter. "He could be a problem for ya." Guido looked at me hard. "His *car* could be a problem."

"For me? *Why?*" I replayed the interaction with Mo. *Maybe we get a look at your paper?* I knew where this was going.

"I know what you're in for, hey." He sucked his air through his teeth. "This *hate crime* business. Drugs are fine. Assault, robbery, murder, all good. Chomos are dead meat, already told ya. But your shit, I dunno man. I don't think it's gonna go down well, from what I hear."

A chill ran down my spine.

"Ah, don't worry," he made a dismissive gesture. "I got my eye on it. You keep your head up anyway, hey?"

"I will."

"Your kid put the word out. He knew it'd be an issue. He's smart, that kid."

Vinny.

"Hey, hey...you still with me?" Guido again snapped his fingers in my face. It was one of his more annoying traits.

"Just processing." I shook my head. "I don't know what you been told, but I ain't no fucking racist."

"I know that. Don't worry, I got my eye on it."

"Thanks."

"Final lesson for today. The guards."

"Right."

"Show respect and be polite. Do what they tell ya. Beyond that, don't talk to 'em, don't make friends with 'em. Don't let *them* make friends with you. They're the enemy. It's us versus them, never forget it. You talk too much, people gonna think you're a snitch."

I was trying to listen...but I kept thinking about Mo. And his car.

"The new ones get a little chatty, and there's *always* new ones. The ones that been around a while," Guido laughed bitterly, "they're worse than the inmates. They'll make your life hell you give 'em half a chance. Ha, even if you don't. You'll figure out quick who the bad ones are. You better."

He got up to take a leak. It was awkward, but I'd get used to it – the close proximity, the bodily functions.

While peeing: "All that make sense, Tony?"

"It does. Thanks a lot Guido. *Grazie.*"

"Anytime, paisano. Anytime."

I stood. "I think I should take a shower."

"I was gonna say." Guido burst out laughing. "You stink, man."

"You think I don't know?" I laughed with him. "Any advice? This'll be my first time."

"First time what?" More laughter.

"*Not that.*" I laughed again, but with less enthusiasm.

"My advice – wear sandals. Lot of fungus and disgusting shit. We live like pigs. Guys jerking off, shittin' in there." He shuddered. "Worse than pigs."

Jesus.

I'm not gonna lie, I was terrified. I got my towel, my soap, my sandals. All business. I didn't talk to anyone, didn't look at anyone. I felt eyes on me. Appraising. Calculating.

I was sure I'd be attacked, and ready for it. The old *don't drop the soap* line played in my head. Alas, nothing happened. I was in and out quick.

Victory.

For now.

Chapter 42 – Latin America

Prison was no fun. The day-to-day grind. The drudgery. The nasty encounters were almost welcome, just to make life interesting. Not true, but you see what I mean. Way too much time to wallow and stew. Time passed slowly, and I tried not to count the days. That only made it worse.

While I was in, *massive* changes happening outside. Did I say *massive?* Surprisingly, I was able to keep fairly up to date from the wrong side of the bars. If you learn to read the tea leaves, prison's not as isolated as you might think. A lotta shit went down. Hold on tight, we'll blast through a few years.

Globally, things were falling to pieces. You might counter by saying, *when in history were things* not *falling to pieces?* This was different. Outside the Western World – save exceptions like China, Russia, and Eastern Europe – we're talking chaos. Total fucking breakdown.

Formerly functioning countries were flipping to *failed state* overnight, as if a plague had taken hold. The contagion leapt borders and ravaged victims. Like dominoes, they fell. Rendered ungovernable, economically destitute. A humanitarian crisis of biblical proportions was forming. Like a hundred Syrias. A hundred Venezuelas.

Pundits even labelled it *Venezuela Fever*. In a two-year timespan, the virus hollowed out Latin America, and that includes Mexico and California.

Not surprisingly, Africa was also in crisis. That seemed its natural state. Its destiny. By 2025, except for pockets of light in South Africa and Botswana, the continent had gone dark. Wholly reverted to primitive tribalism.

The Western World yawned. When the media deigned to comment, they focused on the refugees, of which there was an unlimited supply. There was also demand, in the form of still-functioning pockets of Western civilization. Thus, unchecked migration continued.

Conservative thinkers expressing concern were shouted down. Did these heartless monsters not care about starving people in Peru and Paraguay? Or persecuted peasants in Senegal and Sudan? Not that there were many critics. To scream bloody murder from rooftops, as I had done, was to end up like me, and others like me. They locked many of us up. Some, they killed.

Western citizens worked hard to tune it out, to live their lives in peace. Their governments assured them all was well. They did this with friendly slogans, statistics, and scientific polling. *Life was good*, they said, *and getting better all the time*. If you can't trust your government, who can you trust?

One country, however, played a different game. The People's Republic of China didn't ignore the world's problem, but they certainly didn't try to solve them. They brought in no refugees. Not one. They had zero diversity. Zilch. China was populated exclusively by the Chinese. Many, many of them.

They'd been on a path to world domination – *economic and military* – for decades. They didn't seek conflict with the United States. Uh-uh. They simply watched and waited as the only so-called superpower self-destructed in real-time. China hovered like a vulture.

Their forays into Latin America and Africa went unchallenged. They came with a helping hand – human capital, expertise, money. But unlike the West, who historically aided the world's poor for benevolent reasons, China had selfish motives.

Strings were attached to their good deeds. You might even call them ropes. Or chains. Lending money to insolvent countries that can never repay let China play the hero – they put boots on the ground and shovels in the earth. But was it secretly a bid for world domination? Modern-day colonialism? China was a loan shark, and few noticed or cared.

When it was time to collect and there was no money to pay, China seized assets. Not cars and boats and houses. *Nope.* Ports. Passageways. Infrastructure. Corporations. They didn't do it through force – that would attract too much attention – they did it with the blessing of corrupt local officials, whom they'd long since been exploiting and bribing.

Their vast military might was largely unnecessary, except for intimidation. Soon, China would have leverage over almost everyone.

Chapter 43 – The Western World

What about my picturesque and once-peaceful hometown? How did mega-multicultural Vancouver fare as the world collapsed into anarchy?

By the early 2020s, Chinese culture was deeply embedded. Chinese-Canadians controlled key sectors of the economy and dominated many areas of the city. Few complained. They were peaceful and industrious. Vancouver remained ultra-Western and ultra-safe. Also eminently desirable to the world's wealthy, and to locals lucky enough to be born there.

However, there was trouble brewing in paradise. Lines were being drawn, and on the wrong side of these lines, the spread of blight and decay was rampant. Potholes, garbage in streets, boarded up-buildings, vacant lots. Scofflaws too numerous to police. Call it the broken window theory, call it what you will – we were slipping.

Immigrant classes claimed laws were racist, not compatible with their culture. Petty crime was suddenly everywhere. Trust within communities, once a hallmark, plummeted.

As for Toronto, Montreal, Halifax, they were worse. American cities worse still. Violent crime in Vancouver remained rare until the mid-2020s. Eventually our luck ran out. The destructive forces – some imported, some manufactured – arrived with fury. Incidents of terror hit. Ethnic violence skyrocketed. Whites and Chinese were preferred targets. They were the softest and the richest.

Meanwhile, Muslims staged noisy and hostile public prayer, they pushed for Sharia, they staked territorial claims. Other ethnic groups did likewise as the competition for dominance escalated.

We became like any other major Western city – London, Paris, Sydney – our streets full of treachery. Realtors described neighbourhoods as edgy and vibrant, which was another way of saying extremely dangerous. Security companies urged people to protect their homes like a fort, difficult under gun laws which ensured only criminals were armed. No one fought that particular issue too hard, not in Vancouver. We never had a gun culture.

Racial violence was impossible to ignore, and people altered their behaviour. They took extreme precautions. Nonetheless, the government propagandized on a bright future for all. They downplayed epic crime rates even as they took steps to ensure continued decline. They focused dwindling tax dollars on issues like diversity training and carbon footprints.

Outside Canada, the descent continued. Chaos and uncertainty reigned. Traditional alliances became murky and diluted. Was England still a friend? What Israel still good? Was America still a beacon of light?

Not anymore. Trump was an unexpected blip. He could not alter the trajectory. Until his messy ousting, at best he postponed the inevitable. People realized this as far back as 2018, when the Democrats recounted their way to sizable midterm gains.

Once back in power, there was a vicious backlash against Trumpism. It was hailed as evil, and supporters were singled out. The tyrants clamped down on guns and free speech, they relaxed the southern border. Incidentally, Trump's infamous *wall* was started but never built.

By 2024, the Dems became a permanent majority. They no longer needed to cheat. What was the old adage? Demographics is destiny.

Over in Europe, the surge of populism was also a blip. The *far-right* parties tried to fight the evil, but the language prison was too powerful. They couldn't fight the R-word smear, and their enemies exploited the weakness.

The contagion ran rampant, and though many perceptive souls sensed imminent collapse, wide-spread panic didn't take hold. The illusion of normalcy was too prevalent. Mainstream media, what remained, aggressively pretended. Shiny happy anchors reassured. World leaders dutifully maintained the charade.

Meanwhile, the elites were devising protection schemes for an emerging new world order. There were power grabs, greed, opportunism, as China's influence came to dominate. It felt eerily reminiscent of the recent collapse of Latin America.

However, no one told the U.S. government, and their actions grew increasingly conflicted and schizophrenic. China handled intermittent American insurgence as one would the antics of a recalcitrant toddler. With patience and a firm hand. The once-mighty America was clearly second fiddle on the global stage.

By now, messengers like me – *guys who warned of the dark path* – were rare. The few there were operated in stealth. Underground. If discovered, and they all eventually were, they were methodically removed and punished. I wasn't the only prisoner of conscience. Not by a longshot.

State-sanctioned virtues were relentlessly signalled. *Diversity is winning*, they said. *But there is much work to be done. Everyone must remain diligent until the last remnants of racism, privilege, and implicit bias are stamped out.*

The reality on the street was different. The masses no longer displayed enthusiasm for the nonsense, partly because financial incentives had dried up. But there was an organic component, too. *Fear.* By now, citizens toed the line. They hoped and prayed they'd be left alone – by government tyranny and violent thugs roaming the streets.

These thugs weren't live-in-your-parent's-basement Antifa. They were racially-aligned gangs – intimidating, robbing, raping, murdering. The media said nothing, but people knew.

They knew the jig was up, the grand charade over. There was no point in pretending. The structure had been pulled down, the patriarchy was dead and gone. The only thing left was survival, and profound regret. As Joni Mitchell sang – *you don't know what you've got 'til it's gone.*

How the hell could it happen? Big tech played a role. They controlled the flow of information with sinister secrecy. Who knew Google's one-time motto, *Don't Be Evil*, would be so prophetic. A lot of people, actually.

Those good folks didn't see themselves as evil, they were censoring and controlling for the good of society. They favoured civility over freedom. *Riiiighhhhht.*

By the early 2020s, tech behemoths were not only in lockstep with each other, they were supplying China with tools to root out thoughtcrime among that country's 1.4 billion citizens. It was the ultimate beta test for big tech's AI-based surveillance and tracking technologies.

But it wasn't enough. *No sir.* Controlling China's race-homogeneous society was child's play. *Give us something hard*, the mad scientists demanded. So by the mid-2020s, the tools quietly rolled out across Western nations and the age of *absolute* authoritarianism arrived. Democracy didn't stand a chance, but governments maintained the façade.

Part of this work was the revision of history. Documents started disappearing. Articles, news stories, even people. Especially the ones that wouldn't shut up. Most were muzzled or banished, but sometimes they outright vanished. Sometimes entire families.

Suffice to say, political rants diminished. Even the tamest comments attracted a scolding. The virtue-signal crowd still ranted, but the most shamelessly nauseating posts were rare. Something in the algorithms seemed to sniff out false virtue. How's that for silver lining in a hyper-police state?

Every bit and byte was scrutinized, de-encrypted, pattern-matched, all in real-time. They had the buy-in of the Telecoms, who had long-since succumbed to Chinese interests, and were beholden to the new masters.

Freedom was gone, never to be returned.

Chapter 44 – Life on The Inside

On the inside, my days ticked by. The same deadly dull routine, over and over and over. The only variable was my level of terror. Always high, some days higher than others.

The snapping of timed locks always set my nerves on edge. For the next fourteen hours, I'd be loose with the animals. Inmates spent their day lounging in the yard, smoking, lifting weights, shooting shit.

Lockdown was at ten, and sixty minutes hence, *lights out*. That's when the shenanigans began. Crazy talk, trash talk, sexual activity. I won't sully you with the depraved acts. By 1:00 a.m., the pod was usually quiet, except for a chorus of snores. My sleep patterns weren't great, but I trained myself to get shut-eye.

To fill time, I took a job mopping floors. It gave me a small sense of freedom. A purpose. A little exercise. It was a segregated gig, meaning I handled my turf, and my turf only. I wasn't about to circulate amongst the Natives or the Indians or the Blacks. That woulda been suicide, especially for me. It turned out I did have a target on my back. Not a *kill-on-site*, but let's just say I was looking over my shoulder.

Meh, life goes on. You get used to anything. Besides floor-mopping, I developed an exercise regimen and stuck to it even when my bad knee ached. Sit-ups, push-ups, calisthenics. It helped keep me sane.

Besides my knee, several nagging issues bothered me, but I eschewed medical attention. That was last resort, said Guido, and he knew first-hand. Medical care, if you got it, was shoddy.

In fairness, inmates were notorious for faking illness to get a field trip, a mini-vacation. Complaints were treated skeptically, and you got the bare minimum, if you were lucky. I didn't envy prisoners with chronic conditions – diabetics, Hep-C sufferers, the cancer crowd. They were all there, and expected to tough it out.

Thank God, no major illness befell me during my incarceration. Passing time was my biggest challenge. The prison library helped. The selection was hit and miss, but I lucked out with a few classics: *Brave New World, Fahrenheit 451, 1984*. Lisa woulda been proud.

The novels were tedious, but they packed relevant messages, especially Orwell's masterpiece, with its prophecies of Newspeak and Doublethink. The slipperiness of words was bang on. Utterly amazing.

Unfortunately, interruptions were frequent and I couldn't always calm my mind to relish the prose. There was no silver bullet to prison life. My loneliness was profound, trumping even my fear. It ate freely into my soul, carving and hollowing and destroying.

I turned to God, as I had done throughout my life. I spent an hour each Sunday with the prison chaplain. It didn't fill the void.

I had few visitors. No one wanted the taint of guilt by association. But every few months, Vinny turned up and put a smile on my face. Took a lot for him to come. He didn't like contact with the law, the justice system, certainly not corrections.

On the morning of my 60th birthday, I awoke feeling old and tired, a little sorry for myself. This was not how I drew up the plan. Would I still be here at 70? 80? Would I die here?

Vinny visited, as promised. He was a man of his word. Later that day, Guido surprised me with a cake. He moved heaven and earth to make it happen and we had a small celebration in my cell.

What a guy.

We talked about family – Guido had a couple kids himself. I reflected that almost seven years had passed since Lisa and Julio were taken. Were they watching over me? Were they proud of me? Was I proud of myself? I found no peace in these ponderings.

When we had the cake, my ever-reclusive cellmate even participated. Over the years, Steve-O and I had shared few words. The guy was squirrely, that was his nature. Outside the cell, he did his best to stay invisible. I looked out for him, but I had myself to look out for too. Hard to be a Good Samaritan on the inside.

His backstory, what I gleaned, was sad. A North Surrey boy, grew up on the mean streets of Whalley. Parents? God only knows, he didn't say much. He got into drugs and crime in his teens, and never found his way out.

Guys like him were a dime a dozen. White privilege didn't do them an ounce of good. If anything, it hurt. Every other colour and stripe had targeted outreach. Special programs for shelter, healthcare, rehab. The white underclass? Not so much.

I coulda done worse for roommates, though. Far worse. Steve was quiet and respectful. Deferential, too. Top bunk was preferred, so a couple weeks in I told him outright, *I'm taking it.* Makes me sound like a bully, but that's how prison works. You skip over the niceties.

A month later, I decided top bunk sucked. Too much of a bitch getting up and down to take a piss. So I switched back, no questions asked, not a peep out of Steve.

But the times they were a-changin'. Mountain was filling up. All Canadian prisons were as real-world chaos manufactured criminals. This was terrible news, because a crowded prison was a dangerous prison. However, it also meant I might get an early release. Or transfer to minimum security.

In April of 2026, Steve-O and I received rotten news. We were getting a third roommate. Wally was mixed-race, half-native, half-white, half something else. He wasn't the friendliest hombre in town, either. He kicked poor Steve out of the top bunk first night, and didn't say boo to me for a week.

Half-breeds were a wild-card. Hard to trust, 'cause ya never knew which side they'd take. Or which side would take them. Truth be told, probably harder on them than anyone.

Mountain was getting viler and more dangerous by the day. More filth, more cockroaches, more people that wanted me dead.

Chapter 45 – Racial Tension

Truth be told, I'd had a target on my back since day one. When word got out I was sent up on hate crime charges, the POC clan – *I called them prisoners of colour* – labelled me a white supremacist.

That was as bad as a chomo, maybe worse, but I had my supporters, my defenders. To attack me was to attack our entire car, and risk all-out racial warfare. The stakes were high.

Prison wasn't known for rational thought, but I had reality on my side: *I was no white supremacist. I was no racist. I was a guy who stood up for his rights, and the rights of all Canadians, including the decrepit motherfuckers I was locked up with.*

Few appreciated that view, and the issue got worse as resentment against whites went mainstream in the outside world. Prison was ahead of curve. Since the dawn of diversity, there was resentment against whites inside. Hostility and violence, too.

I wasn't deemed KOS – *though I mighta been for some* – but I was toxic, even within my own car. Curly woulda tossed me to the wolves, had it not been for Guido. And Vinny-by-proxy. Each night, I thanked God for Vinny.

I was fine so long as the shot callers feared the holy hell of revenge, and Guido assured them it would come. But I never got complacent, 'cause in prison things change in a hurry.

As the pod's population exploded, not everyone seemed aware of Guido's *leave-Tony-the-fuck-alone* memo. I had a run-in with a young Indian punk who got in my grill. I suckered him, and he folded like a cheap tent.

Not a good move, it turned out. He was connected in the Indo-Canadian community, cousin of an MP or some goddamn thing. Next thing ya know, I got a brand-new army of enemies. I was watching my ass every fucking minute, and my luck would surely run out.

Mo ignored me entirely, like I wasn't there. A bad sign said Guido, who had no magic answer to my prickly dilemma. Nor did Curly.

Once again, Vinny to the rescue. He knew the word on the street. He knew his Papa was ass out, and he knew the only way to fix it.

Go to the source.

He went direct to Dhanesh. *Yes* Dhanesh, my high school pal, my blood-brother. Dhanesh was part of the Indian community, *the Indian family*, but he was also part of *my* family. It was genius by Vinny, but it put poor Dhanesh in a tough spot.

When Dhanesh and I had a heart-to-heart several years back, he was a mere rising star. Now he was *bona fide*. An MP, a cabinet member, a highly-touted Prime Ministerial candidate. Dhanesh had the secret sauce, evidently. The X-factor. He was a tenacious campaigner and he played dirty when he had to.

He was in full embrace with his Indo-Canadian heritage. He donned a turban in 2023, and became known for sporting striking colours. He called it an ancestral calling, but admitted privately to Ivan he hated the damn thing.

In his home riding, he dusted off Hindi skills to address largely Indian crowds in their native tongue. His message was inflammatory: *for too long, we were denied a seat at the table. Now It's our turn. We must break free from oppressors. We must seize the moment.* He even paraphrased JFK: *The torch has been passed to a new generation of Canadians.*

Hint: not white ones.

Nobody called him out. This was the new normal.

The NDP was grooming Dhanesh for leadership. He was touted as smart, hard-working, and noble. (My God, if they only knew.) The press took note and filled the echo chamber with puff pieces and fawning headlines: *The Brown Leader Canada Needs* and *The Rise of Dhanesh Singh.* Everyone loved his winning smile.

In a hotly contested fight, Dhanesh edged out a devout Sikh to win the party leadership in 2026. He was officially Leader of the Opposition and many felt a shoo-in for PM. Dhanesh was in demand. No longer a common man.

That didn't stop Vinny. He worked through Ivan to secure an audience with the great man. They played up the old tropes – East Van, the Three Musketeers, brothers forever.

Dhanesh not only took the meeting, he heeded Vinny's call. He pulled strings, he made phone calls. He made damn sure *the hit* on me was called off. Threats were made to any who challenged his authority.

What a fucking guy. *What a powerful guy.*

No kidding, Dhanesh wielded frightening power in the Indo-Canadian community, politically and on the street. They were tightknit, like a family, especially in concentrated pockets like Surrey. They looked after their own.

But like any family, there were rifts. Much of the bad blood was rooted in the old country, in the Sikh-Hindu conflict. Sikhism was a young religion, just several centuries old, and it tended to the extremes. It nurtured a fringe element. Nothing like Islam, but the radicals were there and growing in numbers.

Going out on a limb for me was not universally popular and it triggered a rupture in the community. For this, Dhanesh paid a steep price. His enemies were livid, and were out for blood. This would not bode well for him.

But it sure boded well for me. I sensed a change immediately. So did Guido. He told me Mo was angry, but would honour the agreement. I breathed a tentative sigh of relief.

By the summer of 2027, I'd been locked away six years. That I'd survived was a miracle. *Grazie Dio!*

So much was happening on the outside, so much was changing. I was missing all of it. I was missing my family members, my friends. I even missed Leo.

Chapter 46 – Ferndale

Marked man or otherwise, life inside didn't get much easier. In fact, I felt like it was getting worse. My chats with Guido took an ominous tone. Even he, *the Dalai Lama of Mountain*, was having a hard time finding positive spin.

The problem was over-population. They were packing us in like chickens in a coop. Wally was a terrible cellmate. He was loud and smelly, and he seemed to take up a lot of space.

"I hear you might be getting a fourth," Guido said one chilly October morning.

"Fuck off."

Guido shrugged. "Kelvin told me." A newbie guard, one of the not-yet-permanently-jaded variety.

"They better not try it or—"

"Or what?" A smile played on Guido's lips. "Whatchu gonna do about it?"

"Maybe I complain about you? Last I checked, you got no roommates. *Zero*." I made a gesture with thumb and forefinger. It was true, Guido got a special deal, a *grandfathered* deal. Like I said, the man was connected.

"Don't bother."

"*Ha*, like they'd listen to me."

"Exactly. How's the new fish? *A fish called Wally.*" He burst out laughing. It was the hundredth time he'd used the line.

"Terrible. He's always there, taking up space, messing with my sleep. I don't trust him. I don't like him. I don't want him around."

Guido chuckled. "Tell me what you really think."

"I think he's a fucking plant. I'm worried he's gonna stab me in the night."

"No man, I had him checked out. Besides, you got the Dhanesh Singh insurance policy."

"I don't think Wally knows about it."

Guido made a dismissive gesture. "If he was gonna smash you, he'd a done it by now."

"I suppose."

"Listen, that's not the only thing Kelvin told me."

"No?"

"No man, I'm messing with ya." He bellowed laughter. "There *is* another guy slated for your house. But..." dramatic pause "...that's 'cause they're moving you the hell out."

"*What?*"

"Yeah bud, you're goin' to the country club."

I eyed him skeptically. "You better not be bullshittin'."

"Ferndale, Tony. They got a room with your name on it."

"*Holy fucking shit.*"

"How's your golf game?"

"Whatchu talkin' about?"

"Back in the day, they had a nine-hole course, no fucking kidding." He shook his head. "Sorry pal, they got rid of it. Some people weren't happy."

I grinned. "In that case, I'm not going."

Guido laughed appreciatively. Ferndale was the former name of the minimum-security annex of Mission Institution. The name lived on in prison parlance.

"*Hallelujah,* I'm getting outta here." The news was settling in and I whooped it up a little.

"Calm down, you don't leave 'til Friday. Lots could happen 'tween now and then."

"Shut up."

"Mo was looking extra mean at breakfast."

"You're an idiot, but I'll miss ya, pal."

"I'm sure you'll visit."

"I won't miss you that much."

"I'll look ya up when I get outta here. *In 2047.*"

"Can't wait." I looked toward my cell. "I'll be a little worried about poor Steve-O once I'm gone."

A couple months back, he'd taken a beatdown from a new arrival, a native who despised whites and said so frequently. The guards let it go long, for their entertainment not their safety, and I wasn't close by. Steve was battered and broken. He pissed blood for a month. His left eye would never be the same. But he never got a medical field trip. *Tough it out,* said the guards. After I was gone, God only knows how he'd fare.

"Keep any eye on him, eh Guido?"

"Maybe he's fine once you're gone, hey? Maybe you're the problem. *By association.*"

"Jesus, maybe you're right. Who knows in this godforsaken place?"

"Hey, *va fongool.*" Guido made wild hand gestures. "Eeza mya house you-ah talking about. Doan-a be a sucha snob, hey?"

"Hey, hey," I mimicked the gestures and we both got a chuckle. "Gonna miss you, Guido."

"Likewise."

With three more sleeps to endure, I became terrified I'd get whacked ahead of my release. I didn't sleep a wink the last night. Alas, I survived and after lunch on November 6, 2027, they crammed me in a transport van for the short hop to Ferndale.

Walking out of Mountain, hearing the heavy clang of security doors for the last time, I felt light and free. Drunk with relief. I had the goods on Ferndale – non-violent offenders, very few *incidents*. But that wasn't all.

"Ferndale's under our control," Guido had stated bluntly. He meant HA. "We're the only shot caller in town."

I settled in at my new house. A room, not a cell. I had a private shower, a bed, a desk, a TV. Vinny brought me new civilian wear, a pair of jeans, couple T-shirts. I felt like a million dollars. This was living.

There was no fence or wall, no guards patrolling the perimeter. I wasn't about to walk away, though. Those who did were always found and tossed back in Mountain.

I missed Guido, but I found new ways to pass time. I tinkered in the woodshop, building birdhouses and jewelry boxes. Just like high school shop class. This place had a better library, too.

Best perk of all? Unlimited visitation. Vinny started coming once a week. Sometimes he brought friends. Sometime the friends stopped by on their own. It was like a club. I was getting all the gossip, even the juicy stuff from Mountain. Guido was a legend in these parts, and I shared my own stories.

Vinny's first visit set the tone. He bounded in with his trademark enthusiasm and flopped on the bed like a teenager. "This country club living's better than outside, Papa."

"I doubt it."

"You haven't been outside for a while."

"True."

"It's a mess. How you doin' anyway, Papa?" He sat up and embraced me for the fourth time. "They turned you into a bonerack, I see."

"What can I say, I been on a diet."

He laughed. "You need a good woman to feed you pasta. Like I got."

"You sly dog." I poured us hot coffee. "What's your new girlfriend's name again? Cindy?"

"She ain't new, Papa. We been together four years. Take a look." He held up his phone and Cindy's smiling face stared back at me.

I nodded approval. "She's a beauty."

"Tell me about it. I chased her a couple years 'fore I finally caught her."

"You wore her down, eh?"

"Something like that."

"An Asian girl? Always pictured you with a nice Italian girl, Vinny." I made an hourglass gesture.

He took a few swipes at his phone. "Take a look."

"*Whoa, whoa*, I think Cindy might have some Italian in her."

"Every night, Papa." He made a sexual gesture and bellowed laughter. Nothing finer than locker-room high jinx.

"Something else I gotta tell ya, Papa."

"Oh ya?"

"Big news, Grandpa."

"What the fuck?"

"That's right, *Nonno*."

"Get the fuck out."

"No kidding."

"*Get the fuck out*." I took Vinny in a hearty embrace. "Unbelievable."

"Tell me about it."

"Whadayagot a girl? A boy?"

"You kidding me? I don't fool around, we gotta boy. We called him Julio."

"You called him Julio?" A burst of emotion welled up and my eyes teared.

"Don't lose it on me, Papa."

"When do I meet this kid? I haven't even met your woman. How old's little Julio?"

"Ha, not even a week. We just had 'im. I didn't say nothing 'til I knew you was safe. 'Til I knew you could see 'im."

Vinny was quite a kid. Quite a man, actually. He turned thirty-four a few months back. "Ah Vincent, come 'ere. Gimme a hug."

He obliged with gusto. "I wanna have three boys, Papa. Just like you."

"Well, you got yourself a Julio. I don't recommend a Leo, just sayin'." I laughed heartily, but Vinny drew back. His mood changed on a dime.

"What is it?"

"Papa." Vinny hung his head. "Leo ain't doin' so good."

"Tell me." I took a deep breath. "Tell me everything."

Chapter 47 – The Left Eats Its Own

"I barely saw him in ten years, Papa. After you went in, no glue left in the family. I saw him at a wedding here, a funeral there, maybe Nonna's place at Christmas. We barely said a word." Vinny sipped coffee. "For a while, I don't know where the fuck he's living, not that I'm paying attention. Anyways, I guess he ran outta dough, so he moves in with Nonna and Nonno."

"I heard about that. Four, five years ago. I wasn't surprised. I was bankrolling him before I went in. There was always a job for Leo, right around the corner..."

Vinny scoffed. "Leo never worked a day in his life. He's like Uncle David."

"Both trying to save the world."

"Both useless."

"So what happened?"

Vinny took me through his version of Leo's sad saga, and I've since learned more. A year after I went inside, Lisa's parents took him in. They tried like crazy to help, to get him happy and functioning. But they already had dysfunctional David in their midst. They were birds of a feather those two, but for some reason they clashed mightily. Catfights, Vinny said.

As the years ticked by, Leo kept up his SJW routine, but he also took up partying. He drifted into the gay nightclub scene. Raunchy, risky behaviour, drugs. Not a bad life, if that's what you were into. And someone else was paying.

Meantime, law and order was breaking down. Vancouver was one of the safest Western cities, *if not the safest*, which wasn't saying much.

Leo and his ilk felt invincible, part of the anarchy and thus immune to it. The media still labelled them protesters, even though they were bored, rich kids, desperate to be part of something. They got bolder and nastier. They got up in people's faces, they torched cars, they destroyed landmarks.

The good people of the city stopped wandering the streets for leisure. If you were out, you were going somewhere, and your head was on a swivel.

Was early 2027, just six months back, when things went south for Leo. His troop was out and about, stirring up trouble, harassing taxpayers (what few were left). But something else went off that night. Perhaps it was the full moon, who knows, but a thousand-plus migrants got in on the act – I'll let you guess their country of origin.

The government called them Canadians. I called them barbarians. This particular tribe took over a tent city in Oppenheimer Park. By now, homeless camps were everywhere, and new ones sprouted daily.

As Vinny put it, new shitholes. The Downtown Eastside paradigm was metastasizing throughout the city. On this night, the new arrivals were full of piss and vinegar and savagery. Fresh from their native hellholes, they rampaged. Not their first go, but a particularly feverish bloodlust was triggered. They turned on any whites they found. Citizens, Antifa, didn't matter. They went full tribal. Asians fared no better.

They attacked mercilessly, chasing and beating and stomping. The carnage was epic, and couldn't be swept under the rug, though media and public officials gave that a good run.

Headlines blared: *Disturbance in Downtown Eastside.* Reporters worked familiar euphemisms: *Large swarm of teens wreaked havoc, vandalized property, randomly attacked bystanders.*

The burning of cars, the looting, the rape – glossed over. The death toll wasn't high. Many of the victims were vagrants, low lifeforms, easy to sweep under the rug. No one gave a damn about them.

Leo came face to face with the barbarism he so passionately stoked. In Vinny's vernacular, *Leo got his head kicked in.* He spent a week in hospital, and he was damn lucky to get in. The healthcare system was a shadow of its former self. Like everything else, on the verge of collapse.

"How is he?"

"Nonna figures he suffered a brain injury." Vinny shrugged. "I haven't seen 'im."

"*Where* is he?"

Vinny scoffed. "I hear he's shacked up with a sugar-daddy in the West End. Some old freakin' queen."

I winced. "I don't like the sounds of that."

"Leo's a little gay boy, doin' what little gay boys do." Vinny mimicked fellatio. "Sorry Papa, I know he's your son. Hey, *lui è mio freaking fratello.*" *He's my freaking brother.* "But what a mental case."

Not long ago, Vinny woulda been slammed as a homophobe, but things had changed. Gays were back in hiding, no longer loud and proud, not even in the West End. Flamboyance was tucked back in the closet, gay PDA a surefire way to get hurt. I won't even mention the transgender movement.

Since the mid-2020s, gays were openly taunted, harassed, and attacked. The West End was prime hunting ground. Every resident had a horror story, straight and gay alike. This had nothing do with conservative Christians, incidentally.

On the plus side, no one had been tossed off a tall building. Not that I knew of. This was the Utopia Liberals fought for. Just sayin'.

Vinny was still on about Leo: "...what I hear, he's big into the powder." Vinny shook his head. "He don't have the constitution for it. Look at me, I smoked and snorted every drug in the book." He pounded his chest like Tarzan. "But I take it or leave it. Leo, *ha*, he's a helpless little fucker."

"If I ever get outta here, I'll talk some sense into him. He's not even thirty. Maybe I can turn him around."

Vinny smirked.

"And you be careful, *il mio ragazzo*. I don't wanna hear about you taking drugs, hey?"

"I stick to the booze these days, and not even much of that any more. Hey, I'm a fucking Dad. I gotta put food on the table, gotta buy my kid shoes. I got people counting on me."

"*I'm* counting on you, Vincent."

"Always got your back, Papa. *Always*."

"Ya, I wouldn't be here if not for you."

"Ditto, Papa." We had a laugh. "Speaking of havin' your back, you gotta watch yourself out there now, no matter who the fuck you are. Never used to be like that."

"Was bad before I went in."

"It's different now, Papa. Those crazy foreigners, they gone wild a few more time since the night with Leo. That was the christening. One time they got near my place. Me an' the boys, we let 'em fuckin' have it." He made a firearms gesture. "They won't come back any time soon."

Chapter 48 — An Old Friend
March 24, 2028

Ivan *finally* deigned to visit. Was he still my best friend? In seven years, we'd swapped a few letters, surface-level stuff. Beyond that, I'd seen hide nor hair of the guy.

He was a paranoid sort, and could ya blame him? Look what happened to me. But Vinny put the squeeze on him, basically told him *you're coming*. Vinny knew it'd do me good.

"Nice to see you, pal." We embraced and back-slapped. "Where the fuck ya been?"

"I thought about visiting."

"But you chickened out."

"Sorry bud, these days the wrong opinion gets you fired. Cavorting with the likes of you? Jesus, that gets you killed."

For all his bluster, Ivan was a *scaredy-cat*. The thought of setting foot in prison terrified him. In fairness, it terrified most people. Especially whites.

After I got hauled off, Ivan had panicked. He also conformed. No more Facebook rants. No more Facebook period. He deleted everything. But secretly, he kept informed. He had his ways. He never lost hope.

It was great to see him. Hard to believe, we'd been pals sixty years. You don't find that every day. We kidded each other about our age, *sixty-three*, and how we were both showing it. Ivan had put on weight and lost hair. Me? The hard time was written on my face. I'd aged double the normal rate.

"Vinny says it's bad out there. *Real* bad. What the hell's going on, Ivan?"

"Where do I begin. We're living in *Bizarro World*. Everything I ever warned about..."

"Coming true?"

"And then some."

"Who's winning?"

"There *are* no winners."

"Wasn't that Trudeau's slogan?"

He chuckled. "It shoulda been. Humanity's the fucking loser."

"America's the same?"

"Pretty much." Ivan shrugged. "They still have the First and Second Amendment, the remnants of 'em anyway. That seems to be helping."

"Man, those Americans and their Constitution. They sure as hell got that right."

"No shit. We got nothing like it."

"Any word on Bucky Bradford?"

"Legal troubles, not as bad as yours."

"Oh?"

"Gosh golly, Ah reckon that good ol' boy fixin' da make a run fer it." Ivan's *Southern boy* impression wasn't half bad.

"Seriously?"

"He's on bail. Some bullshit charges. They wanna nail him."

Ivan flinched at the sound of commotion outside my door, some of the younger inmates. "They get boisterous," I said. "Don't worry, they're harmless."

"You got it good here."

"Compared to what?"

Ivan grinned. "You know I moved, eh?"

"I heard you moved outta the East End, ya fucking traitor."

"Had to. White flight, dude. I was way too close to Broadway. That SkyTrain station was a nightmare. Worse now."

"Vinny seems happy."

"He's farther north. Anywhere from Templeton to the docks ain't so bad. North Burnaby's good, too. Vinny's in the stronghold. That's his turf."

"Vinny *is* the stronghold." I fired up a smoke. Yes, I'd taken it up again. "Where you at then?"

"West side, pal. Not far from your old place." He grinned. "We coulda been neighbours."

"No way."

"Two blocks over from Charles Kennedy, you believe it?"

I massaged my temples. The mention of Charles got my ire up. "Expensive?"

"Oh yeah, I'm mortgaged up to here." He waved a hand above his head. "Had to do it for the family's safety. Sasha's still at UBC. At least now, no one's gonna mug him on the bus. Or at a crosswalk. Plus, he's way closer."

"That bad, eh?"

"It's terrible. You're fair game out there, not just in the hellholes – *and there's plenty of those*. People are hunkered down. You don't make yourself a target, if you can help it. Forget about going out after dark."

I sighed. "The bastards did a number on Leo."

Ivan nodded. "Sorry about that, my man."

"He's in bad shape. Brain injury. On drugs." I skipped the sordid living arrangements.

"Know what I think?"

"You're gonna tell me anyway."

"I can't comment on the drugs or the brain injury. But all these SJWs, reality finally hit him 'em in the chops, and they're traumatized."

"Could be. That was Leo's religion."

"Exactly. Everything he believed collapsed that night."

I shrugged. "Maybe and maybe not. He's probably made a million excuses for the attackers. Probably blames himself."

"Maybe, but ya don't see many white kids protesting anymore. They get their asses kicked by the assholes they're *supposedly* standing up for. It's absurd."

"Leo's got nothing to fall back on, either. No hobby, no sport, no spiritual connection."

"And no job."

"Fuck no, he never grew up. Never took responsibility."

"He's like any socialist. He figured the government would solve his problems." Ivan paused. "And pay his bills."

"Actually, that was me. Where's all this going, man?"

"You mean the chaos?"

"Is it gonna be anarchy?"

"*Gonna be?* Dude, we already police our own streets. We're hiring private security. Those guys are thriving. We're like South Africa was ten years ago. We're gating off neighbourhoods."

"Your neighbourhood's safe, ain't it?"

"I'm not taking any chances. When crime hits critical mass, you can't enforce laws. We're almost there."

"But Ivan...we don't need laws in Utopia." I was being cheeky. "There's no need for crime if there's plenty for everyone."

"Pardon me for not laughing. Tell that to Venezuela. Fuck, tell that to Europe. From what I hear, we're still the safest town going."

"Not counting places like Japan."

"Course not. *They're fine.* They have no diversity. But Europe's fucked. America's fucked. Baltimore, St. Louis,

Chicongo? They been fucked since Obama. Now they're dead zones. Not a scrap of white working-class left. Remember, all those years ago, I showed you Colin Flaherty's videos?"

"Yep."

"Well, that's what happens when you ignore a problem."

"How's T-Dot?" *Toronto.*

"Hellhole, just like the States."

"Jesus." I shook my head. "The sickness has taken over."

"Like a fucking plague. And what does it leave in its path?" He didn't wait for me to answer. "Total destruction, and you can't rebuild. Whatever you build during the day gets stolen or demolished at night. They loot, they rob, they burn. Retail's impossible. Buildings are abandoned, they fall to pieces. Squatters and druggies take over."

"And the sickness spreads."

Ivan nodded. "We don't even have tent cities anymore. We got shanties. People pissing and shitting in the streets."

"What happens when the locusts destroy everything?"

"We might find out. I think we passed the point of no return."

"That's okay. I'm sure our government has a plan. They'll save us."

"*Yeah.*" He laughed mirthlessly. "Or maybe the *UN.*"

"I been outta the loop, man. What do the politicians even say? Do they pretend everything's normal?"

"Look at your buddy Charles. He's the master. Still doing the same song and dance. He'll play that charade to the bitter end. Ya know, People of Colour are victims, yadda yadda."

"And he's a *conservative.*"

"I repeat. Bizarro World."

"You said you talk to him, what's he say privately?"

"Do I look stupid? I don't bring that shit up. We talk about the weather, we talk about our kids. You think I wanna get arrested and end up here?"

"This place is nice."

"I've noticed."

"Can we change the subject?"

"Please."

"How's the philandering Hindu?"

Ivan laughed. "Watch your mouth, dude. They'll get ya on hate speech."

"This is a free country."

He chuckled. "We're as free as Danny Boy is ethical."

"What's he up to?"

"Same old, same old, still bilking the public purse."

"Still in Surrey?"

"Oh yeah."

"You guys chat?"

"We keep tabs."

"Say hi for me."

Ivan scoffed. "I don't wanna taint myself."

"Asshole." I said, as I pretended to cough. "I hear Surrey's a gong show. Gang violence everywhere."

"It's not so bad if you're the right colour. Very racially aligned out there."

"Always was."

"True. I'm telling you, East Van's violent *because* it's fucking diverse."

"You can't tell me Surrey's not violent."

"I only know what Dhanesh tells me, and I have no idea why I believe him." We laughed. "It's not like I go there and visit. Yeah, they got issues. Sikhs and Hindus, the Muslim factor – *those fuckers mess everything up.* And they're still top of the totem pole. Top protected class."

"This racial alignment shit, the tribalism. That's how I've lived for seven years. *On the inside.*"

"It's like that on the outside now."

"Awesome." I stood up. "Coffee's brewed, you want some?"

"No beer?"

"Alcohol-free zone here. *Mostly.*"

He grinned. "Coffee, yes please."

"I hear Danny's gonna be the next PM."

Ivan snorted. "I don't know if we'll even *have* another election."

"Come on."

"Politics is bloodsport now. A goldrush for power, and they get it by any means necessary. Danny's got thugs at his disposal, *I know you know.* He told me about your challenges in the Big House."

"That was scary, pal."

"I can only imagine. *Jesus.* I'm not sure Dhanesh knows who he's playing with. He strikes me as naïve compared to the cutthroats he's up against."

"'Cause you know him."

"He worries about himself, too."

"Nothing wrong with that."

"True. He takes precautions. He's always on about *the crazy fucking Sikhs.* He's got enemies. They think he's a phony."

"He is."

"They all are. And they're taking us to hell in a handbasket."

"They're not taking us anywhere. They're bringing hell here."

Chapter 49 – Freedom

Ferndale was a huge improvement. I had books to read, movies to watch, cigarettes to smoke. But I was crawling the walls a few months in. I gave up woodshop. After my tenth birdhouse, it felt pointless.

Prayer kept me grounded, and I got my fair share of visitors. I had fellowship with some inmates, too. I didn't even feel like an inmate. More a guest at a summer camp.

But life had no meaning. I woke up uninspired. Borderline depressed. I had too much time to ponder my shattered dreams. Hey, at least vile animals weren't plotting to kill me. I had that going for me, right?

Or did I?

Ferndale's population was increasing, and I felt a rogue element creeping in. I was looking over my shoulder again. Paranoia had returned.

Maybe one of these guys was a plant? Then again, would a plant not strive to appear inconspicuous? These were the head games I played.

When I mentioned it to Vinny, he mocked me savagely, called me a pussy. He also promised to look into it.

As the months ticked by, I swear the power structure changed. Something was amiss. There were bad apples, guys not on board with...*my team.* Ivan told me prison systems were failing everywhere. They were beyond full. Overflowing. There simply wasn't enough room for all the bad guys. The result? The ones they did put away were the scariest hombres. *The psychopaths.*

Then it happened.

One cool, crisp November morn, Vinny arrived unannounced. He brought a couple henchmen, one a behemoth named Tiny with a massive bald head and no neck. Built like Vinny but fifty percent bigger.

"Today's your lucky day, Papa. You're getting out."

"*What?*" I had five years left on my sentence. "You talk to my lawyer? He hasn't returned my calls in a month."

Vinny placed a beefy arm across my shoulder. "You don't need 'im, I got you a better lawyer."

I shot him a puzzled look.

"You weren't wrong, Papa. This place is falling apart. It's *all* falling apart. Time to get you the hell out. Somewhere safe."

"What's going on?"

"Tell ya later. Right now, we take care of business, eh?" He opened the door and a middle-aged man walked in. He wore glasses, a suit and tie. He carried a briefcase. But underneath the veneer, he looked like he wouldn't be out of place at a street fight.

"This here's Monte. He's got paperwork to sign. All above board, don't worry 'bout it."

"What is it?"

"Discharge papers."

"Is this legit? Isn't there supposed to be a hearing?"

"I got connections, Papa. We run this place, right Monte?"

I didn't ask any more questions. When I signed, I noticed a few snippets of language. *No threat to community. Model prisoner. Low risk to re-offend.* If this was a charade, it was a good one.

I followed instructions, I packed my things. I skipped heartfelt good-byes, not that I was especially close to anyone. This felt suspiciously like an escape.

If Vinny could do this, how lawless had society become? I was confused. Had the line between good guys and bad guys blurred? *Or disappeared?*

Vinny and the boys were all business. They were edgy and hyper-alert. Vinny patted his pocket several times. *I got my little friend here, just in case.*

On the drive to Vancouver, Vinny was stone-faced behind the wheel. Was he worried about a roadblock? Or some other malfeasance? I rode shotgun while Tiny and the other goon crammed themselves into the back seat.

In spite of the foreboding mood and lurking uncertainties, my spirits soared. *I was free.* I watched familiar landmarks pass with intense fascination and déjà vu. Abbotsford. Langley. Surrey. The Port Mann Bridge.

It was midday, but the sun was low in the sky. The dashboard reported a chilly five Celsius. I didn't care. I wanted to hang my head out the window like a dog. I wanted to breathe the crisp November air, to feel the wind in my hair.

We exited at Willingdon and I noticed a dusting of snow capping the North Shore Mountains. A sight to behold. I never felt more alive.

Did people still ski Grouse Mountain? I wondered. *How about Whistler?* Probably the very rich, I decided. The most insulated, the Charles Kennedys of the world.

I had catching up to do. Amid the chaos, what societal institutions had survived? I heard the NFL dissolved. Self-destructed under the burden of its kneeling controversy. As revenue evaporated, the movement doubled down and eventually the league went tits up. New leagues rushed in, but never captured the public's attention or pocketbook.

How about the Canucks? I couldn't imagine Vancouver without pro hockey. But who the hell attended games? For that matter, who the hell played? The elites? The Charles Kennedys?

When we crossed Hastings, Confederation Park came into view and memories of my soccer-playing youth sprang forth. Was that really fifty years ago? Seemed impossible, though not when I considered all the water under the bridge.

The pitch stood empty. The park, too. Even the streets, I realized, were near-deserted. This was not the city I grew up in.

"You gonna tell me where we're going?"

"Almost there, Papa."

Vinny was in charge. Without him, I was helpless. I had no money, no prospects, no connections. Thank God for Vinny. How often had I said that this past eight years?

We navigated twisty, turny streets, butting up against the Burrard Inlet before Vinny pulled into the driveway of a modest two-storey home.

"Welcome home, Papa. You'll like it here."

"Looks good to me. How's the neighbourhood?"

I was kidding around, but Vinny answered in earnest. "We control this territory. Nothing but good folks round here. Trustworthy. You got a water view, you can walk the trails. What more you want? *Buono.*"

"*Buona lavoro.*" Good job. "But how 'bout something closer to the Drive?"

"We gonna keep you incognito awhile, hey?"

"How come?"

"Don't worry, no one's gonna do nothin'. But why wave it in their face? We just keep you outta sight awhile."

I hopped out to survey my new digs. *I loved it.* The place had character. I didn't have a clue what I'd do every day, but at least I'd be in a nice place.

Vinny came up behind me. "Papa, you're shuffling like an old man."

"I *am* an old man."

"Ya, but you're free. You gotta walk like ya own the world." He pranced around for emphasis, and burst into laughter when I attempted to mimic his moves.

"Come on, I show you around. This is one of my favourite safe houses."

Vinny sold it like a realtor – the deck, the scenery, the location. The place wasn't ramshackle, but it could use some TLC. I saw the makings of a decent garden out back. My own Papa would have approved.

It was also a fortress. Every door was a solid-core beast secured by six-inch triple deadbolts. The windows were tinted and bullet-proof. Automated surveillance monitored the grounds and perimeter. The security system was governed from a control room with screens capturing every nook and cranny of house and yard.

"Impenetrable," said Vinny.

"If the neighbourhood's so safe, why we need all this?"

"Insurance, Papa." He roared with laughter, and I couldn't help but join him. "It's our turf. We got spotters, informants, but ya know what? I still want you to keep this around." He handed me a pistol.

"Does it come with a user guide?"

"Haha, point and shoot. This is the new law and order, Papa."

I shook my head. "What's going on out there, Vinny?"

"Business as usual."

It dawned on me – the descending chaos, the anarchy, the violence – none of it was new to The Vin Man. It'd been his way of life since day one. The gangster life. A subculture beneath the civility. I always thought of Vinny as an honourable gangster, if there was such a thing. Either way, he'd been preparing for this nonsense his whole life.

While Vinny made a few calls, I freshened up. Had a quick shower, a quick shave, took a long look in the mirror. I was down to a buck seventy-five in Mountain – the prison food sucked, but it was also the stress. I'd put some weight back, but *Jesus* I looked like shit.

My hair had thinned, and what was left was a dull shade of grey. My face was hollow and gaunt, the light in my eyes gone. Does that ever come back? Would I ever reclaim my youthful glow?

I admonished myself. *You're sixty-five years old, man. Nothing youthful about that number.*

I heard raucous shouts and laughter in the living room. Sounded like a house party. Typical Vinny. I put on the new jeans and T-shirt he'd laid out for me – *was there no end his goodness?* – and ambled out to meet the hooligans.

The afternoon sun was perched low over Burrard Inlet. It would soon disappear behind Stanley Park. What a dazzling sight.

"I could get used to the view."

"Have one of these, Papa. The view gets even better." He poured me a shot, and I downed it without hesitation. "Attaboy." He poured another.

We didn't have a rager, but it was the most excitement I'd seen in a while. Plenty of guests, plenty of laughs, plenty of booze. What a welcome. I'm not a big drinker, but I indulged mightily. Was my first go at the drink in eight goddamn years, and I went well beyond pleasant buzz.

Vinny brought in a feast, too. Steak and chicken and seafood – nothing for the Vegan crowd. To top it off, Cindy showed up with my new grandson. She was a sweetheart, and Young Julio was a beauty and a terror. Ten months old, already walking and stirring up trouble. A chip off the old block.

I slept like a baby that night. Or should I say, like a free man. No nightmare haunted my slumber. I didn't even wake to take a piss. I could get used to this. From Mountain to Ferndale to North Burnaby. I was moving in the right direction.

Chapter 50 – Commercial Drive

I was irritable and jumpy the first few weeks and Vinny took pleasure in mocking me. I didn't mind. It was coming from a place of love. The neighbourhood was peaceful, as promised, and blessed with wonderful walking trails. I got out as much as possible amidst the wet, green foliage, but blizzards in December and January kept me housebound.

Vinny stopped by frequently. He was always on the go, and I often wondered where the hell he went, but I didn't pry. Why start now?

I was working hard to live like a human being. Eight years of prison left scars. This was evident the day Cindy took me Christmas shopping at Brentwood Mall. *Yes*, we still had Christmas, and *yes* we still had malls. They had a massive security presence, but the number of *incidents* was growing.

Still, people showed up and spent money. Too many for my liking, and that was the problem. I felt its twinges in the parking lot, but the panic didn't take hold until we entered. The swarming crowds, the racial mashup, the lighting, the chaotic unruliness.

It was too much to bear. Danger lurked, I was sure. I hyperventilated, my heart raced, sweat beaded on my brow.

My nervous system was a shambles. Cindy helped me to a bench and rushed off to get a cup of water. I tried to breathe, tried to calm myself. I prayed. Somehow, I pulled it together.

That was the end of the excursion, though. We got out of there quick as we could. I guess I'd accumulated some pretty intense PTSD during my incarceration. The constant brutality, living like an animal. Hard to walk away unscathed.

I probably should have done therapy, but I was too old school for that crap. Maybe one day. I didn't wanna live in a bubble, though that's what Vinny had in mind when he parked me here.

I was fine with some crowds – family, friends, Italians haha. White people in general. Asians didn't bother me, either. Sounds racist, eh? Try spending eight years in prison. See how you fare.

By the spring of 2030, I'd made progress. Panic attacks were less frequent, as were moments of intense foreboding. I was getting outside almost every day and I felt the old vigour coming back into the bloodstream.

Trepidation, I told myself, was unwarranted. *I preached it.* The fears were in my head, rooted in my overactive imagination. It was a tough argument, because reality was close by. Why would Vinny give me a gun if there was no danger?

I prayed each morning and every night before bed. I asked God for strength and courage, for the safety of loved ones. My relationship with Him kept me grounded. So long as I followed His will, He would guide me and keep me safe. My faith was strong.

Ivan and I rekindled our bond, but at first only through electronic means – geography precluded face-to-face meetups. Vinny didn't want me driving, and because I lived under his roof, I lived by his rules. Talk about role reversal. As for Ivan, he was a big chicken. He rarely ventured from the safety of the West Side, certainly not to Burnaby. To get to me meant transit through the entirety of East Vancouver, a hazardous proposition.

Eventually, we found a compromise. We'd meet on the protected territory of Commercial Drive, hallowed ground for me. My own Papa drank coffee and bullshitted with pals here in the '50s and '60s. A block away, he and his friends played bocce and sipped wine until sunset. The Drive was in my blood.

Vinny dispatched a driver for Ivan, and Tiny would be my chauffeur. Tiny was a great guy, but quiet as a mouse. Fine with me, I was slightly stressed on the drive in. Commuting around town was dicey. You had to be ready for anything: infrastructure failure, criminals, random violence, the occasional police roadblock. Law enforcement was no longer trustworthy.

We still had a skeletal public transit system – SkyTrain lines plus a handful of ancient buses. But thugs preyed on passengers, and you were taking your life in your hands. Absolutely not recommended.

Our SUV had bullet-proof windows and tires. Nothing to worry about, Vinny assured me. Fucking guy. Ivan took some convincing, but he got the same security assurances from Vinny and relented.

We met at a cozy little coffee house called *Café Maria*. The proprietor alone was worth the price of admission. Maria was a powerhouse, vivacious, entertaining, and damned attractive. She had meat on her bones, too, in all the right places.

We immediately clicked, though I confess, she clicked with everyone. She laughed at my cheek, then gave it back twice as hard.

Ivan and I had a couple hours to enjoy lunch and catch up. We got our drinks – double-espresso for me, caramel macchiato for Ivan. *He was such a woman.* "Tell me twinkle-toes, how's life on the other side of the tracks?"

"Feels like I'm on the edge of a goddamn civil war. How's life in the burbs?"

"Dull as paint, but peaceful."

"Let's hope it stays that way."

"What you talking about? Civil war?"

"That's what I'm hearing. You probably know as much as me, on account of Vinny. Maybe more."

"How you staying up to date, pal? I barely go online. Big Brother's keeping tabs, no?"

"No ifs, ands or buts. They watch *everything*." He leaned in close, his voice became a whisper. "But my kid's a security guru. Works for the government. I got mega-encryption going on. Data comes in from all over the place, only my decoder has the key to put it back together."

"Sasha's a smart kid, eh?"

Ivan smiled. "We're proud of him."

"The apple didn't fall far..."

"Do I detect a compliment?"

"I toss 'em out now and again, even to a chooch like you." We chuckled. "What do ya see there on the dark Web?"

"Hard to find reliable sources, I tell ya. Not like the old days when we were spoon-fed. Now you have to hunt and filter, and double-check. But I ain't exaggerating on the civil war comment."

"No?"

"Hell no. A civil war with many sides."

"Isn't it *People of Colour* against *The Evil White Man*?"

He laughed. "That's true in some countries. Around here, some areas have no whites. And the various factions are at each other's throats."

"Sounds like prison."

He nodded. "Take LA. Blacks and Hispanics going at it."

"That's not new."

"It's worse now, trust me. In Chicago, it's Blacks v Blacks."

"Also, not new."

"An ugly mess, and we're no different."

"We're better off than LA and Chicago. We have to be."

"For now. But we're on a knife's edge, dude. *Everywhere is*. Germany, England. Australia."

"You think it's gonna blow up one day?"

"What do I know." Ivan made a sour face. "We take everything for granted, even now. The smooth workings of society. We figure stores will always have food, cops will keep peace..."

"They don't."

He continued unabated. "...water will pour out of the taps." He sipped his girly drink. "What if one day it didn't? What if one day, we had no power? No Internet?"

"That's what happened in South Africa."

"South America, too. Are we next?"

I shrugged.

"If you don't maintain First World infrastructure, it disintegrates. How long would you last if the taps ran dry? If there was no food in the stores?"

"I might last awhile. I got Vinny. We got supplies."

"You're lucky. I'm set up, too. I'm like a prepper. Have been for a while."

"What do you got, water? Dry goods?"

"Everything. Toothpaste, toilet paper. First aid. *Ammo*, obviously. Gas for the generator."

"I better check with Vinny."

"Yeah, if they choke off the supply, we're fucked. Who even works the docks these days?"

"They laid off a lotta guys. But they still operate, far as I know. Shit's going in and out."

"Well, I'm ready for Armageddon. Just in case."

"Shouldn't we be reminiscing about the good old days instead of all this doom and gloom? Don't you wanna hear about my grandkid?"

"He's a bruiser, I'm told."

"You surprised?"

He shook his head. "But bringing kids into this crazy world? That takes balls."

"Vinny's got 'em. What I find truly amazing is..." I grinned mischievously, "...I don't even look like a grandfather."

Ivan bellowed laughter. "More like a great grandfather."

"What do you think Maria?" My timing was perfect. She'd just arrived at our table, and I struck a pose. "Do I look like a grandfather?"

Her laughter filled the room. "What's wrong with being a grandfather? Look at you, so handsome. So big and strong." She gave my shoulder a friendly squeeze, the first feminine attention I'd received in years. My grin was ear-to-ear.

"She works on tips," Ivan said. "You know that?"

"Then obviously you're not getting a compliment. *Alligator arms.*"

Maria held up her hands. "Boys, boys. It doesn't matter. I'm just happy you're here. You need anything else? It's on the house."

"She's something, eh?" I said to Ivan, but the message was for Maria.

"That she is." Ivan dramatically retrieved his wallet. "We're good, Maria. Just the cheque please. I got this."

I feigned shock, as Maria giggled and hustled off.

Ivan paid in US currency. After repeated bouts of hyper-inflation, the *loonie* was on its deathbed, worth pennies on the American dollar, if that. Our money was Monopoly money.

The recent collapse of markets and monetary systems made the 2008 meltdown look like a tea party. As assets haemorrhaged, Western citizens panicked. They became desperate for safe havens.

Unfortunately, everything was high risk. The 2027 bank run was so devastating, the Canadian government had to regulate withdrawals, a strategy that did nothing but provoke alarm. People hoarded cash and stopped using credit cards.

The Federal Reserve was exposed as a sham, and one by one our banks failed. Two of the big five still pretended to operate. What exactly they did was anyone's guess. Mortgage defaults were common, though actions weren't always taken. Home ownership was about occupancy and protection. To bastardize an old adage, *protection was nine-tenths of the law.*

Protection rackets exploded. On the West Side, things were more civilized, but Ivan confided he'd stopped paying his mortgage at the bank. Instead, he paid a mysterious new creditor.

By 2030, a small number of currencies had become standard fare, including the greenback. In places like Richmond and Metrotown, the Yuan was de facto standard. In fact, Chinese currency accounted for eighty percent of global commerce at this precarious juncture in time. In Third World countries, it was the only game in town.

Vinny's ilk operated on bartering systems involving various contraband – drugs, booze, cigarettes. Also, unpleasant tasks, the settling of scores. That had been part and parcel of their business for decades.

After exiting *Café Maria*, I wandered a few doors down and fired up a smoke. For some reason, I didn't want Maria to see me smoking. I was trying to cut down, but quitting seemed a preposterous notion.

"Still smoking?" Ivan sneered.

"I quit for thirty years."

"And look at you now."

"After your gloomy updates, I might as well smoke. We're all gonna be dead soon by the sounds of it."

"Don't blame the messenger."

I grinned at him. "We're gonna do this again, right?"

"Of course, was good to see you, brother. Been too long."

I took him in a bear hug. "Love ya, brother."

The lovefest didn't last, Ivan wasn't that kinda guy. Besides, our respective drivers were anxious to hit the road so we'd make it home in one piece. It was almost five and darkness was imminent.

That's when the animals got restless, I was told.

Chapter 51 – Bad News

Coffee on The Drive did wonders for me, and my renewed spirit had as much to do with Maria as Ivan. Possibly more. Life throws curveballs. Not in a million years did I entertain the prospect of finding love again. Partly out of loyalty to Lisa. I also figured that aspect of life died in prison.

Look at me getting ahead of myself, like a silly teenager. Heck, she's probably got a boyfriend, I figured. *She must.* And she probably thought I looked like a grandpa, which I was.

I pegged her for early fifties, a decade south of me. Too much of a gap? Didn't stop me from indulging the dream with gusto.

Unfortunately, a few days after my encounter with Maria, I received devastating news. A Tuesday afternoon, just back from a walk by the inlet. I'd been daydreaming about Maria and castles in the sky.

Vinny was waiting at the front door, his demeanour downcast. Something was wrong, and my first instinct was Julio. *Oh my God, has something happened to Young Julio?*

Vinny wasted no time. "Leo's gone, Papa."

For a split second, I rejoiced it wasn't Julio – *I'm not proud of that* – then the news settled and spread its darkness. Another child gone. I sat down on my favourite chair. Collapsed would be more accurate. I felt old and weary. This was too much to bear.

"What happened?"

"Typical bullshit. Bad drugs. He was in it up to here." Vinny made a hand gesture.

"An accident?"

Vinny sighed. "Yeah Papa, *an accident.*" His face turned sour. "Don't worry, we took care of the guys who did it, if ya know what I mean." He waited for me to acknowledge I did, in fact, know what he meant. "They knew it was bad shit." He patted my shoulder roughly and gave my arm a solid squeeze. A show of comfort and affection that I greatly appreciated.

As the afternoon wore on, the sharp sting of grief dulled. I began to see perspective as Vinny and I talked. I'd lost Leo many years ago, and in many ways, I'd already grieved the loss. There was a sense of relief. I could stop worrying, I could make peace with the past, and pray for Leo's soul. He never found what he was looking for. He never found happiness.

Vinny was also philosophical, but in a gruffer way. "With everything goin' down, maybe it's for the best..." He didn't elaborate.

"You're all I have left, *il mio ragazzo.*"

"You got Julio and Cindy, too. We ain't goin' nowhere." He stood. "Know what? We gotta drink a toast to Leo. Poor kid, he never fit in. Either did I really." Vinny burst out laughing. "But Leo, he, uh...he had challenges. He was blood, though. We loved 'im. Right, Papa?"

"Of course, we did."

Vinny's melancholy was over. Swashbuckling Vinny was back. After a couple shots, he was full technicolor and I was trying to keep up. We shared old stories. We reminisced. There were no more tears.

The following weekend, we held a ceremony at a church off Commercial. We had to commemorate Leo's life. It was our duty. The event was a reunion of sorts, with Lisa's parents and brother in attendance.

I hadn't seen my former in-laws since I went to prison. They never reached out, and I didn't blame them. As years passed, I thought of them often. We were close and friendly back in the day. They were good people, the Millers, and their beloved daughter was cruelly taken.

We made amends that day. Hugs, words of solace. We didn't delve into my activism, or nine years of no contact. It was too awkward.

I said a few words at the ceremony. I had to, Leo was my son – but I struggled. I didn't know what to say so I kept it simple. *Leo lost his way. I never stopped loving him. I never will.* I went on awhile, but that was the essence.

David also took the podium and made up for my lack of substance. His goal, evidently, was to honour my son's *legacy.*

"Leonardo was committed to the struggle. He wore his shame on his sleeve, the shame all whites feel. David was a tremendous ally to People of Colour, right to the end. He understood what they went through, and what they still go through to this day."

Jesus.

"Does David understand what I go through listening to this BS?" Ivan whispered. "I wonder if ne nauseates *himself.*"

I stifled a giggle. David said nothing of the hostility between himself and Leo. Not that he should have, but it added to the hypocrisy.

From his insulated bubble, David's delusions had grown worse. He was over sixty now and not about to change. If the unwashed hordes invaded his home, he'd find a way to blame himself.

His diatribe marred the event slightly, but no one called him out, not at first. Outside the church, there was a confrontation between David and Ivan. Bad blood still lingered, the resentment was sharp in David's spiteful brain.

He attacked with ancient talking points: *you're losing your white privilege, you're the patriarchy's dying gasp, diversity's killing you off.*

When David ran out of steam, Ivan grinned smugly and clobbered him with wit and wisdom. Would David never learn? Of course not. Like Leo, he'd go down with the ship. A subservient ally to the bitter end. A useful idiot.

We held a small wake afterward, minus the Millers. I cornered Ivan. "Couldn't leave it alone eh?"

"*He* came at me. I wasn't gonna, I swear. I wanted to walk away. But it was too easy."

We laughed together, but piled on no further. Leo was gone. It was not a day for rancour or ridicule. To lose a son was devastating, no matter the circumstance. I felt the loss deep in my soul, but I was done grieving. I had no remaining resentment or guilt. Leo suffered a form of insanity, a mental illness over which he had no control.

"When we connecting again on The Drive?" Ivan asked.

"Anytime."

"This weekend. Same time, same place?"

Ivan nodded. "I'm in. Now how about we do a proper toast to your kid?"

We hoisted a few that night. We reminisced, we took playful shots at Leo, and each other. We sent my boy off properly.

Chapter 52 – Maria

I was thrilled to be back at *Café Maria*, in close proximity to the lovely proprietor. I'd become obsessed.

The date was July 1, 2030. *Canada Day*. There were no fireworks, no cultural displays, no concerts. Not a single event to commemorate my country's 163rd birthday. The government stopped bothering. There was no need, and more importantly, no point.

That didn't stop Maria. She had Canada flags everywhere, including one on each cheek. She put up posters up of old-time hockey heroes – Crosby, Lemieux, Gretzky, Orr. She also Canadianized her menu for the day, adding specialties like poutine and Nanaimo bars. I felt a stirring of patriotism, among other unfamiliar stirrings.

I played it smart, arriving early to allow flirting time. How long since I'd courted a woman? Forty, fifty years? If I won Maria's heart, would I know what to do with her? I'd cross that bridge when the time came. *If* it came.

My strategy worked, I arrived during a lull. Maria greeted me with customary warmth. "Look who's here." Her smile was as bright as the sun, and she marched forward to give me a hug.

"I'm way early, Maria. Hey, join me for a coffee? My treat." You get what you ask for in life.

She laughed like it was the funniest thing she'd ever heard. "Oh, why not, I'm the boss." She glanced around. "I could use the break."

We spent forty-five minutes swapping backstories. Maria's daughter Isabella handled customers like a pro, God bless her.

Maria was cheerful, but also a no-nonsense Italian. She could speak her mind. She might even tear your head off, if you crossed her. She was rough and crude at times, but in a charming way. So different from Lisa, and this was essential. If she reminded me of Lisa, it'd never work. Even so, I felt a twinge of betrayal. I didn't let it rule me, nor would Lisa want me to.

Maria was fifty-six, nine years my junior. I didn't ask her age, she volunteered it. How stupid do I look? She was of sturdier stock than Lisa. Voluptuous, a little junk-in-the-trunk, as they say. So very Italian. Her gaze was steady, and a twinkle played in her eyes. She wore hair up, and I wondered if that was only during work hours.

Isabella was eighteen, a stunning brunette. Well-mannered and clearly well-raised. But no father. Like me, Maria was a widow.

Her family lived in North Vancouver for generations. The great grandparents settled there in the '50s, and promptly opened a delicatessen on Lonsdale. The family business prospered.

Not an ounce of crime then, certainly nothing violent. But in the 2010s, it crept in, and got real bad by the 2020s. North Van followed the classic script. Enclaves aligned by race and culture. Lonsdale went Muslim, as did much of the North Shore. Halal restaurants and mosques dominated. Females, regardless of ethnicity, didn't dare stroll about without a hijab. Full burqas were not uncommon.

Business at the deli held steady, but all was not well. There were break-ins, vandalism, anonymous threats. *They called us dogs and infidels. They threatened to rape me. They threatened to rape my daughter.*

Maria and Bruno were frightened obviously, but they dug in their heels. This was Canada. A free country. *And we were here first.* They confronted the danger head-on. Bruno barred up the windows and installed a fancy security system.

They trained staff to be diligent, and they hired several Muslim workers, thinking to bridge the cultural divide. They befriended neighbouring businesses, they attended events at the local mosque. None of it mattered. The intimidation became more brazen.

For every incident, they painstakingly filed police reports. They went to court frequently, but never got justice. The courts were lenient, and the cops didn't care.

"Right before it happened, we'd already decided to leave," Maria stated. "We were scouting locations in East Vancouver. Right here on The Drive."

"What happened? You wanna tell me?"

She turned to see if Isabella was in earshot. "One night, Bruno's closing up late. The parking lot's dark. Course, he's aware of the danger. He'd had a few run-ins. He even had a gun for protection. *He wanted me to get one.*"

"Welcome to the new Vancouver."

"He was attacked by a mob, it's all on video. They came outta nowhere, he couldn't get the gun out in time. Bruno was a big guy with a booming voice. He was intimidating, ask anyone. But they were too many." Her voice caught. "I only watched it once. They beat the hell out of him. They beat him so badly," she was sniffling now. "He was on life support for a week, but he didn't make it. He was *never* gonna make it."

I put my hand on hers. "I'm so sorry for your loss." I didn't know what else to say.

After a few moments: "It's been five years."

"Twelve since I lost Lisa." I'd already shared my highlights. *And lowlights.* Maria actually remembered the story. She'd followed my rise and fall.

"When does it get better?"

I sighed. "I'll let you know when I find out."

"I don't know how you went on," she said. "You lost a child, too. I thank God every day I still have Isabella. Don't know what I'd do without her."

I shrugged. "I still have Vinny."

"He's a beauty." Maria knew Vinny, if you can believe it. Cindy, too. They weren't regulars, but they'd been in the cafe. Vinny was memorable.

We had ourselves quite a heart-to-heart, Maria and I did. Amazing what you can learn in a short time. Hard to believe we were both widows for essentially the same reason.

The door opened and in walked Ivan, precisely on time. You could set your watch by that guy. Maria fussed over him. She was a hostess to reckon with.

After we got settled: "Ain't she a little young for you, grandpa?" Ivan missed nothing.

"Not this again."

He grinned evilly. "You're making moves, aren't ya?"

"Maybe."

"How old is she?"

"None of your business."

He chortled. "She looks forty and you look seventy-five."

"You look like shit at any age."

"I'm married, dude. Doesn't matter what I look like."

"Good point."

Truth be told, for the first time in a decade, I cared about my appearance. I tended to it. This strange new behaviour started the day I met Maria. I was like a teenager all over again. Crazy, eh?

Chapter 53 – Impending Doom

Shortly after Ivan's arrival, the lunch crowd descended and kept Isabella and Maria hopping. "I love this place," said Ivan. "Coffee's great, Maria's great. But maybe next time you wanna come to my place? Some of the riffraff out on the street. Jesus."

"You're such a chicken."

"I watch out for myself, nothing wrong with that." He sipped his caramel macchiato.

"I see you ordered the vente, today. Does that mean you got your period?"

"Look at this, the Tony of old. *He's back.* She's really got your spirit fired up, eh buddy?"

I tried to suppress laughter.

Ivan didn't relent: "On the way over, I saw a fucking building on fire just off Main. Huge fucking blaze. You musta saw the smoke?"

"Do we still have fire departments?"

"They were there, squirting water on it."

Maria squeezed her ample derriere past our table, and Ivan grinned at me like a caveman.

"Easy pal, back off."

His hands shot up in mock surrender. "Anyway, I worry man. East Van's going off. I don't really feel safe here."

"Relax Nancy. You mentioned some news?"

Ivan buried his face in his hands for a long time. When he finally emerged, he regarded me solemnly. "Not good, Tony. I don't think you know, or you woulda brought it up."

"Jesus Ivan, you're worrying me."

"It's terrible." He drew an enormously deep breath. "I hate to hit ya with this…"

"Just fucking tell me."

"Danny Boy was shot dead last night."

"What?" I put a hand to my forehead. *"Jesus Christ!"*

"I know, man. I talked to him not a week ago. He told me he was worried. Said he feared for his life."

"For good reason, apparently."

"Those crazy fuckers he's up against, they live in the past. Some feud from back in India. Some old score to settle."

"Dhanesh didn't care about that shit."

"Maybe that was the problem." Ivan paused for a sip. "A lotta these hit jobs lately. A lotta guys suffering the same fate."

"Politics ain't no picnic. Not anymore."

Maria wandered by and frowned at me, as if to say *what's upsetting you?* I gave her an *it's all good* gesture, which she didn't buy.

"You know the details?" I asked.

"They ambushed him in his driveway. They were laying in wait. Boom, boom, two shots to the head. Mafia style, eh? Killed his bodyguard, too. Probably got him first. At least they didn't go after his wife and kids."

"Who was it?"

"I hear it was a rival from the same party."

"Jesus."

"Who told ya?"

"Charles Kennedy, who else. He said it was retaliatory."

"Whoa."

"Hasn't made the news yet – *they cover this shit up all the time* – but this is too big. They're gonna make a big deal of it, Charles told me. Call it an assassination, a national tragedy. His star's gonna shine brighter in death. Charles' words."

"Those bastards." The media, I meant.

"The police'll vow to find the killer, they'll spout the usual platitudes."

"Awesome."

Ivan went for a bathroom break, leaving me to ponder the fresh horror. Man oh man, I was still reeling from the shock of losing Leo. Now this. The carnage was coming fast and furious, and adding to my sense of impending doom.

This one hurt, I hate to say it, more than my own son. *Danny Boy.* I loved the guy. Loved him with all my heart. He saved me, too. I was dead meat. Mo and his boys were gonna nail me. What does Dhanesh do? The fucker goes out on a limb to save my ass.

Something else clicked, something Vinny mentioned a few months back. There'd been a riot at Mountain, and Mo got whacked. Taken out by his own car. What a sordid mess. And now prison-yard protocol ruled the streets. And the political class, evidently. *Jesus.*

Ivan returned and lunch arrived. Pastrami on rye for him, a BLT for me. For a few precious moments, Maria cast her spell of bonhomie. She cheered me up, and distracted me from the icy shadow of death. The food helped, too. Maria was all that, and she could cook. *Bravissimo.*

"You see a lotta Charles Kennedy these days, eh?"

Ivan washed down a mouthful with a gulp of ginger ale. "Couple times a week maybe. He's chattier than he used to be. Asks about you sometimes."

"He does, eh? What's his deal?"

"Fuck if I know. Government guy. Still on the payroll."

"Are guys like him gettin' whacked?"

"Guys like him?"

"Pasty white conservatives."

"Ah, I see." Ivan grinned. "There ain't too many of 'em still in politics."

"*Cuckservatives*," I corrected myself. "He's as cucky as they come."

Ivan nodded. "His principles are definitely flexible."

"Exactly." I scoffed. "They're whatever they need to be. Goddamn *mangiacake*." I hadn't used that word in years. Took me by surprise, and came across as small and petty, even to my ears.

"You're still jealous of him?" Ivan chuckled.

I scoffed again, which seemed to prove Ivan's point. *After all these years, I still was. What the hell's wrong with me?*

"How's he do it?" I asked. "I mean, he's the classic straight white male. Guys like him are supposed to be despised, aren't they?"

"There are exceptions. Charles plays the game well. He adapts, he kisses the right asses."

"He's always been the type. Kinda guy who rails against white privilege, and somehow keeps his job."

"He's smooth, gotta give it to him. Expert with the PC dogma. Always up-to-date with the lingo, which is always changing. They gotta keep people off balance."

"It's all bullshit. Charles is a bullshit artist."

Ivan smiled broadly. "You *are* the Tony of old. Jesus, Maria's like a drug for you. Like you been snorting coke."

"Fuck off." I was laughing as I said it.

"To answer your question, I don't know what the fuck he does. He's always flying off to Ottawa on mysterious business."

"How you know it's Ottawa?"

"That's what he tells me. Heck, for all I know it's Beijing. Charles' lifestyle hasn't changed much, I'd say."

"Sometimes I wonder if *he's* the enemy."

"You haven't seen the guy in ten fucking years."

"He just seems...*evil.*"

Ivan chuckled. "That's why I stay on his good side."

"Put in a good word for me, eh?"

"What, and let 'im know I got friends in low places?"

"Bastard." I polished off the last of my sandwich. "What else ya got to say for yourself?"

"Rome's falling, dude."

"Tell me something I don't know. How'd it happen?"

He pondered for a moment. "Altruism and indifference, I'd say. The Achilles heels of any Judeo-Christian society."

"I think our biggest problem was the useful idiots. That and the fear of being called racist. That fucked us over big time."

"You're not wrong." Ivan nodded.

"It made us vulnerable, allowed the evil in. The people intent on destroying civilization."

"And once they're in, they use the system to destroy the system. Ironic eh?"

"Makes my head hurt." I checked my phone. "Hey what the fuck, I got no service."

Ivan snatched his phone. "Me neither."

Just then, a commotion erupted in the street. Shouting bodies running past the storefront. I stood to get a better look.

What I saw struck fear in my heart.

Chapter 54 – Chaos

The street was thick with bodies. A riot? *Or a stampede?* Waves of rampagers, hundreds it seemed. The noise was deafening. Not so much shouting as cries of war.

They brandished clubs and sticks and knives. The swarm was so sudden, bystanders were swept up in the fray. Beaten, trampled, savaged. One ominous character wielded a machete. Another a hatchet. The weapons were not for show. People were brutalized as they scrambled for cover.

I saw one man viciously clubbed. He collapsed instantly. A fatal blow? I had no time to ponder, as fresh horror piled on. An elderly woman was bowled over by a joyous reveller. A toddler snatched by the ankle and hurled ferociously against a concrete wall. The attackers didn't dwell, they moved toward new adventure and havoc, and more aggressors kept coming.

I watched aghast. We all did. It was so quick. A few shots rang out. The rampaging or the rampaged? I couldn't tell. Bodies piled up, and the onslaught continued.

Some had faces covered, but not all. Those I saw were gleeful, maniacal, homicidal. There was no mistaking them – they were African. This form of mayhem, this *feral-ness* had the unmistakable stamp. I'd not seen such primitive barbarism in any other group. I doubted others capable of it.

I felt a flare in my cerebral cortex. *Racist.* Even now, the old patterns lived. I ignored the message. It served no purpose. I'd seen these raging mobs in places like Melbourne and Dublin, and of course South Africa. The media rarely reported them, and when they did, they spoke of *troublesome teens.* But footage was there for the curious. I'd seen it on Rebel Media, I'd seen it on Colin Flaherty's videos.

This is what Leo faced. Youths with no empathy, no understanding of consequence. I'd seen them up close in Mountain. They looked to be Somali. Their numbers had swelled in North Surrey and pockets of South-Central Vancouver.

But not here. This wasn't their turf. They had no business here.

But they kept coming, wave after wave. Was there no end? People desperately tried to escape. One man pushed his way into a hair salon. Several Somalis followed.

I was stunned by the violence – we all were – but the incident snapped me to attention. "*Jesus Christ,* we gotta lock up, Maria. We gotta lock this place up." As if to confirm, a brick smashed through the window. Thank God it was barred.

"Oh my God, the keys are in the back." She rushed off.

"Hurry," I said, as an immense figure materialized in front of the now-broken plate glass window.

Tiny.

He was fighting off three smaller attackers, one brandishing a knife. Tiny's right hand was oozing blood. The men circled, taunting and hopping. They had mob madness in their eyes, greedy and murderous.

We had to let Tiny in. Among our assets, I spotted two hardy young lads. Twenty-somethings. Maria was on her way back, I heard keys rattle as she pushed through. She also sported a baseball bat. *God love her.*

As she started to lock the door: "Hold up, Maria." I blocked her. "My boy Tiny's out there. We can't leave 'im. *They'll kill 'im.*" The kid with the knife took a wild swing which Tiny dodged, backing him into our door. He neatly stepped forward and socked the attacker in the jaw. Tiny was surprisingly quick, and the youngster crumpled and retreated. His cohorts also scattered.

The respite was temporary. They came back angrier, more determined to take down the big white man. I took the bat from Maria without asking.

"Oh my God, Tony. What are you doing? *You can't go out there.*" Her voice was panicked.

The bat was a Louisville Slugger. It felt good in my hands, a good weight. "You guys." I pointed to the strapping kids. "Back me up. I'm gonna scare these fuckers so we get Tiny in. *Alright?*"

The bigger of the two stepped forward. "You got it, sir. My name's Matt. This here's Nathan." The smaller one was less enthusiastic but didn't shy from duty. I spotted Ivan from the corner of my eye. He'd retreated several layers back. I'd give him a ribbing, later. *If there was a later.*

No point hesitating. I opened the door and stepped out. I tried to appear big and threatening, yet invisible to the remaining hordes. Their numbers had dwindled, I noticed.

"This way Tiny," I bellowed. "*This way.*"

He recognized the help and backed up slowly. As he did, I stepped forward brandishing the bat. The attackers laughed. They pegged me for an old guy, easy pickings. Maybe they were right. One of them feigned attack, and I flinched badly. Their mocking laughter was blood-curdling.

However, their faces changed when my young friends appeared. Matt pretended to throw something, and this time the attackers flinched. Was a good bluff, not something we planned.

"Get inside," Maria yelled, and we didn't have to be asked twice. We all bolted in and got the door shut just in time. Maria took charge. She locked up tight, throwing a series of deadbolts.

The laughter turned to rage. They tested the door with fists and feet, and I was sure it'd give. But it held. We didn't taunt, we didn't make eye contact. After a few minutes, they lost interest.

"You okay, Tiny?" His right hand was covered in blood.

"*You saved my fucking life.*" He hugged me in appreciation.

"Don't mention it," I said. "And you're getting blood on my shirt."

"Oops, sorry." Tiny held his arm aloft. His sleeve sported numerous incisions, but none had penetrated the thick leather. "My coat saved me, too," he said. "They got me good here, though."

The gash was on the back of his hand. Not devastating, but it could use stitches.

"I'll get the first-aid kit." Maria rushed off. The panicky edge in her voice was gone, and that did wonders for my spirit.

"What the fuck's going on, Tiny? You heard anything?"

"Shit's going down everywhere. Right before my cell died, I heard they raided the Burnaby house. Vinny said don't go back."

"Where is Vinny?"

"No idea."

Maria was tending to Tiny's hand. Some gathered around. Others huddled in their own private conversations. The number of rampagers outside had further thinned.

"What happened out there Tiny?"

"I'm in my car, next thing I know they're everywhere. Some running over top of the damn thing. I couldn't drive without mowing 'em down, and I fucking thought about that. So I don't know what to do, an' I see Rocco get out.

Then *he's* getting attacked. I figure I'll help. I get out, and *boom* they're on me, I'm getting swarmed. I take a few shots." He tilted his head and showed bruising along jawline and cheek. "They're like little ants – I'm swatting 'em left and right." Tiny attempted a gesture and Maria scolded sharply – she was tending his wounded hand.

"Sorry," he said with a grin. "An' I left my gun in the glovebox. *Fuckin' rookie.* Anyhow, I get my back to a wall and I'm fightin' 'em off, inching my way towards youz guys – *Vinny'd kill me if I let something happen to you.*"

I nodded appreciatively.

"Then *you* end up saving me. Crazy. Can't thank you enough, Tony."

"Don't mention it," I said. "What happened to Rocco?"

Tiny sucked air through his teeth. "Dunno, man. Wasn't looking good."

"What are we supposed to do now?" One man called out in a tone that could easily incite panic.

"Hey, *relax.*" I said. "We're safe here."

"We have to wait it out," said Maria. "We've had riots before. They always fizzle out."

"Like this?"

"Not like this." She laughed bitterly. "Never seen anything like this."

The man retreated to his seat. People spoke in hushed tones, they checked phones that didn't work. I heard a helicopter flying overhead.

"It's stopping," Matt announced. He'd been standing vigil at the window.

He was right. Just like that, it stopped. No more stampede. No more shouts and cries. Like someone turned off a tap. It felt like forever, but the chaos had lasted only a couple minutes. An eerie calm descended.

"Is it safe to go out?" The panicky man hollered.

"Better wait awhile," I said. Heads nodded.

I scanned up and down the street. Bodies were strewn, but not as many as I'd feared. I counted twelve. Most had escaped. I looked into storefronts and saw other heads peering out cautiously.

What to do?

Wait it out, was my instinct. *Wait what out?* Wait for the rule of law to be restored? Good luck with that. I suppose just wait and see what happens, if anything.

Then what?

They raided the Burnaby house, Tiny had said. He didn't know where Vinny was. My phone didn't work. No one's did.

I took a headcount. Fourteen of us, seven adult males, one of whom was Ivan, and he didn't count. Then again, Tiny counted for two. I chuckled mirthlessly.

We had a baseball bat. We could probably dig up knives in the kitchen. No guns. Hopefully this wouldn't come to a fight. I didn't like our chances.

"Holy fuck," Matt yelped. *"What the hell is this?"*

Jesus Christ. A convoy of military vehicles in tight formation made its way down Commercial. Heavily armoured and decked in army camouflage. They appeared indestructible.

Shock and awe again, but the rigid order and symmetry was in stark contrast to the earlier chaos. If these guys weren't friendly, Tiny wasn't gonna fight *them* off.

The formation paused as soldiers poured out to retrieve the dead and wounded. They worked their way down the Drive with machine-like efficiency. Before long, the procession was out of sight.

Who were they? Where'd they come from? Questions floated around in whispers. They wore green uniforms with red trim. They were armed and jack-booted. Every single man was Asian. I doubted they were Canadian. *Nor American.*

Ivan was suddenly at my side. "That was interesting."

"Who the fuck—"

"Definitely Chinese," he said. "The uniforms were a giveaway."

"What's going on, dude?" I stared at him intently. Maria and Isabella hung nervously in the background.

"When I saw the anarchy," he started, "*and then my phone's not working* – I thought this is it. *The Singularity.* Ya know, when the computers finally take over. I always figured they'd just turn everything off and let the dregs run wild."

Ivan was the smartest guy in most rooms, but this was ridiculous.

He laughed briefly. "A silly thought, really. I'm lost without my phone."

"You were shitting yourself, pal."

"I still am."

"Those weren't fucking computers running down the street. *The Singularity.* What's wrong with you?"

Ivan ignored me. "The prophecies say the Second Coming shall be sudden and unmistakable, *like a flash of lightning.* That riot, whatever it was, that would qualify."

"What have you been smoking?"

He continued to ignore me. "This theory made more sense. The anti-Christ has been among us, perverting us, inspiring sin and depravity."

"You mean Leftism?"

He looked me in the eye. "What did Father Fazzio used to say? *The devil doesn't come with horns and hooves.*"

"And he's a liar. The devil I mean."

"We could use Jesus right now," Maria said.

"Amen," Ivan agreed.

"Look," I said. "We can say our prayers soon, but seriously Ivan. Put the crazy shit away. What do you really think?"

"I think we picked a bad day to meet for coffee."

"No shit."

"I'm glad you're here," Maria said.

I put my hand on hers. "Me too."

Ivan was staring at his phone. "It's working."

"What?"

"My phone. *I'm online.*"

"Get the fuck out." I snatched mine from my pocket. "Aw Christ, I'm not."

"Me neither," said Maria.

We soon deduced that only West Side residents had been bestowed access. They got busy sending texts, making calls, perusing propaganda. Meanwhile, Ivan was all over the Dark Web, trying to piece things together.

He finally looked up. "It's a global event," he said. "Chaos everywhere."

Shock and disbelief.

"Lots of gossip and rumour." He was tapping and swiping as he spoke. "Those military troops, they're calling 'em *Peacekeepers.*" He smiled an ugly smile. "Hopefully they live up to the name, 'cause lots of atrocities going down. Ugly stuff. Rape, torture. People dying."

"We saw it with our own eyes."

"Worse than what we saw." He shook his head. "Women are always the spoils of war. An age-old truth."

I patted Maria's hand protectively.

"It's everywhere. America, Europe, Australia." He flipped through some more screens. "They're saying arsonists and looters will be shot on site."

He finally looked up. "It's almost as if..." he was thinking hard, "...the rampage was staged. A stunt to scare us, to put us off balance. They used the same pattern everywhere. Like a stick of dynamite. Architected chaos."

"What's happening in North Burnaby? Can you track down Vinny?"

"Sorry pal, I been looking. No one's online."

"Fuck."

"Don't worry, if anyone'll be fine, it's Vinny. You know that."

I said a silent prayer for Vinny and Cindy and Young Julio. I prayed for us, too, singling out Maria and her daughter for special protection.

It dawned on me. I hadn't asked after Ivan's family. He rarely talked about them. "Hey bud, how's Petra and Sasha? You made contact?"

"Thanks for asking. They're good." He shrugged dramatically. "The streets are safe my side of town. No fighting, no riots. Nothing."

"Lucky you."

"*Lucky me?* I'm here, aren't I? Rumour is, the West Side's some sort of protected zone. Those soldiers, *Peacekeepers*, whatever they are...they're *guarding* it."

"What the fuck?"

He nodded emphatically. "Looks like they have them everywhere, all the cities."

"Protected Zones? What is this, the wealthy circling the wagons?"

"The wealthy ain't that smart, trust me. This isn't natural, it's not organic. It's orchestrated. Part of some grand fucking design."

"Why you say that?"

"In London, the chaos was Pakistani Muslims. A million of the fuckers took the streets. They went insane, they swarmed everywhere. It was Muslims in Brussels, too. And Cologne."

"What, are you Islamaphobic? You go to prison for that."

"There ain't no prisons, dude." He scoffed. "*Or maybe we're all in prison?* Anyway, in Paris it was the Africans. In New York, Chicago, Philly, the Blacks. The Sudanese in Melbourne."

"For us, it was Somalis," I said. "I'd bet money on it."

"They used different triggers everywhere, different groups to incite the panic. All to the same effect, of course."

"Did they use any white people?" I asked.

He grinned. "Not to stereotype, but I think whoever pulled these puppet strings looked at tendencies. I'd say they picked groups with a penchant for this type of thing, if ya know what I'm saying."

I nodded.

"Some places had it real bad. Correction, *still* have it bad. These Peacekeepers are ruthless, but apparently they haven't shut down all the turmoil yet. Not everywhere."

"Like where?"

"Houston. Atlanta. Miami. Those southern cities."

"'Cause of the Second Amendment?"

"No man, 'cause they got lots of criminals. Prisoners running loose everywhere. If you ain't in a protected zone, you're fucked. 'Specially if you're white."

I said a prayer for Bucky Bradford and his family.

"People are going out on the street," Matt announced.

We looked out the window in unison. "Speaking of not being in a protected zone," Ivan said. "I think it's time for me to head home."

Since the military sweep, an hour had slipped away. Everyone was restless. Some were testing the waters, the panicky man included. "Time to go," he said. "I live a few blocks away. I need to check my house."

"Careful, my friend," I said. What else was I gonna say? I had no idea if he'd be safe. If his house had been raided. Evidently mine had.

"I need to check my house, too," said Maria.

"Where do you live?"

She nodded south. "Ten blocks that way."

Ivan shook his head. "It's bad up near Skytrain. Even the public feed is saying so. And they're trying to pretend everything's normal."

"My street's usually good," Maria protested. "We look out for each other. It's always been like that."

She didn't sound convincing, and I pondered my own situation. I wasn't about to go home, *but where the fuck was I gonna go?* It was past six-thirty. Darkness wasn't far off.

Matt appeared at my side and whispered. "We're gonna make a move, Tony. Seems like the thing to do."

"Where you guys live?"

"West Side," said Matt. "We took SkyTrain."

"Hey Tiny, how many can we squeeze into your SUV?" An idea was forming.

"Eight. More if we need to."

We numbered seven – me and Ivan. Isabella and Maria. Matt and Nathan. And Tiny, of course. "Perfect. Let's take a road trip."

"Where we going?"

"Where else? The West Side."

Chapter 55 – Escape

Before we left, we raided *Café Maria's* kitchen, stocking up on food and water. Adrenaline was flowing, but I wolfed a spicy Italian panini and some pasta salad. It would stick to my ribs, as Lisa used to say. The others ate, too, except Ivan who was nervous as a kitten.

"Time to get the heck outta here," I announced. "Where you parked, Tiny?"

"One block that way." He pointed north.

"Perfect. Gimme a chance for a smoke on the way."

"You smoke?" Maria shot me a scolding glance.

"Sometimes." I gave her a wink, and shook one out of the pack. "I'm almost out, *damnit.*"

"Hopefully the car's okay," said Ivan.

"Lighten up, brother." I placed a hand on his shoulder. "We're gonna be fine."

I had no playbook, no idea what to expect. My thought was to make our way to Ivan's place, but I hadn't told him yet. Or maybe Matt's? Whether we could navigate there in one piece was anyone's guess. Were we in danger from roving gangs? The Peacekeepers? We'd soon find out.

But my confidence was surging. I was in God's hands. I felt His presence and the others responded to my leadership without challenge. They sought my guidance, *they craved it.*

Out on The Drive, Ivan couldn't hide his terror. I was scared, too. I won't lie. The sun had set but we still had nautical twilight, and streetlights. They still worked.

I spotted another group across the street, but this was no Sunday stroll. We ignored them and beelined for our ride. We passed a trail of devastation, broken glass, trashed storefronts, rubbish. We gave a wide berth to a car on fire. Maria wiped away tears. Commercial was her territory. Her home.

Perfect timing, we arrived at the SUV just as I finished my cigarette. Tiny opened up and went straight for the glovebox.

"Ahhhh, still here." He lovingly cradled the pistol. "Finally, I can relax."

I got no pushback from Tiny when I suggested Matt take the wheel. I liked this kid. He was on the ball, not phased in the least by the situation. Not showing it anyway. My affection for him felt almost paternal, and I conjured an image of Julio. A pang of sadness hit, but I pushed it away. Grief was a luxury.

I put Ivan shotgun, though he wasn't keen. I wanted West Siders up front. Maria, Tiny and I took the middle row, Isabella and Nathan piled in the back. Off to the races.

I figured we'd take side streets to Clarke, then zip up to Great Northern Way. From there, scoot unscathed to the apparent safety of the West Side.

A block from the Drive, we encountered our first hiccup. The roadway was blocked with assorted debris – shopping buggies, a park bench, cardboard boxes. When Matt came to a stop, the bad guys descended.

"It's a trap," Tiny hollered.

They numbered at least ten, and scared the daylights out of us. Forget sticks and pipes, these bastards had guns. They pointed them at us, they rapped them on our windows, they screamed threats and obscenities. I had no idea what they wanted, and no desire to find out.

No faces covered here, and they weren't Somali. They were a mashup – Hispanic, Asian, Middle Eastern? A mixed-race mob, every bit as mean as the Africans.

"The sidewalk," Tiny screamed. *"Take the sidewalk."*

Matt didn't hesitate. We hopped the curb and he floored it. The gunfire was immediate, and everyone ducked, except Tiny.

"Hey, we got bullet-proof glass. We got bullet-proof *everything.*"

As he said it, more bodies emerged, these ones blocking the sidewalk and firing at us. We were in a shooting gallery.

"Holy fuck." A twinge of panic in Matt's voice.

"Don't stop," Tiny said. "Run 'em over if ya have to."

Matt showed his nerve and complied. At the last second, the goons dove out of the way, but one poor sonofabitch got clipped. The thump made me cringe.

"Don't worry 'bout it." Tiny patted Matt's shoulder. "They're scumbags."

Tiny was a true East Ender. I was glad he was on my side. "Maybe I shoulda let you drive, Tiny."

"The kid's doin' fine."

He was. I glanced back to make sure no one was in hot pursuit. *Nope.* And already we were approaching the iconic East Van Cross on Clarke.

Matt grinned. "Hopefully that's the end of it."

It wasn't. We encountered more stray thugs along the way, some white ones even. We were taunted and harassed. They threw rocks and bottles. They shot at us.

"Where's a cop when you need one?" I quipped at one point. It got a laugh.

Stoplights – *amazingly, they were still in operation* – were a frequent hazard but traffic was eerily light, and we started running reds. Thank God for the bullet-proof everything. We woulda been screwed otherwise.

In between bouts of drama, Ivan kept a close eye on his phone. "The Peacekeepers have a roadblock at Second and Main. We should probably take a detour."

I agreed, and we zipped up to 6th Avenue. Miraculously, we crossed Main with no challenge. A couple blocks later, Ontario. We were on the West Side, at least technically. The true West Side didn't start 'til Oak Street.

"Jesus, they got roadblocks everywhere. Cambie's like a giant wall."

"Pull over, Matt. We better think this through."

Ivan glanced around nervously. Despite the streetlights, it was dark enough to provide cover for an assault. So far, no more bad guys, but we weren't about to get out and stretch our legs.

"Where we going anyway?" Ivan finally asked, a noticeable whine in his voice. I knew it was on his mind.

"You got room for a few guests, pal?"

He shrugged, not good-naturedly. "You think that's a good idea?"

"You got a better one?"

He sighed miserably.

"Where you guys live, Matt?"

"Tenth and Blenheim. Not a lot of spare room, though." Nathan confirmed with a nod. They were privileged white kids, attending UBC, living in a bubble.

"*Chez Ivan*, it is." But was that possible? They were looking to me for direction, and I felt the weight of leadership. It was more a puzzle than a burden. "What's this about a wall?"

"See for yourself." Ivan held up his phone and showed me an impressive military-style presence. Vehicles, armed personnel, flashing lights. "That's Cambie and 16th. They're calling it a security check. They're asking for ID."

"I'm not going," Tiny announced. "No way, no how. I don't think you should either, Tony. Just sayin'."

Tiny had a deep distrust of law enforcement. Who didn't, these days? But his had been honed across a lifetime.

"We don't have a choice—"

"What the hell?" Matt cut me off. A young boy peered cautiously at us from across the street. He was mostly hidden behind a tree, but I'd seen a flash of movement. His hair was impossible to miss. It was blonde. *Almost white.* Judging from his body language, the poor little guy was petrified.

I unrolled my window. "Hey kid, you okay?"

No answer.

"We won't hurt you. What you doing out here?"

"You want me to get him?" Matt offered.

Ivan started to protest but I silenced him with a glare. "Yeah go. That kid needs our help."

The youngster tried to run when Matt got close, but didn't get far. Matt scooped him up, and the kid struggled only for a moment. He seemed to sense no immediate danger. Matt led him back to the SUV.

"Who's this little guy then?" I said it jovially, hoping to break the kid's shell. Didn't work. He was frightened, and a little beat up, too. He seemed close to tears. Maria's motherly instinct kicked in and she took him in her arms, and rocked him gently. He sobbed for a few minutes, but snapped out of it.

"What's your name?" She asked.

"Spencer."

"How old are you, Spencer?"

"Ten."

She spoke in soft tones and slowly drew him out. He'd been living with his family near SkyTrain. It was never great. *Not many kids like me*, he explained. *I got picked on. We all did, but especially me on account of my hair. Always been like that.*

When the chaos struck, his family was attacked in their home, his sisters and mother raped in front of the father.

They were all tortured, and eventually killed. Young Spencer hid throughout the ordeal and escaped later when the bandits left. He didn't see the horror, but he heard it.

I didn't bother asking who did it. I'd heard enough. Poor Spencer was scared and alone. Heartbroken over the loss of his family members, and racked with guilt, to boot. Maria comforted him. No way we were letting him back out on his own. He wouldn't stand a chance.

Earlier, Spencer had got within a block of Cambie. *I heard it was safe there*, he said. When he saw the checkpoints, the armed soldiers, the military vehicles, he couldn't work up the nerve to approach.

We picked up a few other choice tidbits. He was an observant lad. He had to be to stay alive. The area near his house was mixed-race, a few lone whites. They were scared like him, and they mostly stuck together. But even they were dangerous to Spencer.

Racial alliances came and went, he said. Whites were always outnumbered, always a target, singled out for violence by the competing factions – Indians, Chinese, Blacks. Spencer wasn't specific, but confirmed some groups were crueler than others, more prone to attack. Some were defensive, they huddled. After today's theatrics, I assumed, if anything, the situation was worse.

It was the Wild West. Survival of fittest, where the weak and infirm perish. For poor Spencer, everyone was a threat. Every place, hostile territory. He was a boy without a home. Without a country.

Maria asked him if he was hungry and he looked up shyly and nodded. She passed him a ham and cheese sandwich, and he scarfed it like he hadn't eaten in a week. When he accepted a second, I saw a hint of a smile. He was a shockingly cute little bambino.

We were fascinated with Spencer, but also restless and uncertain. Especially Ivan. He desperately wanted to be home in bed hiding under the covers. I didn't blame him.

Meanwhile, Tiny steadfastly refused to engage the Peacekeepers. "I ain't going. Period."

"What do you wanna do?" I asked.

"I got a place in mind. Off King Ed and Alberta. I know a guy. Vinny knows him, too. Obviously, I can't call...and no guarantees...but it should be good. I'll take my chances. I think you should too. *All a youz.*"

"I don't wanna go, either," Spencer announced.

"They're not *arresting* anyone." Ivan pointed at his phone, as if for evidence. "The worst they do is say no. But they'll let *me* in. *I* live there."

"Lucky you," I said.

"Let's go to my buddy's place," Tiny said. "It's close to Cambie. You guys can walk from there."

A plan crystallized. We parked at the safe house and Tiny made contact. There was some debate and handwringing. I suggested perhaps Maria and Isabella remain with Tiny. "I got nothing to lose," I said. "I've been in prison."

Maria was adamant. "If you're going, we're going."

In the end, Spencer and Tiny stayed while the rest of us trekked toward Cambie on an imprecise mission. I was tempted to call it off, but we'd come this far. I was curious. I had to see this for myself.

If we made it to the other side, Ivan's wife would be waiting to whisk us away. If not, we walk back.

Easy peasy, right?

Whatever. I was ignoring a million concerns and I knew it. I had no choice.

Chapter 56 – The Peacekeepers

During our approach, doubt and fear gnawed but I kept my resolve. I sported a confident air to inspire the others, but Ivan didn't seem to need it. He was walking tall. Not so much as a whinge since we left.

I assumed he was excited about reuniting with his family, and the rest of the hypocritical liberals. Is that what they were? Was that concept still valid?

I felt a slight resentment. The West Siders had functional Internet and armed security. Another example of the rich isolating themselves from the consequences of what they created. Was that actually true? No idea. At this point, I didn't know up from down.

15th Avenue was a leafy side street, but commerce was close by and there would normally be sporadic traffic and pedestrians. Not today.

Once we crossed Yukon, the military presence was evident. We heard voices, we saw reflecting lights. We were *this close* to the so-called *wall* and my anxiety flared. When I got a glimpse of the Peacekeepers, it got worse. They looked anything but peaceful.

I tapped Ivan's shoulder. "Maybe we could sneak in?" It was the East Van in me.

"Are you kidding?"

"Just an idea."

"A dumb idea." Ivan consulted his phone. "These guys will be ruthless if you play games."

I resented his tone. What the hell had gotten into him?

The full spectrum of Peacekeeper presence became apparent. Cambie was flooded with light and a fleet of armoured cars gathered at the intersection. Some of the larger models resembled tanks, with built-in turret and machine gun. *Jesus.*

Soldiers stood in clusters. I expected five or six, maybe ten, but there had to be near a hundred. They wore body armour and wielded assault rifles. We wouldn't fare well in a fight, or a chase. Nor would any East Side street gang. They'd figure that out, if they hadn't already.

If the display was meant to intimidate, it was working. The soldiers were aware of our presence, but made no move to engage. I could hear them speaking, and it wasn't in English. When we got close, one of their charge emerged. He wore a slightly different uniform, and possessed an air of authority. Top man, I assumed.

He approached slowly, followed by several minions. "Can I help you?" His English was heavily accented. His tone did not convey an intent to help.

Ivan lost his nerve, but managed a response. "I, uh, live in, uh, Point Grey. My name is—"

"I know who you are." The Commander waved him off and consulted a tablet. "I know all of you."

I thought seeing them up close would humanize them. *Nope.* The soldiers were neat and trim and clean-shaven. All male, all roughly the same height – a couple inches shy of six feet. They were expressionless, like robots, clones of each other. The uniforms were immaculate, finely pressed with razor-sharp creases. They bore a five-star red flag on one armband and Chinese characters emblazoned on the lapels.

The Commander stood out. He was older, and wore a ribbon bar with an impressive array of awards and medals. He was clearly a higher rank, some sort of section-leader, perhaps.

"We have been monitoring your progress," the Commander proclaimed. He turned and spoke sharply to nearby minions, then consulted his tablet.

Finally: "You, you, you." He pointed at Ivan, Matt and Nathan. "Go with them. *Go now.*"

They complied, but as Ivan stepped forward, he meekly pointed at me and blurted: "He knows Charles. *He knows Charles Kennedy.*"

The Commander eyed Ivan suspiciously. So did I. "Charles Kennedy said it'd be okay if, uh, if they, uh—"

"Silence," the Commander barked. "I have my instructions. Not on list. See." He waved the tablet rudely in Ivan's face. "*Not on list.*" He was a humourless man. I doubted he'd respond to any charm I might drum up, not that I was feeling the mood.

"I can call Charles." Ivan's whingy tone was back.

The Commander sighed in exasperation. It was the most human thing I'd seen him do. Whatever Ivan had cooked up – *in secret, the bastard* – hadn't worked. We weren't getting in, that was obvious. We'd need to go further up the ladder of command.

Ivan glanced back, a look of sorrow and grief and guilt. Also a shrug that seemed to say *I tried.*

Now I knew why he was confident earlier. He'd sorted out details ahead. He *knew* he was getting in.

But Ivan wasn't done. "I'll talk to Charles," he hollered. "I'll call you."

Finally, I spoke: "Uh, my phone's out. Remember?"

"Oh fuck, that's right." He turned and spoke to the Commander, I presume explaining the situation. For the first time the Commander hesitated. He consulted his tablet, his minions, then his tablet again.

He turned to me: "Give me phone. *Give me.*" I handed it to him and he swiped and tapped for about thirty seconds, pausing occasionally to consult his tablet. "Here. Phone works."

I wanted to ask if he could do Maria's, too, but it seemed unwise. The man's patience was thin. He again pointed to Ivan, Matt, and Nathan: "You come now." Then to us, a dismissive wave. "You go."

Suddenly 16th Avenue toward the west was flooded with bright light. Ivan's wife was waiting in their SUV. Our eastward path also awaited, and we went our separate ways.

We said nothing until we re-entered the leafy and hopefully still-safe side street. It took a moment for my vision to recalibrate from Cambie's intense lighting.

"That was interesting," Maria offered.

I scoffed, as if to say what an understatement. "At least we didn't get arrested."

We laughed out loud, Isabella too. It was an emotional release, an expression of relief.

"And your phone works," Maria said cheerfully.

"That's right. Hey, I can check Facebook."

"You think he'll call?"

"Ivan?"

"No, the Pope. *Of course, Ivan.*" Maria's fiery spirit was back.

"Hope so. Meantime, at least we got a roof over our head tonight."

She nodded. The safe house was in sight, dimly lit and unimpressive from the outside.

"Tiny's looking out for us, too."

"We have to look out for each other," Maria said, and winked at me.

"You bet we do." I pointed to my phone. "Maybe I can get hold of Vinny?"

We made it to the safe house without incident, though Tiny had fallen asleep and neglected to inform the other occupant of our potential arrival. He was a shady-looking character. White, possibly a hint of Italian. Eventually, Tiny descended from his slumber and got us sorted. He was relieved by our arrival. Like a weight off his shoulders.

Young Spencer was still curled up in a blanket at the foot of Tiny's bed. He'd insisted, evidently, on sleeping in the same room. Understandable. He was a frightened child.

The house was sparsely furnished, but comfortable. Miraculously, in the middle of *Armageddon*, everything worked. The electricity was on, the gas fireplace pumped heat, clean water flowed from the taps. An additional bonus, the fridge and pantry were overflowing with food. Even Maria was impressed.

It wasn't a big house, perhaps 1,600 square feet, but there were spare bedrooms – one for me, one for Maria and her daughter. No awkward sleeping arrangements to deal with. I'd been wondering about that, I won't lie.

Tiny had no news, but was keen for our update. When I described our interaction, the extent of Tiny's feedback was *glad I didn't go*. But when I mentioned the functional phone, his eyes lit up. He was desperate to get a hold of Vinny.

We tried to no avail. Tiny tried several other associates. Nothing doing. Just 'cause we had a phone didn't mean they did.

I had no fancy dark Web access, either, so all we got was government feeds. A lotta bullshit propaganda – law enforcement working to restore order, curfew in effect, everyone remain calm. You get the idea.

By midnight, we all retired to respective sleeping quarters. I was exhausted. Tiny assured me there was no danger. The house had airtight security. I must have believed him 'cause I was asleep before my head hit the pillow. I slept dreamlessly and uninterrupted 'til past 9:00 a.m.

I needed it.

Chapter 57 – The Safe House

The next day, I awoke with a start – *a where-the-fuck-am-I* panic. I felt edgy and irritable. It was déjà vu from my time behind bars, when shock awakenings were the norm.

I shook off the cobwebs as reality settled. I had an unspecified sense of dread, but also an inkling of optimism. An uplifting of spirit which I traced entirely to Maria.

By the time I showered and shaved, I felt a thousand percent better, even though I had no clean clothing. I wandered toward the kitchen, lured by the smell of freshly-brewed coffee. As I poured a cup, I spotted Spencer peering around the corner.

"Hey, *buongiorno!*"

He smiled up at me.

I savoured a sip. Stronger than I liked but no complaints. I heard the allure of feminine voices and made my way toward the living room.

"Morning, lazybones," said Maria.

Wow, did she get better-looking overnight? "Morning ladies, sleep okay?" I took a seat at the opposite end of the couch.

"Definitely. Though the bed was a little crowded," Maria mock-glared at Isabella. "This one needed cuddles."

"Don't we all," I said with a cheeky grin. "Where's Tiny?"

"He and the other fellow ducked out. Said they'd be back by noon."

"Hmm."

"How's your appetite? Isabella's volunteered to make brekkie."

"I'm starving."

"Any requests?" Isabella asked.

"Ah, I'd love a salami foccacia. And a nice Biscotti, for after."

She giggled. "I don't think they have any."

"How 'bout bacon and eggs then? And more coffee."

"That I can do." She marched off on a mission.

"Spencer, be a good boy and give her a hand would you?" He didn't have to be asked twice. "Such a cute little boy," said Maria.

I nodded. "Isabella's quite the kid herself."

"I know it."

"Gorgeous like her Mamma."

Maria bowed her head and covered a smile. "You're gonna make me blush."

"Ain't a guy allowed to tell the truth?"

"I guess it's okay." She gathered herself. "I'm not used to male attention since…"

"Bruno?"

"It's old news, but I still miss him."

"Tell me about it. Not a day goes by when I don't miss Lisa and Julio."

She sighed. "Isabella's the same, I worry about her with Bruno gone. And now," she gesticulated, "with the world gone insane."

I leaned over and took her hand. "I'll keep an eye on Isabella, okay?"

"Oh, Tony," she squeezed my hand with astonishing strength. "I appreciate that more than you'll ever know."

"Course it'll be easier if we can figure a few things out." I looked at my phone. "Anything new at your end?"

She shook her head. "You?"

"Nada." I tried Vinny again, no answer.

Then, as if by some divine intervention, my phone rang. We stared at each other in amazement.

"*Ivan,*" I confirmed. "What's up, pal?"

"You survived?"

"No thanks to you."

"I tried."

"You were keeping secrets, that's what you were doing."

"I had to."

"So what's up?"

"Good news, bud. Actually, *great news*. I met with Charles Kennedy. He wants you in, and he's gonna do what he can. Those are his words."

"Wants me in *where*?"

"*Tony, Tony,*" he chuckled, "you got so much to learn." Smug Ivan was back. "Tonight, 6:00 p.m. He's sending a car, bringing you in for a chat."

"This is weird, Ivan."

"You're up for it, eh? Can I tell him?"

"I'm bringing Maria."

"No can do."

"Fuck it, I'm not going then."

"Dude, come for a talk. No strings."

"Not without Maria and Isabella."

Massive sigh. "Here's the thing. They're coming to get you one way or the other."

"*What the fuck?*"

"I'm serious. They're picking you up at six."

"And if I'm not here?"

"They'll find you." A small sigh. "Come in and listen. I swear it'll be okay."

"And I should trust you why? *Mr. Secret Keeper.*"

"'Cause we go back, man. I'm loyal and you know it. We're two of the three musketeers."

I scoffed.

"You gonna be there?"

"Maybe."

"I'll take that as a *yes*. And I'm telling Charles."

"Anything else you can tell me?"

"Not now. Not on the phone." More chuckling. "Talk soon, pal."

I hung up and stared at Maria. "You get all that?"

"I heard everything." Her voice was flat, the shine in her eyes gone.

"Don't worry, I won't desert you guys."

"What if you have no choice?" A hint of hysteria.

"Wait and see." Another squeeze of her hand. "Hey," I hollered toward the kitchen. "*How's brekkie coming?*"

"Come and get it," Isabella sang out. She sounded uncannily like her Mamma.

Isabella had wrangled up quite a feast – scrambled eggs, bacon, sausage, toast, hash browns. Enough to feed an army.

"Hope ya like it." She was proud of her handiwork.

"Think you made enough?"

She giggled. "Tiny's coming back. I, uh, I figured he'd be a big eater. You too, Mr. Fierro."

"Call me Tony. And what are you saying?" I patted my belly.

"I didn't mean—"

"No worries. Let's eat."

"I made all the toast," Spencer announced.

"Nice work, son." I ruffled his hair.

We tucked in mightily, and it tasted as good as it looked. I was pouring myself a second cup of java when we heard the rattle of keys.

A familiar voice boomed, and it wasn't Tiny. "Papa. Where you at Papa?"

Chapter 58 – Vinny's Back

I hugged Vinny almost as hard as he hugged me back. I was with him three days prior, but it felt like a lifetime ago.

I started to make intros, but Vinny already knew Maria and Isabella. He was charming in his trademark rough and coarse way. There was nothing refined about him. Young Spencer took to him straightaway. "Who's this little guy then?" Vinny mock-glared at me. "You have another kid while I wasn't looking, Papa?"

I laughed heartily and explained. Everything tumbled out, the stampede on Commercial, the Peacekeepers, the strange call with Ivan. Vinny processed it like a champion. He asked a few questions, but he had it figured out in no time. He was especially interested in the situation with Maria.

"What's your story?" I finally asked. "Where you been hiding? How's Cindy? *How's Little Julio?* And how the hell'd you connect with this guy?" I pointed at Tiny. "You got no fuckin' phone, pardon my Italian."

"Hey, one question at a time." He waved his hands wildly. "Cindy and Julio are good, I got 'em sealed up tight, not saying where, but don't worry 'bout it." He fished in his pocket and retrieved a shiny iPhone. *"And who says I got no phone?"* He bellowed laughter. "Why you never call, Papa?"

"I called many times."

He grinned. "New number."

"I got a new phone, too." Tiny added.

"We got lotsa new phones," Vinny said. "I gotta guy, *smart guy*, real Brainiac. He got the unlock process figured out, but we get new numbers. And, sometimes we get shut down." Vinny shrugged. "Whatever, we got a black market going. Why not? We're using it to our advantage, put it that way."

Maria, Isabella and Spencer were enjoying Vinny's animated delivery. So was I.

"But yeah, I was SOL for a while. And we had some drama, probably worse than you guys."

"You hungry Vinny?" I pointed at a side table, where stacks of food remained.

Vinny wandered over. "Already ate, but what the heck." He wolfed down a sausage and grabbed a strip of bacon.

"Courtesy of Isabella," I said.

"Not just a pretty face, huh?"

She blushed.

"Where was I?"

"Drama."

"Right." He nodded vigorously. "People panicked. These new cops – *whadaya call 'em? Peacekeepers?* Whatever, I got stories about those fuckers." He belted out a laugh. "They came strutting through the hood, raiding random houses – like your place, Papa. They picked on some of our guys, not too bad though. They fuckin' *nailed* the Muzzies, I hear. And the Somalis. All the troublemakers," more laughter. "They beat those fuckers down."

"Ha, the things I *don't* read about on here." I waved my phone in the air.

"I hear the local Chinese – *the Richmond crowd, South Van, ya know* – I hear they're petrified of the Peacekeepers."

"Interesting." I said, and tried to make sense of that revelation.

"And I heard about the action on Commercial. They set that shit up, eh? They herded the fuckers in and set 'em wild." He gobbled down another sausage. "There were tough battles all over the East Side, too, and I'm not talking Peacekeepers – *everyone ran from them*. They had helicopters and tanks. I thought they might start dropping freakin' bombs, no kidding. But we battled our turf lines. People got hurt, people got, ya know..." he made the *throat slice* gesture. "We did okay. We lost two guys, God bless 'em. Up by Skytrain – that was the worst. Just a couple blocks from where you crazies had to be." He burst out laughing.

"I'm there every day," said Maria. "I work there."

"Not anymore."

Her smile vanished. "I guess not."

"Wait and see," said Vinny. "I can't tell up from down. No one can."

"What's happening today?" I asked. It was almost 3:00 p.m.

He shrugged. "Everyone's layin' low. The Peacekeepers ran a couple patrols, but they left us alone. I tell ya, though. I started worrying about our people. How they gonna eat? Where they gonna get food and water and shit?"

"Some planned ahead, Vinny. Preppers. They been ready for a while, for when all hell breaks loose. When shit hits the fan – that's what they like to say. Ivan told me about 'em."

"Well, I guess I'm one of 'em, 'cause I planned ahead, too. I got this place stocked up eh? You check the freezer downstairs? No one's going hungry here, hey Isabella?" He winked. "But how about the people who didn't plan? They gonna get desperate damn quick."

I nodded.

"But here's the thing," Vinny shook his head in amazement. "You ain't gonna believe it, *whadayaknow*, stores opened up. They're all guarded and shit by the Peacekeepers, but ya just walk in and get your shit. They call 'em *outlets*."

"Who pays for it?"

Vinny shrugged again. "It's fucking free. They don't take no money. An' they don't take no bullshit, either. Start something and they'll shoot ya. And they track everything. Who you are, what ya get. They got limits. Vito told me all this shit. It's a helluva system."

I shook my head in wonder. "Socialism."

"Call it what you want, it ain't fuckin' Venezuela. The shelves are full. They're truckin' shit in, right through the ports, eh Papa?"

"Must be." Vinny was smarter than I thought. *Jesus.*

"Problem is, things like booze, cigarettes, weed. A lotta guys ain't getting' enough, me included. Nothing's perfect, eh?"

A light bulb went off. "Guess they gotta make sure there's *something* to fight over. Keep the tribalism alive, even with Peacekeepers around."

"Oh, it's tribal alright, don't worry. Nothing new there. And if ya ain't protected, you're fucked. Especially if you're white." He pointed at young Spencer. "Don't go running off, eh?"

"You think the racial stuff's gonna get worse?"

"I don't see it gettin' better."

Vinny's turf was mostly white – *over sixty percent* – yet it was also the most ethnically diverse in the Lower Mainland. They had Chinese, Indian, plenty of mixed race. Other areas had become extremely polarized by 2030 – Indians with Indians, Chinese with Chinese, Blacks with Blacks. Certainly, Muslims didn't tolerate non-Muslims. Our city was a microcosm of the planet – only whites tolerated non-whites. This was what lefties called diversity.

"I feel bad for folks stuck in the wrong neighbourhoods," Vinny continued. "Geez, if they thought it was bad before..." He tailed off. "The mixed-race crowd, too. Some of 'em can't find a home. We take in some, but we can't take 'em all."

"Why not?" Maria asked. She was a compassionate soul, I was learning. "Too crowded?"

Vinny shook his head. "It's not space, it's trust. I can't be looking over my shoulder. I don't want some asshole comin' in my turf so he can kill me and skip off. We don't need traitors, only brothers and sisters."

"How do you decide?"

"Simple. They gotta know someone. They gotta get *vouched* for." He shook his head again. "Some gonna get left out in the cold. And they won't last." He sighed. "Not fair. But since when was life fair?"

"So sad," Maria said. "Must be so many frightened young people out there, just 'cause they don't look like us. Or they're not Indian or whatever."

"Hey, we try not to discriminate, but we're mostly white, ain't gonna lie. I ain't no supremacist. Fuck that, I don't want those fuckers. Who says *they're* not gonna kill my girlfriend? Or my kid for that matter."

"I wish everyone could just be nice to each other." Maria said, a silly comment but I wasn't about to say so.

"Blame the government," said Vinny. "They threw people together, they got everyone at each other's throats. What did they expect?"

"I brought that up fifteen years ago, Vinny, and they threw me in jail."

"Just saying."

"So was I."

Vinny's phone rang. "I gotta take this. *Yo, Carmine.*" He wandered down the hall bellowing. The last thing I heard was *what da fuck, those motherfuckers.*

It was a welcome disruption and Isabella brought in tea, coffee, and a selection of biscuits. She was her mother's daughter.

"Ever think about opening a café?" I teased.

She giggled. "Maybe one day."

"If I keep hanging around you guys, I'm gonna outweigh Tiny." I gestured toward him. "No offense, Big Man."

"None taken. While you're up, pass me a chocolate chip cookie."

Ten minutes later, Vinny stormed in. "Yo Tiny, we gotta take a drive to Burnaby. Couple incidents."

Tiny was on his feet in no time, a loyal servant.

"Papa, what time you leavin'?"

"Six."

Vinny frowned. "I should be back. You guys'll be fine, but don't answer the door, eh?"

"Everything okay?" I asked.

"A day at the office, Papa. Takin' care a business, that's all. Watch the fort while I'm gone, hey?"

"Will do."

Vinny looked at Maria affectionately. "One question before I go. What's for dinner?"

Maria laughed out loud. "I'll surprise you."

"You any good with pasta?"

"Is the Pope Catholic?"

"*Hahahahahaha*, I'll hurry back, don't worry. Maybe I bring a nice bottle of Italian wine."

"That'd be wonderful."

Once Vinny and Tiny departed, the room became much quieter. We lounged and nibbled and sipped. Isabella discovered the TV was functional and flipped channels like a good teenager.

The propaganda was relentless. One channel showed clips of various American cities – Chicago, LA, Philly, Houston. The violence was extreme, according to the narrator, but she assured viewers order would soon be restored. They cut to a shot of a marching army, columns of goose-stepping soldiers. An intimidating display of military flamboyance and power. I suggested to Isabella something else might be more appropriate.

She settled on a decades-old SciFi flick. *The Terminator* seemed oddly appropriate, since we were in the middle of our own Dystopian nightmare. Isabella and Spencer became engrossed immediately. Maria and I half-watched, half-chatted. A nice moment. I actually relaxed for the first time in God knows how long.

All good things come to an end. At four, Maria bolted upright. "Time to start dinner. Hope everyone's got an appetite." Off she went.

I didn't plan to, but I napped the next hour away on the couch. When I came to, it had gone five. In an hour I'd be talking with Charles Kennedy in the Protected Zone, whatever the hell that was.

I spruced up. Vinny had brought me a few essentials – a change of shirt, underwear, socks. What a kid.

The familiar smells of Italian cooking clobbered me with déjà vu. Roasted garlic and olive oil, onions, peppers, all the aromas blending. Maria was preparing a feast, just like my Mamma used to. Too bad I was gonna miss it.

I entered the living room. Spencer was perched by the front window. "I'm watching for the car," he announced. They knew I had to leave. Two minutes to six. *Oh man, my ride was due.* For some reason, I knew the driver would be punctual.

Maria came out wearing an apron, her face shiny from the kitchen's heat. She never looked better. "I'll save you a plate. *A big one.*"

"Aw, thanks." I desperately wanted a hug. I wanted a whole lot more. But I had business to attend to.

"Be careful would you?"

"There's a car out front," Spencer called out.

"What's it look like?"

"It's huge." He made a fish-sizing gesture with both hands.

"'Kay guys, time for me to go. Back in a couple hours."

"Did you hear me? *I said be careful.*"

I gave Maria a warm smile. "I will, don't worry. Vinny texted, he's on his way."

"Ciao, see you soon," she said. The kids bellowed out good-byes.

I don't know what came over me, but I blew Maria a kiss. She gave it straight back, along with a glorious "*Mwah.*"

What a send-off.

Chapter 59 – Behind the Curtain

The driver was smartly dressed. Asian, of course. He drove a large, grey sedan, a make and model I'd not seen. Similar to an S-Class, but bigger and sturdier, which was saying something.

The insignia on the door was China-branded, the five stars of the flag artfully integrated with Chinese characters. Subtle, but powerful once you spotted it. Like an unmarked police cruiser, the vehicle had an air of state power.

Car and driver were cut from central casting, perhaps a spy movie from the '60s, with a modern twist. The whole scene was surreal. He wasn't chatty, didn't offer his name nor did I ask. We swapped minimal small talk. His English was accented but otherwise perfect.

Transit was uneventful. We crossed Cambie without fanfare. The same Commander waved us through, the same minions stood by. Traffic was non-existent.

When we entered Point Grey, déjà vu struck with a physical force. My neighbourhood hadn't changed. The same leafy streets, the same stately homes. I saw kids playing in parks. I was in a time machine.

We pulled into Charles Kennedy's estate and the sprawling grounds welcomed us. Charles' freshy-polished

1962 Aston Martin gleamed and glistened under the driveway's bright lights.

Charles was privy to the world's horrors, but they never got near his family. They existed in the abstract. He was insulated.

He greeted me as he had a decade prior – with a warm smile and a firm handshake. His dress was casual, his demeanour cordial.

"Welcome Anthony, it's been a long time."

He'd aged, certainly, but with commendable grace. Far more than me, I hated to admit. He was slim and straight, with wispy white hair and an unlined face. He'd be boyish 'til the very end, when one day old age would strike as if overnight.

"You thought you'd seen the last of me," I said.

"And vice versa." He smiled. "Let's go inside. We'll have a drink and a nice chat. How's your son?"

"He's, uh," I chuckled, "he's keeping busy."

"I have no doubt."

"And yourself? How's young Landon? And Brett? He must be pushing thirty now."

"Everyone's well, thank you for asking." His face took on a pitying expression. "My continued condolences on the loss of Julio and Lisa. I mean that from the bottom of my heart."

"Thank you, Charles." I noticed he didn't mention Leo. "Lots of water under the bridge since then."

"Yes, but such a tragedy."

We wandered through his home's elegance before settling in the study where the walls were lined with books. I took in the north-facing view. Grouse Mountain's lights shone in the night sky. I found this reassuring.

"Care for a drink?"

"Why not? I could use one, and I'm not driving."

He poured us each a finger of whiskey. "I assume you have questions."

I smiled a genuine smile. "Like why am I here?"

He laughed. "We'll get to that. First, maybe I can share a little about what's happened the past few days. Give you some context."

"The past few days? How about the past few years? Or decades?"

More laughter. "We've lived in interesting times." He sipped thoughtfully and gazed out the window. "Let's go back a ways then. It will be fun for both of us." He cleared his throat. "Back in the 2010s, we all knew the world was crumbling, you weren't unique in that respect. You happened to experience it firsthand, unfortunately. Some say it started in the '60s. The hippies had their fun, they sowed their oats – peace and love, turn on, tune in, drop out. Were they sowing the seeds of hell for future generations?"

"I've heard the argument. Hedonism over God."

Charles nodded. "Others blame immigration."

I scoffed. That was my lane, and Charles knew it. "Who knew bringing in people who hate us would be a problem?"

"You must realize, Anthony – *I'm sure you do* – the progressives of fifty and sixty years ago had a vision, they truly believed goodwill and gratitude would prevail. No one predicted the clouds of hatred and resentment."

"I did."

"Sure, *eventually* people did. By then it was too late. We were on a ride and there was no getting off. it was a crazy experiment gone awry, and we were in it for the long haul. It spawned unusual behaviour."

I wanted to call him out, but bit my tongue.

"People like me, I admit, we pretended everything was fine. It was our way of life, our mantra. The more we pretended, the more the anti-white zeitgeist festered. History was being rewritten. The demonization was in textbooks, on the news, in pop culture. The jabs were no longer subtle, especially against us." He indicated me and him.

"White males?"

He nodded. "The ideal of a single Canadian identity, where race didn't matter, it was once fashionable, and it worked for a hundred years."

"Worked like a charm when everyone was white," I said.

"And the thing is, whites did *everything* asked of them. They accepted, they tolerated, they bent over backwards."

"It was never enough."

"After Obama's tenure, everything slipped away fast. No one could stop it. There was no defense."

"I tried."

"Look where you ended up."

"I'm surprised to hear you say all this, Charles."

"Times have changed."

I turned away so as not betray my feelings. I hated Charles in that moment. How many times had he betrayed his people? Sold his soul? Yet here he was, still playing the game. I had to give him credit, he was wilier than most. Only the wiliest white man could make it this far. He even outlasted Dhanesh.

I faced him. "So what have they changed into?"

He wandered to the bar. "It's rather astonishing what has happened, Anthony. Another drink?"

"Why not?"

He handed it to me and remained standing. "I'm not permitted to say much yet, but I'll tell you this. China's running the show. *Everywhere.* You probably figured that out."

"What? Canada? The US?"

"Everywhere. *Globally.* We have the one-world government everyone wanted," he paused to chuckle, "but it's not what they expected."

"How?" I frowned and tilted my head. "How could—"

"They control everything. They *literally* control every person on the planet. Even people that think they're off the grid."

I shook my head.

Charles smiled a sinister smile. "Of course, they grant more privilege to some – I call them the chosen few. Everyone else, in the Unprotected Zones," he scoffed, "they keep a lid on them. It really has come down to *us and them*. The *haves and the have-nots*. Here," he made an extravagant gesture, "we have protection. We have order. We have freedom. Basically, we have civilization. Everything we know and love. There?" Another sinister smile. "Chaos. Hedonism. Savagery. Madness."

"The East Side?"

"That's how it plays out in Vancouver. Every city is thus divided. They all have their own patterns."

"And *there*...every man for himself?"

He shrugged. "The Peacekeepers will keep the peace, to a degree. They'll certainly make sure the savages never threaten *us*, that they're docile to the master. No one particularly cares if they're peaceful to each other. Honestly, I think some of the Chinese power brokers see them as entertainment. How's that for sick and twisted?"

"So that's my world – chaos and savagery?"

He held up a hand. "That depends on you, Anthony. Let me explain. Here," he pointed at the ground, "we're part of a thin elite. It'll be a nice life, I believe. We have ultimate freedom, provided we're beholden to the master."

"Isn't that a contradiction?"

He chuckled. "I don't let it bother me."

"Of course not." My words dripped with bitter sarcasm.

"None of this was my idea, Anthony. Just so you know."

I scoffed rudely. *No, it wasn't your idea Charles. But you're here aren't you? You were always destined to be here. You were always a shadowy swamp creature, a sociopath, slithering and sneaking about. So, you weren't the mastermind. You were still privy to process.*

"We're essentially an experiment," Charles continued. "And not the only one. I mean, God only knows what they're doing with their own people."

"I could hazard a few guesses."

"You know what else, Anthony? You'll appreciate this. They've cut off migration. A hundred percent halt on everything. Wherever you are is where you shall be. They want the DNA dust to settle, so to speak. That order came straight from the Chairman, by the way. But they're not changing settled populations, so if they're fighting and segregated down there – let them fight it out. Here in the Protected Zones, mind you, we're not segregated. We don't fight. In fact, we'll treat identity politics like cancer. It'll be excised immediately. No more PC nonsense."

My mind was swimming. "How do they control everything?"

"It's not that hard, Anthony. China has unlimited manpower. To make this happen, they deployed *millions* of servicemen all over the world. *Literally millions.* I don't have the figures. Maybe five million, maybe ten, maybe twenty. It's nothing to them. A drop in the bucket."

"How many in Canada?"

"A hundred thousand maybe. At least a million in America. They've been shipping them in slowly for months. Don't forget, China had economic leverage over everyone – the entire Western World, including the mighty U.S. of A. Post-Trump, America fell fast, as you know. China sat back and watched."

For some reason, he laughed out loud at this. Despite myself, I joined him. It was all starting to make sense.

"When the time was right," Charles continued, "China simply waltzed in and took over."

"How?"

He shrugged. "It wasn't difficult. They took control of the police, the military. They appropriated the weaponry. They already *had* their people in place. I'm over-simplifying. There were definitely hiccups, lots of small battles, probably more than I know about. But good Lord, American cities were in ruins. Like *actual* ruins, not metaphorical. Detroit and Baltimore, St. Louis, I could go on. They were dead. Not to sound racist, if that word still has meaning, but the Blacks were so unmanageable, *so violent*, no one could live there. Not even other Blacks."

"Not all cities."

"You're right. The heartland, flyover country. China had challenges there, too. They still do from what I hear. Blame it on the good old Second Amendment. But the Peacekeepers will eventually get everyone in order. Only a matter of time."

I sighed. "What about Europe?"

"Europe was easier, most of it anyway. Places like the UK, Sweden, Germany? They just rolled over. Like Canada did, by the way."

I nodded. "Yeah, we were weak. An easy target."

"So was Europe. Divided, fighting with each other. No unity. Just a bunch of competing factions. Some countries put up a fight. Italy went down swinging, you'll be happy to know."

"*Dio benedica l'Italia!*"

"They still went down, though. *Eventually*. The tide was too strong. The population of Africa was exploding, set to double in, what, twenty-five years? Two billion by 2050, four billion by 2100. And no ability to sustain themselves. It was a refugee factory. The flow to Europe never dented the supply."

"I was fighting this ten years ago."

"It got worse after you, uh, *went way*. The hordes kept washing up, like the tide, a never-ending flow. Europe was becoming Africa. At the same time, America was becoming

Hispanic, Canada Asian. And Islam was everywhere stirring up shit, protected and shielded from scrutiny." He threw his hands in the air. "Guess what. China put a stop to it."

"Why?"

He shrugged. "They figured migration was like entropy, the destruction of order. You familiar with the concept?"

"Ivan explained it to me once."

"Migration was an irreversible experiment. For the sake of the West, they had to stop it. It was a benevolent act."

"Yeah, the Chinese are known for that."

He smiled at the sarcasm. "They fixed the African birthrate thing, too."

"How?"

"Simple. They stopped sending aid. Without Western money, food, and medicine, nature's taking its course."

"Wow."

"Sounds cruel, eh Anthony? Racist, too."

I nodded.

"At the same time, imagine a world where white societies aren't being systematically destroyed."

"But have we already *been* destroyed?"

"Europe's sixty percent white. North America close to fifty." He gauged my reaction. "We're actually *allowed* to have a conversation like this, Anthony. Remember what I said? No more PC. No more rewriting of history. We're *allowed* to speak truth, to have open discussions. We can cherish heroes and celebrate excellence without guilt. It's very freeing."

"I bet some topics are still off-limits."

He laughed. "I suppose. Hey, nothing's perfect. There has to be *some* limits. Like social media. That's gone. It was a failed experiment. All it did was foster hate and division. And envy."

"Interesting." I was processing a lot of information. "I still don't know why I'm here, Charles."

There was a knock at the door. "Come in," he bellowed.

An Asian man in formal attire entered. He addressed Charles in what I assumed was Mandarin. To my great shock, Charles responded fluently in the same language. They spoke for several minutes, before Charles turned to me: "Anthony, I'd like you to meet Wei Ming. He's liaison to the Premier. He's been instrumental in coordinating the, uh, events here in Vancouver. We're extremely lucky to have him. Wei Ming, this is my dear friend, Anthony Fierro."

"A pleasure, sir," I extended my right hand.

"The pleasure is mine," he replied in accented English, then smiled broadly. "The infamous Anthony Fierro."

"We have a planning session tonight," Charles announced. "Believe it or not, there are many loose ends floating around. Normally, we meet at my office, but I had this rather important meeting *here* tonight." He winked at me, but I was still reeling from the *infamous Anthony Fierro* remark.

"I have to step out for a moment." Charles stood. "Help yourself to another drink, I'll be back shortly and we'll get down to business." He smiled. "*Finally.*"

After they left, I took a slow, deep breath. I massaged my temples. So much to ponder, and still more to come.

For the past thirty years, I'd watched my way of life erode. To hear it confirmed should have been no big deal. I knew it was happening. But to have it explained so clinically – my heart was breaking all over again.

We'd lost the war. Western civilization was dead. Everything our ancestors fought and died for – gone. Replaced by some strange new world order.

I felt sick.

Chapter 60 – Negotiations

Charles entered without knocking. "Sorry Anthony, won't happen again." He poured us another drink, and I made no protest.

"How does that man know me?"

Charles smirked. "They know everyone. They know every*thing* about everyone. They know the troublemakers, the phonies, the sycophants. They know what's in people's hearts. You'll have to get used to that, Anthony."

"But he said the *infamous* Anthony Fierro."

"Ah yes." Charles moved his chair close to mine. "Wei Ming knows about the, uh, work you did. The work that got you in trouble. He knows about your *movement*. He also knows about your *following*."

"That's ancient history."

"People have long memories."

"Wei Ming and his people?"

"Yes, and people in the Protected Zones. That's precisely why we brought you here."

I sipped whiskey and savoured its comforting warmth. "I'm not following."

"At one time, most of the Western World knew your name, and you had huge favourability. You were a man of the people. They admired you, they looked up to you. Because you stood for something. You were special. A folk hero. That's why you're here."

"I'm not connecting the dots."

"We want your help, Anthony. Plain and simple. We ask respectfully and humbly."

"Help with what? What can I do?"

"Use your voice."

"To say what? And to who?"

"Remember, this is an experiment. And China wants authenticity. They *want* it to work. Without inspirational leaders like you, people might not fully embrace the vision with their hearts and minds. They might pretend, go through the motions."

"Experiment?"

"Don't let the word bother you. *Everything's* an experiment. In 1776, America was an experiment. A good one. North Korea? Not so much. We want this to be a good one – *a great one* – and you can help. You can be a spiritual leader. That is, if you wish to be one of the chosen few."

"*Chosen few.* Are you listening to yourself Charles?"

He smiled. "I get carried away with the language. But we need you, Anthony. To calm the people, to coax them along, to inspire them to greatness."

"In Vancouver?"

"Not only Vancouver. Your name resonates all over the world. Will you do it?"

"I'm not sure I know what *it* is."

He smiled. "Essentially, we want you to preach the same message you preached ten years ago. Only under a different framework."

"Not sure I believe that."

"It's true."

"I need to think about this. I have so many questions."

"You don't need to decide today."

"The chosen few," I muttered. "So I'd live here? On the West Side?"

"We could probably get your old house back, if you want it."

"What about Maria? Do you *know* about Maria? And Isabella?"

He nodded brightly. "Of course they're welcome. Spencer, too."

"You even know about Spencer?"

"I told you, no secrets."

"What about Vinny?"

Charles smiled condescendingly. "Vinny won't come."

"He's changed, he's got a family now."

"We know, and his family's welcome. But not Vinny. He'd never be allowed, but it's a non-issue. He'd never come."

"Why would he never be allowed?" I was indignant.

"Anthony, I'm not sure you know the extent of his misdeeds."

That set me off. "I don't know the extent of yours, either."

We got heated after that. Okay, I got heated. Charles was calm. Finally: "Let's put that on the backburner," he said. "I'll look into it. See what I can do."

"I'll never desert, Vinny. He never deserted me. I wouldn't be here if not for him."

"Fair enough, just don't assume I have the authority to grant any old wish." He looked doubtful. "But I'll make a few calls."

"Thank you." I was still stewing.

"We're counting on you, Anthony."

I scoffed.

"You can make a difference."

"How?"

"Remember, *we know* what's in people's hearts. We've done our analysis, we've run the simulations. They *will* listen to you. What's more, they'll *believe* you."

He was playing me like a fiddle, and it was working. I felt a surge of the old spirit flare, fierce and savage. Heck, maybe I could champion the spread of good.

"Exactly what is my message? Will I have control over it?"

"*To a degree*, certainly. The message we want you to share is the message in your heart. Western Man's message. Family, the sanctity of life. Freedom of speech, freedom of assembly – but also law and order. Respect for rule of law. It's a delicate balance. We want safe streets, polite discourse, a high trust society."

"We had that a few decades ago."

"And how quickly it went away." He wagged a scolding finger. "But not this time. We won't let it happen. And the results will be glorious. Beyond anything we can imagine."

"You're losing me again."

"We want the flowers of free thought to bloom in all their glory. Science and technology. It'll be a new age of exceptionalism."

"We're doing this for the Chinese?"

"For everyone, Anthony. We're all on the same team. Do you remember what it was like before Western man was silenced? Before he was put in a thought prison?"

I shrugged.

"It was a golden age, Anthony. Putting men on the moon was a priority. We want that spirit back. We want to put science ahead of virtue-signaling. Imagine the advances we'll make in quantum mechanics, virtual reality, artificial intelligence. *In medicine.* Maybe we'll start living much longer?"

"Sounds exciting. Also a bit scary."

"How so?"

"Perform for the master, *or else.*"

"It won't be like that. They know tyranny won't work, they're giving us full freedom, but with limits."

I didn't point out the contradiction.

"This is not the end, Anthony. It's the beginning. A new beginning, an era of infinite possibility. No more tearing down monuments, no more policies that limit human potential. No more bashing people with white privilege or unconscious bias. We'll value hard work, humility, personal responsibility. We'll have a true meritocracy."

I'd never seen Charles so animated.

"Imagine what we can accomplish. Space travel, eradication of disease. If a scientist discovers something inconvenient, they won't have to abandon it. Nothing will be off-limits."

He was capturing my attention, I must admit.

"We'll grow our culture, too – art, music, literature. A complete revitalization."

An image of Lisa sprung forth. "That all sounds pretty great." I jerked my head eastward. "And *down there*, as you put it. What about down there?"

"That's an experiment, too. A more volatile one. We'll keep a lid on it, keep the peace. I honestly have no idea what direction it goes. Just glad I'm not a part of it."

"Like my son."

Charles sighed.

"*Exactly*," I said accusingly. "I need to think about this, Charles."

"Understandable."

We sat in silence for a long spell, and I pondered. I'd be a man of the people, but insulated from true power? I was skeptical. The whole notion seemed utterly ridiculous, yet I was excited.

"While you're thinking, I'll throw in a few reminders. Quality of life, Anthony. Access to clean water, healthcare. Up here, you get your drug prescriptions, you don't have to fight for them. Your heart meds are getting low, aren't they?"

He was right – *and I was worried* – but I tried not to react.

"Down there, it'll be a black market. *Nothing will be easy.* That's how they engineered it. Always a slow boil. A massive underclass of the downtrodden, *the agitated*, neatly aligned by race, everyone full of hate and mistrust."

"You're talking about my kid again, you realize that?"

"Don't get stuck there, Anthony."

"I *am* stuck. Vinny's my son. The only one I got left."

"I understand. I'll look at it."

"You better, or it's a deal breaker. Julio, Cindy *and Vinny.*"

"Won't be easy, but I'll see what I can do. Trust me."

"How can I trust you, Charles?"

"Because I'm the only game in town." His face brightened. "My goodness, look at the time. I must get to my meeting. Wei Ming and the others are waiting. And you have much to think about."

I scoffed.

"There's a lot here, Anthony. We want you, and we need you. You're a leader. You can do great things. I mean that sincerely."

I shot him a look of skepticism, but he was undeterred.

"I haven't told you everything. There's more to the vision. Great things. Really great things. Should you come, should you commit – *and I know you will* – you'll be privy. Eventually, you'll be privy to everything."

Chapter 61 – Soul Searching

Charles was right about Vinny. I knew in my heart he would be. I gave Vinny a version of the story – *the Protected Class*. The *us and them*. I pitched hard and he listened attentively. When I made my final play, he laughed in my face.

"That sounds terrible." He roared with laughter. "I'd be bored silly. Reminds me of the fancy schmancy school you sent me to in grade three."

"But it's safe, Vincent. Come on, think about your old man. I worry about you." It was pointless, but I kept fighting.

"Hey Papa, don't lay the guilt trip on me eh? It don't work." He wasn't laughing any more. "I got people to protect, people counting on me. I was born in East Van and I'll die in East Van. You know that, Papa."

"I suppose I do."

"Don't worry, I know how to take care of myself. And you think it's so great on the West Side eh? Well *fuhgeddaboudit*, we do alright on the East Side, too, I promise ya. 'Specially me." He burst out laughing again.

I didn't doubt it. "You be careful though, eh? You're my only son. Heir to my vast fortune." A small joke.

"I'm already rich, Papa." He scoffed. "Besides, they'd never let me in."

He was smarter than I thought. I know I keep saying that. "What about Cindy and Julio?"

"What about 'em? My wife and kid go where I go. We're a family. I'm livin' the dream."

Vinny was gonna do his own thing, I shoulda known. The only uncertainty was my own. What would I do? The question kept morphing into *what would we do?* I had Maria now. And Maria had a child. And what about Spencer?

I was already formulating negotiating tactics – *to be used on Charles* – for visitation with Young Julio. I wasn't about to give up seeing my only grandson.

Across several days, I agonized over possibilities, I tried to anticipate future outcomes. It was a torturous time. Charles called every day. Ivan, too. I had no doubt where they stood.

I confided in Maria. Told her every last detail. I gave her a song and dance about wanting to be noble, about staying in the trenches to fight the good fight. Told her I'd rather *die on my feet, than live on my knees.* Not my line.

She saw through the façade. "You're no good to anyone dead."

"Neither is Vinny. You don't see him running away to hide."

"That's Vinny's world, not yours. You said it yourself, maybe you can do some good up there."

She nailed me at every turn, but never in a haughty, gloating way. She was simply being pragmatic. A realist. Also, an *optimist.*

No two ways about it, I was getting on in years. I didn't wanna say old, but I was *this close* to sixty-six, and feeling my age. I needed my medication and Charles knew it.

And hadn't I already served time in the trenches? Not to mention prison – a decade inside had left me fearful and anxious, not that I would admit it. Maria was slowly coaxing me out of the wilderness, making me feel human again.

Was it cowardice to accept Charles Kennedy's offer? Would I be a sellout? *Vinny wasn't a sellout.* That thought kept playing in my head. But Vinny was thirty-six and it *was* his world. What about this role Charles had for me? And his bosses – who were they? What was this new world order?

Did I even *have* a choice? What if I said no? Would I be marked? Targeted? Would my *ranking* go down? Maybe there were gulags? Maybe one day, I'd disappear? I didn't trust Charles, not with his track record.

If you haven't already guessed, I knew I was going. The only uncertainty was how to justify it to myself. The story I used, at least my working hypothesis, was that I'd get more done there. I'd be more effective. A catalyst for the greater good.

Lame, I know.

There were details to sort out – the fine minutiae of my obligations, where we'd live (*my old house*), visitation arrangements. We stayed on in the safe house almost a month. The time was uneventful, and I mean that in a good way. I have a feeling the Peacekeepers had something do with that.

There was uncertainty with Young Spencer. He'd taken a liking to Vinny, and Vinny showed no inclination to steer the youngster toward safe waters. On the contrary, Vinny romanticized life in the danger zone.

But Spencer was ten years old, and such a decision was too much to put on a kid, a traumatized one at that. Maria put her foot down and Vinny relented without a fight. Spencer would live with us.

The day of parting was a celebration. Vinny hosted a barbeque, and I saw many old friends. We were into August and summer was in full force. Vinny and I shared a last shot of whiskey, and we did this multiple times throughout the evening.

It wasn't a farewell – we had plans for visits and phone calls – but it felt like one. My son wasn't much for sentimentality, but he got emotional. For a moment, I thought he might even shed a tear. Then he planted a kiss on my cheek and started laughing.

"Things'll work out, Papa. They always do."

Chapter 62 – Settling In

Life settled into place. I was sleeping well, and not alone. Maria and I were living idyllically. We felt stable and secure, as if world peace had finally been achieved.

It was an illusion, of course. Certain parts of our planet were murky, probably anything but peaceful. What was happening in the Middle East, Africa, South America? God only knows. And when I say God, *ha*, I mean China.

The illusion also required we ignore the massive underclass across town, which was carefully engineered never to touch or threaten us. But through Vinny it did (touch not threaten). I got regular reports. We'll get to that.

I still didn't trust Charles Kennedy. Probably never would. We were neighbours again. Business associates, too. I saw him frequently, but we never became close. Was it a grudge cultivated fifty years ago, one born of envy? Charles was the white kid with wealth, privilege, and Gentile arrogance. He hadn't changed a bit.

He was always flying off somewhere, meeting dignitaries and other leaders. The way he placated his Asian masters reminded me of, pardon the expression, an *Uncle Tom*. But who was I to talk? I was jumping through hoops myself, and it wasn't all bad.

I held up my part of the bargain and was happy to do so. I encouraged citizens of the *Protected Western World* to go out and live. I was even a rebel at times, sneaking in old-school references. It was a good gig. So far, I hadn't been censored, or even scolded.

The hours were short, the pay exceptional. I was sixty-six. I had status and social currency in a land of plenty. With luck, I could do this another twenty years or more.

I focused on the important things – *family, friends, and faith.* Except when I talked to Ivan that is, which was daily. He was still up-to-date on everything. He still scoured the dark Web, what was left of it. He was still paranoid.

Many mysteries were revealed that first year. I pressed Charles for info, but he rationed me admirably. Ivan, on the other hand, was a fountain of information. Some things never change.

The two of us pieced together practically everything. Big tech, the multi-nationals, they were co-conspirators. The companies – *which I won't bother naming* – were beholden to no country. Only to an ever-changing set of false ideals, and the prodigious egos of their owners.

Through the late 2010s and into the 2020s, they forged ties with China and began collecting data on everything. Every action, every nuance. Nothing went unrecorded. It was the era of *smart cities.* They studied the data. They sliced and diced and scrutinized. They ran it through algorithms, and feedback loops, and they patiently built their plans.

Meanwhile, racial divisions sharpened, and rough outlines of Protected Zones formed across Western populations. It was a thoroughly engineered process, carefully designed to appear organic.

"I still find it shocking China didn't conquer us through war," I said to Ivan.

"Why bother? They knew we'd self-destruct."

"Amazing eh? They just sat and waited."

"I know. Some people think it was some grand Machiavellian masterplan." He scoffed. "China just saw it happening. Okay, maybe they *encouraged* it here and there. But they were more opportunists than strategists."

"I get it with Canada. I mean, the Chinese have dominated us forever, especially in Vancouver. And especially with Trudeau. That clown loved China. He probably sold us out, eh?"

Ivan laughed. "I give Trudeau credit for nothing but buffoonery. He wasn't bright enough to plot anything. He was a willing patsy, that's all."

"Remember the populists? Trump was the grandmaster, obviously. But we had Salvini, Le Pen, Bolsonaro—"

"After getting stabbed no less."

"We never had one in Canada, though."

"We had Bernier."

I chuckled. "He tried, I'll give him that much."

"And don't forget Faith Goldie."

"Yeah," I nodded. "She got banished, just like me."

"Wouldn't have mattered, anyway. Nothing matters when the hordes are pouring in."

"We never stood a chance."

"Nope."

"Did Charles tell you any more about the, uh, digital breach?"

"He's cagy." I smirked. "Says it was hardware infiltration – backdoors, unauthorized access, intel-gathering, that sorta thing. They were entrenched in our banks, corporations, airlines. Our government, obviously. They only used a fraction of what they could've. They coulda turned our lights out forever."

"And all they had to do was disable communications for a few hours."

"They did more in some places, I promise you. But they had a *kill-switch*, and the Western leaders knew it. China got a lot done with threats and bullying."

"What a moment, eh? When they finally pulled the trigger."

"I didn't think so at the time, being on the Drive and all. But yeah it's impressive, looking back."

"We had a front row seat, dude. They take down communications, incite fury, then they trot out these Peacekeepers, like they're the good guys. How brazen can you get?"

"And they already got their army here – guns, ammo, fancy armoured trucks, whatever you call 'em."

"Easy enough when you control the ports. You know about that."

"Don't forget, my last shift was twelve years ago, and I didn't exactly go out on a high note. But yeah, I heard a few rumours from the old gang. China controlled everything. *Not only here.*"

"And what were our leaders doing?" Ivan scoffed. "Setting up safe spaces, working to eradicate white privilege. They were totally asleep on the job."

"Unless they were in on it," I corrected. "Like Charles."

"True."

"It's so impressive that they did it all over the Western World, *all at once.*" I snapped my fingers. "*Boom.* A new world order."

"No war, no hostile takeover, no fucking resistance."

"What do you call that, a silent coup? A bloodless coup?"

"Not totally bloodless."

"True enough, there was blood in the streets."

"But as far as *coup d'etats* go, this was unprecedented in size and scope."

"And America, with all their fancy space-age weapons, their military might. It was all useless."

Ivan nodded. "*The supreme art of war is to subdue the enemy without fighting.* Sun Tzu said that a couple thousand years ago."

"Amazing."

"No shit. They caved without so much as a dying gasp."

"The neocons must be turning over in their graves."

"It'll go down in history, that's for sure."

I laughed. "We still tracking history?"

"I am," said Ivan. "I never stopped. I knew exactly what was happening the whole time you were locked up. But I also followed *the news...*" big air quotes "...they had explanations for everything, always a presentable message for the common man."

"Not that the common man was listening."

"You'd be surprised. A shitload of people actually took comfort in the fake news. Right to the bitter end."

I shook my head. "People's ability to self-delude is staggering."

"Orwell called it *Doublethink.*"

"That's what got us in this mess in the first place."

"Then there were the rebels."

"Ha, that was me in my heyday. I guess in some ways, I was lucky I got taken down when I did. Otherwise..."

I didn't finish the sentence. I was referring to one of the more sinister aspects of Transformation, a shakedown in the Protected Zones. The *wrongthink* crowd was easy to find and the worst of their ilk unceremoniously removed, no questions asked. They simply vanished. I was concerned for Ivan, but he was fine. He was an info junkie, and otherwise harmless. He was also scared of his own shadow, and they knew it.

"Yeah," Ivan continued, "nowadays the pecking order's clear. You're under China's thumb or you're living in chaos."

"Or both. Hey, you think Vancouver was favoured 'cause of our high Asian population?"

"Maybe. Most of Charles' power team is Asian, and they ain't all from China. Not sure if you noticed, but there were plenty of Communist China supporters in Vancouver. They didn't hide it. They flew the flag proudly and no one said a peep. That was diversity. A beautiful thing, eh?"

"On the other hand, I hear a high percentage of those *thought criminals* were Chinese-Canadians. Surprising eh?"

"Or *not*."

"Good point. One thing's for sure, Trudeau was the perfect useful idiot."

"Oh, fuck yeah. And now they got no use for him." Ivan scoffed. "What a sock puppet."

I switched gears. "Tell me again about Eastern Europe. Whadaya been hearing?"

"China hasn't touched 'em, and it looks like they won't. Some kinda special deal with the Kremlin maybe? Remember, countries like Poland and Hungary, they didn't wallow in white guilt and shame like the rest of us saps. Hell, they were behind the Iron Curtain fifty years. They had first-hand knowledge of the Left. They knew what a communist regime could do. They knew it well."

"I wonder what life's like in Budapest and Warsaw?"

"I'd say pretty decent. Population's very white, very Christian."

"What do you mean, special deal with the Kremlin?" I asked.

"I'm just speculating. Look, Russia's a minnow beside China, but they're tough, and they don't back down. Why would China want the trouble? They're having too much fun experimenting on us."

"Interesting. How 'bout Africa, anything new?"

"About what you'd expect. A steady return to the precolonial state."

"Tribal and violent?"

"*And primitive*. This might sound bad, but you can't fool Mother Nature, no matter how hard you try."

"That *does* sound bad. Whatever happened to Wakanda?"

He chuckled. "China hasn't changed their strategy. They're still colonizing Africa in their own insidious way. You know, mining away for precious metals with *zero* concern for the environment or the workers."

"But...but...*what about the Paris Accord?*"

Ivan laughed appreciatively. "Like China took that seriously."

"No one did. Except Trudeau, but he was a moron."

"True. Where was I?"

"Africa."

"Right. Yeah, the Chinese never took bullshit from the Blacks. They're not burdened with the old altruism gene like us."

"You mean altruism curse," I said.

Ivan nodded. "They're tough taskmasters, that's for sure. They have no patience for African ineptitude."

"Ha, the natives are gonna miss their old colonial masters. Say what you will, the European Man pampered them. Back in the day, I mean."

"To his own detriment."

"Oh, fuck yeah."

"Speaking of whites, South Africa's an exception." Ivan paused to chuckle. "Those fucking Boers, man. Never count those bastards out. *Never.* They had no Peacekeepers, but they circled their own wagons. I hear they're making a go of it, carving out their own little country, and China's lettin' 'em."

"God bless 'em." I drained the last of my beer. "And no more migrants spilling into Europe?"

"Nope. China figured out what we already knew. If you don't protect Western society, it gets infiltrated and destroyed. Israel figured that out a long time ago. No more Latin America seeping into the States either, though Trump never did finish his wall."

"Not for lack of trying."

"I'm getting another beer, you want one?"

"Is the Pope Catholic?"

"The Pope's dead."

"Is he?"

"I have no idea," said Ivan and headed for the kitchen. I pondered the race issue while he was gone. So many problems caused by mass migration, and the Western World's insistence that race didn't matter, when everyone secretly knew it did.

If you don't believe that, I'm sorry you read this far. I told you this was a book about race. For the record, I still believe multi-race societies can be viable, but not when whites are incessantly demonized. Sorry, if I sound sensitive.

I like to think we don't care about the colour of skin in the Protected Zones, certainly not here in Vancouver. We care about what's in your heart, and I still have *kumbaya* in mine.

Vancouver was one of the most multi-ethnic cities in the world, and we made it work for a long time. Especially compared to some. Post-Transformation, some cities actually had multiple segregated protected zones, just to keep the peace. *Imagine.*

Ivan was back with the beer, and keen to keep exploring. "How about China itself? Still trouble in paradise?"

"I hope not, or we could all be fucked."

"What'd Charles say, exactly?"

"He pawned it off as run-of-the-mill dissention in the ranks, basic disagreements. They're piloting *innovation farms* within their own population, which is how they see us, by the way."

"I know, they want us to innovate. To be creative, come up with shit. Be inventive."

"That's the Western way. And they know innovation never happens in a repressive society. So they wanna leverage our model."

"You mean steal our ideas, like they've always done."

"Yeah, that's a whole new discussion."

"No shit. But maybe one day we'll spawn another Steve Jobs. An Edison, a da Vinci, an Aristotle?"

"Didn't seem likely before Transformation, not with the sorry state of academia." I took a healthy swallow. Beer was a such a blessing. "Anyway, China wants to combat discontent within their own people by trying to foster innovation. Give the people some hope."

Ivan chuckled. "They're basically packaging up the American model. Always stealing from us."

"There's differences of opinion at the top. Lots of movement within the power structures. Charles says he doesn't know details. Not sure I believe him."

"Ha, maybe one day they fall apart, and we take over?"

"My buddy Bucky Bradford talks about that. He figures one day we'll throw up another flare of freedom. Create a new America, 1776 all over again."

"He's a dreamer."

"*We broke free of our imperial master before, we'll do it again.* That's him talking."

Ivan laughed. "Tell him to be careful, *thoughtcrime* and all."

"The Chinese probably let it go out of sheer fascination."

Just another of our many spirited discussions. Ivan loved to analyze and there were so many compelling issues to unravel in our post-Apocalyptic world.

Like LGBTQ. They foisted it on us pre-Transformation. It was a sacred cow. Truth is, *the movement* was never really about people. It was a political platform. A tool to divide and control and destabilize. Like how the Paris Climate Accord had nothing to do with climate change.

Anyway, LGBTQ was back in the closet, where it belonged in my prudish opinion. This is not to say gays and lesbians didn't wander about freely. *They did.* No one persecuted them, but nor did they flaunt their sexuality or stage perverted parades. There were certainly no silly laws or make-believe pronouns. I dare say, these changes triggered negligible suffering.

Our new overlords had no patience for the ridiculous, like sovereign claims of the Indigenous, or Islam's push for a global caliphate. Toxic rhetoric like that was taboo, a sure-fire way to find the master's wrath.

Terms like *white privilege* and *unconscious bias* were likewise scorned. That didn't mean their utterance was forbidden – like the N-word was pre-Transformation – it meant application of the underlying concepts was treated appropriately. Like garbage.

Removing nonsensical language and behaviour allowed sanity to prevail in unexpected areas, too. Take Canada's Indigenous. Through the 2020s, they didn't fare well. Their place at the top of the victimhood pyramid was threatened as new minority groups vied for power.

Victimhood was a competitive industry, and the Indigenous were yesterday's news. Vibrant new victim classes began sucking up tax dollars, especially as they gained political power.

Our Chinese masters saw things differently. They believed the path to dignity and success was self-sufficiency. Taking responsibility for your actions. In other words, no government handouts, not even to the Indigenous. However, the Chinese did recognize the unique rights and freedoms of Canada's First Nations peoples, and they encouraged tribes to live and prosper on their reserves. To live off-grid in remote communities, if they so desired. The government would no longer interfere.

What a concept. And it was working. Substance abuse plummeted. Leaders emerged. Free of the shackles of victimhood, and blessed with responsibility, they were thriving. Not all, but some.

I found the story inspirational, and found myself thinking *if they can do it, why can't we? Why not indeed?* I entertained wild fantasies of a rebirth of Western civilization. Maybe it had be torn down before it could be rebuilt.

We could grow the Protected Zones, share best practices with fellow travellers around the globe. We could meet, hold conferences, spread the word of God, and unity, and freedom.

We could reclaim the American spirit, the knowhow, the ingenuity. We could demand our inalienable right to life, liberty and the pursuit of happiness. I'm aware I was never American, by the way. But I've long envied their fierce love of country, their get-shit-done attitude.

It was a vague dream, with many flaws. How was it possible when we were but a foreign power's plaything, who already knew we entertained such thoughts, because they knew all?

It was Bucky's influence, no doubt. He planted the seed. He preached we bide time, we connect with like minds. He used words like patriot and MAGA often. I loved the guy.

He and his family had been through hell. After Trump's tenure, the backlash against Southern whites (Republican or otherwise) was immediate. *And violent.* Much of the South was a no-go zone. Once the Dems took power, the onslaught began.

Without the Second Amendment, or at least its remnants, the carnage would have been far worse. It was the last stand, and it proved stubborn.

Like many white families, the Bradfords fled Louisville taking what they could. They ventured west in search of a new home. Pockets of safety were forming in states like Oregon, Idaho, Montana, and the Dakotas. Bucky settled in a Portland suburb, which became a Protected Zone after Transformation.

I'd yet to meet the man face to face, but it would happen. We were separated by a six-hour drive. I'd invited him many a time, but I'd likely have to make the trek. Even after all that had happened, Bucky still knew in his heart the world revolved around the magnificent US of A. Land of the Free, Home of the Brave.

Epilogue
Vancouver, B.C.
July 10, 2031

The summer of 2031, Vancouver experienced one of its patented heatwaves. We get one every year – it's been like that since I can remember. Nothing to do with global warming.

Vinny and family visited regularly. Getting in and out was no problem. Peacekeeper presence at the *borders* was down, not that they ever gave Vinny issues. He had privileges, as per my special deal, but the Vin Man didn't need them. He knew the regulars, he joked with them, even the ones that didn't speak English, which was most.

Vinny soon earned the option of *retiring* to the Protected Zone, and I pestered him on occasion. "You kiddin' me?" He would say. "Too much work to do. *E me piace.*" *And I like it.*

His home in the wilds of East Vancouver was insulated from the chaos. Post-Transformation, there were many needy kids like Spencer. Vinny took in a bunch. His place felt like an orphanage, so said Cindy.

Blessedly, the chaos had tapered. Equilibriums formed and tempers cooled. But violence still flared, and sometimes it was frighteningly barbaric. Some groups seemed intent on conflict, as if it was in their DNA. Vinny instituted an eye-for-an-eye policy. Sounds equally barbaric, but *ruthlessness was essential*, he said. I didn't ask for details.

Maybe one day, he'd make the move. Hopefully before I was dead and gone, which wouldn't be for thirty years if I was lucky.

Besides the ugly stuff, Vinny's lifestyle was pretty darn good. He enjoyed himself. On his turf, people found ways to be useful. Most everyone had a skill and artisans were prized. Plumbers, electricians, guys that could tune a car. We needed that in my neck of the woods, too, and we *borrowed* their expertise on occasion. Post-millennials were mostly clueless – they didn't know a hammer from a handsaw. Couldn't fix a leaky faucet to save their life.

What else?

Ivan remained a political junkie. People don't change their stripes. Between diatribes and paranoid delusions, he still dreamed of a glorious future. Travel was opening up, and he was primed. That was his pre-Transformation hobby, and his options were no longer limited to terrestrial destinations. Recreational space travel was a thing. I told him he was too old, but that didn't quell his enthusiasm.

Good on him. He liked to explore, even all those years ago when he dragged me to England and well...you know what happened. That was a lifetime ago. I held no grudge.

Back then, Lisa was my wife, my partner, my soulmate. When I lost her, part of me died. I figured we only got one true love, but I was wrong. Maria and I came together in crisis. Our bond was forged in fire. We were lucky, a match made in heaven.

Our lives were joyous and full. Who knew at sixty-six, I'd adopt a daughter *and* a son. Isabella and Spencer were both in dire need of a father's love, and I wouldn't let them down. How quickly Spencer won our hearts. He stood out in a crowd with his blonde hair, and he had the same sunny disposition of Julio – *my Julio that is.*

Spencer never shied from the spotlight. He was whip-smart and full of mischief. He'd already grown a few inches, and puberty would soon descend. What a delight to have him in our midst.

School was school again. It focused on subjects that mattered, like the three Rs. It taught values and traditions. Spencer and Isabella recited the Lord's Prayer to start the day, as I had back in the 1970s. But not everything was the same. For example, they were learning Mandarin.

We settled into new routines, a new way of life. Maria had infectious energy and zest. She loved to cook and, *buono*, I loved to eat. I still felt like a loner at times, and I put that down to a decade in prison. Maybe I'd get better?

I needed a hobby. A passion for my energy, what little I had left. Some enjoyed sailing, others skied. I would have played soccer, but my knees – *and various other ailments* – begged me not to try.

Maybe I could coach? Spencer would be a helluva player. And Young Julio? Couple more years, he'd be good to go. If only there was a league.

"You always say that," Maria scolded. "Enough already. *You* start one."

"Ah, if I were younger and more energetic…"

She cut me off with one of her looks. I took no offense. It came from a place of love and honestly, I needed her tough love.

"Maybe I'll try."

"I'll believe it when I see it."

"I'll think about it over a glass of wine. Join me?"

She nodded brightly. Maria was a light drinker, like me, but a glass in the evening with a little Sinatra in the background – you couldn't beat it. I even serenaded her on occasion, though I'm not sure she loved that.

Not a lot of new music so far Post-Transformation. Maybe that would change?

"Our era had the best music, eh Maria? Full of hope and love and freedom. Especially the '70s."

"What do you mean our era, grandpa?"

She loved to tease, and I didn't mind. When *My Maria* came on, I serenaded her along with the great B.W. Stevenson. A more apt lyric I could not find.

She blew me a kiss – *mwah* – and I felt it clear across the room. Her aura was strong. I felt a familiar stirring in my heart and loins.

I never imagined such a life, nor to live in such interesting times. I'd been pushed to the edge, but luck had been on my side. I'd seen good times and bad, I'd loved and been loved. I'd lost.

The good fortune I have is a treasured gift. My heart is full of love and hope and gratitude. I don't focus on the state of the world, or where this good earth will go, or that the rug may one day be pulled out. I let Ivan and Charles worry about that.

Had I reached the autumn of my days? I hope not. How many more years would God grant? Ten, twenty, thirty?

Didn't matter. He had blessed me with a good woman, good friends, a good life.

I was peaceful and fulfilled. I felt no fear. What more could any man want?

A Note to the Reader

I'm not of Italian heritage, but my upbringing was similar to Tony Fierro's. Rough and tumble East Vancouver, which went from mostly-white to hyper-diverse as I progressed through school. I was a classical liberal. I trusted the system. I thought our way of life would last forever.

I was wrong.

All Thy Sons paints a disturbing vision of our future. Do I believe we'll descend so rapidly, and in such a manner? Generally, no, I think the unravelling will take longer and be much messier. But who can say? If you described today's divisive climate to a 1990s conservative, he'd never believe you. When I see what's happening in Europe or, *my goodness*, South Africa, I wonder if we'll go down far quicker.

ATS is a conversation-starter. The window of opportunity for uncomfortable conversations is shrinking. Governments curtail free speech, universities suppress debate, and our children are immersed in Leftist groupthink – not to mention drugs, porn, and toxic technology.

What do I hope to achieve with this novel? First and foremost, to entertain *you* the reader with interesting characters and provocative (yet credible) storylines. Beyond that, awareness of the dark path we're on. Hopefully, enough to motivate people to speak up.

My wishes and wants are not extravagant: safe streets, equal opportunity for all, freedom – like we had a few decades ago. Let it be known, *ATS* is not an attempt to incite racial conflict, *it's an attempt to prevent it.*

People say the Canada I miss never existed, but I know differently. I was there. It was a simpler time. It wasn't perfect, but it was peaceful and idyllic. People had reason for optimism. Even white people ☺.

Maybe this story is way off-base. Maybe we're in some awkward transitional phase en route to a glorious multicultural Utopia – like the globalists preach. I suppose it's possible. I only hope getting there doesn't involve the persecution, torture, and slaughter of people that look like me. You know, like what's happening in South Africa, and has been since 1994.

Society tells me I'm not allowed to talk about race. Only *people of colour* are bestowed the privilege. So I speak through my characters. I give them the freedom to report what they see, and react to the absurdities around them. Don't blame me for what they say. Who says *I* agree with them?

ATS is a work of fiction, but the events are not outside the realm of possibility. I'm not so arrogant to think it can change the course of history. But if I can't save the Western World, at least I can document its demise.

I think of my novels as comfort food for conservatives, and red pills for liberals. I see no other author of fiction authentically capturing today's distressing realities – the absurdity, the obliteration of freedom, the blatant demonization of whites. I feel obligated to continue. I sleep better at night for doing so.

I'm optimistic we can turn things around, but we need drastic change in government very soon. If you feel the same, I suggest you speak up. One way to do that (self-serving as this may sound 😊) is to tell others about *ATS*. Word-of-mouth is everything to book sales and political movements.

If you were entertained and/or found value in this novel, let the world know. Leave a review on Amazon, tell your friends, share the link on Facebook. Do something. *Anything.*

Thank you as always, *dear reader*, and feel free to contact me directly at kmbreakey.com.

About the Author

K.M. Breakey was born in Toronto and educated at Simon Fraser University in Vancouver, BC. He has previously published *Never, Never and Never Again*, *Johnny and Jamaal*, and two other novels.

To learn more, visit kmbreakey.com.

Also by K.M. Breakey

Never, Never and Never Again

Audrey is a starry-eyed Brit, Pieter a tenth-generation Afrikaner. At the height of Apartheid, they fall in love. A life of splendour awaits, but the country is shifting underfoot. The winds of change fan revolution, and Michael Manzulu's rage boils. He is hungry, and will risk everything to destroy his oppressor.

When white rule gives way, trepidation is tempered by precarious optimism. Mandela will make the miracle happen. Or not. Twenty-three years on, South Africa has suffered unprecedented decline. The country unravels and fear is pervasive. Fear of persecution, land seizure, slaughter. Pieter and Audrey march on. They navigate the perpetual threat. They pray the wrath will not strike their home.

Recently, voices of protest cry out, none louder than the bombastic scholar, Kaspar Coetzer. World leaders cautiously take note, but will they take action? More importantly, can they?

Never, Never and Never Again is a story of vengeance, greed and corruption. A story the world ignores, but a story that must be told...before it's too late.

Johnny and Jamaal

Two athletes from different planets are on the verge of greatness. Johnny's a carefree Canadian making his mark in the NHL. Jamaal's set to follow LeBron and Kyrie out of the ghetto. When their worlds collide, the catastrophic clash ignites racial conflict not seen since Ferguson. The incident tests the fledgling love of Johnny's best friend Lucas and his African-American girlfriend Chantal, and sets them on a quest for truth and justice in the perverse racial landscape of 2016.

As chaos escalates across American cities, an MLK-like voice rises from the ashes. Wilbur Rufus Holmes may be salvation for Luke and Chantal, but can he stop society's relentless descent into racial discord?

Johnny and Jamaal is awash with sports, violence and political taboo, as America's seething dysfunction is laid bare.

Creator Class

Decades have elapsed since The Creators inflicted their vision on the planet. The population menace is tamed, resources are plentiful, and climate concerns abate. A sustainable world order has been achieved.

But the rigid restrictions of P-Class torment Shawn Lowe. Movements are tracked, conversations scrutinized, conformity enforced. It's wrong. The Laws of Earthism are wrong. When a treasonous outburst cements Shawn's fate, an unexpected communication from Creator Class sparks changes he could never have imagined.

A new life. A new family. Boundless opportunity. Destiny, it seems, has been rewritten. But an evil nemesis emerges, and a lust for vengeance points Shawn down a treacherous path.

A powerful idea has descended on 30-year old Lane Craig, a corporate gunslinger who dreams of greatness. Simple beyond belief, powerful beyond measure, the idea won't go away. Lane knows that if managed properly, a new electronic organism will emerge and transform the Internet and his life forever.

He also knows he can't do it alone. Fortunately, suitable partners are nearby. Best pal Johnny is a glib slacker coasting in life's fast lane. Thomas is freakishly brilliant but has grown surly and awkward. What's he hiding? It's only the addition of hard-charging newcomer Gino that galvanizes momentum.

Will the idea triumph? Will it derail in a tumult of testosterone and alcohol? A brave face cannot mask Lane's self-doubt and paranoia. Nor can new love interest, Cat.

But as the saying goes, even paranoid people have enemies. Especially when it comes to Internet riches.

41137155R00236

Made in the USA
Middletown, DE
03 April 2019